Sweetbriar Hope

Brenda Wilbee

Fleming H. Revell
A Division of Baker Book House
Grand Rapids, Michigan 49516

©1999 by Brenda Wilbee

Published by Fleming H. Revell
a division of Baker Book House Company
P.O. Box 6287, Grand Rapids, MI 49516-6287

Printed in the United States of America

Library of Congress Cataloging-in-Publication Data

Wilbee, Brenda.
    Sweetbriar hope / Brenda Wilbee.
      p   cm.
    ISBN 0-8007-5695-9 (pbk.)
      1. Denny, Louisa Boren—Fiction. 2. Frontier and pioneer life—Washington (State)—Fiction. 3. Women pioneers—Washington (State)—Fiction. 4. Seattle (Wash.)—History—Fiction. 5. Denny, David Thomas—Fiction. I. Title.
PS3573.I3877S93 1999
813'.54—dc21
                                                  98-41196

For current information about all releases from Baker Book House, visit our web site:

                http://www.bakerbooks.com

This book is affectionately dedicated
to my very dear friend

Shirley Doop.

Acknowledgments

I would like to thank the Bellingham Public Library. At one point I had forty-seven books checked out in about three different batches with three different due dates. They were very kind and often, throughout my process of writing this book, overlooked late fees and permitted me to renew books time after time. And a special thanks to Pam!

I would also like to thank my daughter-in-law, Katie Boice Kent, for her willingness to trot books back and forth to Western Washington University's library. Thanks a bunch, Katie!

I especially thank my mother, Betty Wilbee, for her many hours of painstaking edits. Someday I just may get it through my head that it's bloodcurdling (not blood-curdling) and that it can be all right or alright, though I know I shall never figure out whether it's lay, lie, or laid.

Finally, I would like to thank Susan Champness, a reader, for pointing out that Guthrie Latimer was not Louisa's uncle, but her cousin. As a historian, it can be difficult to "join the dots." Information can be missing, misreported, and very often contradictory. It's up to the historian to try and make sense of the hodge-podge. With Guthrie Latimer I made a wrong leap in logic. So thank you, Susan, for the family tree and helping me fill in the blanks! Mercy, *et merci*.

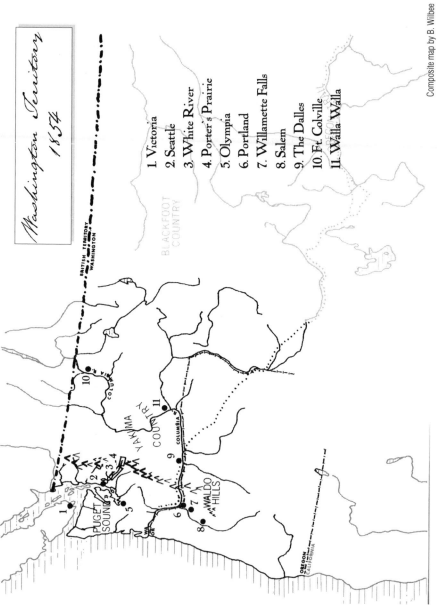

Washington Territory 1854

1. Victoria
2. Seattle
3. White River
4. Porter's Prairie
5. Olympia
6. Portland
7. Willamette Falls
8. Salem
9. The Dalles
10. Ft. Colville
11. Walla Walla

BRITISH TERRITORY
WASHINGTON

BLACKFOOT COUNTRY

YAKIMA COUNTRY

COLUMBIA

PUGET SOUND

WALDO HILLS

OREGON
CALIFORNIA

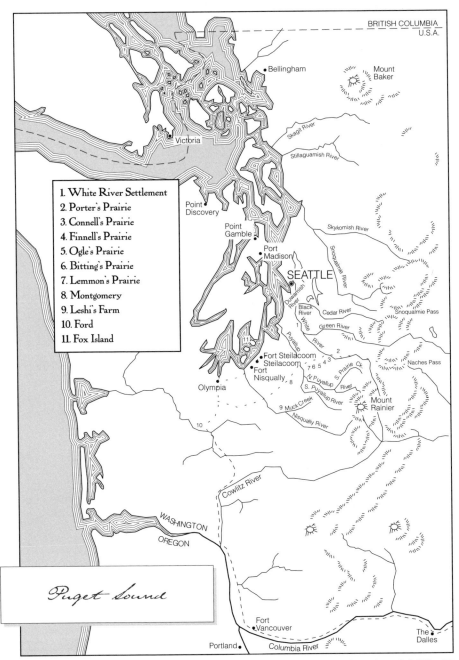

BRITISH COLUMBIA
U.S.A.

Mount Baker

Bellingham

Skagit River

Stillaguamish River

Victoria

Skykomish River

Point Discovery

Point Gamble

Snoqualmie River

Port Madison

SEATTLE

Duwamish River

Black River

Cedar River

Snoqualmie Pass

White River

Green River

Naches Pass

1. White River Settlement
2. Porter's Prairie
3. Connell's Prairie
4. Finnell's Prairie
5. Ogle's Prairie
6. Bitting's Prairie
7. Lemmon's Prairie
8. Montgomery
9. Leshi's Farm
10. Ford
11. Fox Island

11

Fort Steilacoom
Steilacoom

Fort Nisqually

Puyallup River

N. Puyallup River

S. Prairie Ck.

Mount Rainier

Olympia

S. Puyallup River

Muck Creek

Nisqually River

Cowlitz River

WASHINGTON
OREGON

Puget Sound

Fort Vancouver

Portland

The Dalles

Columbia River

Composite map by B. Wilbee '98

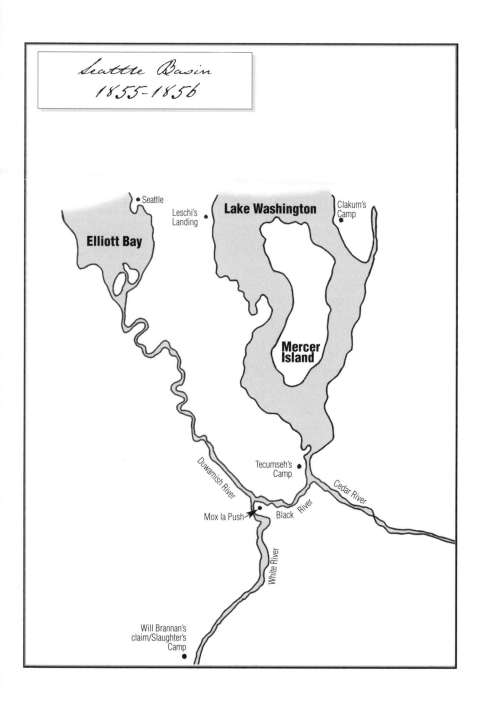

Seattle Basin
1855–1856

Seattle

Leschi's
Landing

Lake Washington

Clakum's
Camp

Elliott Bay

Mercer
Island

Duwamish River

Tecumseh's
Camp

Cedar River

Mox la Push

Black River

White River

Will Brannan's
claim/Slaughter's
Camp

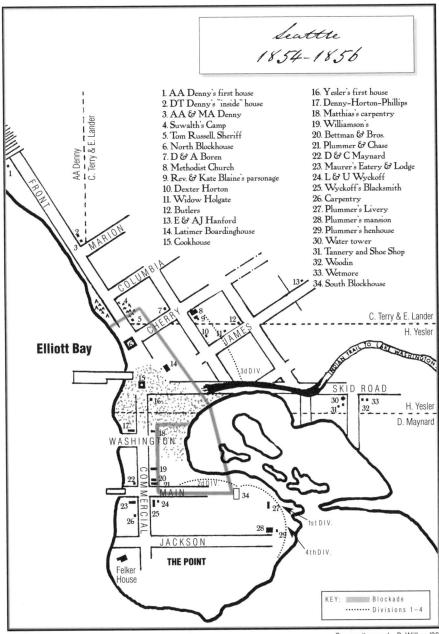

Seattle
1854-1856

1. AA Denny's first house
2. DT Denny's "inside" house
3. AA & MA Denny
4. Suwalth's Camp
5. Tom Russell, Sheriff
6. North Blockhouse
7. D & A Boren
8. Methodist Church
9. Rev. & Kate Blaine's parsonage
10. Dexter Horton
11. Widow Holgate
12. Butlers
13. E & AJ Hanford
14. Latimer Boardinghouse
15. Cookhouse

16. Yesler's first house
17. Denny-Horton-Phillips
18. Matthias's carpentry
19. Williamson's
20. Bettman & Bros.
21. Plummer & Chase
22. D & C Maynard
23. Maurer's Eatery & Lodge
24. L & U Wyckoff
25. Wyckoff's Blacksmith
26. Carpentry
27. Plummer's Livery
28. Plummer's mansion
29. Plummer's henhouse
30. Water tower
31. Tannery and Shoe Shop
32. Woodin
33. Wetmore
34. South Blockhouse

AA Denny

C. Terry & E. Lander

FRONT

MARION

COLUMBIA

CHERRY

JAMES

Elliott Bay

C. Terry & E. Lander

H. Yesler

INDIAN TRAIL TO LAKE WASHINGTON

3d DIV.

SKID ROAD

H. Yesler

D. Maynard

WASHINGTON

COMMERCIAL

MAIN

2d DIV.

1st DIV.

JACKSON

THE POINT

Felker
House

4th DIV.

KEY: Blockade
          .... Divisions 1–4

Composite map by B. Wilbee '96

THE BORENS AND DENNYS

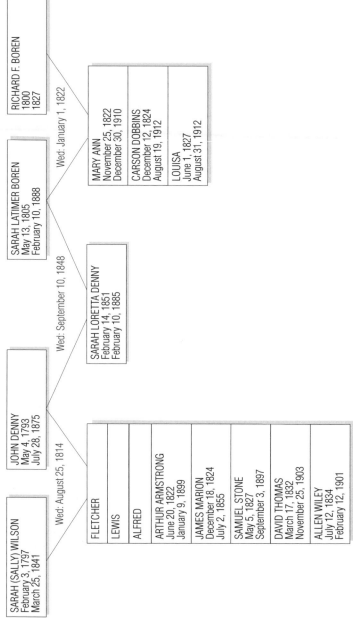

SARAH (SALLY) WILSON
February 3, 1797
March 25, 1841

JOHN DENNY
May 4, 1793
July 28, 1875

SARAH LATIMER BOREN
May 13, 1805
February 10, 1888

RICHARD F. BOREN
1800
1827

Wed: January 1, 1822

Wed: August 25, 1814

Wed: September 10, 1848

SARAH LORETTA DENNY
February 14, 1851
February 10, 1885

MARY ANN
November 25, 1822
December 30, 1910

CARSON DOBBINS
December 12, 1824
August 19, 1912

LOUISA
June 1, 1827
August 31, 1912

FLETCHER

LEWIS

ALFRED

ARTHUR ARMSTRONG
June 20, 1822
January 9, 1899

JAMES MARION
December 18, 1824
July 2, 1855

SAMUEL STONE
May 5, 1827
September 3, 1897

DAVID THOMAS
March 17, 1832
November 25, 1903

ALLEN WILEY
July 12, 1834
February 12, 1901

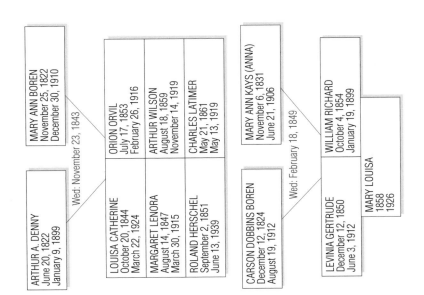

LOUISA BOREN
June 1, 1827
August 31, 1912

DAVID THOMAS DENNY
March 17, 1832
November 25, 1903

Wed: January 23, 1853

EMILY INEZ December 23, 1853 Unknown	**ANNA LOUISA** November 26, 1864 May 5, 1888
MADGE DECATUR March 16, 1856 January 17, 1889	**DAVID THOMAS JR.** May 6, 1867 October 4, 1939
ABBIE LUCINDA August 25, 1858 June 25, 1913	**JONATHON** May 6, 1867 May 6, 1867
JOHN BUNYON January 30, 1862 Unknown	**VICTOR W. S.** August 9, 1869 August 15, 1921

ARTHUR A. DENNY
June 20, 1822
January 9, 1899

MARY ANN BOREN
November 25, 1822
December 30, 1910

Wed: November 23, 1843

LOUISA CATHERINE October 20, 1844 March 22, 1924	**ORION ORVIL** July 17, 1853 February 26, 1916
MARGARET LENORA August 14, 1847 March 30, 1915	**ARTHUR WILSON** August 18, 1859 November 14, 1919
ROLAND HERSCHEL September 2, 1851 June 13, 1939	**CHARLES LATIMER** May 21, 1861 May 13, 1919

CARSON DOBBINS BOREN
December 12, 1824
August 19, 1912

MARY ANN KAYS (ANNA)
November 6, 1831
June 21, 1906

Wed: February 18, 1849

LEVINIA GERTRUDE
December 12, 1850
June 3, 1912

WILLIAM RICHARD
October 4, 1854
January 19, 1899

MARY LOUISA
1858
1926

PART 1

1855

It cannot be doubted that the hurried treaties negotiated, in 1855, with the tribes of eastern and western Washington had a good deal to do with fomenting discontent of the Indians, which culminated in bloody uprisings all over the country, causing the death of many innocent and unsuspecting settlers and the destruction of immense quantities of property all over the territory, retarding its development for many years.

The provisions of some of these treaties were exceedingly unjust to the Indians; notably the one executed at Medicine Creek; likewise at Walla Walla.

—CLARENCE BAGLEY, HISTORIAN
IN *HISTORY OF KING COUNTY, WASHINGTON*

1

*Monday Evening,
November 26*

Toward the latter part of November, Captain Hewitt's company was ordered to establish a post at the forks of the White and Green Rivers and there await orders from Lieutenant Slaughter of the regular army. The women of the village gave a supper for the volunteers the night before they left and presented them with a handsome flag.

—Roberta Frye Watt, Katy Denny's daughter
in *Four Wagons West*

*M*oonlight spilled from a cloudless sky the night of November 26, 1855, picking from the darkness the jagged outline of Seattle's many stumps and bracken, her scattered cabins, her stores, the unfinished steeple of Reverend Blaine's church, the shadowed hulk of Mr. Yesler's noisy little sawmill. It was a cold night, alive with moonlight and shadow and rich with the pungent scents of earth and sea, forest decay, the tease of salt. Alive too with the squeal of the saw, the gurgle of an outgoing tide, the lap of waves playing hide-and-seek with the sturdy pilings that held Mr. Yesler's creaking wharf in place. Suddenly, from behind his mill, high-spirited applause erupted, and for a moment the boisterous, spontaneous laughter and loud clapping drowned out the play of water, even the high-pitched whine of the whirling saw.

The rowdy applause had emerged from Yesler's cookhouse, a boxy, twenty-five-by-twenty-five-foot log house seated on the Sawdust southeast of the mill. Inside its square-timbered walls the tables were packed, with most everyone in Seattle squeezed in for supper. The ladies had prepared a fine meal for their men, and seated with her husband and daughter, her sister, and her sister's family, Louisa Boren Denny smiled a little at the fun the men were having this evening. Tomorrow they were off to war, and their excitement knew no end. It was when Ursula McConaha Wyckoff, the blacksmith's wife, presented an American flag to Captain Hewitt of Seattle's very own Company H that the wild frenzy of patriotic furor erupted. The crowd, though their stomachs were stuffed with duck and pheasant and oyster soup, nonetheless hooted and hollered, stamped their feet under the tables, and whacked their hands together like there was no tomorrow. Louisa clapped too, but with little enthusiasm. Two thoughts dominated her mind. *David was going away in the morning* and *the sloop of war was already gone.* Without the men and without the *Decatur* how would they get on?

The *Decatur* was the U.S. warship that had providentially put in to Seattle within days of the Yakima Indian Nation declaring war the month before. Louisa had grown accustomed to the safety the warship offered—her sixteen thirty-two-pound guns mounted on her sides; her ninety-six navy men and eighteen marines aboard; the kindly, wise Captain Sterrett in command. But the warmongering Haida of British territory had recently become bolder, coming down from the north in their huge war canoes with no purpose but to menace, steal when they could, and, if finding men in isolation, kill them. A month ago they'd slit the throats of two men on Bellingham Bay, and three days ago they'd been seen near Steilacoom. Captain Sterrett was gone to scare them off.

As for her husband, whom she loved more than life itself, David was one of Seattle's fifty-five volunteers. Like most of these men tonight he'd be leaving first thing in the morning and would be gone a long while—until January 25, when their term of enlistment was up. Company orders were to rendezvous with Lieutenant Slaughter of the regular army at White River thirty miles away. They were to build and occupy a fort as a defensive position to prevent the hostile Indians from descending the river into the Sound.

"Do you want to go home?"

Startled out of her reverie, Louisa turned sideways to meet her husband's familiar brown eyes and dark lashes.

"I think it's pretty much over," he told her, smiling, recalling her gently back to the present. "A few speeches left, nothing we need to sit through."

"Yes," she answered, frowning a little, for she was disoriented between her worries and the prevailing atmosphere of gaiety and fun surrounding them. "But what about the dishes and cleaning up? I can't leave everything to the others."

"The rest of us can manage," her sister, Mary Ann, interrupted. "Your back must be a torment."

Louisa was nearly six months pregnant. Her back *did* bother her.

"Come on," said David firmly, settling the matter. Somehow he managed to swing his leg over the bench without kicking Sally Bell in the ribs. It was far more difficult for Louisa to manage. Finally everyone nearby politely looked the other way so she could hike up her skirts and get the job done. David bundled Emily Inez, their two-year-old daughter, into her hat and coat.

19

"My no want to go home, Papa," she protested, though she allowed him to feed first one arm, and then the other, into her coat.

"But if little girls will have roses in their cheeks," he told her, leaning down to touch noses and crossing his eyes to make her giggle, "they must do as roses do—"

"Go to bed whiff wiwwies!" she shrieked, jumping up and down on the bench.

"And?"

"Get up whiff moaning gories!"

Go to bed with lilies, get up with morning glories. Louisa smiled indulgently at them both.

"Auntie, good-bye!" her nieces and nephews called across the table.

She blew kisses to each of her sister's children. One, two, three, four. *Katy. Nora. Rollie. Orion.* "And good-bye to you too," she said, bending down to kiss each of the Bell girls lined up in a row on her side of the table. "Laura. Lavinia. Olive. Virginia." She counted each one. "And Austin, can't forget Austin." She gave the baby of the Bell family *his* kiss. One year old, he was sound asleep in fourteen-year-old Laura's lap.

"I vos yust looking in de voods!"

Louisa glanced up. Mr. Maurer, seated at the next table, was telling a story, his high, excited voice commanding attention. "Such a vine pig cedar tree I see!" he all but shouted. "So I go round him to look! Ya, there is a hole in him, by the ground yet. I stoop down so—to look in, and py golly—it got someting inside yet!"

Louisa caught David's eye and smiled, unaware of her particular beauty tonight. By daylight she was always a pretty woman: porcelain skin, luminous eyes as brown as a good cup o' tea, her ma once said; her "midnight" hair drawn off her brow and left to fall in black, glimmering ringlets the full length of her back. Yet this evening she was all the prettier—her beauty made more fragile, more ethereal—her delicate features softly captured by the warm glow of the table lamps.

"Ya, it someting inside all right!" shouted Mr. Maurer. "Ya, it someting black, mit hair on it! I look closer—it got no head, no tail, so, I gives it a poke mit my gun, and py golly I soon find out vot it is!"

"Ya, vat is it?" hollered Lewis Wyckoff, the blacksmith, three heads down and daring to imitate Mr. Maurer outrageously.

"Vy, it's a big black bear—so pig as a cow! It shump up! An' say 'gr-r-r' an' den he comes right out at me! Mein Got—I vos dot skert—I run all de vay 'ome!"

Oh, such happy laughter! thought Louisa, her worries vanishing. With loving pride she watched her handsome husband clap Mr. Maurer warmly on the back.

"Why didn't you *shoot* him, Maurer?" demanded David.

The German proprietor of Maurer's Eatery & Lodge looked up vacantly.

"The bear!"

"Vell, py golly," sputtered Mr. Maurer sheepishly, wiping his forehead with his sleeve. "I never tink of dot! I vos yust too busy gettin' out of 'is vay!"

Laughter to peel paint from the ceiling! Louisa put both hands to her eyes to wipe the tears.

"May all our men be as brave!" someone hollered.

"To bravery!"

"To bravery!"

"Ready?" David asked Louisa, though they were still laughing uproariously at Mr. Maurer.

"Oh yes! Oh dear yes," she said, and had to wipe her eyes again.

Finally, with Emily Inez slung over his shoulder, his right hand against the small of Louisa's back, David steered her toward the door. Pride in him rushed through her limbs and heart like a wind. Was there a woman anywhere married to so fine a man as her David Denny? So kind? So gentle and strong? So wise? She turned to see him. *How tall he is! How broad his shoulders!* And when he swiveled around to hail a friend, exposing his handsome profile, her pride swelled to burst her heart! And then to see his eyes, crinkling at the edges, turn back to look at her?

Walking tall, she nodded with happiness and joy to all their friends as she squeezed between the tight benches, sometimes bumping her knees into people's backs so closely was everyone seated. The Hanford men, Ed and Seymore. Widow Holgate and her daughter Abbie Jane Hanford, Ed's wife, as well as her younger, unmarried children, Lemuel, John, Olivia, and Milton. The loggers from Salmon Bay—Edmund Carr, William Strickler, Frank McNatt, John Ross. Mr. and Mrs. Yesler. The Butlers. Uncle Tommy Mercer and his daughters. The Neelys. When Louisa passed Diana Collins she felt a pang of pity. Diana's husband had taken up with an Indian mistress. The news was all over town.

"Hello, Mrs. Russell, Mr. Russell, how are the children?" she asked, stopping at the Russells' large family table to inquire after the three orphans they'd taken in after last month's White River Massacre.

Mrs. Russell, herself a refugee from White River, dabbed her eyes with an old sodden, balled-up hanky. "The poor dears. They ain't here. Mr. Russell said not to bring 'em, to leave 'em at Tom's." She nodded across the table to her son, Seattle's sheriff with whom she, her husband, and their three unmarried children were staying. "They scare easy," she sniffed. "And what with all this talk of fighting and whatnot . . ."

"Now, Mother, you know Mary Jane's with 'em," said Mr. Russell firmly, a chubby man dressed in overalls and a stained flannel shirt. "Mary Jane's our eldest, do you know her?" he asked Louisa. A sparkle suddenly glinted in his eye, and he elbowed the two girls seated on either side of him. "Nancy and Emma here, they up and married out of turn."

"Now, Pa, you just hush!" hissed Nancy, married to John Thomas. "That's old-fashioned!"

Emma, married to Jim Crow, merely rolled her eyes, and David urged Louisa on.

Wisely, he skirted around the table where the Do-Nothings sat—the Wetmores and Woodins and some of the other newcomers who, despite everything, still pooh-poohed the Indian troubles. Louisa ignored their stony glares. Last month David had shamed Ben Wetmore in a fight. They hated him.

At the preacher's table she said, "Kate Blaine, you're looking lovely tonight."

The preacher's wife, seven months pregnant, turned awkwardly on the bench. "I might say the same of you, Louisa."

"Then do," said Louisa, teasing her.

But Kate Blaine had no sense of humor and didn't understand.

"How are you feeling?" Louisa hurried to ask.

"Like I swallowed a stone. And you?"

"My back's tiresome."

"It'll be over *one* of these days," sighed Kate.

"How long? Two more months?" Louisa asked.

"Seven weeks."

"At least *three* more months for me, maybe four."

Kate frowned with puzzlement.

"March. *My* baby is due in March."

"Yes, of course."

David gave her a nudge. Mr. Plummer, proprietor of Plummer & Chase, and Seattle's postmaster, had clambered up on a bench and was proposing a toast for "our gallant boys!"

"Whew, but it's good to be outdoors!" said David two minutes later, moonlight bathing their faces and putting a pearly glow to their skin. "I was feeling a little smothered in there."

Louisa reached for his hand, at the same time idly patting Watch, their black Labrador hound, who'd been waiting in the cold for them to come out. She heard a soft, rushing sound. A hostile Indian? Louisa froze.

But it was only a spotted fawn, bounding out from behind the mill, leaping up through the clearing toward the church and parsonage, alive with speed and wild loveliness. "Oh, look!" she cried in relief, pointing, smiling at the pretty picture the baby deer made. A flying glimpse of moonlight made flesh! Suddenly an Indian dog careered out of the trees, baying, giving chase. Another. And another.

"Watch!" warned David. "Come back here."

Reluctantly Watch held back, but the Indian curs kept on, tearing after the deer, barking and baying their way deep into the woods. Soon both the dogs and deer were gone, hunter and hunted. The sound of the chase died away through the moonlit woods.

2

Still Monday Evening, November 26

In October, 1855, [Seattle] numbered fifty souls and about thirty houses, including a church, hotel, boarding-house, five or six stores, and a blacksmith and carpenter-shop. Within a radius of thirty miles the white population amounted to about one hundred and twenty—making a total of one hundred and seventy men, women and children in Seattle and vicinity.

—Lieutenant T. S. Phelps, *Decatur*
in *Reminiscences of Seattle*

o you want to go down and take a look at the water before going home?" David asked in the quiet that followed the flight of the deer, closing his fingers tightly around Louisa's icy cold hand.

"Yes," she answered hesitantly. "I think I would."

"Liza . . ."

"What?"

"It's the way of the wild."

"I know. But it makes me sad anyway."

He drew up her hand and kissed her fingers, and was gratified to see her slowly smile. Moonlight caught in the whites of her eyes, and in the flash of her perfectly even white teeth. "That's better," he whispered. "What? Again?" He laughed, for she'd lifted her fingers back to his lips. "You're shameless, Mrs. Denny," he whispered, obliging once, and then twice.

"One more time?" she cajoled.

"Guess I'll have to do this proper." He juggled Emily Inez a little so he could lean down and kiss his wife on the lips. "We'll catch our death," he murmured, "standing here like this."

"I don't care."

"You will when your nose starts running."

"Silly."

Moonlight dappled the Sawdust—the yard immediately surrounding the mill. They crossed without tripping over any of the ugly stumps or stubbing their toes on the various-sized wood chunks that hadn't yet been picked up and tossed into the incinerator. But David did pause at one of the higher stumps. "Pig as a cow," he said, and then smiled to hear Louisa burst out laughing.

"I like to hear you laugh!"

"Mr. Maurer *was* funny, wasn't he?"

"Yes, he was."

He paused, letting go of her hand to shift Emily Inez again. She'd grown heavy in his left arm. The scent of hemlock and cedar suddenly came to him, surrounding him. The smell of evergreen woodsmoke, too, and the sweet perfume of fresh-cut balsam. The combination brought an unexpected and heady rush of elation. *This is why I left Illinois,* he thought in a rare moment of exuberance. Raw land! Beauty! Challenge! At moments like this, suddenly everything made sense—why they were here, what they were doing. Lately he'd been wondering.

Why *had* they abandoned everything, he'd questioned himself all summer and fall. Why *had* they left their comfortable homes and family and friends in Illinois to build an uncertain civilization along this lonely shore, blanketed by millions upon millions of cedar and pine and hemlock and Douglas fir? Why? This was an isolated corner of the earth embraced by danger. And not just from the hostile Indians either. George McConaha, a promising young attorney, drowned in a storm on his way home from the first territorial assembly in Olympia. Ursula Wyckoff's little girl was killed by a cougar on her way out to the necessary house. He'd never forget the day the Hanford and Holgate boys had dropped the giant cedar tree right on top of Widow Holgate's old house, nearly crushing Emily Inez to death inside. Or when the cougar had jumped Louisa.

What a flimsy thing this was, this civilization they sought to build, he scoffed to himself and not for the first time. Nothing more than a thin coat to shield them from hunger and wind and thirst and cold. A flimsy coat drawing the line between them and death. And if a man grew careless? The enemy was there to win. And sometimes did. The hunter and the hunted.

But tonight, smelling the forest decay and the sweet sting of fresh-cut lumber, the old sense of manifest destiny surged again within him. *Manifest Destiny.* The same sense of destiny kept thousands of men just like him tramping the Oregon Trail, planting their farms, building their towns. They were all building civilization.

Give a man a pile of sticks, a wagon of bricks, he built. Men built bridges and barns and towns just as beavers built their dams. For no other reason than it's just what men did.

No, he thought now, *there are reasons.* Civilization isn't just the coat that keeps off the wind and holds hunger and thirst at bay; it brings music and art and study. Without civilization a man has to grub in the dark for fuel and food and look over his shoulder. With civilization a man can sing and paint and learn.

He'd known this before of course but was glad to know it again. And gratefully he stood breathing in the colliding elements of his life on the Sound: the savage and civilized, the wild and tame, the forest's rich mulch and Henry Yesler's new-cut lumber. The Indian troubles in which they were immersed slid from his thoughts; his troubled mind found rest. This was home, this was Seattle. This was the town he and everyone else intended to put on the map.

The mill, a constant whine twenty-four hours a day, was, for the moment, mercifully quiet. Break time. But it was the mill that dominated and defined the town. It sat on an open platform near the water, its huge circular, steam-powered saw sheltered beneath a high, corrugated tin roof. To meet San Francisco's insatiable need for lumber Mr. Yesler ran his mill around the clock, with two twelve-hour shifts, midnight to noon and back again, the fires never letting up.

Surrounding the mill was the Sawdust, the triangular, sea level clearing that marked the center of town. Three years before there'd been nothing here but dusk and moon rising to meet the unbroken forest. Now there were nearly two hundred people, David realized, living in and around town.

North of the Sawdust—interspersed with more stumps and an occasional tree left standing, and here and there nearly a dozen of Subchief Suwalth's Indian shanties—lay the narrow residential area. Six or eight log and frame houses lined the narrow stumpy trails, an invisible track of streets his brother Arthur had platted and filed on paper two years ago: Front and Second, crossed by Cherry, Columbia, and Marion. The Latimer Building, a two-story boardinghouse built by Louisa's cousin during his short stay in Seattle last year, stood a stone's throw northeast of the mill, shelter to many of the town's numerous bachelors—men like George Frye, David and Walter Graham, Bill Gilliam. The new blockhouse, hastily but stoutly built, claimed the knoll at the foot of Cherry.

South of the Sawdust—across a spit of land widened and heightened by even more of the endless supply of sawdust—was the Point, Doc Maynard's claim, a bluff of land that eased out of the tideflats to a height of thirty feet above sea level, surrounded on three sides by water. It had taken Hillory Butler and Bill Gilliam over two years to clear the firs for Maynard, and Maynard had sold the land faster than the trees could come down. Cheap, ten dollars a lot. Now the Point was a denuded bluff—gawky and ugly, but the very core of the business district. Here were the stores and mercantiles, the carpentry and blacksmith shops, the livery, the ornate Felker House, Mr. Plummer's mansion, plus another half dozen or eight little houses scattered here and there.

True, the town wasn't much to boast of—yet. Yesler once called Seattle a mud-and-puddle town. Mud-and-puddle it was, with its stumps and mud and eternal sawdust. And when the wind was right the smell of sulfur, like rotten eggs, blew off the lagoon behind the Point. *But we're only getting started*, David thought. *As for Seattle making her mark in the world*, he had no doubt.

One, Puget Sound was the shortest route to China, beating San Francisco by two hundred miles. Two, Elliott Bay was the deepest natural harbor on the Sound, able to accommodate ships from anywhere in the world. Three, Congress was ready to underwrite the transcontinental railroad to the first seaport that could most economically connect the States to the Orient. One plus one plus one? It was only a matter of time.

But first—his elation vanished as quickly as it had come—they needed to settle with the Indians. One man's civilization was another man's demise, or so it seemed. The hunter and the hunted. But it didn't need to be that way. He felt strongly about this. There was plenty of room for everyone, though it certainly wasn't the way things were working out.

"What's the matter?"

"Just thinking of Jim and George Seattle, wishing things were different. Maybe even wishing," he said with a sigh, "they were going with us tomorrow. I know I'd feel better having men along who knew the countryside."

"I don't expect Jim and George want to get caught off the reservation and run the risk of getting shot. They are Indians, remember."

"Sometimes I forget." He took her hand as they started for the beach.

The idea to move his people over to the new reserve had, at first, been Chief Seattle's. Satisfied with the reservation assigned his six allied tribes at last year's treaties, he'd wished to leave October's explosive eruption of Indian hostilities to those with complaints, namely Leschi, chief of the Nisqually. But lest his own friendly people be mistaken for hostiles, he'd come over last month from Port Madison—his ancestral home and site of the new reserve—to encourage his many tribes and bands living on the east side of the Sound to make the move. But this was before Acting Governor Mason had announced, as part of his new war campaign, that *all* Indians had to be interned on their assigned reservations and that any Indian found off his reserve would be considered hostile and would be shot. Chief Seattle's good idea suddenly soured.

Hundreds of his people, having voluntarily come into town to begin preparations for their move—primarily the laborious, time-consuming task of carving large enough canoes to carry themselves and their possessions across open seawater—found themselves suddenly under white man's mandate . . . and schedule.

Suspicion flared. The government really meant to ship them off to the Land of Darkness. *Polakly Illahee!* A fearful place where the sun never shone, where mosquitoes were so big a single bite could kill the strongest man! No, assured

Doc Maynard, a man they trusted and who'd fortuitously been appointed subagent responsible for their removal. Still, *how did he know?*

Excuses set in. *November was a bad time to move their household goods by canoe.* Doc Maynard said he'd get a schooner. *There's no time to build winter shelters.* Doc Maynard said the government would supply lumber. *Food,* they argued, *was short.* Doc Maynard said he'd see to it they didn't starve. In the end, it was only because they trusted him, this friend of their chief, that the task was ever done—in two large shifts over a period of three days during the third week of November. Using Doc Maynard's brand-new barge and a rented schooner, a thousand men, women, and children were moved before it was over, and with very little trouble. Though Suwalth, the subchief in Seattle, refused to go. So did Subchief Clakum. He took his band back to Lake Washington. And Subchief Tecumseh of the Black River Duwamish returned with his band to their old home.

Tonight, holding fast to David's hand, Louisa glanced up and down the emptied beach. An eery, surreal scene. The iridescent moonlight picked up the skeletal framework of the Indians' abandoned cedar-bough shelters and dampened campfires and, scattered here and there, the piles of fish bones and entrails not yet washed away by the tide. "It's so quiet with everyone gone," she whispered.

The quiet, in fact, was profound. David tightened his grip on her hand, and she followed him carefully down to the very edge of the dark water, easing around the tossed-up logs, some large, some small, the shingle crunching harshly underneath her feet. Mr. Yesler's wharf seemed almost to climb past her shoulders as they descended the landfall. The pier of course was horizontal, it was the ground that fell away.

The tide was in retreat. They stood toe-to-toe with the black curls of receding waves, in full shadow of the wharf, listening to the soft lap of the water before them. Watching, too, the soft translucent moonlight from behind ripple across the inky black surface of Elliott Bay, Puget Sound.

Louisa shivered. "It's lonely and scary out here."

"Scary?"

"With the *Decatur* gone."

"It's not like Captain Sterrett's gone for good," he reminded her. "He's still on the Sound. And not likely," he added, "to leave anytime soon."

"I know."

"You're not worried about us leaving tomorrow, are you? We all have guns now."

"It was nice of the British to give us so many. And to send the *Otter* to help patrol the Sound."

"I doubt it was the British as much as it was Sir Douglas."

"Sir Douglas is British. He's Hudson's Bay, that's British."

"Yes. Well, it's going to be a blow for the Indians. Soon as they figure out the English *King George* have sided with us American *Bostons*. I'm sure they were expecting some measure of support from their time-honored friends."

"Do you think they really believed the Hudson's Bay Company would help them out?"

"The Company has always treated them well. Why not?"

"Too bad Governor Stevens didn't," she said bitterly.

"There's no use talking about it, Liza."

This she knew. The treaties were made, Governor Stevens was a thousand miles away, Indians everywhere were up in arms—and nothing could be done now. Except try to protect themselves. Which was why David had to leave. She felt the sting of tears and willed them back. David had enough troubles to worry about without her crying every time he turned around.

"At least Pat Kanim and Seattle are still staying out of it, Liza."

"Is he going to come back?"

"Pat Kanim? He says yes, when the governor returns. He wants to fight on our side, he has a hundred warriors—"

"Noooo, not Pat Kanim!"

"Chief Seattle?"

"No, Captain Sterrett!"

"Oh! Well yes, I expect. Soon as he can encourage the Haida to get along home."

"He can't chase them clear up the coast, where they belong."

"True."

"Do you think he'd have gone away if he'd known the volunteers were being ordered upriver?"

"Someone's got to keep an eye on the Haida."

"But Captain Sterrett would never leave us women and children alone, without protection," she persisted.

He smiled down at her. "You've got the Do-Nothings."

"Oh, David, don't joke."

"I'm sorry. But really, you needn't worry. The blockhouse is finished. The friendlies are all on their reserves. Well, most of them anyway, and soon we'll be guarding the river. And we've got the new soldiers at Fort Steilacoom now. And Major General Wool I guess will get things organized."

"Who?"

"General Wool. Chief commander of the Pacific army. He came up from California last week. Remember?"

Yes, she'd read it in the paper. "But he's in Fort Vancouver. That's practically Oregon."

"It's not a cheerful picture, I know," he offered, "but it's not hopeless. Things *have* looked worse."

She didn't answer.

"Ready to go?"

"I guess."

Emily Inez half asleep in his arms, they started back up the beach. "I've asked Uncle Tommy to keep an eye on you while I'm gone, Liza."

"I know, he asked me to move in with him and the girls, on the Point."

"It's not a bad idea. You might consider it."

"I have, and I won't. Besides, what would I do with Mandy?" Mandy was Yoke-Yakeman's *klootchman*. David had hired the Indian woman to help out with the chores that were becoming difficult for Louisa to manage while pregnant.

"You could fire her."

"I can't do that!"

"She's not that helpful," he pointed out. "My shirts only get clean in the middle, she completely forgets to do the sleeves."

"I'm not going to fire her, David."

"Well, maybe she'll learn."

"I'm sure she will."

They retraced their steps to the Sawdust, then turned in behind the mill and headed north, uphill past the Latimer Building and along the trail called Front Street toward what they called their "inside" house. David had built the little board cabin two years before, during Seattle's first Indian scare. Their real home—where Louisa *really* wanted to be—was two miles north of town, abandoned now because of the war.

"I didn't get the new inside cabin done, did I?" said David when they passed the empty lot across from the newly finished blockhouse.

"I've told you a million trillion times I can manage to run two blocks to the blockhouse if there's trouble."

"Still, I wish I'd gotten it done."

"You couldn't possibly. There're only so many hours in a day."

"Never enough," he answered with a sigh, and she knew to say no more.

They'd entered the woods—two more houses to go before reaching their own. "Mynez asleep?"

"My not asleep!"

Louisa laughed softly and reached up to lightly pinch her daughter's cheek.

"No, no, My no like that!" sniffed Emily Inez, and she pushed Louisa's hand away.

This time David laughed. "Have you locked up your chickens yet, Missy Mynez? I think it's your turn tonight."

She reared up. "My *never* do chickens, Papa! My a little girl!"

"Yes, well I guess that's right! You *are* a little girl!" He grinned and pulled Louisa close to himself. She snuggled in, near to his heart, breathing deeply of his rich, cold scent, and relishing the very substance and strength of him.

Dear God, she prayed in a rush of panic. *Don't let him go, please don't let him go. What will I do with him gone so long? How will I live if something happens to him?*

3

Midnight Monday, November 26

It is difficult to conceive of a situation more unpleasant, or better calculated to inspire thoughts of danger, than the one which the two companies were placed during the night. . . . Encamped upon a small prairie, completely surrounded by thick woods which were swarming with Indians . . .

—*Puget Sound Courier*
November 30, 1855

Fifty miles to the southeast and at midnight there was no moonlight. A heavy fog instead shrouded the tight cluster of dirty tents pinned to the muddy banks of Bitting's Creek. No moon, no stars, not even your own hand—even when held an inch from your face! *Bad enough to be out in the beastly wet woods all day,* Lieutenant Slaughter thought to himself, *thickets and trees so wild and dense they completely hide a man at twenty feet! But to have to endure this kind of fog all night as well?* The very wetness of the air crept in wher-

36

ever it could find space—between his cuffs, his wrists, his collar, his neck, his ears, his hat. It seeped into his sinuses, his throat. *Camp Misery*. This is what the lads had called *every* camp. And misery it was. The whole *war* was misery. Definitely *not* what he'd been taught at West Point, this hide-and-go-seek search for Indians skulking in the woods, and then enduring bursts of potshots coming at them from dense foliage! The good Lord knows, he breathed reverently as he stared into the murky darkness, they could've *all* been dead awhile back. At that first encounter up by Mike Connell's place, God rest his soul, it was fortunate the Indians had been lousy shots, aiming high so their two-ounce balls fell short. *Thank the Lord for tender mercies.*

Outside, closer to the creek, down in a gully protected by a copse of fir and pine, forty-five horses and twelve mules stood huddled for warmth on their picket lines, heads down, obstinately enduring the fog. Suddenly one of the horses pawed the mud. Two or three others whiffled through their nostrils. David Hall, standing guard in the swirling darkness, stiffened.

Lieutenant Slaughter inside his tent stiffened too, intuitively sensing something wrong. Tense, he strained to hear. Nothing. He found himself ruminating.

When William Alloway Slaughter graduated from West Point the summer of 1852, marching orders for an aspiring soldier couldn't have been more disappointing: Fort Steilacoom, Puget Sound. *Where in the world was that?*

He pulled out his atlas. Even after tracing his finger clear across the country, Atlantic to Pacific, he couldn't locate the post. Not until he pushed his finger up the west coast, due north, almost to British possession on the 49th parallel, did he find it. Fort Steilacoom sat midway between two towns called Olympia and Seattle. He'd never heard of them either.

He was ordered to proceed immediately via Cape Horn. The voyage took seven months. He was seasick the whole way and arrived at army headquarters in Benicia, California, more dead than alive. Bad news awaited. He'd been reassigned. He was to return and proceed with all haste to the Great Lakes.

Again seasickness beset him. And again he discovered himself reassigned—*back to the west coast*. When rerouted a third time, a friend from West Point discovered him at anchor in the bay of Panama, a vision of misery and dejection. Slaughter sat at a table, chin in his hands, and lamented to his fellow West Point graduate that he should have listened to his father and joined the navy. "That way," Slaughter quipped to Ulysses S. Grant, "I wouldn't have to spend so much of my time at sea!"

When he finally did get to Fort Steilacoom (no orders to the contrary!) his suspicion was confirmed. Wilderness posts were not known for heady fighting or rapid advancement. He did what he could to pass the time and dispel his boredom. He built a home for his wife and children. He helped lay out the streets in town, a mile southwest of the fort, edging the Sound. He took part in the local Masonic rites. He did stints as quartermaster and commissary. In Captain Maloney's occasional absences he commanded the isolated post. As a military man, he kept abreast of the European War and followed with growing concern the escalating civil tension in Kansas. Mostly he waited for his own destiny to unfold. *Did he have a destiny?*

He'd just about reconciled himself to oblivion when the Yakima of eastern Washington slit their agent's throat and declared war. In short order he found himself marching out of Fort Steilacoom.

So here I am! he thought to himself, straining to hear through the muffling fog and shivering uncomfortably in his damp bedding. *And still doing the old army shuffle—one step forward, two steps back.* It was all so disappointing. He and Maloney had been on their way to the mountains and beyond, to help the Oregon forces. The Indians had declared this war, and though the first battle—three days of a hard fight between Kamiakin of the Yakima Nation and Major Haller of the U.S. Army—had ended in favor of the Indians, there was ample time to show those dirty savages some Yankee mettle. Which is exactly what he and Maloney had intended to do!

He should have known better. This was the army, after all. A day's hike off the mountain pass and descending into Yakima to reconnoiter with their superior and reinforcements, word had come that Major Rains had been delayed at The Dalles far to the south. *So much for showing mettle.* Between Slaughter and Maloney they had but three hundred men, fifty of them inexperienced volunteers. The Indians numbered anywhere from fifteen hundred to six thousand seasoned warriors. Mettle and stupidity were two different things. So it was back through Naches Pass, terrain all too familiar. His only consolation was that Maloney intended, upon returning to the fort, to head down to Fort Vancouver, east up the Columbia River to The Dalles, and in this way make the reconnoiter with Major Rains—and send those Yakima packing! Yes sir!

Ah . . . but coming off the western foothills onto Connell's Prairie they'd stumbled across the mutilated corpses of four white men—two of them their own scouts. Which is when all this miserable skirmishing started, and thoughts of glory vanished.

Dirty buzzards *this* side of the mountains had declared their own kind of war, cat-and-mouse. Just cowards popping off sneaky shots, shooting you in the back. No real glory in this. Of course the buzzards had waited for him and Maloney to go fight the Yakima in the east and leave the Sound unprotected. *Double cowards. Well, they'd come back, hadn't they? And hadn't he and Maloney gone after their tails?*

White River Skirmish, Green River Skirmish, South Prairie Skirmish. Three skirmishes in about as many days. Chasing Indians through dense, wet trees was not his idea of war. A man usually liked to *see* what he was shooting at. Better yet, what was shooting him!

California's reinforcement had finally arrived, Company M, Third Artillery, led by Captain Keyes. He had immediately taken over the command and ordered them all—regulars, volunteers, and conscripted animals—into the field and out to every point of the compass. This war, yes sir, was going to get organized yet! No more shiffle-shuffle!

Maloney, with the main body of regulars, was headed for Frank Montgomery's big log house on the Nisqually Plains. Within easy reach of both Forts Nisqually and Steilacoom, and within striking distance of favorite Indian camping grounds along the Puyallup, White, and Green Rivers, Montgomery's was to be the central station for war operations.

Olympia's Company B was making tracks for the mouth of Muck Creek on Nisqually River, near Leschi's abandoned farm and ranch, to round up reluctant friendlies and force them onto the Fox Island Reserve.

Slaughter was assigned White River, where he was to rendezvous with Seattle's volunteers and build a fort—and defend it. This was their last night at Bitting's Prairie, tomorrow they'd head for Stuck Creek and beyond. *It'll be nice,* he thought, thinking of the fort they were to build, *to sleep in a real bed, a dry bed.*

What's that?

This time he sat up, rubbing his eyes and trying in vain to see through the blackness. *Lousy, stinkin' war! Can't see a dadgum thing!* He thought of the four dead in his command, the four wounded. He had no idea what kind of casualties he was inflicting. *What kind of war was this? When you can't tell who's winning, and who's losing?*

To top things off Keyes had reported the campaign in eastern Washington a complete fiasco. Lead out of his boots, Rains had finally marched out of The Dalles with 334 soldiers and six companies of Oregon volunteers, a total of 750 men, only to drag his heels at every encounter with Kamiakin. A few minor scuffles, two or three of his own boys dead, and all he'd managed to accomplish was to burn down the Catholic Mission on the Ahtunum! The *mission?*

As for Kamiakin, Rains allowed him to cross the Columbia River and disappear! Unwilling to give chase and force a showdown, Rains simply went back to The Dalles! Abandoning the *real* war, the *glorious* war, to the Oregon volunteers who'd stayed behind in the field. A preposterous state of affairs! What Kamiakin might do next was nothing *he* wanted to think about!

Maybe it's just as well I'm stuck over here. At least we're shooting Indians, he told himself, feeling better. *Not burning down churches!*

A high, yipping howl suddenly surrounded his camp. He hardly had time to lunge for the tent flap before general gunfire exploded. David Hall came stumbling in from the picket lines, tripping over tent pegs and screaming, "They're after the horses!"

"Get down to the picket lines!" Slaughter bellowed. Pandemonium broke. Guns in hand, everyone plunged into the murky blackness toward the picket line and the frantic, neighing horses, bumbling over tree roots, crashing into trees, all the while blindly blazing away at whatever might be in front of them.

This is not *good,* thought Slaughter. "Hold your fire!" he screamed. "They only want the horses!" Just then a bullet lifted his hat.

4

Early Tuesday, November 27

Early in November General Wool arrived at Fort Vancouver, bringing with him from California one company of artillery ... and two thousand stands of arms. This addition to the defenses of the territories would have done much to encourage the settlers, if Wool had permitted them to be used.

—Clinton Snowden
in *History of Washington,* vol. 3

*I*n Seattle the next morning Louisa awoke before daylight. Her window, facing east toward Elliott Bay, was still so dark she saw nothing of the minute droplets of rain beginning to chase each other down the warped glass. *Today David is leaving.* Sighing, she turned over in their rumpled bed to see his face—so familiar, so dear to her. She knew each angle, each line, the fine texture of his forehead, the way his cheeks went slack in sleep. Gently she stroked his lips, warm to her fingertip. *His lips can say more without speaking,* she

42

thought, *than most men can with words.* The message came in the way he smiled at her, in the way he kissed her, in the way his mouth turned up at the corners when he watched her on the sly. These lips she traced ever so slightly suggested always and in many different ways, "I love you."

He opened his eyes and smiled. But when she smiled back, he closed his eyes again. Such peace. She slid into his arms, arms that welcomed her even as he slipped back into unconsciousness. *Even asleep, he loves me. So I will lie here and be loved.*

Captain Sterrett of the *U.S. Decatur* was a man of middle years with coarse, graying hair and steel blue eyes—eyes that, if necessary, could hold a man uncomfortably to the wall. Short by way of height though formidable in stature, he sat unhappily on a bentwood chair inside the officers' quarters of Fort Steilacoom, listening in dismay as Captain Keyes of Company M, Third Artillery gave him a full report on the war. Through the window Sterrett could still detect a pale pattern of stars against the gradual lightening of the sky. What time was it getting to be? Six? Seven? Too early, certainly, to be listening to such a sorry state of affairs. But he was leaving at sunrise for Nisqually and needed the briefing. Captain Erasmus Darwin Keyes, the army's new commanding officer on the Sound, was in direct communication with Brevet Major General Wool and was the man to do the briefing.

"The real truth of the matter," Sterrett finally spoke up, his emerging anger blunted by the astonishing dismay he felt, "is that Major Rains threw the war in eastern Washington to the Indians."

"It seems that way, yes. Though he's blaming everyone else for his abysmal failure," answered Keyes, a man Captain Sterrett pegged to be an efficient and sufficient, if not astute, sort of man. Seated at the desk he had been invited to share with Fort Steilacoom's Lieutenant Nugen, Keyes leaned back in the solid oak chair and gave Sterrett his full attention. "Rains's officers are preferring charges against him. He, in turn, is preferring charges back against them."

"And Major General Wool? What's he say?"

"Wool is blaming the volunteers."

Sterrett was so taken aback by the statement that he lurched forward, nearly spilling his coffee. "If it weren't for the volunteers," he gasped, arm up, leveling his cup, "the Yakima and Walla Walla Indians would have annihilated every white man, woman, and child in *both* Oregon and Washington by now. And not left a grease spot, I might add!"

"I'm only saying Wool doesn't like volunteers. Considers them uncouth and undisciplined. He dismissed them—"

"He can't do that!"

"The Oregon volunteers he can."

"But he can't," said Sterrett decidedly. Just as decidedly he set aside his coffee cup. *Army* coffee.

"He can, he did."

"How so?"

"The Oregon boys were never sworn into the regular army, unlike Washington's men."

"Right, right." Sterrett waved a dismissive hand. "And if I remember correctly, Rains made quite a fuss about it at the time. He wanted them under his thumb."

"You may know more of this than I do, but Acting Governor Mason, I was told, made Rains Brigadier General over Washington's volunteers if he consented to let the Oregon boys tag along. Wool is furious he fell for such hocus-pocus. He has no use for volunteers and made short work of dismissing them. Wool *also,*" Keyes rushed on, "disbanded another Washington brigade Mason put together to fetch Governor Stevens and escort him home."

"Someone's heard from the governor then?" said Sterrett, surprised.

Keyes nodded.

44

"So where is he? What's he doing?" This, at least, was good news!

"According to Mason he's at Coeur d'Alene."

"That's only halfway," Sterrett mumbled, elation gone in a breath as he pictured the five hundred miles and two mountain ranges yet to be traversed. Mostly through Yakima and Walla Walla territory. Dangerous ground where one paper reported "a thousand blood-crazed warriors lurking behind every hill, hiding in every swale, waiting to kill the governor and wipe out his train."

"Peo-Peo-Mox-Mox sent him a message," said Keyes.

Sterrett felt his eyebrows go up.

"A slave was promised his freedom to deliver it."

"I assume he's a free man?" A rhetorical question. As to the message, he hardly needed to ask. Peo-Peo-Mox-Mox, along with Kamiakin and Five Crows of the Cayuse, had made it clear who their number one enemy was—and whose scalp they wanted.

"Peo-Peo minced no words," said Keyes.

Sterrett inched forward on his chair. "Did Wool know this when he disbanded the governor's brigade?"

"He did."

"You've a fool for a boss!"

"A navy man might say so, sir."

The officer warranted a smile. Sterrett did not give him one. "What does Wool suggest Governor Stevens do?" he snapped instead, his anger surfacing.

"I think he's of the opinion that the governor can look out for himself. Though he did suggest Stevens hop a boat on the Missouri and flee for safety to St. Louis and New York."

Sterrett popped to his feet, stunned. He found himself pacing, rubbing the back of his neck. "What in the world?" he thundered, turning on Keyes, all pretense at calm gone. "He lets Rains get away with tossing the war to Kamiakin! He dismissed the Oregon volunteers! *And now he's telling the governor to go back east?*"

45

"He may hate the volunteers, but he despises Stevens. Loathes him."

"It must be some doozy of a quarrel, to play so lightly with so many lives!"

"They're sizing each other up like a couple of gamecocks."

"Is war the place to stake their wagers?"

"No, sir."

The navy captain went over to the dark window and stared bleakly outdoors, rubbing and rubbing his neck. He was getting a headache. The army captain briefly explained the origins of an old quarrel, something about a boast Wool had made in regard to his role in some battle during the Mexican War, a boast that Stevens publicly castigated his superior for as an exaggeration.

"Makes no sense," Sterrett muttered furiously. The sky, he noticed, was at last beginning to fully lighten. Though threatening clouds stood by to the north.

"There's more," said Keyes.

Sterrett gave him a brief glance.

"While Rains and six of the Oregon companies were playing peekaboo with Kamiakin, Peo-Peo and his allies stormed Fort Walla Walla. Did it up right too. Plundered over thirty-seven thousand dollars' worth of stores, both government and Hudson's Bay. Then they burned down the Umatilla mission and some of the Oregon settlers' homes. That's when the two Oregon companies at The Dalles got their dander up—and went after him."

Sterrett stopped rubbing his neck long enough to hold up a hand, like a schoolboy waiting to ask a question.

"From the original eight," said Keyes, clarifying. "Governor Curry of Oregon sent Rains eight companies total."

"Right. But you said Wool sent them all home."

Keyes sighed and flopped backward again into Lieutenant Nugen's office chair. Arms clasped behind his neck, he said, "Let's start from the beginning," and made eye contact with Sterrett.

46

"All right."

"Eight companies."

"Right."

"Six go with Rains after the Yakima. Two are left. They go after Peo-Peo and the Walla Walla."

"Right."

"Then Rains gives away the war."

"Yes."

"When he returns, he finds Wool at The Dalles, and Wool is livid. He dismisses the Oregon men on the spot."

"So you say."

"But no one in Oregon is beholden to him, Sterrett. They can do as they please. Which they did. Half went home in pretty bad shape. Without suitable clothing or tents to protect them from the winter weather, they'd all suffered, frostbite mostly, but some were so severely disabled with rheumatism they simply weren't fit for duty. Most of their horses weren't either. Complaints over their treatment ran high. Consequently, some asked Colonel Nesmith, their elected commander, to be discharged, while several others were discharged by orders of Nesmith's surgeon. A few had urgent business requiring their personal attention. These Nesmith furloughed. Command was then turned over to Colonel Kelly."

"Why?"

"Nesmith had to go back too—he's been elected to the legislature."

"So Kelly's in charge."

Keyes nodded. "He reorganized the men who were left—enough for two companies. Plus the two already gone after Peo-Peo."

"Who are now stuck up the Umatilla on their own," said Sterrett grimly, beginning to follow.

"Up a creek without a paddle, literally," said Keyes, easing forward to clasp his hands together on top of the desk. "With Rains and the regulars pulled out of the fray Kamiakin and the Yakima were free to reinforce Peo-Peo and his Walla Walla."

Sterrett felt his heart drop. "Are you telling me that Major General Wool isn't sending the *regulars* to support the volunteers against Peo-Peo-Mox-Mox?"

"No. I mean, yes. You're right, sir. He is not."

"And Major Haller? Major Rains? They're to sit this out at The Dalles? While settlers are in danger and Governor Stevens has to somehow wade through five hundred miles of hostile territory on his own?"

"The volunteers at The Dalles have already sent two urgent appeals to Wool for more guns and reinforcement. Wool refuses. *Despite* the fact that we brought up from California two howitzers, three hundred tons of stores and ammunition, and two thousand stands of arms. But not one gun, not one bullet for the volunteers, Sterrett. That's just the way it is."

Sterrett turned back to the window. "It's his *job!*"

"His quarrel with Stevens is stuck in his craw, he's out to settle a score. He's shifted all blame for the war onto Stevens—"

"It hardly matters who's to blame!" stormed Sterrett in a thunder of fury. "We have a war on our hands!"

"Wool says the war is of Stevens's own making—"

"And I'm sure there are any number of settlers who will agree with him!" snapped Sterrett. "From what I hear Stevens all but jammed his treaties down the Indians' throats! Kamiakin and Peo-Peo-Mox-Mox, Leschi, the whole bunch— they're bound to gag! That's not the point! What's done is done! It's war now! Wars have to be *fought!* With *men!* With *guns!* Who is Wool to sit on both?"

"He says the settlers over there aggravated everything. Any movement against the Indians is punitive, he says, unworthy of civilization. If the settlers will just leave the Indians alone, he says, the Indians will leave them alone."

48

Sterrett smote the window frame with the heel of his hand. "Knock a beehive loose and the bees won't attack if you mind your own business? Is that it?" he thundered, so angry that in his mind he was already dashing off letters to Washington City.

"I suspect that what Wool is saying is that if you knock a beehive loose you can expect to get stung."

"Kamiakin declared *war*," Sterrett answered coldly, turning to Keyes.

"I am well aware of that."

"He vowed to kill every white man, woman, and child—even if it took him five years. As for Peo-Peo-Mox-Mox, you said yourself that he's ransacked government property, that he's boasting about murdering the governor. Sometimes a beehive *has* to be knocked loose! And Major General Wool is *obligated* to protect the settlers in this country! He is *certainly* obligated to ensure the life of the governor!"

Keyes sighed. "I'm only playing the devil's advocate, Sterrett. Maybe he knows something we don't. After all, some of those volunteers, you have to admit, are a little short on brains and awful long on bravado. And Wool did *not* get to where he is by being a *complete* fool."

"He's old! He's traded intelligence," Sterrett angrily tapped his own head, "for pride! He needs to be put out to pasture!"

Keyes leaned heavily over the desk and thumped his folded hands softly against the desktop. "Well . . . that's what's happening on the *east* side."

"The *east* side, yes," agreed Sterrett, going wearily back over to his chair and sitting down. The east side. None of his business. Better to save his energies for this side of the mountains.

"What I'm saying here," said Keyes, and Sterrett jerked up, startled afresh by a dark edge to the captain's voice, "is that Kamiakin might send his warriors to help out old Peo-Peo-Mox-Mox."

"I'm sure he will. I'm sure he *has*."

49

"Or . . ."

Sterrett felt his eyebrows shoot up. "Or?"

"Or he might spare a few for Leschi, here on the Sound."

Sterrett swore. He should have seen this one coming. He was still trying to absorb this when Lieutenant Nugen came through the door and startled them both.

"Bad news, Captain Keyes. Slaughter's been attacked on Bitting's Prairie. About five hours ago, middle of the night sometime. One man's been killed, three or four more injured. Some of the tents were perforated by balls, a bullet pouch was hit. But it seems they were mostly after the horses. Thirty-two were stolen, and all twelve mules, sir."

"Leschi?"

"Yes."

"How many Indians involved?"

"Fellow that came in says near as anyone can figure, two hundred."

Keyes and Sterrett caught each other's eyes at the same time. Leschi had but a hundred warriors. Kamiakin hadn't wasted any time. *But it could always be new recruits,* thought Sterrett. *There were hundreds of unaccounted Indians living off the reserves.*

Keyes drew up the orders. A company of his infantrymen would leave immediately to reinforce Slaughter. "He'll of course be reinforced by the Seattle volunteers," he told Sterrett, "once he gets to White River—"

"You ordered *Seattle's* volunteers into the field?"

"It's logical. Yes."

"But—"

"I'm not Wool!" snapped Keyes, sensing judgment. "Anyone willing to fight, I take. I don't care if they're West Point graduates or blackguards with a prison record—so long as they have a gun and know how to shoot the blamed thing. Besides, Washington's volunteers were sworn into the service of the army. To use *your* word, I am *obligated*—"

"Keyes, you've left women and children unprotected."

50

"No one's complained about me using the volunteers out of Steilacoom and Olympia."

"That's because the Steilacoom citizens have the fort and Lieutenant Nugen here to protect them. And Olympia's got *two* companies. One works under you, yes, but the other serves as home guard."

"Confound it, Sterrett, this is war. I don't have enough men as it is—"

"*Wool* has the men! He has them sitting on their fannies, blowing smoke out their—"

"But *I* don't have men!" Keyes shouted back. "What am *I* supposed to do? And if any of those Klikitat/Yakima warriors are headed for here, pushing through the pass, I've *got* to have a fort at White River to plug 'em up! It's the only way."

Sterrett threw up both hands in the universal language of submission and agreement. "I know, I know. I mean no criticism. We're between a rock and a hard place here, Keyes. All of us. It's just that Seattle is the most vulnerable city on the Sound. I hate thinking about those women and children— they're sitting ducks, Keyes."

"But if there's a fort blocking the river—"

"What about the Haida? Attacking from the water?"

"That's *your* job."

"You know that the band bothering you folks last week hit Fort Nisqually yesterday. I can't go back to Seattle, I've got to go down there now—"

"Captain Keyes," put in Nugen, reminding them of more urgent business. "Slaughter's requested a surgeon. Their doctor was shot, the injury is serious."

Sterrett glanced sharply at the window. The clouds had closed in, a soft rain had begun to fall. He had to get going. "I'll loan you my assistant surgeon, Keyes," he said, easing to his feet and heading for the door. "Will it work if Taylor reports here for duty within the hour?"

"Thank you, Sterrett." Keyes came around the desk.

"Keep me posted." Sterrett took Keyes's hand. "And if the army gives you any more trouble, let me know. Maybe there's something more the navy can do to help you out."

"I appreciate that. Thanks."

Sterrett headed for the muddy road that would take him down to the harbor a mile away, rain picking up just enough to ensure him a good dousing by the time he got to the government pier. Never mind the rain. He needed the walk to work off his anger. *Was Wool's quarrel with Stevens to bring similar woe to the Sound,* he wondered darkly, *as the dispute between Agamemnon and Achilles brought to Troy?*

The Oregon volunteers, those who were left, ignored General Wool and rallied, setting out to reinforce their exposed comrades. But being left to their own resources, they were compelled to continue with insufficient arms, clothing, camp outfits, and sundry supplies. Nevertheless, they went.

They followed the Oregon Trail east a hundred miles, out to the Umatilla River and Fort Henrietta, and Major Chinn. Three hundred seventy-five men, ill-equipped but willing. Anxious to relieve their fellow volunteers, open the country for Washington's governor—and most of all, to go shoot some Indians!

5

Early Tuesday Morning, November 27

When they came to the trail's end and entered a high, grassy meadow, the clean, peeled logs of their new, unfinished cabin stood before them, bathed in morning's first glow of light. . . . *It's the most beautiful house on the Sound,* Louisa thought with pride.

—Brenda Wilbee
in *Sweetbriar Summer*

Louisa stood atop a beached log, gazing absentmindedly out to sea. Last night she'd dreamt the war was over, that she was back at home in the Swale. The war, of course, was not over. But still, she thought, toying with an idea while watching a steamer slowly emerge out of the rain. It was too dangerous, *but still . . . it would be nice if I could!*

"Come on, Watch! Time's up!" she hollered suddenly, stepping off the log, moccasins soft around her feet and quiet against the crunchy shingle. Seconds later Watch came bounding out from beneath an overhang of wet foliage to leap all around her outstretched hand, throwing up sand, seaweed decay, and bits of mud. "Acch, go on!"

When he raced up the beach, past the trail to her house, she yelled, "Hey! Come back here! Watch! Come onnnn!" she pleaded. "It's pouring rain!"

He paid no mind. "Watch!" she shouted again. "Watch! It's *raining!*" He looked up, tail wagging, as if to say, "So what else is new?" But he'd heard the tone in her voice and dutifully came trotting back.

"Good boy!" She gave him a push up the trail, grabbing the low brush and ferns to draw herself along after him, toes digging into a web of protruding madrona roots. "And no sniffing the milk!" she hollered.

David's brother Arthur had inherited her own brother's cows last summer—when Dobbins left Seattle in search of his runaway wife. Cresting the cliff, Louisa rattled off the cows' names in her mind: *Hay Barn*—never got enough hay; *Hardy Axe Handles*—a hard milker; *Texas*—the only longhorn; *Loco*—the crazy one; *Portia*—yellow milk, rich cream; *Juliet*—thin, blue milk; *Pied*—a high kicker. Sometimes her nieces Katy and Nora liked to play it dangerous and give old Pied a tug on her tail when Arthur wasn't looking. *Ah, one of these days,* Louisa thought to herself, *those girls will get caught and be sorry! Hay Barn, Hardy Axe Handles, Texas, and Loco,* she chanted, turning up the trail. *Portia, Juliet, and Pied!* Each morning Arthur had the girls set a bucket of the milk on her doorstep, and sure enough, her milk was waiting on the stoop, rain dripping into the rising cream. Smiling, she picked up the pail and eased indoors.

Still smiling and feeling exhilarated by her run up the hill, Louisa draped her wet coat on the spike beside the door, hung her bonnet on the back of the door, and then tiptoed across the small crowded room to bend over the bed. "Good morning," she whispered, her happy smile growing tender

54

as she gazed down at this man she loved so dearly—and who would so soon be leaving her.

He opened his eyes for a second time that morning. "Where've you been?" he mumbled sleepily, reaching up to cup her neck and bring her face down to meet his.

"To let Watch out," she mumbled back between their kisses.

"What's the weather like out there?"

"You can't hear it?"

"I was hoping I was dreaming."

"There's a steamer coming in."

"The *Traveler*?"

"No, Captain Parker is already here, tied up at Yesler's. Came in early, I guess. Everyone's there, getting her loaded. This is a different ship, coming in from the north."

"Maybe it's the *Beaver*," he said hopefully, sitting up and swinging his legs off the bed. "Sir Douglas said he might send it after the *Otter* if he could. If it is, maybe Captain Sterrett can come back to Seattle. Let the British take care of the Haida. They *are* British."

"Maybe," was all she was willing to speculate.

Gingerly David set his bare feet on the cold cougarskin rug. "Burrrr," he complained, grinning over at Louisa. Despite being clad in his red woolen long johns, he was freezing. It wasn't the cold, though, as much as it was the biting dampness of winter coming on.

Louisa tossed him the socks she'd draped near the fire before going out. "Flapjacks?" she asked, fixing her mind on breakfast. Mynez would soon be up.

"If they'll stick to my ribs. It's looking pretty miserable out there."

"At least you won't have to walk. Like the last time you went up."

"Oh, we'll walk. Plenty. The *Traveler* can't get all the way upriver. You making those flapjacks with buttermilk?"

55

"Of course. David, I've been thinking," she said, going over to the table to bend down and draw out her flour bucket from underneath. "There *is* a silver lining to every cloud."

"You have a particular cloud in mind?" He glanced over at his clothes hanging on the bedpost.

"Your leaving, the *Decatur* gone."

"Oh?"

"I was thinking—"

"Here, let me do that," he objected, leaning off the bed to stop her. Six months pregnant, she had no business bending or lifting anything anymore. He told her so.

"I'm not an invalid."

"Still, let me do it," he insisted, pulling out the twenty-five-pound tin and then lifting it off the floor to the crowded shelf that was her work space. "How can you stand it?" he said, looking around at the crowded room. "You haven't room to sneeze. One more week and I could have built the house, closer to the fort."

"You didn't," she interrupted, prying off the rusty lid with both hands. "So leave it be. I'm getting tired of your talking about it all the time."

He went back to the bed to finish drawing on his socks. "You were saying?"

"Every chance you get, you talk about it, David. It's a never-ending story with you."

"Not the house. Your silver lining."

"Oh!" She laughed, and started to measure out her flour. "I was thinking. Well, I was wondering, with you gone and the *Decatur* gone, what protection do I have here that I don't have at the Swale?" *There, it was out.*

He was off the bed and across the room before she even had time to turn around. "You're *not* going out there. I'm not even going to talk about it!"

"Since when did you start telling me what to do?" she asked, bewildered a little by his anger.

"Since White River, since the massacre."

"David, I'm talking about the Swale!—a whole different direction! And it's off the ocean, the Haida have no reason to go back there. And the Klikitat, they're all with Leschi now, or gone back to Yakima—"

"I *saw* what was done to the women, Louisa! Things only the devil could do! Do I need to tell you? *Must I put their suffering into words?*"

Fear etched his eyes. She realized instantly how silly, how stupid she was to even think of leaving town! She'd been thinking only from her perspective, not from his. *What a start I've given him!*

"It was only a thought," she told him quickly, giving in, trying to ease the terrible fear in his eyes. "I just miss the Swale, that's all. I miss my cupboards, my sink, my water pump. I miss my big stove, the hearth you made. I miss my pretty wall bordering—"

"You could make some for here," he offered, glancing around the top of the walls.

"But I don't *want* to make anything new! Don't you understand?" she heard herself burst out. "I just want all the things I *do* have back! I want my pretty dishes, I want my front porch! I want my garden! And with the weather being so mild, I could be—" Suddenly she was crying, tears out of nowhere. "Oh, David," she wept, covering her eyes and tipping her head into his chest. "I just want to go home! You, me, Mynez—the three of us. I want to be home. I want the war over, I want everything to be the way it used to be."

He pulled her into his arms, so hard and so strong, and she could feel the warm comfort of his hand press her head against his heart. "Oh, Liza," he whispered tenderly, "don't you see? That's all the Indians want too."

She reared up, staring into his face. *Yes, this is all Kamiakin and Leschi want, nothing less, nothing more.* She pushed her nose back into his chest. "I think," she whispered, "I could be happy enough here. I could be content, if you didn't have to go away. If you were here too."

"But I have to go. You know that."

She felt him shivering from the cold.

"You know that, don't you?"

She nodded into his red undershirt.

"There can be no peace until the Indians are defeated. It's a terrible thing, but there you have it."

"But I don't want you to go, David. I'm afraid for you. I'm *really* afraid."

He lifted her chin and smiled down into her eyes. "A secret?"

"What?"

"I'm a little afraid too. But remember what you said when I came back from White River the first time?"

"I say a lot of things. I hardly remember what I say anymore, I get so scared when you go off."

"You said God can be trusted both sides of the grave, and in this we have our hope."

"But you were home then, David. That was *easy* to say. But now you're leaving."

He chuckled.

"It's not funny."

"I'm sorry, but whether I'm coming or going, it's still true."

She thought about it. And she did remember saying it. The idea had come from her sweetbriar and the tryst she'd shared with Pamelia, her dearest friend in Illinois. Dear, sweet Pamelia. *She'd* known the eternal hope of their favorite flower. *Spring will always come,* Pamelia had said. *And we shall be together someday! If not in this world, in the one to come!*

Oh, but how easy to say, how hard to believe. Yet Louisa knew it was true. They *were* in God's hands. And in the world to come they would never be called to part. *This is my hope,* she thought now. *This I can cling to.* She sniffed and dried her eyes.

"David," she said, stepping back, "we need more firewood. You're absolutely freezing to death. And if you must die—" she stepped back into his arms and banged her head into his chest, "I'd prefer it wasn't anything so mundane as a cold."

He hugged her. "You're funny."

"I am not."

"You are!" He laughed.

She smiled down at his stomach.

"Are you all right then?" He brought up her chin, searching her face for any trace of lingering sorrow.

"I'm fine—for five minutes anyway. No telling after that, the way I've been lately. Now will you get more wood? Or do I need to go out?"

"Let me get my pants on first."

She laughed out loud, surprising herself and David. He chucked her under the chin firmly. "You're so pretty when you laugh, Liza!"

"I can just see you out there," she giggled foolishly, their quarrel happily ended, "with just your red long johns on!"

"Hey! I have my socks on!"

"Yes, you do!"

He seized her face with both hands. "You scared me. Promise me you won't go out to the Swale. Promise."

"Keep kissing me, I'll promise anything."

"Promise?"

"Don't stop kissing me."

"Promise?"

"I promise, I promise!"

6

Later Tuesday Morning,
November 27

It was an anxious day in the life of the village when the volunteers left for what, as everyone thought, would be their quarters for winter. Adjutant General Tilton sent the Steamer *Traveler* to transport them up the river. One can picture the little stern-wheeler chugging noisily away from Yesler's wharf where the pioneer men had gathered to see them off while anxious women watched from every hillside cabin.

—Roberta Frye Watt, Katy Denny's daughter
in *Four Wagons West*

The ship Louisa had seen coming in was the *Ben Franklin* from San Francisco. On board was Charles Terry, one of Seattle's original pioneers, returning from his trip back east where he'd gone to see his dying brother. After the surprised but happy reunion between him and the other Seattle originals—namely the two Denny brothers and Mr. Bell—Charles joined the small huddle of men who'd come out in the miserable rain to say good-bye to the volunteers headed for White River. Men like Henry Yesler who had to keep the mill going, and Uncle Tommy Mercer with his four motherless children, and Mr. Bell whose wife was dying of the same consumption Lee Terry had suffered. Congregated at the end of Yesler's long wharf, rain drumming down around their ears and pelting their backsides, these faithful few promised to keep a good eye on the womenfolk. David gave his friend Charles a last bear hug, then knocked his hat off.

"What d'you do that for?" chortled Charles, returning the favor.

David laughed, and bent to retrieve both hats.

"Hey, let's swap! Wha'd'ya say?" said Charles. He reached for David's toque.

"Yes, well, but wait, I don't know . . . Louisa knit this one for me. No, no, let's do it," he vacillated. *A fine thing it would be*, he thought, *to go off to war wearing his old friend's raccoon-tailed hat!*

"You sure?"

"Yeah, that's fine. I'd like that!"

"What about Louisa? She won't mind?"

"If she does, we'll trade back when I get home."

So they made the exchange and then stood grinning foolishly at each other.

"Boy, I hate to go, Charles! There's so much to catch up on!"

"I warrant more on your end than mine. But you better shake a leg, Denny! Boat's leaving without you!"

It was true! Crew members were throwing up the lines. Quickly David scrambled aboard and leaned over the amidship's rail, engines rumbling below his feet, Charles's raccoon tail bobbing pleasantly off his shoulder. "So long!" he called out. "Good to see you home! *Real* good! Hey, my friend? Do me a favor! Help Uncle Tommy keep an eye on my wife, will you?"

61

"If she's as pretty as she ever was, Denny, me and every other man in town!" teased Charles.

David's brother Arthur sidled in next to Charles.

"Hey, Charles!" shouted David.

"What?"

"Mary Jane Russell's back in town!"

Charles Terry blushed beet red, Arthur chuckled. Playfully he punched Charles's upper arm. "She's living at her brother Tom's place. You remember Sheriff Tom, don't you, Charles?"

"I remember Mary Jane!" Charles started backing off the wharf with a grin big enough to reach his ears.

"Across from the blockhouse!" shouted David after him. He and Arthur both burst out laughing when Charles waved, turned tail, and ran.

"Well, Dave, looks like this is it!" Arthur thrust up his arm. "Good luck!"

"Thanks!" David reached down. A few words passed between the brothers as they shook hands, their arms linked over the churning, frothy water between the pier and the ship's hull. Clearly, Arthur regretted not going, but he'd been elected to the territorial assembly for a third time in a row and would be leaving at the end of the week for Olympia. The Assembly was slated to convene the following Monday, December the 3rd. "Good luck! And keep that gun dry!" he shouted, leaping away as the idling engines suddenly burst into full throttle.

"Thanks! But I don't know who needs it the most! You or me! Don't let those Democrats bamboozle you, Art!" shouted David, waving.

Arthur threw back his head and laughed. So did a lot of other men. The Denny brothers were the only Whigs in town!

There were no women to slow the departure. They'd already said their good-byes in the privacy of their homes, and when the little stern-wheeler chugged away from the wharf on schedule with a wild churning of waves and a sharp blast of its horn, they watched from their lonely little hillside cabins, straining to see through rain-streaked windowpanes until at last the mist and rain and distance took the ship and their men from view. In the far house on the north end of town, Louisa turned from the glass with a little choking noise.

"Mama, you cry?" Emily Inez wanted to know. She was sitting in the middle of the unmade bed looking at her picture book.

"Just a cinder in my eye," whispered Louisa, struggling to get hold of herself. "Is there something—" her voice caught. "Something special," she tried again, "that you'd like to do this morning, Missy Mynez?"

"Do cutting?" the little girl asked hopefully.

Louisa smiled to see the sweet trust in the face of her child. *That God would watch us all and protect us,* she thought.

"Can My?"

"May."

"*May* My?"

"Of course. Climb up and get your scissors and paper."

Such a happy smile! Emily Inez threw aside her book and scrambled to reach the shelf on the wall beside the bed. "Mama, you get mazageen!" she shouted excitedly.

Mazageen for magazine. Such innocent mistakes of language and words brought the stinging tears back to Louisa's eyes. *What happens to the children during war?* She envisioned the shelled-out city of Sebastopol half a world away where the Turkish war raged on and on. The last newspaper reported two thousand bodies floating in the Tigris. Some of those bodies had to be children.

"Mama!"

"Yes!" she answered with a guilty start.

"You not get mazageen? My need pichers, Mama! And My need glue!"

"I'm getting your magazine, Mynez. Hold your horses." She scooted Watch out of the way, then pulled the September issue of *Lady's Repertoire* from the grass basket Salmon Bay Curley's *klootchman* had woven for her. She missed Madeline. How close she and the Indian woman had become last spring out on the Swale. Every day picking camas, drying berries, rooting out her garden . . .

Down off the bed, Emily Inez went over to the table. Up on her toes, she pushed her scissors and paper onto the tabletop. "Mama, you cry 'gain?"

"A cinder in my eye, darling."

"You say that before!" cried Emily Inez indignantly, whirling around and standing flat on her feet to accuse her mother. Then, "What a cinder?"

"Something that keeps getting in your eye."

"Oh." Emily Inez clambered up on the chair, chattering away to herself.

Louisa drew another deep breath, this time resolute. It was going to be a long, lonely winter. She had better get used to it.

"Mama, My need glue now. You make glue?"

As for David, the familiar shoreline of Seattle receded all too quickly from sight. He'd dreamed often of war and glory as a boy, picturing himself the hero his grandfather had been in the Revolutionary War, fighting the British redcoats, charging Bunker Hill, crossing the Delaware with General George Washington. Or like his father fighting Tecumseh during the War of 1812. But something was wrong with the spirit of the thing now. Though some of the men were wild enough, boasting about how many scalps they were going to take.

These were simple men, David knew. They viewed the world in a clarity of black and white, good and evil. The trouble with such clarity was that it blinded a body from seeing the mix of shadow and light, the truth that all men are a combination of both. It no more occurred to them that *they* were evil than it would to admit the existence of a *good* Indian. At times David envied them; he did this morning. Simplistic notions weighed nothing on their minds, everything was clear, their duty defined. They were free of encumbrance while he suffered the burden of unanswerable questions.

What bothered him most was the growing proof that Leschi had not been responsible for the White River Massacre. It had been Leschi, in fact, who'd sent the messengers racing down through the Puyallup Valley and over the Nisqually bottomlands that same night to warn the downriver settlers of further danger. David had no reason to disbelieve this. From the beginning Leschi had made it clear he had no quarrel with the pioneers, only the government and soldiers, and that if the settlers simply stayed on their farms and minded their own business they would not be hurt. Yet it was hard to ignore the fact that the first settler killed, Jim McAllister, *had been Leschi's friend.*

More alarming was the reality that out there, somewhere, Indians *were* armed and they *were* killing and they *weren't* sparing the women and children. For David this had become a war not against Leschi and the bigger issue of land rights, but a war to protect his wife and child. At least this was the logic he used when he allowed himself to sign on as a soldier. But now, listening to the jocular boasting of some of his friends, he was troubled. Theirs was a duty of honor, heroics. His, nothing so fine. His was a bleak duty, embittered with the salt of Louisa's tears still on his lips, her dear pretty face troubling his memory, her heartbreaking silence louder than the rumble and roar of the engines below his feet.

Was this protecting her? he wondered now as Captain Parker angled the *Traveler* southwest across the bay to the yawning deltas of the Duwamish River mouth. Leaving her six months pregnant, and not a doctor in town? Maynard, of course, was at Port Madison with Seattle's Indians and Henry Smith had come along with the volunteers as company doctor. There was Doctor Williamson, he realized, an Englishman retired from the Hudson's Bay Company. Williamson owned one of the mercantiles on the Point. *But did he ever practice medicine?* David couldn't remember.

"Louisa will be all right," said Henry Smith, standing beside David and picking up easily on his troubled thoughts. "She's a strong woman."

"Strong, yes," admitted David. "But that didn't save her when she had Emily Inez, Henry. You did."

"Seems to me Doc Maynard had a hand in it too. Somewhere along the way."

"He did. You both did. That's why I'm worried, going off like this."

Dr. Henry Smith, a tall, slim man—handsome, blond hair and beard, sparkling blue eyes—was, at twenty-five, two years older than David. Unmarried, he kept himself busy at his nursery out on the north end of Elliott Bay where he was grafting different kinds of apples—trying to cross them, he said, and develop a new hybrid. He was also one of the few men in the area who knew any of the Indian languages. Like both David and Doc Maynard, he was a natural-born linguist and had picked up the Duwamish tongue easily, quickly. And, like David, he was learning other dialects. "When's she due to deliver?" he asked. "From my corner she doesn't look ripe enough to worry yet."

"Springtime. March. My birthday, actually."

"Really?" Henry laughed. "St. Patrick's Day!"

David turned to his friend.

"I can't help it," confessed Henry. "I have a head like an elephant. Ask me what the weather was like June 5, 1849."

"All right, what was the weather—when did you say? June *what?*"

They both laughed. "You know, Dave? With any luck—" Henry slapped the wet rail in front of them with both hands and closed his long, thin fingers around the steel, "—the war will be over by St. Paddy's Day and we'll both be home when she needs us."

David hunched deeper into his parka. "I sure hope so," he said, staring past the six canoes of supplies they were towing, into the mist that hid from view everything he'd left behind. "Hey, Henry."

"Yeah?"

"You know what she told me this morning?"

"I can't imagine."

"She told me she wanted to go back out to the Swale."

"She was serious?"

"All excited too."

"That's a good woman you have, Dave."

David blinked. He didn't know if it was rain or tears getting in his eyes.

7

Wednesday Evening,
November 28

On the day after our company started, an express arrived informing us that Lieutenant Slaughter's company had been attacked by probably 200 Indians, one man killed and three wounded, and that the Indians had succeeded in driving away about 30 horses and mules, and directing Captain Hewitt, commander of our company, to take a secure position where he could remain until he should hear from Lieutenant Slaughter.

—Kate Blaine, the minister's wife
in a letter dated December 1, 1855

ouisa dropped her supper dishes into a basin of hot, sudsy water. Watch, lying by the fire, growled low in his throat.

"Auntie! Auntie!"

What in the world? Quickly she caught up her apron to dry her hands, and flung open the door. Her eldest niece

68

burst through in a whirlwind of rain and dripping-wet red braids.

"Oh, Auntie—" Eleven-year-old Katy stopped short, spotting Mandy. *"Klahowya!"* she greeted, flashing a smile at the Indian woman stirring something on the stove.

"You in big hurry tonight, huh?" Mandy wanted to know.

"Yes!" Gasping, freckles all but popping off her nose, Katy turned again to Louisa. "Auntie, Mother says to come at once! Lieutenant Slaughter of the regular army was attacked!"

Louisa clasped her throat.

"One man is killed, lots are wounded! Forty horses are stolen! Father must go warn the volunteers! They're in the gravest peril, he says! Mother needs you to help pack his things! Oh, Auntie, I'm so scared! Father is frantic, he says—"

"Curb your tongue," interrupted Louisa, not wanting to hear any more, but moving quickly to ready herself—despite her pounding heart and trembling limbs. "It's a wonder any of us are still alive for the stories told!"

"But it's true! Lieutenant Drake—"

Louisa spun around. "The *Decatur* is back?"

"No! Captain Sterrett, when he heard—" gasped Katy, still trying to catch her breath. "Oh, Auntie, just as soon as Captain Sterrett heard we were all alone, he sent Lieutenant Drake and eight marines to guard us! He's our guardian angel, Mother says! And it was Mr. Drake who brought Father the message—"

"Finish the dishes for me, Katy. I need to bank the fire before we go anywhere." She could hardly think beyond David's danger. For of course he was in peril! If the regulars had been attacked, if the Indians—*No!* she told herself severely, setting two logs onto the flames and piling up the ash and embers, *No what ifs!* This was something she and David had promised each other a long time ago they would never do. They would *not* entertain their imaginations. But she couldn't help herself. *What if the volunteers are attacked too?*

69

What if David is dead? STOP THIS! "Mandy," she asked, slipping into her coat, "can you stay with Mynez for awhile? I'll be right back."

"Halo." Yes.

"Keep stirring the caramel, don't let it boil. No, Watch, you stay," she said, dashing out. A minute later, with Katy flying up the stoop just ahead of her, Louisa entered the small, noisy house next door. In this two-room log cabin lived her older sister, Mary Ann, who happened to be married to David's older brother Arthur. As usual, the crowded quarters struck Louisa as intolerable. Poor Mary Ann. In addition to her own family of four children between the ages of two and eleven years old, Mary also had the Neelys, refugees from White River, and *their* four youngsters living with her. Though, of course, Mr. Neely, second lieutenant for the volunteers, was gone for now. Nonetheless it was crowded quarters, and tonight a beehive of disorder, the eight children everywhere, abuzz.

Arthur, Louisa could see, wasn't exactly frantic, but he was focused. For a moment she stood undone by the sheer energy of her brother-in-law's purposeful striding back and forth between the back bedroom and front table, fetching his socks, a shirt, a second pair of woolen long johns, laying everything on the table next to a growing pile of food Mary Ann hastily wrapped.

Arthur was taller than David by two or three inches, thinner, and as fair as David was dark. But unlike David, he was a driven man, restless, a visionary who possessed the will and energy to pursue whatever he set his mind to do—and he'd set his mind to do a lot, sometimes without thought to cost. In the past Louisa had found this difficult to tolerate; she sometimes still did. His moral indignations, his unarguable "rightness" irritated her. At times she longed to slap him, but usually settled for an exchange of caustic repartee. But he was also a man whose instincts were for good, and she knew this. He always sought the betterment of individ-

70

uals and society. It was Arthur who doggedly pushed for temperance in the legislature, for women's suffrage, for the rights of free "mulattoes" to secure title to their homesteads. He was a man of keen intelligence and wisdom, a rare combination, and even though it wasn't always possible to agree with him, everyone did look up to him. He was a leader. His mind, his energy, his instincts, his moral foundation, these were of sterling worth and without match. Watching him now, striding back and forth between the bedroom and Mary Ann's table, Louisa could see that his amazing mind was at work.

He was measuring and weighing, embracing, discarding. He was not planning his clothes, however, she knew this. He was planning how he'd get to White River, who would go with him, how long it would take. If this was already determined, he was punching holes in the plan. Trying to figure ahead of time how things might go wrong, what might be done to fix them.

Irene Neely, she saw, normally efficient and helpful, stood weeping by the fire, a quiet mewing—a terrible distraction that grated instantly on Louisa's nerves. *Things must be very bad,* she thought in a seizure of new fright.

"You best put these on over your other pair," Mary Ann told Arthur, handing him back his long johns. "You haven't the packing space."

"But if I get both pairs wet, what then, Mary?"

"Should I take everyone up to the loft, Auntie?" Katy whispered to Louisa.

"It's probably a good idea." Louisa shrugged out of her coat and hung it up.

"Louisa! What do you think?" Mary Ann asked, seeing her, raising her voice over the din of children beginning to whine about being urged upstairs.

"About what?"

"Should Arthur wear his long johns. Or pack them?"

"He'll need something dry to sleep in, Mary," she said flatly. "Will someone please tell me what's happened? Is it bad? How bad?" Louisa glanced again at Irene.

"Lieutenant Slaughter was attacked two nights ago," Arthur told her without fanfare. He laid his long johns back on the mounting pile and faced her directly. His blue eyes, she saw, were dull with worry, the ridge between his brows stood out. "At least one soldier is dead. More are injured. Thirty horses, twelve mules were taken. A combined force of over two hundred Indians—"

"Two *hundred!*" Louisa gasped, reeling.

"They were after the horses—"

"Where?" she interrupted. "Anywhere near here?"

"Bitting's Prairie."

A glimmer of hope twinkled. Bitting's Prairie was miles away. "Do you think our men are safe then?"

"No," said Arthur, mincing nothing. "There's worry that some of those two hundred Indians might be Yakima."

"But I thought Major Rains went after Kamiakin."

"Major Rains left the field, Louisa. He retreated."

She clamped her mouth shut. First Haller, now Rains? She could hardly think!

"Things over there are a mess," Arthur said, "I can't go into it right now. I'm in a hurry."

The Yakima triumphant *again?* Hope blinked out, and she started to shake in the cold darkness that was left.

"The new captain at Steilacoom is sending Slaughter re-inforcements. When they connect, they'll try to reach our volunteers as quickly as possible. In the meantime, I'm to take up the orders telling them to dig in where they are and secure a point of safety for themselves—and to wait for Slaughter. Liza?" he asked suddenly, sharply. "Do you need to sit down?"

"I don't think I do feel very well," she admitted, shivering with cold and letting him ease her into the chair he'd yanked away from the table.

"I'll get you some tea," offered Mary Ann quickly. "You too, Irene," she called over to the woman still weeping by the fire.

"Then if you'll excuse me," said Arthur, "I need to keep moving." He started for the bedroom, but a sharp knock on the door checked his direction. "Dr. Williamson," he greeted, ushering in Seattle's portly, bald Englishman and proprietor of Williamson's Mercantile. "Come in, come in. You found a river canoe?"

"Turned out Tom Pepper had one."

"Everything is loaded? Ready to go?"

"Aye, but Denny, there's—"

"I gotta go!" Arthur called over to Mary Ann. "Just pack what we have, it'll have to do!"

"Did you bring the bread, Louisa?" Mary Ann asked.

"What bread?"

"I asked Katy to—"

"*I forgot, Mother!*" shouted Katy from the loft.

"That girl," muttered Mary Ann, "she'd forget her head if it wasn't screwed on."

Louisa automatically started up.

"Sit down," Arthur told her. "I'll grab some hardtack at the cookhouse. Rollie? Did you get my boots polished, son?"

"Yes, Pa," answered three-year-old Rollie in a wobbly little voice from the loft overhead.

"Where'd you put them?"

"The hearth, Papa!" Rollie started to cry. Louisa heard eight-year-old Nora rush to comfort her little brother. "He's only going for a little while. He'll be back, you'll see."

"Will the Indians kill Papa?"

"Not if you pray."

Out of the mouth of babes, thought Louisa.

Irene, still sniffling but no longer openly weeping, handed Arthur his boots. But before he could take them, the storekeeper said, "I'm trying to tell you, Denny, it's been decided I go, not you, old boy. The boys think you're needed more in Olympia."

Arthur took the boots from Irene. "Thank you," he told her. To Dr. Williamson he said, "We've been through this. It's Wednesday night. I don't have to leave for Olympia until Saturday morning, which gives me two days to find the volunteers."

"But—"

"But nothing! They've only been gone a day. I can catch up."

"But Denny, they went by steamer." Dr. Williamson irritably spelled out, tugging off his hat. "You're going by canoe."

"I can go farther in a canoe," said Arthur with equal irritation. "Whereas they have to walk after a certain point. The *Traveler* can't take them the whole way." He sat down to his desk, boots in hand. "As for the trip back, it's downriver. I'll be back, don't worry."

"But—"

"Don't worry!"

"Denny, it's all been decided."

"What's been decided," interrupted Arthur, "is that I'm going. It's my brother out there, and a man takes care of his own. If you want to come along, fine. I'd appreciate the company, Williamson, but I'm going and that's that."

The women exchanged anxious glances. Irene crept over to the table and sat down opposite Louisa. The two of them stared at each other. Upstairs, in the loft, the eight children were as silent as frightened mice. Even Rollie was still.

"Denny," said Dr. Williamson, trying again, nervously twisting his hat around and around in his hands. "Yesler, Bell, Plummer, Russell, Terry—they all think it's best you leave for Olympia on that Hudson's Bay boat, the *Fox*—the *Weasel*—*whatever it's called*," he erupted irritably, "Friday as scheduled."

"*Not until* I find my brother. Olympia can just wait. I don't mind, I've said it before. If I miss the *Otter*—" Arthur jammed his right foot into the corresponding boot, "—I'll go by canoe.

74

If the weather cooperates, and if I can find a couple of reliable Indians, a day and a half is all I need to make the trip."

"If the weather cooperates—If I can find a couple of Indians—Confound it, Denny!" shouted Dr. Williamson all of a sudden, his patience snapping. "We can't take the chance! You're needed in the Assembly come Monday morning at nine a.m.! That's why we elected you!"

For an answer Arthur calmly stuck his left foot in his left boot and tied the laces. He got up, found his yellow oilskin amongst the crowd of coats on the back of the door, and slid into it. Quietly he announced that if anyone wanted to give him a kiss good-bye, now was the time. Katy, Nora, Rollie, and two-year-old Orion tumbled down the loft ladder. Mary Ann helped him on with his backpack. For the first time ever Louisa watched Arthur kiss her sister. It was a tender kiss, intimate. Louisa had to look away.

"Good-bye, Louisa," Arthur called over to her. "Do you have a message for David when I find him?"

"Mrs. Neely! He's *doing* it again!" shrieked Katy. "He's swallowed the string again and is pulling it out of his mouth!"

"Make him stop, Mrs. Neely," whined Nora. "Ma! He's making me sick!"

Louisa looked up. Eight-year-old Jonathon Neely was leaning off the loft, tugging slobbery wet twine from his mouth. When he wasn't gagging, he was laughing at the girls down below.

"I think I'm going to be *ill!*" Katy shot past her father and a flabbergasted Dr. Williamson and flung herself through the door into the rain.

Louisa got up. "I'll take the girls over to my house. I have Mandy stirring caramel for a taffy-pull. If Jonathon doesn't have an audience you might get some peace around here."

"Taffy!" yelped everyone at once.

"Good-bye!" hollered Arthur over the sudden eruption of squeals and cries. The door slammed shut.

"Oh, Ma, can I go?"

"Can I, Ma? Can I? Can I?"

"Taffy! Oh, Ma, can I have some?"

"Ma, please let me go too!"

"Only Katy and Nora," Louisa insisted over the rumpus, only now realizing Arthur had left in a huff without a message from her for David. That was just like Arthur.

"But it's not fair!" wailed four-year-old Sammy Neely. "I wasn't swallowing string!"

"Katy and Nora will bring you some taffy," she promised him, forcing herself to forget her distress and concentrate on the children. "If you're very very good."

"Oh *I'll* be good, Mrs. Denny!" he said with a smile.

"I'm sure you will be." She pinched his nose, smiling a bit at his impish little face and quiet manner.

"Do I get any?"

"Yes, if you're good, Jed. Taffy for everybody who is good."

"What about me? Do I get any?"

"No, Jonathon, you do not!"

"No fair! Nobody told me!"

Outside in the night Nora tucked her hand into Louisa's. "Do you think Katy went to the necessary house, Auntie?"

"We can look there first."

"Do you really think she was sick? Or do you think she's just making it up?"

"Well, if she *is* sick, taffy will cure it. Taffy cures everything."

"I bet it cures bad behavior," Nora singsonged, looking up at Louisa with a sweet, mischievous smile.

Dear God, take care of us all! The little ones especially!

"KAAA-ty! Oh, KAAA-ty!" hollered Nora, her voice dissipating quickly in the dark rain. "We're going to Auntie's house for a TAAAA-fy pull!"

8

There were sleepless nights until messengers returned from Hewitt's camp . . .

—Roberta Frye Watt, Katy Denny's daughter
in *Four Wagons West*

*W*ednesday night, Thursday, and all day Friday passed in a blur of uneasy waiting. All the while a cold, determined rain fell from a ceiling of cloud pressed so low to the earth that it made the daylight hours fearfully dark and ominously bleak.

Thank goodness for our ladies' prayer circle, thought Louisa. They met each afternoon at Widow Holgate's three-room cabin up in the forest behind the mill. Seattle's only Baptist had started the meetings last fall when the war first broke out. Numerous times their prayers had been answered, and such hope sustained them now. Mary Ann, Irene Neely, Abbie Jane Hanford, Mrs. Phillips, Mrs. Horton, Mary Jane Mercer, Mrs. Russell—twenty-three women and their children came and went as they could, reading the Bible, praying, visiting. Widow Holgate was a woman whose faith was such that the rest of them drew strength and encouragement just from being around her.

In looking back though, Louisa found she remembered little else of these final November days. She *did* remember Nora knocking the lamp over on Wednesday night, spilling the dogfish oil into the taffy and necessitating a brand-new start. She remembered Mrs. Wetmore's blackened eye and swollen, split lip. (Mrs. Wetmore said she fell, but no one believed her—not when she was married to the likes of Ben Wetmore.) She remembered, too, Emily Inez's determination to eat charcoal from the fireplace. *When had that started?* Nothing could dissuade her—scolding her, putting her in the corner, spanking her—nothing worked. The minute Louisa turned her back Mynez popped yet another chunk into her mouth, telltale smudges marring her lips and fingers. Louisa thought, too, of the *Otter* putting in and leaving Seattle this afternoon as scheduled. Arthur had not returned. The other House members and Seattle's councilman had to go to Olympia without him.

This last night of November she went to bed deeply troubled. Arthur should have been back by now. *Where was he? Had he run into trouble himself? Had he gotten lost? Were the volunteers lost?* And then, suddenly, in a lonely burst of despair, *Where is David?*

On her back, hands behind her head, she stared into the dark emptiness overhead. Tears began to leak from her eyes, and slowly she retracted a hand, sliding it palm down over the icy sheet, feeling the even greater emptiness in the bed beside her. Watch must have heard her crying for he came over to the bed and whined, pushing his nose into the covers. "Oh, Watch," she whispered. "You're *such* good company." She patted his nose. "Go to sleep now, good boy. I'm okay."

Two blocks south and one block east of Louisa's house, Kate Blaine couldn't sleep either. Her first child was due in less than six weeks, and she was so miserably uncomfortable that she finally gave up sleep altogether and went into the front room to write a letter to her mother. She struck a match, lit the table lamp, then sat down, pen in hand. Feeble lamplight flickered across her stationery while outside the night owls hooted back and forth in the forest. From under the cabin she could hear the scamper of raccoons or possums, maybe mice. The unabating rain pounded the roof overhead. A rotted tree branch suddenly snapped like gunfire, crashing with a thud onto the forest floor.

Hostile Indians making their way toward the village? She listened carefully, her hands cold and clammy. Another owl. A dog barking somewhere. In the bedroom, her husband gently snored. It both irritated and comforted her. *How can he sleep when there's so much danger?* With a sigh she began her letter. "King County, W.T., November 30th, 1855," she wrote, then checked the clock on the fireplace mantel. She crossed off November 30th and wrote "December 1st, 1855."

My dearest mother,

The unpleasant situation of Indian affairs renders it so disagreeable. It is impossible to tell what is in store for us, but certainly there never was a time in the settlement or any part of the country when things presented a more serious aspect than now.

As yet, we have been unmolested in the towns, but many of our citizens who have gone out against them have fallen. The Indians sustain but trifling losses as they have so decided an ad-

79

vantage in numbers and in their knowledge of the country, by which they are enabled to retreat to their hiding places.

We are now feeling some anxiety about our company of volunteers who left here Tuesday last to proceed up White River a few miles above the scene of last month's slaughter.

There are three other companies within a few miles of that place and it's been designed that they act in concert. But the other night an express from Steilacoom arrived with a dispatch to the captain of our company to remain in a place of security until he should get further orders as one of the companies had been attacked on three sides, had all their horses taken and sustained other damage. This word was sent up to him with all speed, but I fear it may be too late, as the volunteers are likely to be in a place where they cannot defend themselves from sudden attack.

The day before they left the ladies presented them with a very handsome flag and gave them a supper in the evening. Their absence, together with that of the Decatur, the sloop of war, has made the town seem rather lonely.

I try to keep as cool as I can about the whole matter, and I think I succeed pretty well, considering everything, but I cannot help thinking about these matters much more than I want to.

"Kate?"

Her hand jumped. Ink flew from her pen nib. *If I was a swearing woman, I'd surely swear,* she thought, staring with sharp annoyance at the messy blot on her otherwise neat page.

"Kate? It's the middle of the night, what are you doing up?"

She put the pen away, capped her ink bottle. Taking the lamp with her, she crossed the front room to the bedroom. Shadows trailed, leaping along. Her house used to be the envy of everyone in town—until Mr. Plummer built his resplendent mansion for Ellender. *That* house stood two stories tall with gingerbread lattice in all its peaks and crevices, green shades in all the windows, a wide, sweeping veranda that wrapped around three sides! Tonight Kate's shadows leaped and dragged over the flocked wallpaper she'd once taken such pride in, angled off her expensive, factory-built furniture imported from New York around the Horn to San Francisco, then up to Puget Sound. Now it was all so second-rate. She yearned for the plush opulence of Ellender Smith Plummer.

Her husband was propped up in bed, leaning on an elbow, his red and white striped night cap disheveled. He blinked moronically, his wits dulled by the hour.

Kate went over to the bed and sat down with care, set the lamp on the nightstand. "My back's complaining. Thought I'd write Mother."

"You should have told me. I'll rub your back. Same place?"

"Isn't it always?"

"Get in."

"I didn't want to disturb you."

She settled into the bed. Her husband leaned over and blew out the light. She gave herself over to him, sighing with relief as he worked his hands over her tight, painful muscles. "I think," she mumbled, face in the pillows, "that God deliberately designed these last few weeks to be so utterly miserable that we women would actually look forward to childbirth." The next thing she knew it was dawn.

9

Saturday Morning, December 1

Ever since the arrival of Mrs. Stowe in Europe, negotiations have been in progress to procure money from that quarter to secure the triumph of the abolitionists in the United States.

The triumph of the Allies at Sebastopol has stimulated the governing classes of Europe to assault the great works of the federal constitution—to attempt, by the aid of an alliance with the abolitionists of this country, to overturn the government of the United States.

—from the *New York Herald*
reprinted in *Pioneer & Democrat*
December 7, 1855

ncle Tommy's real name was Thomas Mercer, but the middle-aged widower with four growing daughters was so universally regarded for his kindness and fair dealings that in Seattle he'd simply become known as "Uncle Tommy." He hailed from Illinois, leaving a year after the Dennys and Borens. When he arrived in Seattle the fall of 1853 (the first and only person to forge through the forests and to ferry the rivers and bays with a Conestoga and horses), he took up a claim just north of David and Louisa. Because of their shared isolation, the two families were close. Nevertheless, Louisa was surprised to hear Tib and Charlie whinnying just outside her door Saturday morning at the crack of dawn. Just seconds later came Uncle Tommy's quick, distinct knock.

"You're awful early to be checking up on me," she told him, drawing open the door. Watch bounded out.

"I'm going out to the claim today and need to get a good start," he explained, stepping indoors and doffing his cap, then chuckling with amusement to see her disheveled hair and her face still swollen with sleep . . . or lack of it.

Flustered, she looked down at herself, her wrinkled nightgown, her moccasins tugged on in haste. "You caught me just getting out of bed. It was a long night, I didn't sleep well," she mumbled.

Truth was, when she hadn't been able to sleep, toward morning she'd stoked the stove and lit the lamp to read the *Courier* brought yesterday on the *Otter* from Steilacoom. A mistake. Nothing but frightful news everywhere. In Europe the Russians were refusing to surrender despite the fall of Sebastopol. *Russia never makes peace after disaster,* the Czar had declared. In Kansas the illegal free-soil legislature had called for elections in December and the Missouri Ruffians were pouring into Kansas, amassing an army just south of Lawrence. Someone named John Brown was giving the Free-Soilers free "Beecher's Bibles"—the new breech-loading rifles being sent to Kansas in wagonloads by Henry Ward Beecher, the famous preacher back east. *Who, curiously enough, was also brother to Harriet Beecher Stowe, author of* Uncle Tom's Cabin, thought Louisa. And in Southern Oregon? How many settlers had the Rogue River Indians killed? Thirty? She thought about Ma and Pa and their cozy home tucked into the Waldo Hills. Thank goodness they were nowhere near Rogue River country! As for eastern Washington, a small but significant article stated that the gold mines were paying well and that by summer "we expect to see a renewal of the good old times!" *The good old times?* That had been the final straw. In a mix of anger and fear she'd dropped the paper onto the floor beside the bed and blown out the lamp. *Hadn't it been the gold miners pouring through Yakima and Walla Walla last summer that had started the war? Inciting the fury of Kamiakin and Peo-Peo-Mox-Mox?*

"Well I only stopped by to say I can swing by the Swale," Uncle Tommy repeated. "Anything you want brought back?"

"Let me think. Have you had coffee?" she asked.

"Yes, but I'd enjoy another cup if it'll give you time to put a list together. And Louisa, I was wondering if I can borrow *Uncle Tom's Cabin* again."

"If I can find it. I know it's around here somewhere," she told him.

Louisa fed more wood to the live coals in the stove, adding warm water from the kettle to her brand-new, blue enamel coffeepot.

Will Arthur get back today? she wondered while taking down her coffee tin from among the various boxes and jars cluttering the wall shelf. Carefully she measured the allotted grounds into the already hot coffeepot. She added another stick to the fire, making sure the coffee was coming to a boil.

"Why do you want to read *Uncle Tom's Cabin* again?" she asked, hastily gathering up the scattered newspaper and clearing away her knitting from the rocking chair. She motioned him to sit down.

"Just want to refresh my memory. So much fuss is being made about it."

"What fuss?"

"The whole South is up in arms. The hue and cry is fierce and gathering wind. Someone's written a scathing rebuttal. It's selling like hotcakes," he told her, taking the chair. "The

84

South is claiming Mrs. Stowe made everything up, that slaves aren't mistreated. That to beat a slave is counterproductive to their purpose."

"It makes sense, when you think about it," she said.

"Except human beings don't operate on sense. Ever see a man flog his horse?"

She had, plenty of times.

"And horses don't come cheap."

"No, they don't," she agreed.

"Horses and men cost lots of money. Yet there's nothing like abusing either of them to lend their owner a sense of authority and mastery. Why else does Ben Wetmore kick his dog?"

"It's not just his dog he kicks, Uncle Tommy."

He looked up with a grave face. "Wetmore's beating his wife?"

Louisa didn't answer. She didn't want to think about poor Mrs. Wetmore. She didn't want to think about slavery, either, or the war. *Where was Arthur?*

"I don't know," sighed Uncle Tommy sadly. "The Bible says the love of money is the root of all evil. But it goes deeper than that, I think. The desire for *power* is the root of all evil. Money only buys you the power. Goodness, listen to me." He rocked back in his chair, still frowning, fingering his beard.

"Some folks have decided the abolitionists are trying to overthrow the government. *News to me.*"

Was there something in his voice?

"Are you an abolitionist, Uncle Tommy?"

"Yes, though I've stopped thinking about myself that way. No need to, not out here."

"You really are an abolitionist, then!" she exclaimed, whirling around.

"A friend of mine, Daniel Bagley, he and I used to work with Elijah Lovejoy in the early days of the movement—"

85

"The printer? The man who was martyred in Alton," she interrupted, "when the proslavers threw his presses into the river?"

"The same. A good man. A terrible, senseless death."

"Oh my," she breathed out. "That was quite some time ago. I was only a little girl when it happened. But I can sure remember the ruckus."

"Way back in '37."

"I was only nine or ten then. Were you there?"

"I was."

"It must have been a terrible experience!"

His gray eyes darkened with the memory. "Well I'm glad we don't have to contend with slavery here, on top of our Indian troubles."

"Why are you going out to the claim?" she asked, changing the subject and putting another stick in the stove.

"I had to let the hogs run wild, but the girls got a hankering for ham come Christmas. If I can catch one, we'll have a month to fatten it."

"Arthur's promised to have Yoke-Yakeman butcher one of Dobbins's cows for *our* Christmas."

"Hardy Axe Handles, I hope!"

She laughed. With Arthur gone, Uncle Tommy and Charles Terry were stuck with the milking. She piled the newspapers down in behind the stove box. "Odd, isn't it?" she said, looking over at him.

"What?"

"In Illinois we always had to have something wild for Christmas dinner. Here, surrounded by the wild, we want something domestic."

He grinned and tugged on his beard. "I guess we just like a change when it's time to celebrate."

"Maybe you're right. There, I think the coffee is ready." She passed him a cup, and while he nursed it they sat at the table and visited awhile. Louisa tried to discipline her mind as to what she might want from the Swale. *The two blankets in the*

86

drawer under her bed would be a help. It would also be nice to have the pictures of Ma and Pa from off the mantel. And if there were still a few carrots in the garden, he could bring those. She wrote them all down.

"Thanks for the coffee, Louisa, but now I need to get out to Tib and Charlie."

Shoving back his chair, Uncle Tommy picked up the list and smiled his farewell. He stopped in the open doorway, his attention on a disturbance outside.

"What is it?" she asked anxiously.

"I think it's Arthur."

Arthur!

She raced outdoors, without a thought for her coat and dodging around Uncle Tommy on the stoop. "Arthur! *Arthur!*" she shouted. *"Did you find David?"* She lifted the skirt of her nightgown, running clumsily through the mud and driving rain. "Did you find him? Is he all right?"

"What the deuce—" Arthur started toward her at a trot.

"Did you find him?" They met just outside Suwalth's shack. Winded, trying to catch her breath, she suddenly felt the icy rain.

"Yes, I found him," said Arthur disgustedly, watching her shudder from the sudden penetration of cold. "Are you *nuts?* Come on, let's get you indoors." He lifted her into his arms and started back up the trail. A bouncy ride. She had to throw her arms around his neck to hold on.

"Oh, Arthur, he's really alive?" she squealed.

"Yes, he's alive! They're all alive! Though I can't say the same for you!" he panted. "Holy Moses, but what are you doing here? You're liable to catch your death!"

She didn't care he was angry. *David was alive! He was alive! He was alive!* Arthur passed his own house, then edged around the astonished Uncle Tommy still standing on her stoop.

Inside, Emily Inez was awake by now, pulling down her diaper in front of the fire. Calmly she stepped out of it, leaving the diaper in a puddle where it had fallen with a plop. She watched her Uncle Arthur lower her mother onto a chair. All the while Louisa laughed and cried with joy.

"You look like a drowned muskrat!" snapped Arthur. He yanked the quilt off her bed and draped it over her shoulders.

"You're sure he's alive?"

"Yes, I'm sure!"

"You saw him with your own eyes?"

"Yes, with my own eyes! Liza, I'm tired and I'm wet! I'm going home!"

"You needn't be cranky, Arthur."

Arthur just rolled his eyes at her and turned toward the door. "Hey there, Uncle Tommy," he said. "You headed someplace in particular?"

"The claim. My girls want a hog for Christmas, and a hog they shall have. Say, but I'm glad you're back. And to hear that the other fellows are all right."

Louisa went over to the door, watching the two men amble off the stoop.

"Do you suppose you can sell me one of your hogs?" she heard Arthur ask.

"Depends. Not sure yet if I can catch one for myself!"

They reached the wagon. Glossy black Tib and snowy white Charlie stood patiently in the rain, heads down. Arthur patted Tib, the more spirited of the two. "I asked Reverend Blaine to sell me one of his hogs. The weasel wanted fifty dollars."

Uncle Tommy clambered up onto the wagon seat. "I'll take forty-nine!"

Arthur threw back his head and laughed heartily.

Louisa shut the door and flopped against the split-cedar planking, laughing herself. David was safe! He was alive! He was all right! And soon Lieutenant Slaughter would be there! They'd be safe for sure then! *Oh, dear God in heaven, thank you, thank you, thank you!* Suddenly she was crying again.

What is the matter with me? Why am I crying? She nearly jumped out her skin when Uncle Tommy knocked again.

"Uncle Tommy, you scared me half to death!"

He regarded her carefully, not sure of her tears.

"I'm just happy," she explained, using the back of her hand to wipe one eye and then the other.

"Well, I just wanted to say I'll pick up the book on my way back, when I drop off your blankets."

"I'll look for it, I promise."

"Don't trouble yourself too much."

"Well, it's got to be around here somewhere."

Door shut again, she suddenly got a whiff of the soaking wet diaper. "Oh, pew!" she gagged. "Glory be, Mynez, but I think it's high time we start putting you on the pot!"

Three hundred miles away in northeast Oregon, just as Saturday's early morning cloud began to break, Oregon's mounted volunteer force coming up from The Dalles staggered into Fort Henrietta. After four days and a hard night's march on the road, they at last traipsed wearily through the opened gates and were greeted by a round of wild cheers and hoarse hurrahs from the men anxiously awaiting them.

Their two officers, Colonel Kelly and Major Chinn, wasted no time. They began at once to get preparations underway to mount their assault against Peo-Peo-Mox-Mox, reportedly camped at the plundered Fort Walla Walla. All going well, tomorrow evening their combined forces of four hundred seventy-five men would embark on an all-night march—another fifty miles to the east, up across the territorial border into Washington.

Kelly tapped his pencil point on the spot marked Fort Walla Walla on his map, then carelessly threw it down altogether. "In two days' time we attack at dawn."

"Lord willing."

"He's willing, Chinn. God's on our side."

In Seattle, Arthur had a hurried breakfast with his family. Assured that David and the others were in a reasonably secure position to await the regulars, he saw no reason to be particularly worried about Seattle just now, and he felt no qualms about leaving his family to attend the legislature. One, the blockhouse of hewn logs stood on the knoll. Two, every man in town was armed. Three, most everyone from the outlying area was in Seattle, close to the blockhouse. Four, marines guarded the outposts. Five, Slaughter and the volunteers would soon have Naches Pass covered. Six, the friendly Indians were either in town or on the reservation across the Sound where they couldn't be persuaded to join the enemy. Finally, the trails crisscrossing the mountains would soon be snow blocked, hindering the Yakima from coming over. Not the best of circumstances, he knew, but not the worst. Breakfast finished, the good-byes all said again, he climbed into the canoe, manned by two of Suwalth's men. Already his mind was on the task ahead: Washington's third Territorial Legislature, due to convene in less than forty-eight hours.

Even as Arthur cleared Alki Point and headed south to Olympia, across the Sound and to the north, Cecil Smith of Port Madison heard his brother's frantic cry, "The yard is full of Indians!"

Cecil seized his rifle and tore out of their log cabin, running top speed for the beach. Coming to the bluff he saw two war canoes, unmistakably Haida, push off below. Immediately he raised his gun, aimed, and fired. *Click.* Dang! His rifle wasn't loaded! There he was, in fair view, and he couldn't shoot!

His brother Jordan came racing back up the other way. "Lost my caps!" he screamed, furious with himself and whizzing past Cecil for the house.

Two hundred yards downshore the Haida pulled in again, took on more of their comrades, then headed out to the open

Sound, raising their sails—both canoes disappearing on the wind before either Cecil or Jordan could get their guns loaded and ready to fire again.

Staring into the empty drizzle, Cecil threw down his hat. "Dang it all, Jordie! I ain't never been so vexed in my life!"

In town they learned the Haida had stripped the revenue cutter *Rival* while all hands were ashore, taking her sails, oars, and compass, as well as a good deal of the crew's clothing.

"That's the third time in as many days," complained Mr. Meiggs, owner of the prosperous little sawmill. "Last time they hit me. Got fifty bushels of my potatoes. What am I supposed to feed my millhands now? Before that? They got old Buzbee here."

"That's right," wheezed Buzbee, spitting a stream of chewing tobacco across the floor but missing the spittoon. "Stole the clothes right off the wife's clothesline. Got off with a hundred dollars cash too. That's the worst."

"It ain't always gonna be *iktas* they steal," said Jordan, using the Chinook word for *things*. "Next time might be our heads. Like those poor blokes in Bellingham."

"We gotta send for the *Decatur*," said Cecil. "Anyone know where she is?"

"Nisqually," said Meiggs.

"Can you send for her, Meiggs?"

"I already did."

"Well that's good. Because the Haida ain't gonna leave us alone, that's sure."

91

10

Monday Morning, December 3

... I received from the settlers at this place a request for protection against Northern Indians, who had assumed a threatening attitude towards them. On the morning of the 3rd I weighed anchor and arrived here the same afternoon.

—Captain Sterrett, *Decatur*
in report dated December 3, 1855

Hon. A.A. Denny has been elected Speaker, and if a Democratic House *must* require the election of a Whig Speaker, we do not think they could have done better.

If the Democratic house can stand it, we can.

—*Pioneer & Democrat*
December 7, 1855

Having received Mr. Meiggs's alarming message at midnight about marauding Haida, Captain Sterrett weighed anchor first thing in the morning and hurried north under full press of sail.

The wind was high, and Captain Sterrett made good time, putting into Port Madison about three in the afternoon. The entire village, he discovered, was teetering on hysteria. Scowell—the most powerful chief in the Territories of Northwestern America—along with eighteen minor chiefs, roamed the muddy streets at will, their faces streaked with hideous war paint, toting loaded guns, belligerently ransacking stores, and shooting off random shots. Discretion being the better part of valor, Sterrett hastily decided direct confrontation was not the answer. Better to invite the notables aboard ship and therein conduct a blunt and very straightforward discussion.

His first invitation for a *wah-wah* was spurned. When pressed later, he couldn't remember everything he'd said, or what he might have promised, but in the end he did succeed in coaxing Scowell and his eighteen chieftains to come on board.

He first gave them an exhibition of the power of his heavy guns, the explosive nature of iron shells, and the destructive qualities of grape and canister. He then sat them down to explain the situation.

"We are at war with Indians in the Sound. The settlers' nerves are in an excitable state," he told them bluntly, using an interpreter. "This should concern you. It has to be abundantly clear to you all that the settlers can't distinguish friendly Indians from foe." They cast sharp, tense looks back and forth. Was he getting through? "For this reason," he said, "I urge you to return in all haste to your own country, and to remain there until the close of these hostilities."

"Before sundown tomorrow we will go." Scowell drew to his feet. "And not return until the war is over."

"No, before sunup tomorrow you will go," said Sterrett sternly. "If you are not gone, my orders are to commence firing. Only this time I will not aim out to sea."

"We will be gone."

"I will stay to make sure you are."

In Olympia, Arthur might have felt fairly confident in Seattle's relative safety, but when elected Speaker of the House first thing Monday, December 3, he couldn't ignore the extreme danger in which they all lived. Danger he believed would be all the more extreme once spring rolled around.

Judge Lander, having sworn in the House officers, announced him. *"Gentlemen! Our Speaker of the House, Arthur Denny!"* Arthur found himself escorted to the Speaker's chair by Mr. Morrison of Pierce County and Mr. McElory of Thurston. Waiting for the applause to dwindle, he cleared his throat and then somberly addressed his colleagues gathered upstairs in Olympia's Masonic Hall.

"Gentlemen, you have this day conferred upon me an honor which I highly prize, and for which I am truly thankful," he began. "But I am well aware of the fact that by conferring this high honor upon me, you have also imposed a weighty responsibility, and I can only lament my inability to discharge the duties you have thus imposed. We are assembled today, under the most discouraging circumstances. Our infant territory is now surrounded by hostile savages, our citizens murdered in our very midst, and our constituents look to us in this hour of gloom to render every exertion, and make every effort in our power to secure assistance and ensure protection. Under these circumstances, I am not expecting too much of you, gentlemen, when I ask your kind indulgence in the discharge of the duties this day assumed, heartily trusting and believing that you will do all in your power to render those duties easy, and thus promote dispatch in the business now required at our hands."

Very quickly the initial business got underway. Mr. Morrison moved that a House chaplain be procured. The motion was seconded. Arthur opened the motion for discussion.

"There is no delegated authority in the Organic Act to raise legislative prayers," Mr. Morrow objected. "And if no authority exists to create the office of chaplain, how can the House proceed to fill the office? I, for one, can't consent to convert this Hall into a religious Session, nor transform the Legislative Assembly into a political prayer meeting."

Where's he going with this? wondered Arthur, not knowing whether to laugh or be concerned.

A hot debate ensued.

Mr. Morrison, originator of the motion, rose to his feet. "I have absolutely no fear," he stoutly defended, "that the union of church and state will result by this House electing a chaplain. And in reply to the question of constitutionality, all I can say is that Congress has set the example, followed by all the eastern states."

"Hear, hear!"

"I quite agree," put in Elwood Evans, territorial prosecutor. "It's been a time-honored custom of our parent government—a time-honored usage which has been handed down from the earliest history of our country—a usage our forefathers followed in the darkest days of the Revolution—a usage which was followed by the men who fought for the Christian blessings which we now enjoy."

"Yes, yes, yes," countered Mr. Scorr, "we're all aware Congress has adopted the practice. But the constitutionality of that right remains doubted by many. The principles of our government are that church and state be entirely separate, that the government have no right to levy any tax for the support of religion."

"We are *not* talking about tax levies for the support of religion," said David Phillips without bothering to stand.

We're at war and arguing about whether or not to pray? Arthur thought of the Oregon volunteers he'd just learned were trying to quell the Walla Walla on their own. Would it really hurt, as a legislative body, to pray for these men? Would it really hurt to pray for the returning governor, whose life was in danger? The safety of all their families? *Would it hurt to pray for a change in attitude on the part of General Wool, whose appalling disregard for the seriousness of the war was only now being understood?* he wondered.

"Mr. Speaker—"

Startled out of his reverie, Arthur gave Quincy Brooks a full ear, forcing himself to pay attention.

"I am opposed to a chaplain saying prayers in the House. Members of this body have enough to think about, besides prayers."

Goodness, thought Arthur, *what would Mary say?*

In the end, when all was said, a majority ruled and Messrs. Morrison, Hale, and Johnson were appointed to inform Reverend J. F. Devore that he'd been elected chaplain of the House. The clerk was instructed to inform the Council that the House of Representatives was now fully organized and ready to proceed to business.

The first item for the joint session was how to finance the war.

For David the war had blurred into days of forced marching through savage wet woods, knee-deep swamps and bone-chilling streams, sleeping at night on beds of wet moss. When Arthur had caught up with them the previous Friday on Moses Kirkland's abandoned claim, the war evolved into a grueling dawn to dusk race of felling trees and piling them into high walls of a makeshift fort.

For a cornerstone they'd chosen Kirkland's half-finished barn; still, it was desperate work to extend the walls and finish the roof. In the interest of weight, teams of two sawed only the tallest and narrowest of trees. Nonetheless, it still took four or five of them to heft each fallen monarch of the forest back into camp. The work was the worst he'd known by far, back-breaking, dangerous, and miserably heavy.

Pulling the saw back and forth, they sweated and steamed in the drizzling rain. Yet when they stopped, they cooled off to near freezing. Every bush, every branch was laden with icy cold water that came showering down on them at the lightest touch. He was, he realized, learning what it meant to be a soldier on the Sound: to get up to gray skies, to spend his days listening to men curse the shrubbery that soaked them, to make camp each night in a blue twilight, thick patches of fog rising up from the freezing ground. He yearned for home. Not the "inside" house where he knew Louisa waited, but the Swale. He, too, wanted life the way it used to be.

Saturday, Sunday, Monday. *December yet?* The walls went up, the cedar shingles were split and laid on. All the while scouts scoured the woods by day for sign of an enemy. At night guards listened for owls that weren't owls. The foe remained a constant, nerve-wracking unseen presence as twigs snapped and night shadows leapt.

Monday night the roof was finished at last—with an overhang out front to give shelter outdoors from the rain. Grateful for shelter and something akin to warmth, David and his friends began to dry out a little and feel more like their old selves. They began to talk too. David hadn't realized they'd stopped. Too busy saving their energy, he supposed. But now they conversed, talking of home, boasting about old war stories, their laughter as muscular as their arms.

Suddenly Captain Hewitt was speaking. "We'll send a detail over to the Coxes' house in the morning. He says he has a shed full of turnips and corn we can have, and I want to save rations where we can." Christopher Hewitt, lawyer and oxbow maker by trade, was a fine-looking man with a broad forehead and clear blue eyes. He sat with quiet dignity in the light from the crackling blaze of the campfire, legs drawn up to his chest, ankles crossed, well-shaped arms wrapping his legs, left hand grasping his right wrist. "McNatt? Neely? Tomorrow you'll scout upriver. See if you can't spot some sign of the regulars, and let them know where we are."

David didn't mean to, but with the roof over his head and the fire before him, the seductive comfort brought back the luxury of thinking, and he got to thinking about the baby coming in the spring. A boy this time? Another girl? Would the war be over by then? Would he and Louisa be back at the

Swale? He hoped so. He and Uncle Tommy wanted to clear out the marsh between their places, and get some wheat planted. But spring and going home seemed a long way off, especially now, watching and listening to the rain cannonading against the new shingles overhead.

"Denny—"

He jumped at the sound of his name.

Around him his friends laughed.

"What?"

"Tomorrow you'll cut firewood with Walter and David Graham."

"Sure. Fine."

11

Tuesday Morning,
December 4

When the doctor came he looked down her throat and said nothing much was the matter. He drank a glass of milk, left some pills . . . and rode away.

—Sophie Frye Bass, Katy Denny's daughter
in *Pig-Tail Days in Old Seattle*

The next morning, something was wrong with Emily Inez. "I think she swallowed some charcoal and is choking on it," Louisa told Mary Ann in a near panic, not bothering to knock on her sister's door. "I don't know what to do, Mary."

"Give her to me." Tenderly, very carefully, Mary Ann eased an almost listless Emily Inez out of Louisa's arms and took her over to the table under the window. The little girl's breathing was shallow and raspy. "Can you open your mouth for Auntie Mary, Mynez? A little wider, that's a girl." Mary Ann

99

peered first one way and then the other into her open mouth. "Someone get me a spoon."

"I will, Mama." Nora leaped up; the doll she was dressing clattered to the floor.

"I don't know . . ." said Mary Ann a few minutes later. "I don't see anything. Were you eating charcoal again this morning, Mynez?"

Emily Inez shook her head no.

"Shall I get Dr. Williamson?" volunteered Irene Neely.

"Do you mind?" Louisa asked anxiously.

"Not at all." Irene dug her coat out of the pile on the door and tied on her bonnet. "I'll hurry," she said, dashing out the door.

"How long has she been like this?" Mary Ann asked.

"A half hour?" Louisa guessed. "I put her on the chamber pot while I went out to get more firewood. When I came in, this is how I found her. I couldn't have been gone more than two or three minutes."

"Maybe she's coming down with something," suggested Mary Ann, touching the back of her fingers against Emily Inez's forehead.

"I wondered that, too, but she's not running a fever."

"No," agreed Mary Ann. She took Emily Inez's hands. Carefully, she examined them. "Liza, look."

"I don't see anything."

"Under her fingernail, right here."

Ash.

Louisa looked at her daughter in fright.

"She's cottoned on," said Mary Ann, "and tried to clean herself up so you wouldn't find out."

"Maybe that's from another time," said Louisa, alarmed at the notion of her daughter lying. "Maybe when I washed off her hands I missed that."

"Maybe . . ." Mary Ann looked intently at Emily Inez, then ran her fingers through the little girl's hair. "What are we going to do with you, Missy Mynez?"

"I shouldn't have left her," Louisa agonized. "I shouldn't have gone out like that and left her alone."

"You can't watch her all the time," said Mary Ann gently.

"I know, but—"

"But nothing," said Mary Ann, her tone more stern.

"But look what's happened," moaned Louisa, watching her daughter struggle for air.

"Nothing's happened yet. And the doctor will soon be here. He'll know what to do."

But Dr. Williamson had nothing to offer. "Nothing at all down there. Her gullet's as clean as a whistle," he declared, standing up straight after bending down to peer into Emily Inez's throat. "She could be coming down with the croup, though I don't know. I can leave some pills just in case."

"But she can't be sick! It came on too suddenly!" protested Louisa. "And she's not feverish!"

"That's the nature of some childhood illnesses," he explained. "But I wouldn't worry, Mrs. Denny. Whatever it is, it can't be serious, or she *would* be running a temperature."

"You're sure she's not choking on charcoal?" Louisa persisted. "Or something else she might have swallowed?"

"She'd be dead by now if that were the case," said Dr. Williamson matter-of-factly.

That sent a jolt through Louisa.

"Well, I better get back to the store," he said, downing a glass of milk.

"I'll see you out," said Mary Ann.

Louisa gathered up Emily Inez and began walking the floor, half listening to Mary Ann and Dr. Williamson discuss milk and eggs. "If you have butter, I can pay a half dollar a pound," he told Mary.

"Cash or war scrip?"

"Scrip."

"That would be only twenty-five cents. Mr. Plummer's paying fifty cents cash."

"Just thought I'd offer."

"Thank you," said Mary, "I'll keep it in mind."

Emily Inez's head lay heavily against Louisa's shoulder, and Louisa could feel each tiny breath of her daughter push against her breast. *Like an injured butterfly, trying to move its wings.*

"Louisa?"

The doctor was gone, and Mary Ann was watching her.

"What?"

"I think it's harder for her to breathe that way."

"You think so?"

"Yes. Her own weight pushes against her lungs. She has to push herself up each time to get a breath."

"Maybe if you sat in the rocking chair," suggested Irene. "If she was sitting up—"

"But she's so weak," whispered Louisa, nearly in tears.

"Let her lean up against you."

They found it *was* easier for Emily Inez this way. But as morning gave way to afternoon, she seemed to grow worse. The other children gathered around, hushed, watching her. She sat in her mother's lap, her eyes closed most of the time. *Whatever is wrong with her, please don't let her die,* Louisa prayed. About two o'clock she overheard Mary Ann and Irene whispering.

"Maybe we should send for David . . ."

"But can he get here in time?"

"I don't know. We have to try, don't we?"

"Perhaps Yoke-Yakeman can go."

Hearing Yoke-Yakeman's name, Louisa suddenly remembered that Mandy was to help her clean the stove this afternoon. "Mary? Can you send one of the children over to Yoke-Yakeman and Mandy's hut to tell Mandy I don't need her today?"

"I'll go," volunteered Katy.

"Just a minute," said Mary Ann. She came over and squatted down in front of Louisa. Quietly she kneaded Mynez's little feet, one foot in each hand. "I think we should send for David, Liza."

Tears burned Louisa's eyes, and she wrapped her arms more protectively around her little Mynez. Yes, she wanted David to come home, but it seemed that if they sent for him, Mynez would surely die. "It's like there would have to be *some* reason," she told Mary, "to justify something so drastic."

"That's silly."

Katy had her hat and coat on. "Shall I tell Yoke-Yakeman we need him?"

"Well?" Mary Ann asked, imploring Louisa with her eyes.

"But Mary, it'll take at least two or three days to find him, and then another two or three for him to get here. By then . . ." She bit her lips shut. She'd almost said "too late." *And if it is too late?* she thought with a start.

"Well?"

Louisa hugged Emily Inez tightly, tears in her eyes. "Katy?"

"Yes, Auntie."

"Tell Yoke-Yakeman to hurry."

After chopping wood all day in the rain, David and the Graham brothers wanted a little more excitement. The three of them grabbed a wood stick and joined Lewis Wyckoff and a few of the other fellows down at the river where it ran shallow. They were clubbing salmon for supper.

David waded in. The shock of the icy water racing around his wet boots took his breath and left him gasping. As to the salmon? Whew! Salmon everywhere! *He had to be careful where he stepped or he'd be down on his tail!*

"This is going to taste good after all that salt pork," grunted Lewis, reaching down and whacking a fish with a practiced swing, then tossing it ashore onto a slippery pile.

"What's *not* good," hollered George Frye five yards away, "is we got no hope of starving out the Indians! Not with Mother Nature delivering a ton of salmon like this to their doorstep!"

To David, the Indians seemed far away right now, the war not very real. The *real* enemy was the rain. He was cold and wet and very, very hungry, and if Frye felt badly about the Indians getting plenty to eat, he didn't. Everyone had to eat.

They were still cleaning the fish, squatting or sitting on wood ends under the overhang when Neely and McNatt arrived with the news that Slaughter was camped up at Will Brannan's house. Something like shivers shot down David's spine. Brannan had been brutally killed in last month's massacre, his wife and baby shoved head-first down into the nearby well. If he were the superstitious type . . .

"Slaughter left Lieutenant More with forty men, the horses, and a mule train down at Stuck Creek," puffed Neely, flopping to the ground and leaning up against the fort wall. He let his head flop back too, and brought up his knees and rested his arms on them, hands hanging loose. "But he's got sixty-five of his total force up at Brannan's place."

"How far is that?" Captain Hewitt asked.

Bill Gilliam, sitting next to David, jabbed him in the ribs. "Maybe we can put in a good day's work killing Indians for once, huh?"

"What's that?" asked the captain, cupping his ear toward Frank McNatt. He'd missed McNatt's answer.

"I said, 'bout two miles, I reckon!" repeated McNatt, a small but strong man. He collapsed next to Neely, breathing hard. Both the scouts were covered in mud, their lips blue with cold.

"I better get up there," said Hewitt, "see what's going on. Find out what our orders are."

Next thing David knew he was walking away from his salmon supper with hardtack in his pockets and shouldering his fully loaded rifle. Captain Hewitt had chosen a six-man escort to take him to Slaughter. As corporal he was stuck going along, and he trudged through the tangled brush reluctantly, a bad feeling growing in the very pit of his stomach.

12

Tuesday Evening, December 4

An Indian guide named Puyallup Tom accompanied Lieut. Slaughter through the Green River country where he was to meet with the company of volunteers of which I was a member. It was cold and raining all day. When near the spot where they camped they saw an Indian dog skulking along in the underbrush. Puyallup Tom said that the dog's master was not far off and to "Closhe nanatch" (look out).

—David Denny
in *Blazing the Way* by his daughter, Emily Inez

Somehow David expected the rain to stop when they came on the regulars. If anything, it was coming down harder and had a wicked sting to it. The sun had set, and dusk quietly stole over Brannan's clearing. The soldiers, he saw, were huddled around smoking campfires, trying to get their supper going. But despite the inclement weather and the fact that many of them seemed to have some pretty nasty head colds, their spirits seemed good.

He liked Slaughter right off. The young lieutenant was a frail-looking man, which surprised David, considering the man's reputation as a soldier. He wore a thick mustache. His eyes were round, dark, alert. And as they passed the sputtering campfires toward Will's house it was clear the soldiers liked him too; a lot of bantering bounced back and forth between him and his men. One of them, a man who had to be at least fifty years old, gave a wave. Slaughter detoured over and clapped him on the shoulder. "We'll be all right, Mr. Bills."

"Yes, sir," said the soldier. Only he wasn't a soldier. He was wearing corduroy jeans and a buckskin jacket. A volunteer.

"*Lemuel* Bills?" David asked Lieutenant Slaughter when they passed on.

"That's right. Mr. Lemuel Bills. Oldest man in the field. Fifty-four, but tough as a bull. I borrowed him from Captain Wallace."

"A Steilacoom man then."

"Yes. And a darned good scout."

"Mmmph," grunted David, remembering Lemuel Bills's advertisement last fall in the *Courier* for a wife, and the outrageous response he'd gotten from some woman named Ellen.

Lieutenant Slaughter started to laugh. "You're thinking of Ellen Brooks, aren't you?"

"Yes, sir, I guess I was."

Slaughter threw his head back in unbridled laughter, a marvelous sound that seemed to push away the rain.

The regulars, David discovered, had turned Will and Elizabeth's house into their headquarters, and when he ducked through the door into the darkened room he automatically looked for the blood-soaked ground. But Slaughter had a fire going over the spot. David felt better not having to see his friend's blood, though he didn't feel better when he heard

106

that one of Slaughter's Indian scouts, a middle-aged man by the name of Puyallup Tom, had spotted an Indian dog skulking through the underbrush somewhere along the prairie's edge.

Captain Hewitt tried to persuade the young lieutenant to move his men up to the fort. An Indian dog meant his master wasn't that far away, and they all knew the open prairie was no place to be caught by a war party.

"What's one Indian?" said Slaughter. The bad feeling in David's stomach suddenly got worse. "The men have been hiking since dawn, a miserable stretch. They're tired. If your fort was closer, maybe, but I can't push them another two miles, not in the dark."

So they held their council of war sitting on the floor around Slaughter's blazing fire. With the windows of the house smashed out and the door ripped off there was plenty of ventilation for the smoke, but it also had the effect of making David feel hot and cold all at once. At least he was out of the rain. So while the dampness crept in around his back and neck and the heat of the fire scorched his hands and face, he listened to the officers—Corporal Barry, Corporal Clarendon, Lieutenant Harrison—discuss strategy. For the first time he realized he was in a war. That this was *real*. The whole notion shocked him.

The surrounding area, Slaughter explained, was controlled by Chief Nelson's Muckleshoots. David had to agree. Nelson, said Slaughter, would be the toughest of the war leaders to beat—and it was their task to do it. This made David uneasy. He knew Nelson. Shoot, he *liked* Nelson. But as he looked around at the stains on Elizabeth's newspaper-lined walls, the smashed bedstead, and the overturned tin tub, and remembered finding her bloated body in the well not all that long ago, his feelings and resolve hardened.

"Captain Judge Wallace of Steilacoom," said Slaughter, "is holding the Puyallup Valley. Captain Judge Hayes of Olympia has Muck Prairie. Captain Maloney, the Nisqually Plains. It's believed the main body of Indians have their camp some-where upriver." He took a stick and began etching a rough map in the dirt floor, "somewhere between White and Green Rivers. We're to build a fort at the junction." He tapped the floor where he'd drawn two lines intersecting. "Then leave a company to defend it while the rest of us forge up through here," he waved his stick between the lines, "until we find their camp and flush 'em out. Hayes, Maloney, and Wallace will wall them in for us."

David hadn't counted on going *after* the Indians. Defensive positioning was one thing, but aggressive offense? Did that make him any different than Nelson? But then if they didn't go after the Indians and put an end to this, the war could go on forever. He thought of Louisa, waiting at home for him, of Mynez and the baby coming on his birthday, and he knew he had to do what he had to do.

"Shh! They're signaling each other," hissed Puyallup Tom, suddenly leaping for the door. The men waited.

Whooo-ooh.

Seconds later, closer in, *Who-oooooh.*

The hair on the back of David's neck stood straight up, his heart all but stopped. But when he glanced over to Lieutenant Slaughter, he was surprised to read irritation in the tired man's frail face. "You're mistaken, it's just owls," he told Puyallup Tom. But then seeing all eyes on him, Slaughter shrugged. "We've been chasing Indians for four days and haven't seen hide nor hair. They're hardly going to show now."

"What about the dog?"

"All right, *one* Indian," he conceded.

"Shh!" The scout waved for silence. "There, did you hear it?"

"No," said Slaughter, and David had to admit he hadn't heard anything either.

"We're being surrounded," insisted Puyallup Tom.

"Tom, you're hearing things now," said Slaughter, laughing a little at Tom, amused. "Come on over and sit down."

He patted the ground beside him. "You've done your job. Time to take it easy."

"I tell you, they're out there! If you don't believe me, at least put out the fire!"

But Slaughter refused, and David resisted the temptation to ease back away from the flames. If there *were* Indians out there, they made a perfect target. *Surely,* he told himself, trying to find comfort, *Slaughter has got guards stationed about the yard.*

The young lieutenant did not. Which made it easy for Leschi and his war chiefs—Nelson, Kanaskset, Kitsap, and his brother, Quiemuth—once night came on, to sneak in and surround the camp with their warriors. The soldiers' smoldering fires scattered over the prairie flickered in the black rain. The rounded shoulders of sixty-five men trying to dry their clothes stood out in perfect silhouette, while inside the weathered log house, the blazing fire, visible through the open doorway, lit up the studious faces of the eight to ten men sitting in council.

The first shot, Leschi had explained, was to go to John Hiton, a former servant of Lieutenant Slaughter. Having spent a year hauling beef from the storehouse to the kitchen in the commissary, he was the only one who knew Slaughter by sight. "Because if you kill the big chief," was the way Leschi had explained it, "the rest is easy." And so now Indian John crept in closer and closer, inching his way through the dark wet grass. Closer and closer. Closer. Closer.

"That about covers it." Lieutenant Slaughter eased to his feet, grimacing and favoring his right knee. "I swear, weeks in the rain have rotted my bones. And I got a dozen men down with rheumatism. Think maybe I'm next?" he asked them all, chuckling at himself. But they were grimacing too, struggling to their own feet and helping one another up.

David turned to Slaughter to ask about the guards. A soldier with yellow hair and a red beard burst through the doorway with an armful of piping hot potatoes.

"Ho, Hall!" hollered Slaughter happily. "What have you brought us?"

"Supper, sir! Couldn't find any butter, you have to eat them plain! But I reckon you won't mind!"

Mind? David all but fell on his potato and had it halfway devoured, burning his tongue, when a shot rang out. He looked up and saw Slaughter's eyes widen in surprise. At the same time he saw blood spurting all over Slaughter's potato, hand, and chest.

"Douse the fires!" screamed Captain Hewitt. Lieutenant Slaughter toppled backward without a sound. A second shot rang out—then a third in quick succession. Corporal Barry, snuffing the fire, screamed and pitched face first into the flames. At the same time Corporal Clarendon gasped, spun sideways, slammed into David, then sagged to the ground. David jerked into action. Stepping over Clarendon, obviously dead, he dragged Barry off the dying fire and then helped Puyallup Tom stomp out the last flickering flame. When it was done he stood panting, heart pounding, the glowing embers of the smothered fire glimmering up at him from around his boots in the pitch black of night. All around him he could hear the heavy breathing of the others, the agonized, dying sounds of Corporal Barry—and the terrible volley of gunfire outside.

"Slaughter's dead!" shouted Captain Hewitt from somewhere in the dark. It was then that David realized that he himself was not.

Hewitt stumbled to the door, the rest followed. Outside, soldiers fired back at the Indians while others kicked sod onto their campfires, or beat out the flames with sticks. One by one the coals winked into darkness. And then it was quiet. Without a visible target, and receiving a concentrated return volley, the Indians ceased firing. Though no one believed for a minute they'd gone away.

Captain Hewitt took over the command. He found six men wounded, and while Dr. Taylor, on loan from the *Decatur*, had seven litters made, Hewitt and John Henning organized everyone for a forced march. Everyone would move down-river to the volunteers' fort; for without a doubt the Indians would renew their attack at daybreak.

They'd take the body of Lieutenant Slaughter with them. And though David helped wrap the lifeless body, his mind refused to believe that the likable young lieutenant was actually dead. He was only asleep. He'd wake up, make some joke about his joints. But he didn't wake up, and there were no jokes. Sadly, they had to place his inert body into the litter.

"We'll send someone back in the morning to bury Claren-don and Barry," Hewitt told David. David got the sudden, awful feeling it would be him. "Right now we've got to get going. The Indians are crawling like ants all over the place." As if to underscore the captain's remark scattered gunfire echoed out of the south, then north.

The whole force needed no urging, but traipsed quickly after Captain Hewitt into the woods down the trail toward the river edge, their heavy, stumbling footfall muffled by the night rain. David and a handful of regulars brought up the rear, walking backward, rifles poised. As soon as they, too, moved into the woods and David got turned around, he could hear the jubilant shouts of the Indians swarming through the abandoned camp. He did not like to think about the two bodies they'd left behind.

There was no question that Louisa would remain at Mary Ann's for the night. Emily Inez was wearing out; she'd grown considerably weaker and more listless as the day progressed and the women agreed she shouldn't be moved. They sat to-gether now, the three of them, around the fire. Mary Ann's grandfather clock chimed ten o'clock. The other children had been put to bed. The women didn't say anything, but they knew they'd be up all night.

"Is that someone at the door?" Irene put down her knitting.

Louisa looked up. She'd been running her fingers lightly through Emily Inez's hair. "Maybe it's Yoke-Yakeman at last," she said hopefully. Katy hadn't been able to find either Mandy or Yoke-Yakeman, but had left a message with Suwalth, Yoke-Yakeman's uncle.

"Yes, someone *is* at the door," said Irene.

Mary Ann gathered up her embroidery and went to check. "Mandy! *Klahowya.*" She pulled open the door. "Come in, come in."

"Suwalth say Mynez sick, huh?"

"Yes, yes, she is. Can I take your coat?"

The Indian woman shrugged out of her coat, nothing more than an old dirty Hudson's Bay blanket with a hole cut in the middle for her head. She came over to Louisa. Irene offered her the footstool, which she took, sitting quickly, eyes intent on Mynez sitting inertly in her mother's lap, her lips ringed in blue.

"When I not find you home to clean stove," she said, keeping her eyes on Emily Inez, "I go away, Salmon Bay. Oh. Madeline, Salmon Bay Curley, they say *klahowya.*"

"Is Yoke-Yakeman coming?"

"Maybe. I want see Mynez first, before he go long way White River. See if Mynez bad girl, *cultus tenas.* She eat more—" Mandy couldn't think of the word. She pointed to the fireplace.

"Charcoal?"

"Yes. Maybe in her throat, huh? Make stop breathing?"

"The doctor says no."

"Mmmph," snorted Mandy, a round, plump woman with a missing tooth. "What your medicine man know? I know Mynez eat charcoal. All time Mynez eat charcoal. You give her me," she said firmly.

Louisa hesitated. She didn't want to give up her little girl while there yet remained in her the smallest breath of life.

"Give her me, I fix her," insisted Mandy.

"Louisa," said Mary Ann, "you know she means no harm. Maybe she can even do Mynez some good."

"But what can she do that the doctor didn't?" cried Louisa, nearly sobbing now with fatigue and fear.

Mandy stood up and reached for Emily Inez.

"Let her do what she can," insisted Mary Ann.

Louisa didn't exactly let Mynez go. Nor did she resist. Mandy simply picked her up and started over to the table. Suddenly she had Emily Inez upside down and before Louisa could stop her, had whacked Emily Inez hard on the back. "No!" screamed Louisa, coming out of the chair even as her daughter gagged. Suddenly out popped a small chunk of charcoal onto the floor, a sodden black lump! Emily Inez sucked in a long, shuddering breath, arms flailing—then let out an ear-splitting shriek. But Louisa couldn't move! To save her life she couldn't move! She just stood there, clutching her chest, staring down at the floor and then back up at Mandy in surprise and shock.

"*Cultus tenas!*" Mandy scolded Emily Inez, easing her around right side up. "Bad girl, no more eat dirt!"

Louisa seized her daughter.

Crying, Emily Inez buried her face into Louisa's neck. "Bad Mandy pank My . . ."

Turning Mynez to face her, Louisa spoke gently. "You were the bad one, Mynez, not Mandy. You must *never* put coals in your mouth again. Do you understand?"

"Yes, Mama."

"Oh, Mandy," stammered Louisa, "thank you, thank you!" Suddenly she was weeping with relief, shaking all over. Mary Ann led her back to the chair. She all but collapsed into it, holding her precious child, tears streaming down her face. Irene and Mary Ann cried, Mandy cried. All three of them fussed around Mynez, laughing, crying, laughing again.

"See?" said Mandy, kissing Mynez on the top of her head. "Your medicine man know nothing."

"Let's all have some tea!" said Mary Ann. "Mandy, can you stay?"

"First, I tell Yoke-Yakeman he no go White River now. Tell him Mynez better. I come back." She helped herself to her coat, searched for the hole, and stuck her head through. "You got lots sugar, huh?"

"Lots and lots!" cried Mary Ann.

"I come back!"

As soon as she was gone, Irene gently kissed the top of Mynez's head as well and went back to her knitting. "And Kate Blaine," she snorted, "says the Indians haven't any more sense than a goat."

Rocking her precious little Mynez, so amazingly restored to her, Louisa watched the flames of her sister's fire curl and glow around the woodsticks. She began to hum Brahms's "Lullaby." *Was it possible that only five minutes ago she thought Mynez might die?* In minutes she felt Mynez fall asleep.

"Poor little thing," whispered Irene, "she's all tuckered out."

13

Wednesday Morning, December 5

It was a sad little canoe-procession that brought the body of Slaughter and the wounded soldiers down to Seattle the day after the tragedy.

—Roberta Frye Watt, Katy Denny's daughter
in *Four Wagons West*

*I*n the morning, just as soon as they had enough light to see by, Captain Hewitt ordered the company's supply canoes emptied. Beds were laid for the most seriously wounded, with one man able and preferring to sit up. The body of Lieutenant Slaughter was reverently lowered into the remaining dugout.

David and Lewis took charge of John Cullum, a seriously hurt private. Using the blanket upon which he lay in excruciating pain, they gently lifted him from the ground and swung him over to the canoe. Carefully they eased him in. Despite their care, the movement brought a rush of fresh blood to John's nostrils and mouth, bright red and mixed with foam. "Sorry," said David. "You need anything, John? Can I get you anything?" he asked and immediately felt afraid of John Cullum. Here was Death.

The cold rain thickened to sleet. Lewis, Seattle's blacksmith, hunched into his coat. "Come on, let's get him down to the water."

David took the bow, walking backward, Lewis the stern. Together they slithered and slipped down the steep embankment. David looked over his shoulder to see where he was going and prayed he wouldn't misstep. John started to choke on his blood, a terrible sound. "Nearly there," David assured him. He back-stepped into the icy river, and though he'd braced himself for the shock, he still gasped when the frigid water came swirling up around the top of his boots. *A long, cold ride downriver for a dying man.*

The other canoes were being launched, the moans and sometimes cries of the wounded competing with the rush of the river racing away to the north. David and Lewis eased their own canoe into the swirling current, and held steady. Butler and Neely, designated paddlers, splashed toward them.

"You sure I can't get anything for you?" David asked, wading alongside the bobbing canoe to where the dying soldier lay. He'd stopped choking and was staring up at the sleet and rain with pain-glazed eyes. Once in awhile he blinked. "Anything at all?" David repeated. Getting no answer, he reached over and stroked the man's wet forehead. He wondered where the bullet had struck. The bandaging around John's head was so blood-soaked it looked like a scarlet crusted turban. Suddenly their eyes met, and in the quiet exchange David could see the man's terrible suffering. "God go with you," he whispered.

Neely and Butler clambered in. The canoe rocked and tipped. John winced, then moaned. The canoe then dropped under the added weight, crunched harshly down into the rocky riverbed. John squeezed his eyes shut, as quiet as death. David took his hand. "The worst is over. From here on it's an easy ride."

"We need you to push us clear!" shouted Neely.

"Just a minute!"

Quickly David unbuttoned his coat, wiggled out, and then spread it over John. "It's not much, I know, but it might help," he apologized, tucking the collar up around his face.

"Ready?" called out Neely.

David splashed around to the stern. He and Lewis each seized a side, bent into it, feet braced.

"On the count of three," said Lewis. "Okay?"

"Yup."

"One, two, *threeee!*"

The canoe slid free, caught the current and fish-tailed out to the others. In minutes they were gone, the canoes disappearing around a bend in the river, taking the dead and dying. "Do you think that soldier's going to make it?" Lewis asked David in a solemn voice, sleet cutting into their faces.

"No."

"I don't either."

When they scrambled up the trail to the top of the bluff, both of them soaking wet, shivering, and teeth chattering, Captain Hewitt was waiting. David knew exactly what was coming. He was right. "You can pick your own crew," Hewitt told him.

"What's everyone else doing?"

"Getting packed up. It'll take awhile, though. We have to hand-haul the provisions, and all the equipment. It shouldn't take you too long to catch up, I don't think. Where's your coat, Denny?"

"He gave it to one of the wounded," said Lewis.

Captain Hewitt shook his head. "That's all we need. Two dead soldiers instead of one."

David had no idea whether or not the Indians were still at the Brannans', so he took ten men he knew were good shots.

The trail at least was easy to follow; sixty-five men stumbling through in the dark had left their mark.

A quarter mile short of the prairie he called a halt. "I'll go in and signal if it's safe to come on."

"No," argued George Frye. "We all go."

Everyone nodded.

"But let's take a vote," said Frye, "in case one of us is wounded. Do we stand by the wounded, or do we each look out for ourselves?"

Fear of facing armed Indians was one thing, but the idea of being wounded and left alone to them filled David with abject horror. He was relieved to find the others felt the same way. The vote was unanimous. They'd stay with the wounded down to the last man.

"All right then, let's go," he said.

This last quarter mile they crept single file, pausing, listening with each cautious step, rifles poised and fingers ready on the trigger. At the prairie's edge everything was quiet. They stood a moment listening. *This is it*, thought David, stepping out. The others followed, and they all stared with heart-pounding relief across the forlorn, empty yard.

In eastern Washington, Oregon's volunteers sneaked up on Fort Walla Walla, ready to do battle—but Chief Peo-Peo-Mox-Mox was gone! A broad trail, though, led west-north-west across the plains. Giving themselves a day's rest outside the gates of the fort's ruins, the Oregon volunteers split up on the dawn of December the 5th. Major Chinn, with the baggage and a hundred men, headed west down the Walla Walla River to the mouth of the Touchet River where they would pitch camp and await orders from Colonel Kelly. Kelly, with the remaining men and a day's provisions, cut west-northwest across the frozen plains, following the broad trail of Chief Peo-Peo-Mox-Mox and his allied tribes.

The trail led them straight to the Touchet River several miles away and some ten miles up from the river mouth where Major Chinn would wait. Here they found ninety-eight campfires not yet cold. A mile farther upstream, just coming into the Touchet River Canyon, Kelly called a halt. He didn't like the look of the high rocky bluffs—too easy to be ambushed. He decided to send out a few scouts.

A quarter mile into the rocky foothills, a party of six Indians on horseback came up over the summit. The center figure rode a huge American horse—a big, beautiful bay, with a holster slung over the tooled leather saddle, and a pair of navy revolvers. Rifles up, the scouts ordered the party to stop. The center figure dismounted with all the dignity of a king who knows his importance. He carried a white flag.

He was a big man. Wore a felt hat, with crown and brim. Long black hair hung loose about his shoulders. His nose was monstrously large, mouth too. Keen eyes, set in a face seamed with responsibility, suspicion, and grief, inventoried the white scouts with their raised rifles as they came on, carrying a white flag.

He spoke first. "I am Peo-Peo-Mox-Mox," he said. "Is the agent with you?"

One of the scouts jerked his head back over his shoulder, indicating that Indian Agent Nathan Olney was with the main camp below.

"Bring him to me."

Peo-Peo-Mox-Mox had reason to be suspicious and even treacherous when dealing with white men. In the beginning he'd seen their advantages; and though he was the wealthiest of all Pacific Northwest chiefs, owning thousands of horses and cattle, he nonetheless coveted the white man's superior "medicine."

To gain knowledge of their power he sent his beloved son, Elijah, to be Christianized at the Methodist mission in Oregon's Willamette Valley. Elijah's schooling over, Peo-Peo-Mox-Mox sent him down to California to drive back a large herd of cattle. Somewhere along the way Elijah and his com-

119

rades purchased a string of ponies. A few days later they rode into Fort Sutter, California, and were accosted by a circle of white men accusing them of horse theft. Elijah hotly denied it, and showed them his bill of sale.

The next day was the whiteskins' "medicine" day. Thinking no more of the matter, Elijah stayed over to attend church in the morning. He was kneeling at the altar, receiving holy communion, when one of his accusers came down the aisle behind him, put a pistol to the back of his neck, and blew half his head off.

The sacrilegious aspect of the brutal murder was not lost on Peo-Peo-Mox-Mox, and when no effort was ever made on the part of the whiteskins to punish the perpetrator, hatred for the whole race and their deceiving medicine rooted in his heart. And though he continued to add to his ever increasing wealth by pleasantly trading with the new immigrants passing through his country each year, he was merely biding his time. He would not go to his own death until the murder of his beloved son was avenged.

He watched three of these white men now angle their horses up over the rocky terrain to meet him. He waited, white flag firmly in hand.

Colonel Kelly, Indian Agent Olney, and John McBean, the Hudson's Bay Factor of the plundered Fort Walla Walla acting as interpreter, rode up. *So this is Peo-Peo-Mox-Mox,* thought Kelly, taking a good look at the seventy-year-old chief. Strong-looking, dark features, high cheekbones, a monstrous, wrinkled nose. He wore three brand-new Hudson's Bay blankets over his shoulders and a ridiculous felt hat. *I can guess where he got the duds,* thought Kelly.

"Why do soldiers come into my country?" Peo-Peo-Mox-Mox glared downhill past Kelly's shoulder to the encampment.

"To punish you," answered Kelly sternly, through McBean, "for the wrongs you and your people have done."

"I have done no wrong. I desire peace with the white-skins."

"You pillaged and defaced Fort Walla Walla. You stole government property. You carried away Hudson's Bay goods. You burned the storehouses belonging to the Brooks, Noble, and Bunford Ranch, to say nothing of the settlers' cabins, three of them—"

"I did not do these things!" Peo-Peo-Mox-Mox's black eyes blazed. The icy cold of winter's frigid air vaporized his breath into puffy white wisps.

"You did."

"Some of my young men," he yielded, "may have done these things. It is not always possible to control hotheads."

"But Howlis Wampum," argued Kelly, referring to a notable Cayuse chief and refusing to be taken in by the offended avowal, "says he saw you distribute the goods with your own hands! He says you gave a big pile of blankets to induce the Cayuse to join you in your war against the whites!"

Black, hard eyes stared back. Wrinkled nostrils flared angrily. "I do not want war! I want peace! I will make my people restore what they took!" avowed Peo-Peo-Mox-Mox. "Everything else I will pay. I, Peo-Peo-Mox-Mox, say this!"

"A day late and a dollar short!" barked Kelly.

"I can't translate that!" snapped McBean. "How can a savage know what that means?"

"Not good enough! Tell him that!" He waited impatiently for the translation. Then, "You and your men must give yourselves up! Turn in your guns! All your ammunition! Also, my men are tired and hungry from chasing you down! You must give us some of your beef!"

"We will do as you say. Come to our camp tomorrow. We will give you our weapons and ammunition. We will give you beef to eat."

Kelly turned to the Indian agent. "What do you think?"

"I think he's lying. Look."

At least two dozen warriors had come off the summit and were stealthily advancing their line down around the scouts. Kelly brought up his rifle. He leveled it at the old chief's blanketed chest. "Tell them to back off," he hissed between his teeth, "or I blow a hole through your heart big enough to throw a cat."

The old man barked out an order, the Indians backed up.

Kelly, rifle still leveled, said, "I don't believe you intend to turn in your guns, old man. I believe you intend to buy time to prepare for battle. So if you take your flag of truce and go back to your village to get ready for war, I will be forced to attack your camp and kill everyone in it. On the other hand, if you talk without a forked tongue, you won't object coming into my camp and staying with me until what you say comes true. Take your choice."

Clearly, being held hostage to ensure his promises being carried out was something Peo-Peo-Mox-Mox had not expected.

Kelly repeated his position. "Go, you force me to wage war. Stay, I will see if you speak the truth."

Peo-Peo-Mox-Mox at last nodded. "I will stay with you," he agreed cautiously. "But first, I send a man to my camp to say where I am, to say we talk peace. To say they must get ready to give up their guns."

Given a curt nod, he scrambled lithely up to his mounted guard with all the grace and agility of a seventeen-year-old youth, not a seventy-year-old man. A few minutes later one of his guards wheeled around on a spotted cayuse and started back over the summit.

Everyone else started for the main encampment. One of the prisoners, however, a Nez Perce, hung back and then angled his horse in next to Olney's who brought up the rear. "Peo-Peo did not tell his messenger he was making peace," he muttered on the sly to the Indian agent. "He gave instruction for the camp to pack and go to the mountains and wait for Five Crows."

Five Crows was a notorious chief who'd once held a white woman from the Whitman Massacre captive, determined to make her his wife and submitting her to all kinds of outrages. "Why Five Crows?" Olney whispered back, not liking the sound of this.

"Five Crows brings more warriors."

"Why do you speak?"

The Nez Perce pointed to the encampment ahead. "I am not Walla Walla, I am Nez Perce. I am not a fool."

14

Thursday, December 6

Until the bodies of the dead could be transferred to Steilacoom, they lay in the new blockhouse fort, which was taking on the grim usages of war. One of my mother's most vivid memories was that of Lieutenant Slaughter's body lying under the stairs in the blockhouse.

—Roberta Frye Watt, Katy Denny's daughter
in *Four Wagons West*

In 1931 a Steilacoom woman went walking out beyond her potato garden and found an overturned marble slab in the dense woods on the eastern edge of town. On it was carved:
JNO. CULLUM
CO. M
3RD U.S. ART.

—J. A. Eckrom, historian
in *Remembered Drums*

The very next morning Colonel Kelly and his men marched into Touchet Canyon fully expecting to collect Peo-Peo-Mox-Mox's promised guns, ammunition, and the beef. Yesterday's provisions were gone and they were hungry. But when they came on the Indian camp it was swept clean, lock, stock, and barrel. *Duped!*

The only Indians visible were a ring of warriors along a high ridge of hills. For a time, Colonel Kelly endeavored to get them to come in and comply with the terms of the agreement. But they showed no interest, and seeing that nothing more was to come of his effort, Kelly backed out of the canyon and headed downriver to meet Major Chinn.

Overcome with hunger and knowing they'd get nary a bite until they reached the mouth of the Touchet River, the men marched determinedly all day against a bitter wind, finally arriving frostbitten and ravenous while the dusky hues of night settled down around them.

The same Thursday night, with darkness descending over Puget Sound, Company H dragged into Seattle. John Cullum, they learned, had died somewhere along the way. His body and Lieutenant Slaughter's were both set under the stairs inside the blockhouse. David fetched his coat and asked Lieutenant Drake, who happened to be standing guard, what the plans were.

"Sterrett's been summoned from Port Madison to transport the dead and wounded to Steilacoom for proper burial and medical attention."

"What's Sterrett doing in Port Madison?"

"Haida."

David nodded and started wearily for home.

Louisa was waiting for him. She'd known he was on his way ever since the canoes had come in the night before with the two dead men and five wounded. Now here he was, standing just inside their door, holding her face in his icy cold hands and staring down into her eyes.

She reached up to clasp his cold hands in her own. What did she see in those searching eyes? Sorrow? Sadness? Puzzlement? Weariness, certainly. Fear?

125

"Mynez all right?" he finally asked.

"Yes." *Tomorrow I'll tell him how close we came to losing her. Not tonight.*

He hung up his coat. She saw the blood caked all over the collar but said nothing. He collapsed onto a chair and started to talk. The wet woods. Lemuel Bills. Will and Elizabeth's house. The war council. The shooting. The dead. The frightening trip back to bury Lieutenant Slaughter's two dead corporals. Somewhere in all this he put his elbows on the table and held his head, staring down at the puncheons. "They were both scalped and mutilated by the time we got there," he mumbled. "I don't know why they do that, mutilate the dead the way they do."

In all the time she had ever known him, she'd never seen him so dejected. His clothes were filthy, a ruination. His hair was a mat of mud and pine needles. The worst was his despair. He seemed almost on the verge of crying. Watch sensed his gloom as well and crept over, tail down. Quietly, the faithful dog rested his head on David's thigh, looking up with dark, sorrowful eyes.

"When we went back the next morning," David went on, not even noticing Watch, "yesterday I guess it was—seems like a long time ago—I kept hearing the Indians, the way they sounded the night before. Like a thousand cats thrown across a clothesline with their tails tied together. It's a terrible sound, a sound you can *feel*. You feel it in your ears, in your knees, under your fingernails even."

She sliced leftover potatoes into a frying pan. The fat she'd spooned in earlier sizzled and spat around each slice.

"It was worse than the massacre. The maliciousness, I mean. The sick maiming. We couldn't tell who was who, Liza, Barry or Clarendon. They'd been scalped, their faces smashed in, their ears—"

"It's over, David." Wiping her hands on her apron, she went over to him and kissed the top of his head. "The potatoes will be done in a few minutes. I've got bread and butter. Would you like some jam?"

He nodded.

"I'll get a bath ready while you eat. When you get in, I'll shampoo your hair." She felt like his mother.

"Their ears were cut off, Liza, and their hands—"

"David, it's over now. And you're home."

"Why do they do that?"

"I'll get down the tub."

"The potatoes ready?"

"Let me check."

"Liza, I don't want you pouring the bath water."

"It's all right, I can manage. I'll fill the pail only halfway. Your job is to eat."

"All right then." He was, she saw, too tired to argue, and so while he ate, she transferred the water, half buckets at a time, from the reservoir in the back of the stove to the tub she'd set in front of the fire. It took awhile, but then David did too. As hungry as he was, he nevertheless seemed to have trouble getting the food down.

And once he got into the tub, he stayed there. Even after she'd sudsed down his back, washed his hair, and combed out all the tangles and debris, he stayed put. He sat with his legs crossed, elbows on his knees, holding his head, staring down into the water. Just when she was convinced he'd catch a chill, he looked up.

"Can I have a towel?"

She handed him the one warming by the fire.

He took it, eased to his feet, shook the water first off one foot and placed it on the floor, then the other, and stepped out altogether.

"What?" she said, for he was watching her.

"I'm afraid I'll never forget the look on Lieutenant Slaughter's face. He was surprised."

"I expect he might have been. You said he was so sure there were no Indians about."

127

"His eyes opened wide, he sucked in his breath. And then he was dead. Just like that."

"Do you know what's going to happen now?" she asked.

"No. I guess it's up to the new captain at Steilacoom. Keyes, I think his name is."

"Do you have any guesses? I mean, if the army can't stop the Indians—"

"Maybe General Wool will send us more soldiers."

That was some hope, she thought.

When they got into bed and blew out the lamps, it was she who held him.

"Liza?" he whispered in the dark.

"Yes."

"I've never seen a man die like that before. I hope I never see it again."

"I hope so too. But go to sleep now. You're home." She kissed his cheek. "I'm so *glad* you're home."

"I am too. A nice surprise."

"A *wonderful* surprise."

"It is, isn't it?" And he kissed her.

David was back. At least for now. She had no illusions though. He'd be called out again soon enough.

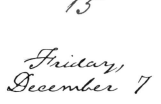

15

*Friday,
December 7*

On the morning of the 7th, Companies H and K crossed the Touchet, leading the column, and when formed on the plain, were joined by Company B. A few soldiers in front were driving the cattle, and a few others were on the flanks, near the foot of the hills that extended along the river. Some Indians appeared in front, and in a short time the whole column, except those detailed to guard the baggage, were in full pursuit of them.

—Clinton Snowden
in *History of Washington*

The reunited Oregon volunteers awoke early Friday morning to a light snow. Breaking the ice off their blankets where their breath had solidified, the men, one by one and then in twos and threes, staggered numbly to their feet and tried stomping some warmth down into their toes. Suddenly, like a blast of cold air that alerts the senses, they

129

spotted Five Crows's warriors lining the hills to the left and front of their camp.

Colonel Kelly ordered two companies to cross the Touchet and form a straight line, another two companies to fall in behind. The remaining companies were assigned the baggage train and prisoners.

It took some time to get the horses across the icy river and onto the plains, and by then more warriors had collected. The first gunfire came from the north. The volunteers fell in and made their charge.

The battle was fierce, a steady barrage that left many dead on both sides, and evolved into a running battle eastward back up the Walla Walla River, the volunteers driving the Indians before them. The dry, fluffy snow on the ground blew up in clouds behind each thundering horse and swirled around in the conflicting winds.

The Indians seemed to increase in number as they neared French Town, a small cluster of cabins some eight miles from where they'd started. Here the terrain funneled between the river to the east and the steep rise of flat-topped, rocky hills to the west. The Indians, fifteen hundred of them now, held a straight line running clear across the plains, from the river to the hilly tableau, with nothing but scabland between them and the oncoming volunteers.

The volunteers, coming into the bottleneck, saw that the Indians carried as flags the scalps of their comrades who'd fallen earlier that day. More scalps from previous victims hung from poles on all the stark, prominent hilltops to the west. Squads of warriors danced fiendishly around them. Enraged by the display of barbarity and mockery, the volunteers met the stand. But the Indians poured such a murderous volley into them that they were eventually forced back.

Fortuitously, and not a moment too soon, Company A arrived with the baggage and prisoners, and with this reinforcement, the volunteers rallied and went back at the enemy with fixed bayonet. Peo-Peo-Mox-Mox and his fellow hostages began hollering to the warriors—and were answered in turn. Colonel Kelly heard the exchange. He had already lost two of his best officers, and now Frank Crabtree was being brought in from the front line with a shattered shoulder and arm hanging loose. So the sight of the hostages screaming instruction and encouragement enraged Kelly.

"I need every man at the front!" he bellowed at the men standing guard. "Tie those prisoners, or kill them, I don't care which!"

Ropes were brought out. The Nez Perce hostage held out his wrists, willing enough, but a large man named Wolf Skin whipped a knife from his leggings and sprang with a demonic howl at Sergeant Major Miller. Miller dropped to the ground with a scream, blood flowing from his arm, sliced open to the bone from elbow to wrist.

Peo-Peo-Mox-Mox tried to snatch the rifle of a second guard. The guard dodged and came swiftly up behind Peo-Peo-Mox-Mox, swinging his gun like a club and striking the old chief such a blow that it knocked Peo-Peo to the ground. Blood streamed from his crown, yet he pushed to his knees and tried to stand up. The guard struck again, driving the chief back to the ground and this time cracking his head open with his bayonet, throwing an arc of spewing red blood against a sky of white falling snow.

The other prisoners panicked. Screaming and tripping over themselves, they made a mad frantic dash away from the gruesome scene. The Oregon guards simply gunned them down, shooting the frightened men in the back and at such close range that their bodies slammed to the ground. Blackened holes as big as a man's fist opened through their torsos to the snow-laced ground below. Almost instantly the snow turned pink.

"Peo-Peo-Mox-Mox! He's crawling away!"

The guards circled and fired their weapons point blank into Peo-Peo-Mox-Mox's writhing body until it moved no more. With a yipping howl, the guard who had cracked the chief's head open reached down and lifted the scalp. "A little torn!" he crowed and guffawed to the amusement of all.

Late that night, with the rest of the Indians driven back for the time being, the guards cut off Peo-Peo-Mox-Mox's ears and then shared his torn scalp, cutting it into small strips.

They laughed at its toughness. "We can make razor strops!" they chortled.

Someone told Colonel Kelly of the barbarity, and he ordered immediate burial of the old chief. But in the middle of the night, while the colonel slept, Captain Benjamen Shaw dug up the corpse. In the black of night, around a low fire, he and the others laughed like demons while they dismembered and further mutilated the old chief's body. They bartered and fought over the mutilated pieces as souvenirs.

Chief Peo-Peo-Mox-Mox was dead, and when Governor Stevens arrived a week and a half later at Fort Henrietta, he congratulated Colonel Kelly, Major Chinn, and Benjamen Shaw and thanked the "fine, brave men" who opened the way for his safe return.

16

Sunday,
December 9

Although his career in the army was brief, it gave promise
that he would ultimately have achieved distinction, had
he been permitted to live.

—Clinton Snowden
in *History of Washington*

I do not remember that we intended to kill them outright,
but to the best of my recollection, we had decided to torture them with a slow death.

—J. W. Goodell
in *South Bend Journal*

ieutenant Slaughter's quest for destiny ended in
death, and as if to mourn the tragedy a piercing rain
fell the morning of his funeral. Rain, however, did not stop
the pioneers from saying their last good-byes. Before the appointed hour, Steilacoom's pioneers trudged along the

muddy road from town out to the fort, their faces averted from the rain's pelting slant. From Olympia they came, from the Puyallup Valley, from the Nisqually Plains. A full military guard stood by, and his Masonic brothers were all present. And when Captain Keyes, his old West Point instructor, delivered the final eulogy, everyone battled tears.

"My heart is sick," lamented Keyes in a choked voice, "when I reflect that so brave an officer and so gallant a gentleman should be slain by the wretched savages."

The untimely death of Lieutenant Slaughter broke the courage of many settlers. The army apparently could not protect them. A deep gloom fell over the Sound as their fear reached new proportions. Fear charged with fear.

Captain Keyes, analyzing the disparate circumstances, realized that to continue a winter campaign was futility at best and only added to the pervasive alarm. That night he wrote Acting Governor Mason of his new direction.

Sir:

It is reported on all hands that it is impossible to operate against the Indians with any effect in the country on the White, Green, and Puyallup Rivers at this season of the year, and I know it to be so from personal observation. To continue such a course will break down all our men and effect no harm to the Indians. Our pack animals are broken down, and we must establish our forces on our own ground, in places where they will not suffer at night, and where they can best protect the settlers.

To this end Keyes summoned Captain Judge Hayes at Muck Prairie to extricate Slaughter's forty men left behind at Stuck Creek, and then ordered the evacuation of all troops

134

from the field, with an idea to reposition them closer to the settlements and along the key river crossings. An extensive web of blockhouses, he realized, would have to be built then linked by well-armed patrols to keep a fence between the settlers and savages. "Brown?" he called out, wondering if his aide-de-camp was still in.

"Yes, sir?" Robert Brown popped his head around the office door.

"Is Captain Sterrett still docked?"

"No, sir."

"No—you don't know?"

"No, he already left. Left for Seattle right after the funeral, sir."

Keyes swore in frustration. "I needed a dispatch taken up to Captain Hewitt."

"Captain Pease will be by in the morning, sir, with the revenue cutter."

"Right. Monday morning run."

"Anything else, sir?"

"Yes. Have someone run this dispatch out to Captain Hayes. Billy Tidd, if you can get him. The country out there belongs to Leschi and his allies now—and from what I hear Billy Tidd's the only man who's met Leschi and come out alive."

His aide-de-camp gone, Keyes propped his elbows on the desk and wearily held his head, staring down at his ink blotter. *How was he going to drive out Leschi?* he wondered. *He had to reclaim the offensive, but for that he needed more soldiers. He had to have more soldiers! Another letter to Wool? Maybe now with Slaughter's death,* Keyes thought bitterly as he reached for his pen, *Wool might yet be persuaded.*

Lieutenant Slaughter's death not only destroyed the pioneers' courage, it also broke the stubborn resistance of the last reluctant homesteaders at Grand Mound Prairie. Hastily they joined their more cautious neighbors at Fort Henness on Chamber's Prairie south of Olympia. Whole families crowded into the tiny rude shelters lining the high pillared stockade, one hundred twenty-five men, women, and children. The living conditions were appalling, the crowding beyond anything most of them had endured. Privacy was nonexistent. Yet by the time Lieutenant Slaughter was buried tedium had set in, and for many of the pioneers this was the worst. For three young boys it was simply not to be endured.

That same afternoon, the weather cleared and they made their escape. The plan was to head down the main road to Jeremiah Goodell's house two miles away. Just what they would do when they got there, they didn't know. It was a fine enough thing just to be ten, eleven, and twelve years old and skipping freely away from the fort, far and away from their parents' close-quarters scrutiny. Splashing through the potholes and jabbing each other in the ribs, they began talking about what they might do should they meet up with Leschi. *For only Leschi and his warriors would be out in the open like this!*

As they went along they became very brave and began to boast of fancied heroism. "We shouldn't kill them outright," said Jeremiah. "We should torture them with slow death!"

"Yes! Yes!" the others cried.

A thicket of oak bushes grew out by the Goodell home, and among the bushes was a main vine, the seed of which grew into a pod about the size of a baseball. Many a sham battle the boys had fought with these pods, using them like snowballs. Someone remembered them now, and the race was on. They gathered them up, the whole lot of them, and piled them into convenient heaps on the roadside. The plan was to attack the first lot of hostiles that came along.

They did not have to wait long.

"Horses!" whispered Jeremiah, hearing a sudden commotion and the clap of horse hooves. He and his pals slithered down on their bellies, noses poking up through the winter grass with an eye on the road. A crowd of thirty war-painted warriors came trotting into view, Leschi out front, sitting tall. Everyone was dressed for battle and seemed in a great hurry.

The boys all gaped at each other in sudden, holy terror. *"Leschi!"* they hissed to each other, wide-eyed and shaking, hugging the ground, and no longer brave but rather frozen by fright. The Indians would have ridden on but for John Metcalf. Up he popped in a moment of insanity, pod in his hand, and fired a fast one straight for Leschi.

Never before or since has a single shot created such panic among the enemy. They couldn't see from whence came the attack, and were thrown into the wildest of confusion.

A few sharp commands from Leschi brought them quickly about-face and suddenly every gun was leveled in the boys' direction.

The three small boys, frozen in mortal terror, awaited their end. But instead of gunfire came the startling eruption of merry laughter. Happy laughter! Joyous laughter! Rich and resinous, musical laughter! Leschi had to throw back his head to let it all out, and he laughed at the sky. He slapped his thigh, wiped his eyes, shook his head, and then laughed some more. Gay, lighthearted mirth! He waved his men to carry on, and they all rode away with Leschi still laughing, leaving three boys with pounding hearts. The laughter slowly faded away—but still lingered in their ears as one by one they wobbled their way, weak-kneed, hearts in their throats, back to the fort.

They were heroes when they arrived. If three boys who couldn't sit down that night could be called heroes.

That night on the Sound, under light sail and headed at last for Seattle, Captain Sterrett retired below to write the navy of his growing concerns. With the exception of Seattle, Steilacoom, Olympia, and a few remote outposts, Leschi now held all the land that had previously belonged to the Indians—land rolling north from the Columbia River to the Skagit, east from the Cascade Mountains out to the sea.

Kill the big chief, the rest is easy. Standard warfare. Leschi had known what he was doing. One bullet through the heart and he'd not only snuffed out the life of a well-liked and admirable leader, but he'd spawned the terrible fear that now ran rampant, leaving the army scrambling from offense to defense and the people barricading themselves in blockhouses in panic, some even fleeing for Portland or California. Slaughter's death was the ticket Leschi had needed to gain ascendancy. Ascended, it was now his to name the next move. Where would he strike next?

No matter how many times Captain Sterrett asked himself, nor how many ways he looked at the thing, he always came up with the same answer: Seattle. Olympia was just too big and had too many men guarding her. Steilacoom had the fort and the soldiers. The villages across the Sound were too far away. Bellingham was too far to the north. *And if Seattle falls, Leschi's victory is complete. The Sound is his.* Troubled, Sterrett picked up his pen. After first reporting his role in the transport of Lieutenant Slaughter's body and the wounded to Steilacoom, he added:

I trust that I shall be pardoned for stating it is my opinion that the war in this territory is assuming a most serious aspect. The number, valor, and prowess of the Indians have been greatly underrated, and the forces now in the field, and, indeed, the whole military resources of the territory, are totally inadequate to conduct war with success or even to afford protection to the settlers. The war in Oregon seems to engross the whole of the attention of the people and press of California and the greater danger to which this territory is subject appears to be unknown. It was, as I have been informed, in conse-

138

quence of information received by Gen. Wool, after his arrival in the Columbia River, that Capt. Keyes's company was diverted to Steilacoom. This timely reinforcement, however, is, in my opinion, altogether insufficient, and it is the opinion of well-informed men here that it will require regiments instead of companies and years instead of months to conquer these tribes.

I am, sir, very respectfully, your obedient servant, Isaac S. Sterrett, Commander.

He was rereading the report when a loud crack rent the air. He seized his desk even as the ship trembled and shuddered. Staggering to his feet, he took the companionway two steps at a time, coming out on deck to a thick, blanketing fog and the sounds of running, surprised shouts, and cursing from the starboard bow.

17

Monday,
December 10

William Webster, pilot in charge, weighed anchor, and while working to the southward against a light head wind, and at about high water, being close in with Bainbridge Island, struck upon a rocky reef making in a south-easterly direction from the land, a danger of which the pilot was entirely ignorant.

—Lieutenant T. S. Phelps, *Decatur*
in *Reminiscences of Seattle*

*C*alamity upon calamity. The *Decatur* limped into Seattle early the next morning with her starboard bilge staved in and her main rail, between the fore- and mainmasts, arched nearly two feet, the seams opened an inch or more. Pilot William Webster, working to the southward against a light head wind, had struck an uncharted reef near Bainbridge Island. And while every attempt had been made to back her off, by the time an anchor was carried out and her heavy guns run aft, the tide had fallen, leaving her draped over a ledge.

She was sustained at two points, the stern and bilge, with the forefoot elevated five feet above the sand. Captain Sterrett ordered the open seams caulked with blankets, and on the next high tide managed to kedge her off the reef and somehow beat her back to Seattle with six feet of water in her hold after a vexing thirty-hour crossing of contending high winds.

The Seattle pioneers, as stunned and frightened by Lieutenant Slaughter's death as everyone else on the Sound, could scarcely believe this double catastrophe. Every able-bodied man in Seattle fell to feverishly to help the marines get the *Decatur*'s topmasts and yardarms dismantled and taken ashore, her hold broken down, and her battery removed to Yesler's wharf. At high tide they hauled what was left of her up onto the beach as far as possible so that when the tide went out she might be "high and dry."

The damage was extensive. The keel, keelson, and side, up to the waterline, were all badly broken, the side completely staved in. On her starboard, from bridle port to mainmast and rail to keel, the frame-knees, lining, and outside planking, excepting an inch of the outer surface, was honeycombed with dry rot. The *Decatur* would have to be almost entirely rebuilt, and Louisa, standing on the beach in the thick, swirling white fog with David and Emily Inez and just about everyone else in town, gazed upon the misty wreckage as if in a dream. Leschi held the country, and the *Decatur* was laid up.

"I can't believe it. I just can't believe it," cried Ursula Wyckoff beside Louisa.

Mrs. Phillips stood with them, wringing her hands. "What is to become of us?" she mewed.

"If the army can't stop the Indians," someone else said, "and with the *Decatur* nothing but kindling . . ."

"Can it be fixed?" Mr. Butler asked a marine.

141

Louisa stole a glance over her shoulder to the surrounding dark woods, expecting at any moment to see war-painted warriors come yowling fiendishly out of the trees. *Where was Leschi? Was he watching even now?* Grabbing the sleeve of the same marine Mr. Butler had spoken to, she asked, drymouthed, "*Can* it be fixed?"

"Like I said, a good smithy—"

"How long?" interrupted one of the Do-Nothings.

A loud toot suddenly came off the water. They all jumped. Emily Inez tilted off her father's shoulders, making a wild dive into his arms.

"It's just a ship," he told her, pointing out to the fog.

She peered along the line of his finger. "Bad noise!" she pouted, finger in her mouth.

"Yes, bad noise," he agreed.

Captain Pease's U.S. revenue cutter emerged a few minutes later and eased in alongside the wharf. A distinguished-looking naval officer disembarked with the well-liked captain. For a moment Pease and the stranger stared disconcertedly at the battery piled up everywhere.

"I wonder who he is?" said Ursula curiously, tossing her thick, golden brown braid over her shoulder.

Mr. Butler said, "Looks navy to me."

"Pretty high up too," agreed Lewis, hand on Ursula's shoulder.

Captain Sterrett scrambled onto the dock and started down, winding in and around the sixteen guns that should be aboard ship. The three men shook hands. *Something's wrong.* She could tell by the sudden stiffening in Captain Sterrett's posture. She glanced at David.

"Something's up," he agreed.

The two naval officers and the customs official started off the wharf. Captain Sterrett spotted David and veered over. "I need to see you and the other volunteer officers in the cookhouse, Denny. Can you round them up for me?"

"Yes, sir."

"Yesler, too, if you spot him."

David passed Mynez over to Louisa. "I'll see you up at the house?"

She nodded but remained behind a few minutes to talk with Ursula and Lewis, the three of them conjecturing the various possibilities of trouble. "Who knows," said Ursula finally, with a terribly long sigh. "It could be anything."

"Whatever it is," said Lewis, "it doesn't look good."

Louisa bid them good-bye. "Let's go see our new house," she told Emily Inez, "before we go home and make supper."

"My no like new house!"

"You will, you'll see."

After hearing about his daughter's near suffocation from choking, David had rounded up his Indian friends and started the house he'd intended to build ever since the beginning of the war. For three days now they'd been working around the clock, felling the trees, laying the foundation, building up the walls. What was unique to the new house was its fireplace. David had built it three feet off the ground—safely out of Mynez's reach.

The cabin stood directly east of the blockhouse, down off the knoll and next door to Sheriff Tom Russell and his extended family (refugees from White River), as well as the White River orphans they had taken in. Louisa stopped one house short of them, stepped in through the open doorway of her own new house, and looked up. Yoke-Yakeman was up over the rafters laying out the shingles.

"Hello, *klahowya!*" she called up.

He grinned down at her. "You like?"

"I do!"

"The ship? Bad broken?"

"I'm afraid so!"

"Not good! Leschi hear soon!"

She said good-bye, her hands suddenly shaking, her heart pounding. The war was closing in on them. She felt her new baby move and stretch inside. Automatically she circled her hand over the spot. Into what kind of a world was she bringing this precious little life? She looked down at Mynez, walking alongside her, trustingly holding her hand. *Help me,* she prayed, feeling almost desperate, *not to forget amidst my fear the miracle of her little life, so graciously restored to me last week!*

An hour later Louisa gaped at David in disbelief.

"It's obviously a false charge," he told her, squatting before the fire and holding his hands to the flames. "It only got this far because the fellow Captain Sterrett executed happened to be the son of the naval secretary."

"But he's to be *court-martialed?* I can't believe it!" Of all the terrible things she and the Wyckoffs had discussed, they had *not* imagined this. Captain Sterrett to be taken away from them . . . *court-martialed!*

"The naval secretary is claiming Captain Sterrett executed his son without a hearing. Lieutenants Drake and Phelps both say it's ludicrous. That the boy was a bad apple, plain and simple. That the evidence of mutiny is all there in the records. Captain Sterrett'll be acquitted of course, of that there's no doubt, but he's still got to go back east and answer the charge." David eased to his feet and grabbed a chair. He turned it backwards and sat down, crossed his arms over the back of it and rested his chin on his arms, watching her.

"The man who came in with this news . . ." she asked. "Who is he?"

"Captain Guert Ganesvoort. The command has been turned over to him." David suddenly chuckled. "That look on his face? When he stepped off the boat and found all the guns piled up on the dock? Can you imagine the *shock?* He thought he had a ship to commandeer! And all he has are a bunch of pieces!"

"It's not funny." Numbly, she picked up her knitting.

144

"No, I guess not. And what a wretched time to lose Sterrett." David gazed off, thinking about Lieutenant Slaughter's death and what Sterrett had said about Seattle's vulnerability. If Sterrett was right, the beached *Decatur* was a direct invitation for attack.

"Well one *good* thing," said Louisa, settling into her knitting, "is that at least *you're* home."

"That's changed. We—"

"Mynez! *No!*" she screamed, dropping her knitting and lunging. *"No, no! Naughty girl!* Spit it out! *Spit it out!"* Not waiting, Louisa stuck her finger into her daughter's mouth and probed for any chunk she might still have in there. "Oh, David," she wailed, "why does she keep *eating* this stuff!" Out came a soggy mess of soot and ash. Louisa threw it into the fireplace. "Any more, Mynez?" she demanded.

Emily Inez shook her head.

Louisa gave another poke around. "You are a naughty girl!" she shouted in her frustration, slapping her daughter's hand hard. Emily Inez burst into tears. "You do that again, I'll spank your bottom! Oh, David! She's driving me crazy! Every time I turn around, she's eating charcoal! You'd think she'd learn!"

He went over to the fireplace and picked her up. Mynez sobbed into his shoulder. "I wonder why she does it?" He pulled her back a little to gaze into her face. "That's a very naughty thing to do," he told her. New tears spilled out of her eyes.

"David, I don't care *why* she does it," said Louisa in tears, bending over and picking up her knitting, "but it has to stop!" She tossed her knitting onto the chair and went over to the stove.

"Did any of Mary's children do this?"

"No." She grabbed her oven mitts and pulled open the oven door.

"Ursula's?"

"No, I asked her. I've asked everyone!"

145

"Well, the new house should be finished soon. Until then we'll just have to watch her like a hawk. Or maybe next time try something my mother once did to Arthur."

"What's that?"

"I can't remember the particulars, but in total exasperation she once dumped a big bucket of cold water all over him."

"But that's awful!"

"Better to sputter and shiver in shock than choke to death, Liza."

"Let's just try to get the house done, all right?" She pulled her pie from the oven. "Besides, I'm not so sure it worked on Arthur."

"Louisa," he chided teasingly. "After everything he's done for us?"

She rolled her eyes. "And what would I do in life if I couldn't give Arthur a bad time?"

"Pick on me? Oooh, shepherd's pie?"

"Yes. Do you want to set the table?"

"Is the pie done?"

"Done to the point of burning."

"What color do you want to be tonight? Your turn to pick."

"Red," answered Louisa.

David opened the checkerboard on the table, and swung his chair around. Louisa had to smile. He always played this way, forearms propped on top of the chair back, resting his chin. He said it gave him a better view of the battlefield.

Oftentimes, after putting Mynez down for the night, they read to each other in the evenings. Sometimes they played cards. Tonight David brought out the checkers, and she set out their tea. "Will Captain Sterrett be leaving in the morning? Hey, you started without me!" she protested, slapping his hand.

David slid his piece back where it belonged. "He already left."

"Already? So soon?"

"He left with Captain Pease. I don't think he really wanted to stick around, accepting our sympathy."

"But I would have liked to thank him!"

"You still can. Yesler and Uncle Tommy are drawing up a protest petition to send to the navy."

"But can women sign it?"

He winced.

"You know, Arthur can redeem himself in my book at any time," she said to David, as if telling him this was something new, "if and when he gets suffrage in this territory."

"Don't hold your breath."

"I'm not."

"Your turn. I'll let you start."

She moved out. Always the same. She liked to begin on the left and work to the right, inching each piece forward its allotted spot until her whole front line formed a new hedge—or until David messed her up. He liked to run it straight. "See your target, aim your rifle, shoot to kill." Such was *his* motto. As for herself, she preferred to keep her defense together. No heroic futility for her.

"Liza?"

"What?" She glanced up sharply.

"We got our new orders, and I have to leave again."

She felt her face drain of color.

"Captain Pease brought our new orders from Steilacoom. But it's not so bad this time," he rushed to say.

"Where? When?" she managed. She'd known this was coming, and had steeled herself. But she still didn't want to hear it.

"Just up to Henry Van Asselt's place on the Duwamish. About a quarter mile upriver from Luther Collins's ferry crossing. We're supposed to build a blockhouse and guard the farmers' harvest. And keep Leschi from reaching Seattle."

Leschi. At first she'd supported him, when she'd learned of the unfair treaty. Then she'd pitied him, Eaton's Rangers dogging him. Now she feared him. Feared him terribly. And with the *Decatur* lying in pieces? What was it that Yoke-Yakeman had said? *Not good! Leschi hear soon!*

David reached over to brush her hair away from her face. "We're only six miles away this time. It's not like before. I can probably come home now and then."

"How soon do you have to go?" she asked, taking hold of his hand and pressing it to her cheek. "And what about the new house?" She glanced over to Mynez, thumb in her mouth and slumbering peacefully.

"I already asked Captain Hewitt. He said I can stay behind until it's finished. I'll get you moved in before I go anywhere. Whose turn?" he asked.

"Yours."

BOOM! She came straight out of her seat. Cannon thunder echoed off the forested hills. The glass in her little window rattled. David had Mynez under one arm and Louisa out the door before Louisa knew to think. "Run!" he roared at her, thrusting Mynez into her arms. "Run! I'll see to Mary and Irene!"

She crashed through the dark in sheer terror, stumbling over the tree roots in the trail, Mynez heavy in her arms, her only thought to get her unborn baby and Mynez into the blockhouse before an Indian bullet found her.

Yes, the blockhouse! She could see it! A hulking shadow against the stars! And the Russells too, just ahead of her! Tom plunging up the knoll with an orphan, Mr. Russell with another! Mary Jane and Mrs. Russell with little Johnny King between them! Panting, Mynez desperately heavy in her arms, Louisa started after them and all the other settlers swarming up the mound from every direction. Suddenly she saw the fire. *Fire?* Yes! Through the trees up behind the cookhouse—a high plume of flame against the backdrop of the pitch black forest! *Oh, dear God, Leschi, the Indians, they're burning the houses!*

She scrambled frantically up the slope to where everyone pushed in through the open fort door. Wincing, she must have twisted her ankle. She was almost there when Mr. Wetmore pushed in front, bellowing, "The d— Indians torched my tannery! Get out of my way!" She felt the blow of his arm. She staggered backward. Reverend Blaine, right behind her and dragging Kate up the hill, caught her, steadied her, then all but shoved her through the fort door and hauled Kate in after them. They found a wall and leaned up against it. Breathing hard, gasping for air, both she and Kate lowered themselves to the ground and held hands. Mynez, Louisa realized, was wailing. Everyone crowded around, shouting, crying. Mayhem! *David!* But Louisa could only bow her head to pray, holding onto Mynez's and Kate's hands, wheezing, tears stinging her eyes.

"The buzzards! They torched my tannery!"

She was sitting next to Mr. Wetmore! She inched closer to Kate. Suddenly a marine stood in the door brandishing a pine knot torch.

"It's all right folks! False alarm! We were just moving a cannon up to the Sawdust and it accidentally discharged!" Louisa gaped. So did everyone else. "Sorry!" the marine apologized. "Didn't mean to startle everyone like this—"

"But the *fire!*" shouted someone out of the dark. One of the Graham boys? Louisa guessed.

"Sorry! We blew the roof off the tannery and the tanning vats ignited!"

Mr. Wetmore was on his feet.

"Shut up, Ben!" someone shouted. "One would think you preferred it really were the Indians!"

"Come on, everyone, let's go home!" *Good, kind Mr. Butler.* "It was a good practice run! We'll know what we're doing next time!"

Fear fragmented into relief, disgust, and irritation. Everyone started out, some grumbling, others laughing in giddy relief.

"It's *not* the Indians, Ma?" a child asked.

"No, darling."

"Are you all right?" Kate whispered over to Louisa.

"I think so. You?"

"I'm fine."

"Do you need a hand back down the knoll, Mrs. Denny?" Reverend Blaine asked.

"No, but thank you. And thanks for catching me!"

"You're welcome. Ready, Kate?"

Louisa wanted only to sit. Sit and feel the relief. *Was there anything so wonderful?*

"Are you all right?" David squatted down beside her a few minutes later in the eerie, empty dark.

"I'm fine. But I need help getting up. I twisted my ankle, I think. Where are Mary Ann and the children?"

"I took them home." He reached for Mynez, then held out a hand and hauled her up.

She grimaced a little but decided the sprain wasn't too bad. She could walk. "It's a good thing you're building that new house," she told him. "I don't think I want to do this again. Two blocks *is* a long run. And don't you say, 'I told you so.'"

"Let's just hope and pray we *don't* have to do it again," was all he said.

18

Year End

On another occasion a cannon being brought ashore from
the ship had accidentally discharged and blown the roof off
a leather tannery.

—J. A. Eckrom, historian
in *Remembered Drums*

Many were the false alarms.

—Roberta Frye Watt, Katy Denny's daughter
in *Four Wagons West*

As it turned out, running for the blockhouse became
such a common occurrence in Seattle over the next
few weeks that even fifty years later pioneers spoke with
undimmed memory of their fear during those final days of
1855.

The *Decatur*'s carpenter crew, having jacked the side of
the sloop of war into place, commenced their repairs, filling
in with new wood, bracing with strong timbers, caulking,

felting, and sheathing the outside. Captain Ganesvoort, proving himself an able commander, prudently dictated around-the-clock effort with huge beach fires and lanterns to light their nighttime hours. But oh, so much to do! Such laborious work! *Ponderous* work! And always the question, will Leschi take advantage and strike while the ship lies undone, the citizens helpless?

Their village stood trapped by the sea in the front and hemmed in from behind by trees towering three hundred feet tall. These trees grew so densely their sweeping boughs interlocked. In places the branches were so enmeshed they completely cut off the sun. Whole pockets of earth never saw the light of day, and no one but the well-armed scouts dared penetrate these darkened woods of Douglas fir and hemlock. Even then they didn't venture far, for no one knew when a horde of howling warriors might burst forth—men who knew these woods and her secret trails.

The nights were the worst. Seattle was a mere sprinkling of candlelit windows along the edge of the tremendous darkness of trees where it was all too easy to hear things. When the *Pioneer & Democrat* reported the unqualified victory of the Oregon volunteers in Walla Walla (nothing said about Peo-Peo-Mox-Mox!), no one cared. It was Leschi they feared, and at the least hint of danger, at the smallest sound, they snuffed the flame of their candles and ran pell-mell for the blockhouse.

Many were the false alarms. Once, three in one night. Nerves frayed. Tempers flared. For Louisa and Kate Blaine, who were nearing the end of their pregnancies, for Sally Bell who was ill and weak with consumption, for the older women such as Mrs. Butler and Widow Holgate, and for heavy women such as Diana Collins and Mrs. Russell, these mad dashes for safety were particularly difficult. And as the days grew shorter, nights longer, and winter skies grayer, the repairs on the *Decatur* dragged on and on. The suspense and ominous quiet increased. *Where is Leschi?*

He'd become a legend. His name was feared above all others. McAllister, so confident, and Slaughter, so determined, had gone out against him and died. Twice the army had gone to meet him, their hopes high, their resolve firm, only twice to return wet, fearful, and defeated. Leschi's name was whispered the length and breadth of the Sound as he stalked the earth like a phantom, seen here, reported there. A farmer milking a cow on the plains east of Steilacoom watched him and eleven warriors cross the night horizon. Small boys watched him gallop by with his horsemen over Chamber's Prairie. Isaac Ebey of Whidbey Island, while hauling seaweed up from the beach one morning, was startled to see him and his warriors paddle swiftly past Ebey's Landing in the fog, a ghost. He was here, he was there. Rumor piled on rumor.

It didn't take long for Indian Agent Doc Maynard and his wife on the Port Madison reserve to figure out that not all of Chief Seattle's people were peaceably disposed. Agitators constantly interfered, and when runners brought news of Kamiakin's second success against the soldiers in eastern Washington and then of Leschi's triumph over the soldiers in their own country—land from which many of them had been dispossessed—the agitation simmered and steamed. And when Leschi and his warriors paddled ashore one night, grinding their canoe onto the beach of Agate Pass outside the huge Suquamish Ole Man House, the seething agitation bubbled hot.

Warned by the chief to disguise themselves, Doc and Catherine Maynard stained their faces dark with berry juice and drew borrowed blankets closely about their heads. They sat with Princess Angeline, Seattle's daughter, at the volatile council. It was, they thought, an impressive squabble.

The first speech was Leschi's, his right as guest, and he stood before the seated, tense crowd. A handsome, passionate man with his aquiline nose, his Yakima mother's piercing dark eyes, and strong jaw. He spoke bitterly against

153

the treaties and railed against Indian Agent Mike Simmons who'd forged his signature on the Nisqually treaty. Most of all he denounced Little Man In Big Hurry and urged everyone to combine their tribes in common cause.

"Kamiakin has it in his heart to help us!" he said. "These are his words: 'I will give you one hundred fifty of our best horses, one hundred head of our cattle, arms and ammunition, and one hundred warriors to help you fight. This I will do if you form a confederacy of all the Sound tribes and arouse them to union through some act of war.' These are his words."

"This act of war, what is it?" someone asked.

"I tell you only this. When you see fire blight the sky, this will be your signal to attack and kill every whiteskin near you. They have scattered us far and wide; perhaps this is our advantage. If every band, scattered as we are, will do this, our victory will be complete."

Chief Seattle's youngest son, George, stood. "Whose coats are you wearing? Whose guns are you using? Whose tobacco are you smoking?" His point made, he sat down.

His older brother stood. "They are our friends. We should not kill them."

Chief Nelson, who'd masterminded the brutal slayings at White River, rose with great flourish. He snarled derisively at the Seattle brothers. "Because *we* are not afraid to kill," he sneered, "we again own our land! From the Nisqually River to the Snohomish!"

"You mistake your enemies!" Jim Seattle was back on his feet, livid. "Who protected you from Pat Kanim of the Snoqualmie in his constant raids against your people? How many have been killed and enslaved by him? You are but a small band! Once you were large! But for the whiteskins you would be nothing! Phht!" he spit. "It is the whiteskins who protect you! *Do you not remember Arthur Denny,"* Jim demanded incredulously, *"at the beach they call Alki? How he*

154

stepped between you and your few warriors and Pat Kanim's many?"

Nelson sheepishly sat down.

"How easy you forget!" Jim scorned with his own measure of derision. "Kill the whiteskins, Nelson, and who will save you from your true enemy?"

A melee of rancor and bitter talk swept through the huge room, and threatened to lead into physical violence.

At that point, Chief Seattle, sixty years old and as strong as he was when thirty, stood with all the majesty and deportment of his position as chief of six allied tribes who were once enemies. Taller than any man present, he pulled to his great height of six feet and squared his shoulders, his blue Company blanket folded as always across his shoulders and held together at the neck with his left hand. In his right he held his staff. Respectful silence stole over the crowd.

"Yes, how easy we forget," he admonished, looking over the subdued throng. "Are we sheep, that we remember no more the days before whiteskins? When the Haida of the north burned and murdered and enslaved? My father did not build this massive fortress," he held out his staff to the supporting pillars of a structure that stood five hundred feet long and sixty feet wide, "so we could sit within its walls and fight each other with words and bitter memories. No, he built this lodge for our refuge, that we might come together and protect our lives from the treacherous northern tribes. Yes, and from the tribes of the east!" he said pointedly and looked directly to Leschi. He held no animosity toward this man. In fact, he admired Leschi. But he carried a deep hatred for Leschi's kin—Owhi of the Yakima. "But all this is no more," Seattle continued, gazing once more over the throng. "The whiteskins have come. We trade our skins and clams and canoes for their guns. We no longer live in fear, powerless, forced to hide and to pray to our *tamaminus* for protection.

155

"I ask, is it better to have one rifle with a Boston behind it as our protector than to return to the old way and live again in terror?

"Last year I made a treaty to be at peace with all white men. My people will live up to that promise. I and my people will not break it."

"You are a coward!" screamed Kanasket, Leschi's war chief.

Seattle stepped forward, black eyes blazing with fury. "When there is cause for shedding blood," he hissed into Kanasket's startled face, "you will find me on the warpath night and day!"

Later that night, the council broke up but the agitation continued unabated. Catherine Maynard nudged her sleeping husband. "Someone's trying to cut the tent," she whispered.

Maynard sat up, reached in the dark for his rifle and cocked it. The "click" sounded ominously loud in the quiet drip of the rain outside. Seconds later came the sound of scampering feet beating a retreat.

If or when Leschi might have left, Maynard didn't know. He and Catherine were but two white people amongst a population of twenty-three hundred natives. To monitor the comings and goings of so huge a crowd was impossible, though Maynard was keenly aware of continued threats against his life. To the disaffected of Seattle's tribes, he supposed he stood between their chief and the united confederacy. Kill *him* and Seattle might be persuaded to join.

In the morning a worried Chief Seattle finally persuaded Maynard to take off his dark suit and wrap himself completely in a blanket. Sufficiently alarmed, Maynard even put aside his octagonal glasses to make it more difficult for the assassins to spot him. But one day was enough before he put them back on, saying, "I'd rather be killed than stumble to death."

At some point he wrote Acting Governor Mason:

156

At half past seven in the evening one of them was discovered crawling about my camp and trying to look in at the apertures. Last night they were discovered again and an attack was expected.

These symptoms of trouble and danger, I must acknowledge, rather absorb all other matters. But with the apparent determination of the Indians to fight when they do come, I am in for one frolic at all events unless I learn their numbers are too small.

Six miles from Seattle, where Company H built and garrisoned the lonely blockhouse of unpeeled logs they called Fort Duwamish, the rumors flew and buzzed like summer flies. Before Christmas Tecumseh from Black River had come in to report seeing hostiles lurking near his camp. Captain Hewitt took a small contingent up to Mox La Push, the river junction, to investigate. When they arrived, they found only a fleet of canoes hidden in heavy brush. The meaning behind such a cache was clear. The Indians meant to strike and were carefully laying their plans. Hewitt ordered the canoes destroyed.

David straddled a particularly handsome dugout, his ax in hand. Few white men knew the time and labor involved in making these magnificent canoes—the careful selection of just the right tree, the laborious hollowing out, the carving, the deliberate design, the attention to detail and decoration. He could hardly bring himself to strike the blow. Nevertheless, to protect Louisa and Mynez, he had to do it. Hands at home on his ax, the smooth surface snug in his palms, he gave a couple of short, experimental chops. Then, arms behind his head, he took a deep breath, shut his eyes, and with a sudden sharp expulsion of air from his gut, he

157

brought the ax whistling down to drive the blade straight through the keel. The splintering cedar echoed in his ears for a long time afterward. *I wonder what Louisa's doing?* He yanked up on the ax handle, and the blade squeaked free.

"Mmm. Nice swing, Dave."

David waggled his right boot. "I once upon a time practiced on my foot, Lewis." The blacksmith chuckled. David tried to picture Louisa in the new house. No image came.

"My mother made a garden," said Johnny King to Louisa.

It was the first time she'd heard the seven-year-old orphan speak of his mother, killed in the White River Massacre.

Though the day was misty and chilly, they were clearing brush from the side of her new house. She wanted to give the sword fern and a spindly huckleberry bush some breathing room. Her nieces, as well as the orphans from next door (seven-year-old Johnny, four-year-old Little Girl, and two-year-old Frederick), had come to help and to play with Mynez. The children were all dressed in yellow oilskin capes and gum boots, making for pretty flashes of bright color amidst the gloom.

"A garden like this," she asked Johnny, "or a real one, with flowers?"

"She had ferns. But I think white flowers in the summer too."

Louisa squatted and brushed away the wet leaves.

Johnny squatted beside her, his freckled face alive with reawakened curiosity.

"These stalks have leaves and white flowers in the spring. They're called trillium. Perhaps they are the same ones your mother grew in her garden," Louisa gently suggested.

"Yes, maybe," he replied thoughtfully.

Johnny poked his fingers at the dead leaves and bare stems. He looked up shyly into her face and said with a big smile, "My mother knew how to make a pretty garden too, Mrs. Denny."

He held out his hand, and she took it. It appeared they were going to be friends. And for the first time in a long while, she felt happy. Like something in this war-torn world was normal. Louisa longed to share this special experience with David. And very soon.

David paced off his lonely patrol outside Fort Duwamish, half frozen with cold. The air smelled like snow. Fervently he prayed it wasn't so. He and the boys had been promised a two-day leave come Christmas, and two weeks of tension and the boredom of their post, in alternating doses, had taken its toll. He was desperate to be with Louisa. Suddenly in the darkness he saw movement. Reflex alone brought up his rifle, reflex alone pulled the trigger. Gunfire exploded, and in the explosion a sliver of light disrupted the night. David saw, *thought he saw*, a flurry of dim figures carrying away a wounded comrade. Then only silence, and darkness. Absolute stillness. *His imagination?*

In the morning he told his fellow soldiers, and when they went out to look, they found a thin trail of blood.

Christmas arrived with a nor'wester howling down the Sound, snow in her breath. A cruel disappointment for Louisa. She'd seen nothing of David in the fortnight he'd been gone, and had been anxiously marking "Xs" through her calendar, counting off each day that remained. Twelve . . . nine . . . five . . . two. Finally, was it possible, only one more day? *How could two weeks*, she wondered, *feel like a whole year?*

But when Christmas came and she woke to howling wind and blowing snow she knew there would be no leave today, or any day soon. By noon a foot of snow banked her house. By nightfall another two feet had fallen. No one dared venture outdoors—except to their necessary houses and woodpiles. Not that anyone in Seattle felt much like visiting or making any fuss over the usual festivities.

The refugees had seen as many as seven years of hard labor on their claims reduced to nothing, and in town, commerce was at a standstill. Everything sold by credit or scrip, little pink slips that cluttered cash boxes instead of coins. Dexter Horton's bank vault from California stood open and empty, revealing to many of the pioneers for the first time that it had no back wall. Food was scarce and of such poor quality that the butter selling at Plummer & Chase for a dollar a pound was something Ursula Wyckoff declared could "walk home."

So Christmas came and went. Louisa wondered if Uncle Tommy had managed to slaughter his pig. Yoke-Yakeman, she knew, had done nothing about Hardy Axe Handles. And though she'd tried to make the day special for Mynez, alone in their little house, Mynez seemed to know nothing was quite right, and couldn't be. It was the memory of better, safer times that got Louisa and everyone else through.

The remainder of the year saw freezing temperatures refusing to rise above seven below zero. The mercury remained steadfastly fixed—yet the awful suspense continued to mount, and rumors abounded.

General Wool was sending help from California. He was withdrawing what troops he had on the Sound and sending them to Oregon.

Two thousand Yakima were coming over the pass to join Leschi. The Muckleshoot and Nisqually had retreated over the pass to eastern Washington.

The governor was at Fort Vancouver. He hadn't been seen since Coeur d'Alene.

You heard everything and believed what your temperament dictated. Louisa found herself believing everything and nothing. Frequently, apprehensively, and filled with growing dread she'd glance to the towering trees.

Where is Leschi?

But the silent forest told no tales.

PART 2

1856

Only by a stretch of the imagination can we faintly realize the situation in the village. From Second Avenue to Lake Washington towered the forest. No one, except well-armed scouts, dared penetrate that formidable wood; no one knew just when it would send forth a horde of yelling savages. The suspense of those weeks was indescribable. Something was going to happen, but when and how, no one knew.

—ROBERTA FRYE WATT, KATY DENNY'S DAUGHTER
IN *FOUR WAGONS WEST*

19

New Year

Leschi was a square built man, and I should judge would weigh about one hundred and seventy pounds. He was about five feet six inches tall. He had a very strong square jaw and very piercing, dark brown eyes. He would look almost through you, a firm but not a savage look. His lower jaw and eyes denoted firmness of character. He had an aquiline nose and different kind of features than these Flathead Indians—more like the Kli[c]kitats. His head was not flattened much, if at all. He had a very high forehead for an Indian.

—Thurston County sheriff
quoted in *Puget Sound Invasion* by Wade Vaughn

By the first of the year, 1856, the emperor of Austria congratulated Queen Victoria and Louis Napoleon on the success of the European Allies, and in faraway Lawrence, Kansas, the December standoff between slave owners and abolitionists was over. Two thousand Missouri Ruffians withdrew from the banks of the Wakarusa River and went back to their own state. The Lawrence "Liberty Guards" disbanded and a man by the name of John Brown returned to his homestead and armory of Beecher's Bibles, filled with a malevolent righteous wrath because no punishment had been meted out to these proslavery Missourian scalawags who'd crossed the border and audaciously murdered one Thomas Barber, the only casualty of the December 1855 affair. But with the immediate threat of the Missouri Ruffians removed, the abolitionists of Lawrence had been able to hold their December 15 election and unanimously ratify the free-state constitution they'd drawn up in their Topeka Convention of October 1855. Thus the new year in Kansas began with two territorial governments, one proslavery, one free-soil, each contending themselves the legal entity. To outsiders, reading of these developments in their newspapers, the "Wakarusa War" was not over. The battle lines had just been drawn. And the unfortunate Thomas Barber, listed as the war's only casualty, was really the first to die in a war over slavery that would escalate, snowball, and within four years engulf the entire nation in civil war, killing more than six hundred thousand men before it was over.

To the west, another war was just getting started.

Before dawn this first day of the year in Washington Territory a warm Chinook came out of the south, sweeping her balmy gale over Puget Sound. The stubborn, subzero temperatures yielded instantly to the gentling touch, and by midmorning, icicles dripped furiously into dimpling snow, their hoarfrost and knobby configurations shedding like snakeskins in springtime. The ice spears rapidly grew sleek, trim, then transparent. Finally they crackled loose from their moorings altogether and knifed silently into glistening crystals of melting snow. Leschi, stirring inside the makeshift lodge of his war camp somewhere in the upper reaches of Green River, smelled the change the instant he opened his eyes, and when he stepped outdoors it was to greet a world far different than the night before.

The whiteskins' New Year, he thought in amazement, and for a moment wondered if the Chinook, coming as it did, this day in particular, portended anything for either race. But he wasn't a man inclined to believe in omens, and decided he was grateful for the change. He could venture out now and perhaps find answers to the increasing questions filling his mind. Four weeks ago he'd driven the soldiers back to their fort, yet for the life of him he couldn't figure out what they were up to. There'd been no show of further aggression. *What were they waiting for? Had they given up?* While waiting out the unexpected cold a new question had formed in his mind. *Did they want peace?*

Before the unexpected snow he'd been far too busy to think this far. Yet now—gazing out to the melting world this first day of a new year—he found himself anticipating spring. His fingers itched to feel the warming earth. He yearned to get on with the whole business of planting seed and potatoes. *Were* the soldiers ready for peace? If so, it was worth finding out!

He and his council rounded up their horses. Cautiously they made their way down to the Puyallup Valley and Nisqually Plains, and for the next three days they rode the abandoned trails. With the exception of the French-Canadian settlement along Muck Creek and the upper reaches of the Puyallup and Nisqually Rivers, where retired Hudson's Bay employees lived with their Indian *klootchman,* the whole countryside lay deserted and desolate, one abandoned homestead after another. House after house stood forlorn, boarded up, the fields left fallow.

Closer to Fort Steilacoom and while watching from a safe distance, they found no evidence of movement toward a fresh assault. Though what a menagerie! Although a fort in name and occupancy, Fort Steilacoom had no stockade, and a tangled herd of horses and cattle, sheep, pigs, and squawking birds the whiteskins called chickens roamed at will over the parade grounds and in and around the outbuildings. Guarding them were dispirited horsemen, slumped in their saddles.

Leschi headed south toward Fort Nisqually, the country of his father and his father's father before him. He wanted to see the land one more time before determining any move.

Nearing the sea, he reined in and came to a stop atop a high, rocky bluff. Two hundred feet below was the old Nisqually House, the Hudson's Bay Company shipping depository. A narrow wharf stretched fifty yards across the water. A much used road wound up the bluff. Quickly it disappeared from sight. Leschi kneed his cayuse pony and trotted on over to the fort itself, where the road emerged from the woods and ended. Fort Nisqually. How well he remembered its construction his seventeenth summer! He gazed with fond memory upon the familiar bastions in opposite corners, the high picket stockade, its center gate taller than three warriors. For a moment he debated about going in to see his old friend, Dr. Tolmie, Chief Factor of the Company.

"The *King George* sided with the *Bostons*," one of his men cautioned. They rode on.

Two miles later they came to the Nisqually Flats—the wide, shallow mouth of the Nisqually River, a boggy estuary where ducks fed on its rich marshes. Across the Flats to the southwest was the broad open plain of the Nisqually council grounds; and through the warm mist Leschi could almost see the two-story home of his friend James McAllister—the very first to die in this war. He, Leschi, had given McAllister this land—and for his trouble had been betrayed. It was McAllister who'd tried to arrest him last fall. Stung afresh by the memory of this treachery, he urged his pony eastward, picking up the familiar trail that edged the river from which his people took their name. The rhythmic clop of hoofbeats fell in line behind him.

In places he and his men had to duck low over their horses' necks to avoid the low-slung boughs of fir and hemlock. In other places along the trail they cantered into the open

166

meadows dotted with bare-limbed oak, ash, and birch. Leschi found himself swept back ten years. This is the way the country had been before the *Bostons* came; open and free. No ringing blows of the white man's hammer, no whining saws. Only the ripple of the wind rustling the trees, teasing the grass. *This is the way it should ever be,* he thought sadly, though he rode proud and tall on his cayuse, his back straight, letting the warming Chinook wind lift his hair off his mist-dampened shoulders.

Half Yakima, half Nisqually, his parentage was what Dr. Tolmie had recorded in the Company log as "high class." His father was Sennatco, Nisqually portage chief; his mother, daughter to the great Yakima chief, We-ow-wicht. For uncles he had Owhi and Tieas, important chiefs of the upper Yakima. His cousin Qualchin, son of Owhi, was the boldest and most daring of the Yakima war chiefs. And finally, Kamiakin, mightiest chief of all Yakima headmen, was his cousin, son of his dead mother's sister. *Yet what does all this mean, now that my father is an old man and his people face extinction?* wondered forty-one-year-old Leschi angrily as he passed his own abandoned farm without a word.

But he knew the answer to that. His royalty dictated he do all in his power to save the Nisqually from extermination. But first, *did the soldiers want peace?*

He bid his men follow. They continued on up past Muck Creek to where the Little Mashel drained into the Nisqually; here at the river junction was Basha-Labsh, his father's winter camp—where many of the women, children, and old men were now hiding from the whiteskins. He and his warriors would rest the night here. Morning was soon enough to make plans.

The dogs caught their scent. Barking, they raced off the highland, announcing their arrival; and the gates of the high palisade swung open even as Leschi and his warriors galloped up the last of the ascending road. They thundered through, the dogs running back and forth, nipping at their

167

horses' fetlocks and worrying them unmercifully. Leschi reined in, dismounted. Before him stood two familiar communal longhouses. He entered the first.

When his eyes became accustomed to the dim light furnished by the fire, he was able to distinguish the many occupants of the house, members of his own family—two of his three wives, their children, his nieces, a nephew by a deceased brother, and his elderly father, Sennatco. In addition were his many slaves. On one of the platform beds that ranged along the side walls lay an emaciated woman, and despite the excited cries of his return and the eager questions that followed him, he went first to her, his first wife.

He'd once thought Sarah a pretty woman. Now he could think of no one uglier, and it pained him to look into her gaunt face, her hollow eyes, and to hear the racking cough that announced her journey to the other world. She was all bird's eyes and bones. He took her hands in his, clasped them warmly, and was happy to see her answer with a brave smile. "Did the medicine man come?" he asked.

She nodded weakly.

This was not good news. He'd spent a lot of money to hire old Luke to come and dance and drum and suck the evil spirits out of Sarah's back. He could see now it had been a total waste. But he'd had to try, hadn't he? A dark premonition suddenly overtook him. *Was this to be the way in everything he tried? High cost, to no avail?*

When he crawled into bed late that night with his third wife, he was eager to ask Mary what she thought of his dark worry . . . and his plan to somehow talk with the soldiers. But she spurned him rudely.

"What is this?" he asked, perplexed. "Does your fancy for me grow cold? Have I been gone that long?"

When she didn't answer, he sat up and looked around. Sluggia, his dead brother's son whom he'd raised as his own, sat by the fire ten feet away, belligerently watching them. He did not even bother to avert his eyes. And when he saw a confused Leschi sit up, he openly smirked. *So that's how it is!* thought Leschi angrily, stung by this new betrayal. He threw aside his bearskin and strode over to the fire and Sluggia.

"You are no longer my kin. From now on your name is Traitor, so do as you will!" he spat. "Or should I say, *have already done?*" He stormed from the house, calling for his warriors, for suddenly, in the heat of his rage, he knew exactly how to approach the soldiers!

Ten minutes later Leschi and his lieutenants and captains sat huddled around a fire in the second longhouse. "When it is light," he whispered so as not to wake the women and children, "we will head for the Puyallup River, find our canoes at Bitting's Prairie, and go out to the Sound. We will find Mr. Swan. He is trustworthy, he will not betray us. *He* can tell us if the soldiers are tired, if they are ready to talk of peace."

"What if they're merely waiting for more soldiers to come?" asked Quiemuth, Leschi's older half brother, his flat face pensive in the shadowy firelight.

"It is possible," agreed Leschi.

"Or maybe it's just been too cold?" said another. "Now that it's warm, perhaps they will take to the warpath again—"

"But maybe they *do* want peace!" interrupted Nelson, the hothead Muckleshoot chief. "It is said by many that the Big Chief Soldier from California wishes to close Yakima country to whiteskins!"

Kitsap the Younger, a cruel man who mutilated his body to convince everyone he was immune to bullets and knives, burst out laughing.

"So why," Nelson shot back defensively, "do his soldiers sit in their forts like old women?"

"Soldiers do not want peace!" Leschi's first lieutenant— and nemesis—contemptuously snorted. "It is their nature to fight!"

"Speak for yourself, Kanasket," said Leschi tersely. "But if this is true, we will proceed as planned."

"*With* the attack," pressed Kitsap the Younger.

"Yes, of course, with the attack," said Leschi irritably.

"With or without Chief Seattle?"

"We do not *need* Chief Seattle!" explained Leschi. "We only need one hundred of his men! And these we will have," he said confidently. "Did we not leave Stuttering George, Econ-O-Lin, and One-Eyed Tom to see to this? But first, do the soldiers want peace? Only Mr. Swan can tell us this."

Concentrated quiet circled the fire. Every man among them knew that Mr. Swan was the Indian agent in charge of the so-called "friendly" Nisqually who'd been herded onto Fox Island like so many animals—and that the island lay almost directly across the channel from Steilacoom. It was a daring move. Full of risk. *What if they were all caught? What then?*

"Who will come with me?"

"I will," said Kanasket firmly, "but only if we can recruit friends to return with us."

"A good plan," Leschi conceded. "What is it that the whiteskins say? Fight with an olive branch in one hand, a sword in the other? Is the plan agreed then?"

Heads nodded all around the fire.

"Then we will sleep," said Leschi. "Tomorrow will come too soon."

20

Saturday, January 5

LESCHI: On the afternoon of the 5th inst., our town was thrown into a high state of excitement by arrival of a canoe from the Indian reservation (Fox Island, three miles distant), opposite this place, with the intelligence that Leschi, chief of the Nisquallies, accompanied by a band of his warriors, was then on the reserve and had Mr. John Swan, the gentleman in charge of the friendly Indians, a prisoner.

—*Puget Sound Courier*
January 11, 1856

Two mornings later, the fifth of January, Leschi and his council put their canoes into the Puyallup River before the sun cleared the eastern trees—though soon a flat gray light began to diffuse over the river in cold, muted hues of charcoal and dust, pewter and gunmetal. Wet, gray riverbanks linked with the rippling gray of the shoreline. Heavy, gray grass and grayer trees tangled with the softer gray of the horizon. *A good day to pass unnoticed along a river as gray as the world that cradles it,* thought Leschi.

But when they passed Adam Benston's claim, Benston, taking advantage of the warmer weather, was out chopping firewood, and spotted them. Retired from the Company and married to a Nisqually woman, he held no fear of Indians, and waved. This was a problem for Leschi. He motioned his men to pull in, then angled his paddle to allow the river current to run him ashore.

"Just to be safe," he explained to Benston after filling him in on what was happening, "I'm leaving a couple of men behind to guard you."

"To be safe? What's that supposed to mean?" protested Benston, offended, struggling with his limited knowledge of the Nisqually language.

"I can't risk tales being run down to the fort."

"Whose side am I on? I'm on your side, Leschi! You know that! Me, and a lot of other folk around here!"

"I'll take my men off your hands when we come back through."

"*If* you come back. And here's some free advice. If it's peace you're after, *wah-wah* with the governor, Leschi, not the soldiers. They can't make the decisions."

"So where *is* Little Man In Big Hurry? I see only soldiers!"

"Don't get in a fret, *tillicum.* All right, I suppose if you feel obligated to leave me someone, then leave me Skookum." Benston referred to his brother-in-law. "And someone who doesn't mind a day's work. I'm putting down a well and could use the help."

In minutes Leschi's flotilla—minus Skookum and another warrior whose grumbling singed the air—angled back into the river.

Late that afternoon they came onto the Puyallup River mouth, paddling swiftly under the high, sheer bluffs and old-growth firs of Point Defiance, a rocky knoll similar to the barren bluff Little Man In Big Hurry had insisted the Nisqually accept as their reservation. But how could people live on such a rock without prairie for farming, without a stream for water? To be sent to such a place was to be like the salmon, ever battling upriver to spawn. Except they should beat their bodies in vain upon the cruel rock until they all smothered and died. Glancing up now at such similar hostile terrain, Leschi wondered what chance he had to make peace, yet obtain livable land.

They rounded the point—their canoes cutting over the shallows and shoaling sand, flat gray flounders ghosting beneath the dugouts—steering into the deepening water to catch the millrace current that ran chaotically through a narrow passage known simply as The Narrows. This spit them out at Day Island. Here they veered away from the little village of Steilacoom a mile or more on, instead heading northwest into the quieter, darker water of Hale's Passage.

Their destination, Fox Island, framed the south arm of the passage, and though evening had begun to close in, the setting sun across the Sound's choppy gray waters shed just enough pink light by which to see. In minutes, the canoes grated noisily onto the rocky shore in front of John Swan's cabin.

Madrona trees hugged the clay banks, bent over the salt water, their satin-smooth bark gleaming red in the last throw of the sun's pink light. Into their leafy shadows Leschi clambered ashore, shaking first one leg and then the other to get the blood flowing again. From the corner of one eye he caught sight of Mollhigh angling off. *Let him go. We need no cowards. Besides,* he reminded himself, *Kanasket's recruits will more than balance the score. But all that later. Here was Swan, extending his hand, exclaiming surprise.*

"*Klahowya, tillicum!*" he greeted, returning the white man's vigorous handshake. "I wish you no harm! You have always been good to us. I come for information, maybe help."

173

"If that's the case," said a very surprised Indian agent in fluent, though markedly accented, Nisqually, "come up to the house. We can *wah-wah* there."

John Swan, a muscular man with bright blue eyes and a quick trot to his step, was a good example of how fast a man's life could change during war. In peaceful times he was a fisherman, using beach seines at the various river mouths to catch the salmon when they were running, and making huge hauls. He and his partner, Peter Reilly, then brined their catch for sale in Hawaii and San Francisco. Now here he was an Indian agent, responsible for 868 Puyallup and Nisqually who had nothing to do with their time but miss freedom and home. It took the patience of Job, the wisdom of Solomon, and, as he said, the luck of the Irish. "Any of you hungry?" he asked Leschi.

The warriors all laughed bitterly at the question.

"That bad, hmm?" said Swan. "Well, war has a way of making us all hungry. Do you think you can choke down some of that pig swill the government feeds your friends *not* on the warpath, hmm?"

They started up the beach, skirting the trees.

"Your soldiers, do they want peace?" Leschi asked as he followed the Indian agent through a narrow opening in a tangle of wild rose bushes.

"Well now, that's a *very* interesting question."

21

Monday,
January 14

He further added that he had been driven into the war, but that his heart was sick now, and he would make peace. All he wanted was land enough to raise a few potatoes. He did not care if the whites took all the rest, only let him have enough for that.

—*Puget Sound Courier*
January 11, 1856

*L*ouisa read all about the surprising affair a week later in the *Courier*—a confusing, exasperating task. *Had anything been accomplished? Resolved?* What exactly *had* happened?

LESCHI: On the afternoon of the 5th inst., our town was thrown into a high state of excitement by the arrival of a canoe from the Indian reservation (Fox Island, three miles distant), opposite this place, with the intelligence that Leschi, chief of the Nisquallies, accompanied by a band of his warriors, was then on the reserve and had Mr. John Swan, the gentleman in charge of the friendly Indians, a prisoner.

With that activity which has ever been displayed when opportunity offers, Captain Keyes dispatched a messenger to Dr. Tolmie, at Fort Nisqually, asking for the steamer *Beaver*, then lying at Nisqually Landing, which favor was immediately granted and the steamer placed at the disposal of Captain Keyes, who detailed Captain Maloney, with a command of thirty men, to proceed to the rescue of Mr. Swan.

Owing to some unaccountable delay, the steamer did not leave until the next morning, when she proceeded to the reservation. Judge Lander, Captain Balch, and several citizens accompanied the command. From a person on board we learn the following particulars:

"That on arriving at the encampment the whole band of hostiles were plainly recognized, foremost among them Leschi. Soon after Mr. Swan was observed coming off the steamer alone.

"After some conversation with Capt. Maloney, he returned to the shore, and after another 'talk' again returned to the steamer; he was entreated to remain on board, but refused, saying that he had been permitted to visit the steamer by promising to return, and as a man he could not break his word.

"Captain Maloney not deeming it advisable to land his men (as the steamer had but one boat, which would carry four or five men), and the whole band of hostile Indians numbering some thirty-five or forty men, all well armed, lined the beach, rendered such a thing impossible.

The steamer retired; consequently Leschi had every opportunity to escape."

It was the "P.S." Louisa found the most interesting—Mr. Swan's side of the story.

P.S. Since the above was in type, we have had a conversation with Mr. Swan, from whom we learn that he was surprised by seeing six large canoes landing on the beach in front of his house.

He recognized Leschi, and several of the leading spirits of the men. Leschi, advancing, saluted Mr. Swan, and told him that he did not wish to harm him; that he (Swan) had always been kind to the Indians, and reassured him that he would not harm him. He further added that he had been driven into the war, but that his heart was sick now, and he would make peace. All he wanted was land enough to raise a few potatoes. He did not care if the whites took all the rest, only let him have enough for that.

He disclaimed murdering the families on White River, saying it was done by some "cultus" Indians and not by his orders.

He appeared to have but a poor opinion of the soldiers, and gave a description of the Indian mode of warfare.

He also informed Mr. Swan that they had a white boy prisoner (George King, Jr.), and intended to make a chief of him when he grew up, and that his parents were killed on White River.

After remaining four or five hours after the steamer left, and some thirty hours in all, the whole party left for the Puyallup, after informing Mr. Swan that if the whites could send him they would 'talk.'

So was Mr. Swan supposed to go up to the Indian camp *to talk peace? But isn't this what they just did?*

Confused, she read the article several times, but managed only to grow more and more exasperated. Where was the *real* information—like what did the *soldiers* say? What did Leschi *propose?* How come an agreement had not been *made?* The abysmal lack of anything specific and straightforward—in contrast to her initial thrill of hope when first seeing the headlines—became more than she could bear, and by the time Mandy arrived to help with Monday morning's wash she railed at her friend in a torrent of frustration.

"How come the paper says Leschi made Mr. Swan a prisoner, when he didn't? And why didn't the soldiers make a deal with him? He says now he doesn't want anything more than a plot of land to grow potatoes! How inhuman are these people running the war anyway?" she all but shouted, question after question spilling out in angry frustration as she mindlessly pulled down the washtub, the washboard, looked for the soap. "How come the rest of us are so helpless? How come we can't stop the war?"

"Only your Little Man In Big Hurry can stop war," sighed Mandy.

"So where is he?" exploded Louisa in a fit of rage, fists clenched. "I *hate* him! I *hate* him, Mandy! We got on just fine before he came, didn't we?"

"Yes," came Mandy's soft answer.

"But then he had to go jam everyone on useless land, and throw together tribes who despise each other! The Nisqually are farmers? he asks. *Put them on land that can't grow garbage!* The Duwamish and Suquamish are traditional enemies? he asks. *Stick them together on one reserve!* He'd do better making a Whig and a Democrat live together under one roof! And is that enough? No! Off he goes to Blackfoot country! To make more of his warmongering treaties! Leaving us all embroiled in a war that none of us want! Who *wants* this war, Mandy? *Who?* You? Me? Seattle? Leschi? I don't think even General *Wool* wants this war! And when any of us tries to stop it, there's no one but *him—that pigheaded, stupid, arrogant Governor Stevens!*—who has the power to stop this madness!" She seized a pan and brought it crashing down on the stove.

178

Emily Inez, seated on the chamber pot in her nightie, burst into tears; Watch, crouched and whimpering beside her, shrank back. Louisa shoved the heels of her hands over her eyes, and tried to breathe long and slowly. "Oh, it's all so useless, so pointless! We're killing each other! I don't know why! I haven't seen my husband for a month! I'm sick of this fear! I'm sick of living like this, jumping at every little sound! And now? *When there was a ray of hope?*"

She started to cry again, harsh, angry tears, and she hid her eyes in her palms, ashamed of herself. She staggered to the wall, banged her forehead into the logs. "Oh why, oh why won't they give Leschi his potato patch? Dear God, why? Now he's escaped, *and there is no hope!*" and with each bang of her head, she cried, "There . . . is . . . no . . . hope."

Yet even as she moaned these words she knew it wasn't true. There was always hope. Guiltily she thought of her sweetbriar—the seeds she'd carried across the country, her tryst with Pamelia, the symbolism the flower represented for them both. *Spring always comes,* Pamelia had said, thrusting the seeds into her hand that long ago day when they'd said good-bye forever in the Illinois spring. *Blossoms cover the thorns. Look for the beauty, Liza. Look for spring. And remember this, dear friend, after our sorrow God will always bring us joy! For spring will always come! ALWAYS!*

Mandy slowly tugged off her coat. "Mynez," she said quietly, "time to finish business. You need bottom wiped, huh?"

"Yes," whimpered Emily Inez.

Louisa drew a deep breath. Either there was hope, or there wasn't. And banging pots around and slamming her head against the wall served no useful purpose except to scare her daughter and her friend. Yes, there *was* hope. She did believe this. God was bigger than the governor, bigger than all of them. Hastily she wiped her eyes, and then blew her nose on her apron. "Mandy, I'm sorry. I went crazy, I guess. If you

179

could just get the water poured, I'll go ahead and take care of Mynez."

"Yes," agreed Mandy.

Emily Inez was a little apprehensive of her mother, but she submitted to the cleanup, and then the rigmarole of getting dressed for the day. Finally, assured by seeing no new tears, she said, "You better now, Mama?"

Louisa forced a smile to her face.

"Mama, you scare My," her little girl sniffed, picking at the scab on her knee.

"I'm sorry, darling. I didn't mean to."

"You cross?" she asked, looking up.

Cross, angry, fearful, lonely. She was all these things. Most of all she was tired. "Do you know how at night you sometimes cry for no reason?"

Emily Inez nodded solemnly.

"Actually, you *do* cry for a reason. You cry because you're tired, and it seems like there's nothing else to do but cry."

"You need nap?" Emily Inez asked brightly.

Louisa laughed weakly. "Yes, I need a nap." She kissed Mynez. "But do you know, big people can't nap when it is only morning. There is too much else to do. And today, Missy Mynez—" she tied up her daughter's moccasins, "—it is 'Clean the Clothes Day.' Do you want to help?"

"My get to find dirty pots?"

"*Ssss*spots."

"*Ssss* pots!"

"Yes, you show them all to Mandy so she can scrub them clean."

Her own little world restored, Emily Inez chattered and sang the morning away. "This the way we wash our clothes, wash our clothes, wash our clothes, This the way we wash our clothes, all on Monday *moaning!*" When she tired of this, she switched over to "Wishy-washy, wishy-washy, up, down, easy, out, wishy-washy-*wish!*"

Mandy, however, remained subdued. With the sleeves of her red calico dress rolled up past her elbows, her sturdy little body bent over the washtub, she stayed at the scrub board with uncommon focus. At first Louisa credited her friend's silence to her own terrible outburst earlier in the morning, and was sorry all over again. But as time wore on she began to see that Mandy carried her own tension.

"What is it?" Louisa finally asked, as they began stringing the clothesline back and forth across the room, a task they did each week, putting it up and taking it down when the clothes were dry.

"Yoke-Yakeman go find medicine man."

"Nancy's worse?"

"*Hyas cultus*. Spit blood now."

Since moving into town Louisa had gotten to know and enjoy Suwalth's fat little sister. Nancy, or Kicumulow, was a cute old woman, all wizened in the face, black, sparkly eyes, a toothless, ready smile. But since Christmas Nancy had been ill with a cold, and the fact that she wasn't getting any better had started to worry Louisa—especially since the weather had remained so balmy. "Do you think maybe she has consumption?" she asked Mandy.

"She spit blood."

"If that's the case, a medicine man can't do anything for her. Your mother-in-law needs a *doctor*."

"Mmmph." Mandy handed the clothesline to Louisa and went over to the raised hearth and sat down, unconcerned about the soapy puddles and soot. Her hands were sore, and she rested them, palm up, in her lap. "What doctor know? He no fix Mynez!"

Well that was true. "But if she's coughing up blood, Mandy, then a doctor—" Oh what was the use? One only had to look at Sally Bell to know a doctor couldn't stay the unrelenting march of consumption. Should Sally live through winter it would be a miracle.

"Yoke-Yakeman go Tulalip, look for Dr. Choush," said Mandy determinedly. "*He* make Nancy better."

Louisa got a headache just thinking about it—the inevitable Indian *tamaminus,* the nerve-wracking ruckus medicine men put their patients through. And they *always* did it at night, it seemed. "When do you expect them?"

"Maybe tonight. Maybe next night."

Louisa scrambled onto the bed and tied the end of the clothesline to a nail in the corner. "Reverend Blaine's going to raise Cain, you know."

Mandy snorted. "Preacher had turn. He pray, say God fix Nancy. But Nancy still sick."

Louisa climbed off the bed, careful not to entangle herself in the lines. There was little point, she knew, in arguing theology, not with their limited English and the two of them coming from such different cultures. She said, "Let's get the clothes hung. Better to keep busy, I think."

"Yes."

Two dresses, three aprons, a nightgown, a shirt, two collars, Mynez's baby blanket, several diapers—the small room began to shrink in on itself. The air grew suffocatingly damp. Finally Mandy pinned up the last sock. Hands on her hips and shaking her head, she surveyed the tidy walls of wet clothing.

"I no understand whiteskins. Why all this trouble? Wash, wash, wash. Indian way better. Smoke dress to kill bugs. That good enough. *Hyas* easy."

Louisa sighed. Yes, it certainly did sound much easier. "Mandy?"

"Yes?"

But she didn't know how to say she was glad they were friends, that it somehow seemed to make the war go away, at least for a little while.

Having left Fox Island without making peace (but with additional recruits to ease the sting), Leschi knew he was right back to the beginning, no other course open but to surge forward with the plans he and his council had decided upon. Benston had proven right. Willing though the soldiers had been to talk peace, it was only Little Man In Big Hurry who could renegotiate the unfair treaty.

He wasted no time. Hastily he sent Klowowit (known as Yelm Jim), his Lower Puyallup war chief, to Yakima. The time had come to accept Kamiakin's offer of help.

The trip would be hazardous, he knew this, for the mountain passes would be filled with snow higher than a horse's head. Yet it must be dared. He'd wanted, of course, to send his nephew Sluggia. Such a journey called for someone young and fearless, recklessly brave. But such a trip required trust, too, and in this Sluggia fell far short. So the task went to Yelm Jim, a man Leschi had come to count on. A competent man; most of all, trustworthy.

Carefully he and Yelm Jim drew their plans. Rather than take the shorter route through Naches Pass, Yelm Jim would go up through Snoqualmie Pass, east of Seattle where the summit was considerably lower. Once through, he'd leave his mount, resort to snowshoes as far as Ki-sit-kees, then borrow a horse and gallop from there to Yakima.

A week passed, nine days passed. By the middle of January Leschi began to get nervous. Had Yelm Jim failed in his mission? Would Kamiakin *not* respond? If so, would he send sufficient force to dare what Leschi and his council had in mind?

Ten days passed, eleven. Runners brought updates on the repairs of the Seattle fire ship. Yes, it still lay beached like a whale, all arms and ammunition storehoused in the blockhouse. At this point, time was on his side. But twelve days passed, thirteen. *Where was Yelm Jim? Where was Kamiakin's promised reinforcement?*

22

Friday Evening,
January 18

On the night of January eighteenth there was a woman's scream and the unmistakable explosion of a gun. The citizens, in their nightclothes, ran to the fort; the marines who had been sleeping there tumbled out of their hammocks and grabbed up their stacked muskets . . .

—Archie Binns, historian
in *Northwest Gateway*

*F*riday evening, January the 18th, Louisa knocked on the door of her brother's old house. "No more *tama-minus!*" she told William Bell cheerfully when he let her, Mynez, and Watch in. "Not tonight or any other night! Dr. Choush just left!"

"Finally! What a relief! Come in, come in! Did you hear that, Sally?"

Three nights of hair-raising tomfoolery—as Charles Terry put it—*over!* Such caterwauling! Beating of drums! Yowling,

184

howling! Why *ever* did they have to do it at night? Particularly when everyone's nerves were so taut?

"I was beginning to worry," William confided to Louisa, closing the door after her, "that Ben Wetmore might take his gun and send one noisy medicine man off to his Happy Hunting Ground. I'm glad to hear we've been spared *that* little complication to our lives."

"I should say so!" Louisa exclaimed, horrified at the very notion. What a pickle they'd all be in then! "Here. I brought your dinner. My turn from the prayer circle. Chicken soup. But I didn't put any onions in it, Sally!" she called over. "I know how they bother you." She went over to the bed. "How *are* you feeling?"

"Surrounded by my family and my friends, you need never ask," said Sally with a sigh, reaching for Louisa's arm. "For the answer is I am always fine." Lovingly, she glanced around the crowded, cheery room to her four daughters, her baby son, and husband.

Once an astonishingly pretty and very dainty woman, Sally Bell now lay gaunt and frail on her pillows, the ravaging effects of consumption taking their last bitter claim. Yet despite her suffering, her sweetness remained, radiating through her smile and eyes. "Laura, darling," she called over to her eldest, "will you take the soup from Mrs. Denny and set out the bowls?"

"Yes'm. But will you have some of it first?" the soft-spoken, fourteen-year-old asked.

"No . . . not tonight, sweetheart."

"But, Mother, you've had nothing all day."

"Please, the rest of you go ahead. The biscuits, I think, should be just about done."

"I'm just getting down the blackberry jam!" called ten-year-old Olive from the stove.

"Come sit beside me," Sally told Louisa, watching Laura take the soup away and put it on the table. "Oh, Olive, sweetheart, when you get the jam, will you fetch your new doll? I think Mynez might like to play with it while you eat.

"Mr. Yesler, such a dear man," she said to Louisa, patting Louisa's hand when Louisa sat down on the bed, "he made each of the girls a doll for Christmas, and Mrs. Yesler knit the dresses. See, aren't they adorable?"

"Oh yes," breathed Louisa, for they truly were. She took in her hands the little wooden doll Olive offered her. Virginia ran to get hers, and Louisa oohed and aahed over them both.

"See, look at their faces," said Sally, struggling to sit up. Nine-year-old Virginia hurried to push the pillows in all around her. "Aren't they exquisite? I don't know how he does it. Such detail. And he's painted them too. Or maybe it was Mrs. Yesler." Suddenly she started to cough, a dry, hacking torment that tore at her lungs. William rushed over to pound her back and hold a hanky to her mouth to catch the bloody phlegm.

Louisa turned away, not so much from Sally but from the awful memory triggered by the heart-wrenching sounds. *James . . . dear sweet James*—Last summer her dear stepbrother had died in her arms, unable to breathe for the suffocation he had endured. Nervously, she pushed a wrist against her eyes. *I musn't cry. It will do Sally no good, or anyone else for that matter.* She leaned over and showed Mynez the dolls. "See how pretty their faces are?" she asked.

"Nose," said Mynez, pointing.

"Where is her mouth?"

Mynez pointed. "Mouth," she said. Her cornhusk doll had no facial features.

Sally's spell was finally over.

"Girls, time to sit up for supper," declared William. "Let Mother and Mrs. Denny visit. Unless, Louisa, you want to join us? You're welcome."

"No, no, that's quite all right. Mynez and I had dinner with my sister. She's leaving for Olympia, did you know?"

"The children too?" exclaimed Sally.

"Yes. The whole kit and caboodle, as Ma would say. Arthur sent them tickets with Captain Alden. They're to leave in the morning on the *Active*."

"Does he think it safer in Olympia?" asked William, a soft-spoken man with kind eyes.

"I know he's worried about the *Decatur*. About the repairs taking so long," said Louisa.

"Aren't we all?" sighed William. Then, "Lavinia, time to put your scrapbook down. Come help me get your brother washed up and into his chair."

"Just a minute, Father! I've only one more picture to glue!"

Sally patted Louisa's hand again. "It'll be lonely for you, I think," she said, "when Mary Ann's gone."

"Yes. We've never been separated before . . . but I have Watch, and he's good company. And!" she said, brightening. "David will be home soon. One more week!"

"Do you want to know a secret?" whispered Sally, her own tired eyes lighting up.

"What?" Louisa whispered back.

"You and I—*Don't tell anyone*—We're married to the two very best husbands in Seattle!"

Louisa grinned. "No . . . we're married to the two very best husbands in all of Puget Sound!"

"Washington Territory!"

They both laughed. "So tell me," said Sally, settling into her pillows. "Do you think Dr. Choush managed to cure Nancy for all the ruckus he made?"

"Are you sure you're all right?" Louisa fussed. "Can I get you anything?"

"I'm fine. Do you know," she said with a smile, "I think that if the Indians had attacked during all that noise we would have never known. At least—at least not until they were right upon us."

"The same thought occurred to me," Louisa confessed. "More than once."

"But we are in God's care, are we not?"

"Still, it is a trying thing to learn."

"Yes," Sally agreed. "Though I think God gives us the faith we need, one day at a time. But will you tell me more about Nancy? Does *she* think she's cured?"

"Absolutely. Dr. Choush, to prove it to her, gave her two packages all wrapped up in butcher paper. He says he pulled them out of her lungs, one from each lung."

"He claims they were *inside* her? She *believes* this?" Sally held one thin hand to her throat in surprise. "However did he pretend to get those packages *out?*"

Louisa couldn't help but laugh. "On that part I'm not real clear!"

"You didn't ask?"

"I was afraid to!"

"Well I should think! What was in them? Did she show you?"

"She did, and it was perfectly disgusting."

"Tell me anyway."

"Do you really want to know?"

"Yes, of course I want to know!"

"Well, the first package was slivers of glass, about two and three inches long—" Louisa held out her hands, measuring, "—all bound together with some very dirty hair."

"Oh, *ugh!*" Sally fanned her face, and scrunched up her nose.

"It was loathsome, believe me! The slivers were all wadded at one end of the hair. The rest of the hair was braided into a tail maybe eight or ten inches long."

"The other package?"

"Same sort of thing, only instead of glass, bits of bone all tied into the hair."

"I believe that's the vilest thing I've ever heard in my life."

"It is, isn't it? But listen to this. Dr. Choush said it was the hair that made her cough. That it was the glass and bone that caused the bleeding!"

"Darling, did you hear that?" Sally called over to William.

He looked up from the table. "Mmm?"

Sally laughed at him. "Liza, he hasn't heard a word we've said! But he's so good-looking we forgive him, *don't we, girls?*"

William blushed. The girls all giggled.

"Oh, dear . . . I'm so tired all of a sudden. Would you mind singing, Louisa? It would be a pleasure to lie here and listen to your voice."

"What shall I sing?"

"How about your mother's favorite?"

"'We Are Climbing Jacob's Ladder?'"

"Yes."

"I'm surprised you remember. The Oregon Trail was a long time ago, Sally. A lo-o-ong time." She dragged out the "o."

"Not really, just four and a half years."

"That's a long time."

"Remember the night, I think it was after The Dalles? It had to be, yes, we were trying to ignore the boatmen, re-member them?"

Louisa shuddered. "How could I ever forget? I wonder if they ever succeeded in killing anyone?"

"Don't say such a thing! Quick, knock on wood!"

"You superstitious woman, you," chided Louisa teasingly, reaching down and rapping the bed box three times with her knuckles.

"That's when I first heard your mother sing, Liza. Such a lovely night . . . the moon full . . . the end of our voyage so close . . . I remember—I remember thinking I'd never heard anything so beautiful in all my life. Like a nightingale your ma sang. But that was before I heard *you* sing, of course!"

"Pish," tutted Louisa. "Where's your brush? I'll brush your hair while I sing—but only if you stop your nonsense. How's that?"

"Liza, I don't want to put you to any trouble . . ." But Sally's eyes were already closed, the bright spots in her cheeks burning redder than ever against her parched, tight skin. Louisa got up and began to poke about, looking for the brush.

The cabin, she realized, no longer resembled her brother and sister-in-law's old home. When Anna had run off last summer, and Dobbins went to find her, David had rented the house to the Bells. They, too, had abandoned their claim. But as sick as she was, Sally had magically transformed the dark, unhappy place into a bright and cheery sanctuary. But that was Sally. Everything tidy, pretty. *I wonder where Dobbins and Anna are?* thought Louisa suddenly. Both the children would have had birthdays since summer. Gertrude in December, she'd be four now. Will in the fall, one year old. *God be with them, wherever they are, whatever they're doing.*

"Are you looking for her brush?" William asked.

She jumped a little.

"Sorry, I didn't mean to scare you."

"That's all right, I was just thinking of Dobbins and Anna, wondering where they were. It always seems so strange to me when I come here and they're not here."

"Has anyone heard from either of them?"

"No . . ."

"The brush, if that's what you're looking for, is on the mantel. Girls, have you thanked Mrs. Denny yet for the soup?"

"Thank you!"

"Thank you, Mrs. Denny!"

"Mrs. Denny, I'd like to get your recipe!"

"Laura! Must you say so?" chided Olive.

"And why not?"

Olive lowered her voice, and leaned across the table. "You might hurt Mother's feelings is all."

Sally smiled. She looked up at Louisa and whispered, "Aren't they just the sweetest?"

"Yes. Now, you rest while I brush your hair." And with that she began to sing.

"*We*-are *climb*-ing *Ja*-cob's *lad*-der, *We*-are *climb*-ing *Ja*-cob's *lad*-der, *We*-are *climb*-ing *Ja*-cob's *lad*-der—"

Her voice rose high and held each note.

"*Sol*-diers *of*-the *cross.*"

190

"Louisa?"

"Yes?"

"I was just lying here thinking . . . about all that business with the hair and glass and bits of bone. I'm thinking it's about as good an explanation for consumption as I've ever heard."

Louisa grinned. "You might be right."

"Do you think I should ask Dr. Choush to come visit me?"

"Don't you dare!"

Sally laughed.

Four hours later a shrill scream of terror brought Louisa straight up in bed. Disoriented, clutching her sheets, she sat in the dark. *Leschi!* Instantly she was out of the bed, out of the house, racing blindly uphill for the blockhouse with Mynez and Watch, a run so familiar she knew the routine by heart. Marines, roused from their hammocks and grabbing their guns on their way out of the fort, rushed forward in a skirmish line toward the blackened forest. Suddenly a single gunshot exploded—and the screaming stopped. Only to erupt in high wailing shrieks of hysteria, over and over and over and over again. Louisa, not yet to the fort, whirled to face the direction of the awful crying. It wasn't Leschi. No, something else was wrong. Something terribly, horribly wrong.

23

Late Friday Night, January 18

The "Decatur's" crew, who were organized in four divisions, with a howitzer's crew in addition, sprang to arms, repaired to the stations assigned in the event of a surprise, manned the guns mounted to sweep the wharf, and awaited further developments, while the women, children, and others, sought refuge in the blockhouse.

—Lieutenant T. S. Phelps, *Decatur*
in *Reminiscences of Seattle*

Widow Holgate's seventeen-year-old daughter, Olivia, had gone to bed deliriously happy. Edmund Carr, her beau—and the only other Sunday school teacher at Reverend Blaine's church—had just proposed. Asleep in one of two back bedrooms in her mother's cozy little house tucked up under the trees, she dreamt fully and happily. Sweet Edmund had promised to build her a real house, with a wooden floor, *and* a front porch. Yes, and as many windows as she cared to wash! They'd have children, of course. Gretchen, Thomas, Zachariah, Martha Ann. She liked these names. Oh, Elizabeth! She must have an Elizabeth! For Mother! Gradually she became conscious of a faint scratching at her window. At first she ignored it. Just a branch, rustling against the glass. Suddenly, she shot up in bed as a primal instinct of danger swept over her, warning her. The hair on the back of her neck stood up, goosebumps crawled across her flesh. *Someone was trying to get in!*

She stared in dismay at the dark corner window. To her horror, the sash slowly creaked up. Slowly, slowly. Inch by inch. Another inch. Up, up, still up, squeaking against the damp casing. A shadow emerged out of the starlight. *Who, what . . . ? An Indian? No, please no.* Someone peered into the pitch black of her room. She shrank into the wall beside her bed. *Oh, dear Jesus,* she prayed, heart in her throat, mouth dry, *don't let it happen! Please don't let it happen!* The shadow of a man suddenly heaved his upper body in over the sill, and she screamed—a shrill, bloodcurdling eruption of terror as she sprang from the bed and seized the sash and brought it crashing down hard against the man's back. Dear God in heaven, he was pinned! Half in, half out of the house! Flailing, bellowing, hurling obscenities! *"Mother! Milton!"* she screamed. *"Oh dear God, someone! Please! Someone help me! Help me!"*

Such terrible confusion! Fifteen-year-old Milton was there, Mother too. Someone had a candle. Mother? Yes, Milton had the musket. The whites of the man's eyes shone in the flickering light as he trumpeted pain and rage. Hand to her mouth, staring at the thrashing spectacle, Olivia could only scream, and keep on screaming.

"Do I shoot him, Mother?"

"Yes, yes, he's trying to kill Olivia!"

BANG! A deafening explosion! The man scissored downward. His head dropped in a rush, thudded against the log wall. His arms hung to the floor, wrists dangling.

Olivia gulped in the sudden silence. She heard her mother hurry over to the bedside lamp. Immediately lamplight and shadow sprang over the floor and up the walls. Milton stumbled to the window, snared a fist of hair, lifted. Glassy blue eyes glittered up at them. Between the eyes, a neat round hole, a trickle of blood running up the forehead. Milton yelped like a wounded animal. Olivia staggered backward, away from the unseeing eyes and empty hole, squealing and screaming and clawing at the wall to get away. It wasn't an Indian . . .

Widow Holgate threw her arms around her stunned, whimpering son.

"I'm sorry, Mama, I didn't mean to kill him . . ."

"No, no. Dear God, I told you to do it, son, it's on my head. No, no, my darling, it wasn't you . . ."

Olivia bit back her hysteria. "Mother, it's my fault . . . I shouldn't have—" But—*Oh dear, what should I have done?* She didn't know!

Captain Ganesvoort found them huddled together, incoherent with grief and terror. But one look in the direction Widow Holgate pointed and he understood. He told one of his men to alert the town it was another false alarm, then barked orders for a second marine to go around outside. When the marine returned, he carried a small box of burglary tools.

"Oh what *have* I done?" wept Widow Holgate, fresh tears streaming down her deathly pale face.

"You've done nothing outside your rights, ma'am," said Captain Ganesvoort firmly, folding his mouth into a thin, straight line. "The man's name is Jack Drew. He's a deserter from the ship. Though it's odd—" He twisted a little to see the corpse draped over the sill. "I would have thought he'd be on Vancouver Island by now."

"He had it all staked out. He knew his business, sir," the marine volunteered, casting hasty shy glances to Olivia. She was a pretty girl, with long, honey-blond hair, wound tonight

194

in a loose braid for sleep. The braid fell off her right shoulder in an easy line of color so at odds with the tearing grief that distorted her face. "The sash, Captain," the marine said, "had a fresh X cut into the ledge. Yes, sir, he had it all figured out."

Captain Ganesvoort drew Widow Holgate and her children out of the room. "Fool . . . sneaking into a house like this," he muttered, more to himself than anyone else. He shut the door as they passed through. "In the middle of the night—armed guards everywhere, Indians . . . Oh, hello, Mrs. Denny."

Louisa eased into the house. "I heard the commotion. Are you all right, Widow Holgate? Milton? Olivia?" They obviously were *not* all right, but she was relieved at least to find them alive.

"There's been an accident," Captain Ganesvoort explained. "A man's been shot—"

Louisa blanched in fear. Fiercely she hugged Mynez. *"An Indian?"*

"No, no, one of my deserters," said Captain Ganesvoort, a tall, thin man Louisa had come to respect and appreciate ever as much as she had Captain Sterrett.

"He was trying to rob them."

Louisa glanced to the marine who'd spoken; his eyes were on Olivia leaning against the wall, hunched over, holding her stomach. The white of her cotton nightgown seemed to glow in the moonlight coming through the window. She looked very thin, and very much like the lost fairy of old Irish ballads.

"Is there somewhere else you can take your friends? At least for the night, what remains of it," the captain asked. "There're things we need to—" He stopped abruptly, not sure how to finish.

"Yes, of course." Louisa shifted Mynez in her arms, and rushed over to hug her dear, weeping friend. "It's going to be all right, Widow Holgate," she said soothingly. "Not tonight, but in time." She hugged Olivia too, taking her arm and drawing her away from the wall. "Come, Milton, I'll take you all to Abbie Jane. Tell me where your coats are."

"Is there another son? Older perhaps?"

"Yes, two. John and Lemuel," Louisa told the captain. "But they're volunteers up at Fort Duwamish. I'll take her over to her other daughter's home—Abbie Jane Hanford."

"I could have someone fetch her sons."

"No," said Widow Holgate, her voice quivering. She moved over to the door as if to stop the captain. "They have a job to do. They needn't be disturbed on account of their mother's folly."

"Ma'am," said Captain Ganesvoort, standing before her and crossing his arms. He looked down compassionately. "The folly is none of yours, but that of a deserter and thief. Waste no time berating yourself."

"He deserves what he got," put in the lovestruck marine, still stealing glances of Olivia. "He was a nice enough fellow, I reckon, but when he drank, and he drank all the time, ma'am, he was a mean son of a—well, he was a—"

"A surly cuss?" offered Widow Holgate hesitantly, speaking around the captain and apparently hoping this would serve in lieu of more vulgar terms.

"Yes'm, I reckon that's what he was all right," said the marine sheepishly.

"We can be grateful," the captain said, his arms still crossed and watching Widow Holgate carefully, "that in his foolishness he took no one with him. Now, if I may?" He doffed his cap, waiting for her to step aside.

"You're a good man," she said, sniffing back her tears.

"I'm a sensible man, ma'am."

On the step outside he paused. "Widow Holgate, I apologize—"

"There's no need—"

"There most certainly is!" he interrupted. "And I most humbly beg your pardon. On behalf of the U.S. Navy I extend my regret for this most unfortunate incident. Particularly you, Miss Olivia. A terrible thing for a young woman such as yourself to go through."

"Such a good man, such a kind man..." whispered Widow Holgate when he was gone.

"Yes, and you listen to him," Louisa admonished.

Midnight or not, everyone in Seattle hurried to Abbie Jane's to assure themselves no worse was done. Seeing everyone in good hands—and Milton even beginning to enjoy his notoriety—Louisa took herself home. With Mynez back in bed but too keyed up herself to sleep, she sat before her fire, feet propped up on the high hearth, suddenly missing David more than she could stand. For all their plans, he hadn't been able to come home once. Not once! Though a few letters had passed back and forth.

He was bored, she knew, now that Fort Duwamish was completed. "Not much to do," he'd written, "but stand around all day while the farmers till their land, waiting for Indians that never come. But better to be safe than sorry. We shoot at every sound we hear." He was glad the weather remained unusually warm, particularly after the sudden snow and gripping cold. "Everyone here is wondering if spring is just around the corner. I dreamt the other night we were at home, Liza. You in the garden, me tilling down by the marsh with Uncle Tommy." The farmers and volunteers, he wrote, slept in the blockhouse every night, which made for close quarters—and testy tempers. But David Graham, he said, kept them all entertained and calmed down by reciting a new psalm each night. He'd memorized them as a child.

Poor Widow Holgate. Louisa thought suddenly, mind jumping from one thing to another. What had Jack Drew been thinking anyway? *Was that his name? Jack Drew?* What was he doing, breaking into a house, armed guards everywhere? Did he think—she didn't know what he thought. *Poor, poor Widow Holgate. Poor Milton. Poor Olivia too.* She felt sorry for the three of them. A terrible tragedy. All three would probably go to their graves feeling guilty. A night owl screeched. She jerked up, gripping the armrests of her chair, palms sweating against the cold wood.

But there was no answering call. Only the slap of the waves against the beach, a rustle in the brush, an Indian dog howling mournfully somewhere. The give and take of male voices, carpenters hard at work on the *Decatur*. Relieved but uncomforted, she slumped back into her chair.

One more week. One more week and David will be home. One week, and his enlistment will be up. He'll be home for good. One more week. One more week. *One more week,* she told herself, climbing into bed.

But she knew she couldn't make it another week—Mary Ann would be gone. It would be only her, struggling to get through each lonely, scary day by herself. *Oh, dear God, what will I do without my sister? The children?*

She climbed back out, and knelt beside her bed.

Oh, dear God, please give me the faith of Sally Bell, one day at a time. Watch padded over to settle himself against her. He looked up and whined softly.

"Oh, dear Watch, you are such a comfort to me!" she bawled, and she buried her face in his silky, cold fur to kiss him.

24

Saturday, January 19

Glorious News! Little bandy-legged "Rough and Ready" is in the field! The governor is back! Ready to take off his coat and roll up his sleeves, and if the Indians do not think the water is deep, just let them pitch in!

—*Pioneer & Democrat*
January 25, 1856

*T*he night Jack Drew broke into Widow Holgate's house was a turning point for the *Decatur*. Working by firelight, the officers and men finished her outboard repairs, and on morning's high tide the next day moved her to Yesler's wharf where they hoisted her spars, guns, and ammunition back on board. By evening she was at anchor, shipshape, and in fighting trim.

In Olympia there was another turning point, of a different kind. After an absence of nine months Governor Stevens was at last back in the territorial capital. The long, anxious

199

wait was over; the people were thrilled to see him home, alive and well, having survived insurmountable obstacles. In the thirteen weeks since he'd been camped on the Teton River east of the Rockies and learned of Kamiakin's declaration of war, he'd traveled over five hundred miles. Stories of his heroic, harrowing trip flashed like scenes in the telling and retelling—verbal daguerreotypes of frontier drama. Stories of crossing mountain passes buried six feet in snow—holding stormy council with the Coeur d'Alene and Spokane Indians—the forming of fifteen gold miners into "Stevens's Invincibles" to act as a bodyguard—traversing hostile Indian country through Walla Walla—enduring temperatures of 27 below, horses freezing at night—scaling ice cliffs on the Deschutes River—riding down the Columbia River one storm-driven night to Fort Vancouver, careering six miles in twenty-six minutes. Such a man was everyone's hero!

Acting Governor Mason ordered the cannon charged to the muzzle, and a thirty-eight gun salute was fired (seventeen more than is even given to the country's president). The roar of the guns boomed off the hills behind the town and reverberated out over the Sound! BOOM! BOOM! BOOM! BOOM! BOOM! BOOM! BOOM! Over and over and over; unending! BOOM! BOOM! KA-BOOM! The citizens thronged the streets, hands over their ears, shouting, cheering, euphoric with their joy. And when the doors of the Masonic Hall opened that night, they surged in, pushing and shoving, to hear what their hero had to say.

Olympia was a Democrat town, the people unswerving in loyalty and praise of their Democrat governor. They held boundless faith in his ability and sagacity, his bravery; and the editor of the *Pioneer & Democrat* was hard-pressed to quiet the throng long enough to introduce to them this man who needed no introduction.

"Please, please!" J. W. Wiley nonetheless tried, throwing up his arms to capture attention. "Please!" he shouted.

"Please allow me to present to you the man of the hour, our deliverer! Our hope!"

"Three cheers for Stevens!"

"Huzzah! Huzzah! Huzzah!"

The crowd took up the cry. *Huzzah, huzzah, huzzah!*

Wiley turned about on the raised platform, looking for something, anything, upon which to stand. He spotted a table, dragged it center stage, and leaped to its top. He threw up his arms again and bellowed, "Ladies and gentlemen! I present to you our deliverer and hope! The man who from this day forward will speedily free us from the evils of Indian hostilities which for months past have cast such a thick gloom over this portion of our beloved territory! Allow me, please—" The crowd kept up the chant, *huzzah, huzzah, huzzah!* "—to present to you our very own! Our governor! The highly estimable, Honorable *Isaac Ingalls Stevens!*"

The applause was deafening! Feet stomping, hands clapping, whistles, shouts! Arthur Denny, one of the few Whigs present, leaned against a side wall, weight on one leg, arms crossed, to watch the unbridled enthusiasm with a perplexed expression. In his opinion Stevens was not—given even the *loosest* stretch of imagination—a deliverer. This weasel of a governor, in Arthur's opinion, was the man who'd single-handedly brought about the "thick gloom of Indian hostilities" by his hasty treaties and callous disregard for the natives.

He was a short man; Arthur guessed about five foot four. He had on what appeared to be brand-new blue jeans—no doubt donated by Mr. Sylvester—and he'd folded the bottom cuffs up six inches lest he trip on the excess. His shirt was new. Red hickory, the sleeves rolled up. Arrogantly and unabashedly, he pitched his bloodthirsty politics to the eager crowd. They lapped it up, shouting "Amen brother!" and "Preach on!" Arthur shook his head at this eagerness for war into which so many of these people allowed themselves to be drawn. He understood none of it. Particularly in light of the fact that Leschi had made such a bold bid for peace only a fortnight ago—though of course the *Pioneer & Democrat* had made no mention of it.

Stevens, however, had been briefed. And Arthur had been present when he'd read Captain Keyes's letter of January 10, informing the territorial government that the army—having heard from Leschi—would be adopting a temporizing course. *I deem it necessary to record my opinion,* Keyes had written, *that a forward movement at this time would not hasten the termination of the war, but might and probably will, induce the hostiles to recommence their depredations.*

But Stevens was out for blood. He wanted war. And war he would have.

"I am ready to take the responsibility of raising an armed force independent of the U.S. Army, if that is what it will take!" he thundered amidst crazed applause. "For the war will be prosecuted until the last Indian is exterminated!" More applause. "I am opposed to treaties! I shall oppose any treaty with these hostile bands! I will protest against any and all treaties made with them! Nothing but death is mete punishment for their perfidy! Their lives shall pay the forfeit!"

Was this really his position, push the natives to the wall and then go for their throats when they shoved back? wondered Arthur. Or was he simply reacting against the army, General Wool in particular?

Not that he blamed Stevens for his animosity toward Wool. Even Acting Governor Mason refused to speak to the general. And already there was talk on the legislative floor to petition Washington City for Wool's removal. His careless disregard for settlers under siege withstanding, the simple fact that he'd turned the war over to Colonel Wright, packed up, and taken the first ship back to San Francisco the instant he'd heard Stevens was on his way down the Columbia was enough to incite hostility in any man—himself included! *But reason has to prevail,* thought Arthur.

"Let not our hearts be discouraged!" Steven was wrapping things up. "I have an abiding confidence in the future destiny of our territory! Gloom *must* give way to sunlight! Gather heart! Do not talk of leaving in our hour of adversity, but stay until the shade of our gloom is lifted! Let us put our hands together," he folded his hands in a dramatic gesture, "and rescue our territory from its present difficulties! So that in the end we may feel we have done our duty, whole and complete, to end the present exigency!"

Two minutes later, moving against the flow of the crowd surging forward to personally speak with the governor, a skinny, whiskered man accosted Arthur. "They say he is sum at sterin up tigers with a long pole! I reckin it will be I. I. Stevens instead of I. I. anybody else! Yis, sir!"

"I'm sorry to say it, but Stevens seems to have hit the nail of public opinion right on the head," sighed one of the few Whigs present, sidling up next to Arthur.

"Amazing, isn't it?"

They pushed out the door into the dark, wet night, and stood side by side on the high porch at the top of the stairs.

"I can't help but wonder," the other Whig said, "what Leschi will do with this when he hears."

"It won't change anything for Leschi."

"How do you mean?"

"What everyone seems to forget," said Arthur with a sigh, "is that Leschi, having failed to reach an agreement of peace, is bound by ancient custom and duty to carry the war forward. He made a bold and surprising move at Fox Island—"

"He did," agreed Mr. Sanders.

"He'll do it again. But without the olive branch this time."

"But where—" asked the dumbfounded Mr. Sanders. "Where would—"

"Seattle."

"You jest!"

"With the *Decatur* out of commission? It's the only logical place."

"What of your family? Aren't—"

"I've already sent for my family."

"They've come! They're here! They're here!"
The night was at its darkest hour when a runner burst into Leschi's huge new war camp on the east side of the *hyas chuck,* the "big lake" tucked in behind Seattle, and edging the foot of the Snoqualmie Pass trail. *"Yelm Jim brings war chief Owhi, kin of Kamiakin! And a hundred warriors!"*

Though sound asleep, Leschi and others were awake in a minute, rolling out of their blankets and diving out through the doors of their wickiups. "Kill a beef!" shouted Leschi, worry dropping off his shoulders, exultation sweeping over him. "The hungry must be fed! Ai, slaughter *ten* beeves!"

Immediately the sleeping camp was full of life—old men, women, children, warriors. It took everyone to maintain existence—an increasingly difficult task since the salmon had stopped running.

The warriors started the slaughtering and butchering. Annie, Leschi's second wife, took charge of the women. Pits were dug for the roasting, fires stoked, buckets of water brought up from the nearby river, stones heated, ready to be dropped into baskets for cooking camas.

Owhi's force did not arrive in one group, however, but staggered bunches lest they arouse the suspicion of any friendlies who might be encamped somewhere along the route. Secrecy was crucial, surprise half the battle.

Arriving first was Owhi himself, surrounded by his council and slaves, led by Yelm Jim. Owhi, looking regal despite his harrowing journey through the snow-choked pass, made no effort to assume a false sense of modesty when he approached his coastal nephew, Leschi. He was a man who knew his own importance. Dressed in a fine doeskin shirt and leggings, both garments elaborately beaded and embroidered with leather fringes, he swaggered over to the council fire with a cocky smile that had not dimmed with age, and threw back his long shiny hair—cut short across the forehead and ears. *Klikitat.* Here was the most feared of all men. War chief of Kamiakin.

"Welcome," said Leschi. "I'm glad to see that you made it through the big snows. I was beginning to worry."

"We had to leave our horses behind, just as you said. We came through the worst on our snowshoes, but we're strong," said Owhi. "Were you able to bring us the new horses?"

"Thirty-two. Sit, eat, take your rest," urged Leschi.

All night they celebrated with bone games, dancing, and more bone games as the others staggered in. All the while Owhi fed his nephew bits and pieces of the news from Yakima. First the triumphs, then the terrible murder of Peo-Peo-Mox-Mox. Hearing it, Leschi was struck dumb. A terrible rage swept over him such as he'd never known, fury so consuming that he trembled, and had to bend over his stomach. The pain, actual and dreadful in its intensity, struck through the core of his being. *Who were these men to do such things? Were they savages? Barbarians? Had they no conscience? Did evil spirits possess them?*

He didn't know, he *couldn't* know. It was licentious brutality at its worst and the fact that it had been done under a flag of truce and by volunteers, not soldiers, made it all the more incomprehensible. One thing was clear, he could no longer hold whiteskins of any rank innocent.

He remembered his promise to the settlers at the beginning of the war that none would be hurt should they mind their own business. That his quarrel was not with them, only the soldiers—and Little Man In Big Hurry. And how emphatically—enraging Kanasket!—he'd insisted there be no killing of women and children like at White River. But now? Did it matter?

What a fool I was! he thought, the beads of sweat on his upper lip turning cold in the midnight air even as his vision of Peo-Peo-Mox-Mox, *that magnificent body desecrated,* turned his heart ice-cold and hard with resolve. *Fool!* he cursed himself. *Knave!*

He recalled the string of his own betrayals from men avowing friendship and kinship. First Charlie Eaton, husband to his little Kalakala—his Flying Bird—*tracking him down as though he were a fox!* His friend McAllister, *riding out to arrest him!* And who gave McAllister the land anyway? The best on the Nisqually River? Wasn't it he, Leschi? Is this the way whiteskins repay kindness? John Edgar! Married to his cousin Betsy—*but scouting for the soldiers!* Dr. Tolmie too—the whole Hudson's Bay Company for that matter! *Supplying the Bostons with arms! Lending them money! Loaning out their fire ships!*

Were there *any* whites who did not betray?

Oh, he understood Kamiakin now, his burning hatred for this race. Truly there was nothing but treachery from them. "Tell me no more," he told Owhi.

By morning the last of Kamiakin's reinforcement under his brother Owhi was present and accounted for. The combined forces gathered at the lake on Chief Clakum's nearby camping ground for the long awaited war council. Leschi knew the Duwamish subchief was *not* pleased, that Clakum wanted no part of this war, that he and his small band had hoped to ride things out unnoticed, living off the many kinds of fish living in *hyas chuck* and the camas growing in the reedy shoreline. But Leschi was in no mood for chameleons. Either stand up and count, or die without complaint!

Of the nearly three hundred men present, fully one-third were the Klikitat/Yakima, the most recently arrived still chewing on their beef ribs and gnawing noisily at the bones, breaking them and sucking on the marrow. The Nisqually and Lower Puyallup were led by Leschi, Quiemuth, and Yelm Jim. Nelson and Kitsap had the Green and White River Indians, plus the upriver Duwamish. Kanasket led the renegade Klikitat from the headwaters of Green and White Rivers. Co-

206

quilton of the Upper Puyallup had a small number, as did Clakum.

When all chiefs present were gathered around Leschi, it was Owhi, Kamiakin's brother and leader of the reinforcements, who spoke first.

"So—the plan? Yelm Jim says it is *hyas* good, but he wouldn't tell me," complained Owhi to Leschi.

Leschi didn't wait for Owhi to ask again.

"The plan," he said, carefully watching his uncle's face for reaction to the announcement of their bold scheme, "is to attack Seattle and then Fort Steilacoom. Both towns have a cache of weapons—" He was rewarded by shocked surprise, then eager, enthusiastic approval.

"How many soldiers?" Owhi demanded with a wide, grinning smile.

"In Steilacoom, three hundred. In Seattle, one hundred twenty *water* soldiers—"

Owhi held up his hand, interrupting. "Do these water soldiers have a fire ship?" he asked anxiously.

"Yes, but it lies on the beach like a whale, and can't fire back at us. All the weapons are stored in their fort. This is our goal—"

"How many white men in Seattle? Not the soldiers," he clarified.

"Only women and children," answered Kanasket with a scowl on his ugly face, clearly annoyed. "And old men. And *lazy* men," he added.

"The able-bodied are six miles away on the Duwamish," explained Nelson of the Muckleshoot. "Guarding it lest we sneak down and surprise them." He grinned under his war paint. "They don't know we're crossing the lake here, that we'll attack from behind the town."

Owhi laughed out loud and slapped his thigh three times in high glee. "You have planned this well! This is wonderful! They guard the front door, we use the back! Good, good! Now Steilacoom. Tell me about the fort."

207

"Here is the plan, if you agree," said Leschi. "You, Coquilton, and Nelson lead the attack on Seattle—"

"I am honored." The handsome Klikitat glanced across the fire to Coquilton and Nelson. "*We* are honored."

"When your victory is complete, burn the buildings to the ground. The great rise of flames will blight the sky and our spies at Port Madison, Chehalis River, Fox Island—everywhere the whiteskins have penned us—will see this and know it's time to make their own attack on the whiteskins nearest them."

"Strike terror all over the country, good, very wise," said Owhi. "But you, Nephew? Where will you be?"

"On my way to Steilacoom with our remaining forces. As soon as your fires enflame the sky, the soldiers at Steilacoom will race to the north, leaving their fort with minimum security. We'll rush in, seize what arms and ammunition are there. Together, we'll then possess most of the weapons on the Sound!"

Knees drawn up, arms around his shins, Owhi smiled at Leschi. "Brilliant!"

Leschi nodded gamely to his council. "A joint effort."

"Still," said Owhi. "Kamiakin will be pleased when he hears of this."

"There is still much to do, before we brag," said Leschi, feeling himself flush from the compliment. He pointed to the lake. "To get in behind Seattle, you and everyone in the camp going with you, must be transported over."

"This could take days . . ." whispered Owhi, gazing across the glimmering surface of the wide, inky black lake.

"Clakum has the canoes," said Leschi, casting the reluctant chief a withering glance. "When the sun comes up, we'll start with the women and children."

"And you? Do you cross?" asked Owhi.

"No, I take the horses and go down around the lake."

The famous war chief pursed his lips.

"Something worries you," said Leschi.

208

"Yes, the fire ship."

"What about it?"

"The water soldiers must be trying to repair her."

"Yes," agreed Leschi. "They work night and day. But the task is endless. My spies say they had to start almost from the beginning."

"But is it possible for them to finish the repairs? Before we strike?"

"Yes," confessed Leschi. "It is possible. Why do you think I have counted the days, pacing the trail, awaiting your arrival?"

Owhi pulled to his feet. "Who is Clakum? Where is he?"

Leschi pointed.

Owhi looked down at the reluctant subchief. "We start now."

Clakum hesitated.

"Now!" shouted Owhi. Clakum leaped to his feet. The war council was over, the great task ahead had begun.

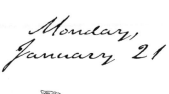

25

*Monday,
January 21*

The effect of Wool's course was to raise an impassable barrier between the regular and volunteers officers, and to leave the conduct of the war practically in the hands of the latter.

—Hubert Howe Bancroft, historian
in *History of Washington, Idaho, and Montana*

I perceive on opening our portfolio this morning that Catherine improved the time while I was at meeting yesterday in writing an improved account of the <u>little incident</u> that happened to us yesterday morning. She seems considerably elated and has a right to be in having presented me with a fine boy, fat and kicking, weighing only 9 pounds, so you have a grandson at last. He seems healthy and good natured.

—Reverend David Blaine
in a letter dated January 21, 1856

Olympia's blockhouse sat in the southeast corner of Sylvester Square, a grassy pasture at the end of the stagecoach line where the town's cattle and horses grazed.

On Monday morning, two and a half days after the governor's arrival and less than eighteen hours after the arrival of his family, Arthur said good-bye to them all at the door of this blockhouse and started for Edmund Sylvester's Masonic Hall, also on the Square. There was to be a joint session of the legislature this morning, with Governor Stevens speaking. He'd be presenting his overview of the war to date and outlining plans for future prosecution.

"Bye-bye, Papa!"

Arthur turned around. Rollie stood in the open doorway waving both hands, flopping them back and forth at the wrist the way little children do. Arthur hastily retraced his steps. "Do you know what?" he said, squatting down to look Rollie in the eye and ruffle his red curls.

"What, Papa?"

"Just as soon as you get your mother all moved in, and the beds all made, I'll take you with me to the legislature so you can see for yourself what goes on there. Would you like that, son?"

Rollie's true blue eyes lit up with a sparkle. "I can go with all the mens?"

"Yes."

"And smoke pipes?" he asked eagerly.

Arthur tried to hide his smile. "Well, I think the pipe smoking may have to wait. Now run along. And don't forget to help your ma with Orion!" he called over his shoulder. "He mustn't be allowed to get in everyone's way!"

"Yes, Papa! I will!" Rollie dove back into the blockhouse. *"Mama! Papa says I can go to his ledge-slater!* But only I can't smoke pipes," he added petulantly.

"May go," corrected Mary Ann with a long weary sigh, hands on her hips and looking all around at the fort's dark walls—and the sagging blankets hung from the rafters in a sorry attempt to provide families their privacy.

"I don't like it here," said Katy crossly from a mat on the floor. "I want to go home."

There was no need to burden Katy with her father's fear for Seattle's safety, so Mary Ann merely said, "It's just for a little while, Katy. Until the legislature adjourns. *How was she to even make coffee?* she wondered, thinking of Louisa—worried sick now that Arthur had told her the real reason they were here. Not that Louisa would have come, had she been told. *Maybe the woman behind the blanket next door can help me with the coffee . . . But I can't ask, can I? What is the etiquette,* she wondered, *for people when they're packed in tight and living in a barn?*

Nora, laying claim to an old potato crate, sat with her elbows on her knees, chin in her hands. Wistfully she rolled her eyes up at her mother. "A little girl four blankets away told me a man here cuts all the insides out of eagles and foxes and even bears, Mama, and he stuffs them all full of sawdust. And he puts marbles in their heads for eyes. And he sticks big, ferocious teeth in their mouths too."

"*Eagles* don't have teeth," scorned Katy, determined to be miserable, equally determined to make everyone else just as miserable.

"Not the *eagles,* Katy! The *bears!* And she says they're real scary to look at, can we go see them, Mama?"

"*Mother?*" Katy clambered off her mat in a rush. "Oh, Mama, don't cry! Please, please! I'm sorry! Mama, *I'm sorry!*" she wailed. "I really do like it here!"

Mary Ann hid her face in her apron. "It's not you, Katy," she mumbled through her hands and the apron.

"Then what's wrong?" Katy stood before her mother, white-faced and wringing her hands. "Oh, Mother, please don't cry."

"I'm sorry, darlings," said Mary Ann, pulling herself together. She wiped her eyes and tried to smile at her worried children. "I just miss my sister." She tugged Katy's braids, and pulled her in for a hug.

Katy threw her arms around her mother. "I do too! If Auntie Louisa was here, it wouldn't seem so gloomy, would it?"

"I know!" shouted Nora, jumping up from the potato crate. "We can *pretend* she's here!"

Governor Stevens's six new volunteer companies, under an enlistment term of six months, were organized into three battalions—North, Central, and South, each covering its own area in western Washington. Also home guards in all communities, and, in isolated areas, wherever three or four families lived within a reasonable distance, a barricade of the most easily fortified farm. This would be the governor's manpower. His strategy? A string of forts, river ferries, and improved roads with well-guarded wagon trains to keep the field forces supplied—and no respite for the Indians. They were to be doggedly pursued until the last hostile was killed or caught, tried, and hung.

"The time to move is *now*," the governor summed up, "while the mountain passes are clogged with snow, preventing the Yakima from crossing over and coming to the aid of Leschi, or Leschi escaping when attacked and closely pressed."

A few questions from the floor.

Yes, General Wool had closed eastern Washington to settlers. Yes, he'd gone back to California. Yes, further troops were on their way. *How many?* The Ninth Infantry had ten companies of 34 officers and 696 enlisted men.

Arthur did a quick calculation. Here was his chance. "Governor," he said, standing to his feet, simultaneously glancing down at his figures. "With the arrival of the Ninth Infantry the strength of the U.S. Army in Washington and Oregon will exceed two thousand soldiers—fully twenty-seven of the available thirty-three companies assigned the army's Pacific Department. In addition, we have on the Sound several armed ships patrolling our waters: the U.S. revenue cutter *Jefferson Davis* under command of Captain Pease; the navy sloop of war *Decatur* under Captain Ganesvoort; the U.S. survey steamer *Active,* fully armed and under command of

Captain Alden; the *Otter* and the *Beaver*, both fully armed on loan from the Hudson's Bay; to say nothing of two further armed transports now on their way from the Sandwich Islands. Considering Leschi's recent bid for peace, these numbers seem more than sufficient—"

"Get to the point," snapped Stevens.

"Why more volunteers?"

Silence descended over the room like cold, falling snow.

"The volunteers you're asking for, Governor," said Arthur, breaking the ice, "are mostly farmers and loggers. If our beleaguered economy is not to completely collapse, we need to get them back to their crops and into the woods. The army—"

"Mr. Denny," interrupted Stevens, "I am certainly willing to cooperate with the army. And I most certainly hope a cordial spirit of cooperation can exist between us. But I'm afraid I must insist upon a force answerable to my own orders, not those of the regular army officers. If you recall, our volunteers sent to Major Rains were badly mistreated and then mustered out. I consider this a breach of faith. Therefore I am prepared to take full responsibility for raising troops separate and independent. And I promise," he added, "that the federal government will sustain me in this—"

"Excuse me, Governor," interrupted Arthur, seeing that Stevens had missed the point entirely. "The past is *moot*. The military is in place. Calling for volunteers appears to be a denial of General Wool's authority to determine military policy."

Stevens leaned on the podium, condescension in both his posture and tone of voice. "Perhaps I should have explained earlier, Mr. Denny, that of the ten companies arriving under the Ninth Infantry, General Wool has, in his infinite wisdom, deemed it best to send eight of those ten companies into eastern Washington to join Majors Haller and Rains in idle garrison of empty forts while only two," he waggled two fingers, "are to be sent to us here in Puget Sound where four thousand settlers live in terror for their lives."

Instant boos rumbled through the room as men turned in their chairs to measure their neighbors' level of outrage. Arthur himself shook his head in dismay. *Eight companies to an area cleared of settlers, two companies to the most densely populated, aflame in war.* "Governor," he demurred, "it does seem we're stuck between a rock and a hard place."

Stevens pulled up straight. "I'm glad you see it that way, Mr. Denny. And now . . ." Wrapping up his speech, he launched into a repeat of his Saturday night closing remarks, beseeching his audience to remain optimistic, to focus on their resources, to steadfastly await their collective destiny, and—above all—*not to desert the territory in her hour of need.*

"That is all, gentlemen."

"Oh, he's so *small!*" cooed Louisa, bending over Kate Blaine's bed to see the wrinkled, red baby asleep in his elated mother's arms. "I forgot how tiny they are!"

"He *is* nine pounds!" bragged Kate, staring lovingly down into her firstborn's slumbering, puffy face.

Gently Louisa wiggled her finger into the baby's closed fist. Even in sleep he grasped tightly. "He's so adorable. Oh, I just love babies, don't you? Especially when they're this tiny? What are you going to name him?"

"I don't know, we haven't decided yet."

"How are you feeling? Ursula said you went into labor the night of the shooting—"

Kate smiled. "One false alarm too many! Things started up and never did simmer down. Look what I ended up with, though." And she bent down to kiss her son.

Louisa grinned. "False alarm for us, the real thing for you!"

They burst out laughing. "Oh, ow! Don't make me laugh, Louisa, it hurts!" moaned Kate. Suddenly the front door banged. The sleeping baby jumped, arms and legs jerking.

"There, there," murmured Kate, tucking in the blankets, jiggling her son back to sleep. *"What's gotten into Mr. Blaine?"*

she whispered at Louisa as her husband stormed into the bedroom. He pulled off his battered old panama hat and threw it at the bedpost. *He must have had a lot of practice,* thought Louisa, tearing her eyes away from the odd hat settling onto the post, and gazing with fright at the preacher's white face and clenched jaw. "What is it? What's happened?" she managed, standing beside the bed.

"Yark-Keman—Yar-ke-ke-man—"

"Do you mean Yoke-Yakeman?" she offered tentatively.

"Yoke-Yakeman! Yar-ke-ke-man! Why can't the stupid Siwash just pick a name and stick by it!"

"But it's not the Indians who change their names," she whispered. "It's everyone else."

"Darling, please," Kate pleaded of her husband, her tired eyes beseeching him. "Just tell us what's happened. What's upset you so?"

"Well *he,* whatever his name is—"

"You can call him Denny Jim," suggested Louisa. "It's what the marines all call him."

"—he just came in with a report for Captain Ganesvoort that a thousand Klikitat have crossed the mountains, *that's* what's happening! Here." He thrust a chair at Louisa.

She flopped down, pushing the heel of her hand against her forehead. *A thousand Klikitat?* But how—"How did they get over?" she asked, looking up. "I thought the snow—"

"Snowshoes," he said bluntly.

Snowshoes?

"And they came over Snoqualmie Pass, not Naches Pass! Leschi's with them! At Clakum's camp on the east side of Lake Washington—*with* Lieutenant Slaughter's horses no less!"

Kate let out a short wail and then caught herself. When Louisa looked over, she saw that Kate's face had gone as white as the pillows behind her head. "Oh, darling," Kate whimpered, "it's the worst, everything we feared . . . Leschi and the Klikitat together . . ." Amazingly, the baby slept on.

"Do you really think Leschi and the Klikitat are on their way *here?*" Louisa asked the preacher.

"I should think that's obvious! Of course they're coming here! To kill us in our beds, to butcher us!"

"He's too little to die," mewed Kate, gazing in anguish down at her little newborn son. "Too little, too little to die . . ."

The preacher hastened to her bedside and knelt, patting the baby, patting her. "Now, now, dear. There, there. I'm going right now to make arrangements with Captain Ganesvoort to see if we can't stay on the *Decatur* until all this is over."

Louisa somehow got to her feet and over to the bedroom door. "Where are they now?" she asked.

"Who?" asked Reverend Blaine, looking up at her.

"The *Klikitat.*"

"How would I know? With *Leschi,* wherever *he* is."

Louisa struck out for the front door, navigating her way through Kate Blaine's fancy living room as if crossing the deck of a rolling ship, so weak were her knees with dread and terror.

"But I don't want to go on the ship, I want to go away from here." she heard Kate moan. "Far, far away. This is no place to raise a baby."

Kate was right. This *was* no place to raise a baby. Louisa let herself out. "Come on, Watch," she whispered, her dog sitting patiently on the porch. Ashen-faced and both hands on her abdomen as if to protect her unborn child, she hurried as fast as she could down the short trail to the Bells' house, Watch loping alongside her, puzzled by her distress. All of a sudden the unbidden image of Elizabeth Brannan and *her* baby came to mind . . . *the two of them thrown upside down and still breathing into the well!* Without stopping to knock, she burst into her brother's old house. "Oh, Sally, Have you heard? The Klikitat have crossed the mountains!"

"Yes, the news is all over town."

"Snoqualmie Pass, not Naches Pass. They must be coming here, to Seattle! And Leschi is with them! *Leschi!* Oh, Sally, what are we going to do?"

"Captain Ganesvoort is moving his men into position, Liza, we aren't without protection. Please, come sit with me and take a deep breath. You mustn't get yourself so upset. You have the baby to consider. Besides, have you forgotten who watches over us all?"

"You're right," gasped Louisa, sitting down hastily on the bed beside her friend. "But I told you, didn't I, this is a hard lesson to learn?" She twisted her coat buttons, vaguely wondering how much the thread could withstand before breaking.

Sally patted her agitated hands. "Liza, it's not so much a *hard* lesson, I think, as maybe it's a lesson we have to learn each time there's new trouble."

Louisa pressed her fingertips against her temples. "Why, what do you mean?"

"Well . . . like dirty dishes." Sally pointed to the dirty stack piled on the counter. "One wash doesn't mean we're done. We're only done until next time."

"Oh, Sally!" said Louisa, laughing a little, and feeling better. But still . . . still she was so *scared!*

Quite suddenly she was aware of the quiet, empty room. *"Where are the children?"*

"They're all right! Relax! Louisa! They're just next door, helping the men with the new addition, that's all!"

"Oh . . ." Yes, she could hear the banging on the other side of the north wall. "How's it coming?"

"William says with any luck the Holgates might move in tomorrow. Go take a peek, Liza. William says the children do amuse themselves in the cutest ways. And they've thoroughly enjoyed the distraction, a blessing really."

Louisa got up and went outside. Right next to the old door was a new one leading into the new house being built for Widow Holgate. It was bigger, but without a loft. *Poor Olivia,* she thought, her fear momentarily distracted by the Holgates' more immediate troubles. The terrible shooting had been two and a half days ago, but the distraught girl was still so terrified of the woods at night that she couldn't bring herself to go home. It was Sally who'd suggested making the addition so the Holgates could be out from under the trees. In the absence of Dobbins, David, and Arthur it had fallen on Louisa to grant permission to renovate her brother's home.

Emily Inez spotted her mother. "Mama! Misser Bell let My hammer nails! See?"

"She's not getting in your way, is she?" Louisa called up to William Bell and the Holgate brothers on the half-finished roof.

Lemuel, a skinny fellow with buck teeth, grinned down through a gaping hole on the roof. "No, ma'am! They keep plenty busy!"

"Mrs. Denny, come see what we're doing," said Virginia Bell.

Louisa went over to look, and had to smile. The children were all pounding nails into the dirt, making stick men and ladies.

"That Mama, that Papa," Mynez announced, proudly pointing out a mishmash of nails that resembled giant sewing pins stuck randomly into a pin cushion.

Standing in the middle of newly constructed walls, the rich smell of the cedar delightfully filling the darkened room, and gazing down at the children's happy play Louisa wondered at the world—how quickly it could become so terrifying, yet so quickly seem so normal.

Which was real?

Nothing confirmed and confusion at an all-time high, Captain Ganesvoort ordered his full force ashore—just in case. Three of his four divisions he stationed around the northeast shore of the Point, the fourth division he picketed up behind the cookhouse. The brass howitzer from the ship was brought ashore and set up at Plummer's mansion, its nine gunners under Lieutenant Morris given orders to sweep the sandbar and operate wherever circumstances demanded.

When night settled in Louisa put Mynez to bed as usual and then lay awake herself for hours in the dark cocoon of the little house that was still so new it didn't feel like her own, listening to the forest and desperately reciting the first chapter of James, trying, *trying,* to control her fear. *My brethren, count it all joy*—Last fall she and David had intended to memorize the whole book; they'd gotten as far as the first chapter. *Knowing this, that the trying of your faith worketh patience*—She could hear Johnny King crying next door; she could just imagine his terror, no doubt envisioning all over again the horror that had overtaken his mother and stepfather. She could envision it herself! The lacerated body of Will Brannan, Elizabeth in the well. The mutilated face of Mrs. Jones. The knifed, charred bodies of Mr. and Mrs. King, their scattered bones blackened with ash and gnawed by wild pigs. *Stop it!*

She sat up in bed and rubbed her face in the dark, trying to concentrate on breathing evenly. She was, she found, trembling from head to foot. *Four more nights. Four more nights and David will be home.*

26

Tuesday, January 22

Mr. and Mrs. Blaine, the pioneer M.E. minister, and his wife, who was the first school teacher of Seattle, went on board the man-of-war on the 22nd of January, 1856, with their infant son . . .

—Emily Inez Denny, David and Louisa's daughter
in *Blazing the Way*

Mrs. Blaine and her new baby were bundled into a rocking chair and taken to the shelter of the *Decatur*.

—Roberta Frye Watt, Katy Denny's daughter
in *Four Wagons West*

y morning, Mrs. Russell had had enough. Reminded of her traumatizing escape from White River just weeks before, coupled with Johnny's disconsolate sorrow, she implored her husband to take their large family over to Port Madison. "Please!" she begged. "Please."

221

"This ain't like before, Mother," balked Mr. Russell. "We got a blockhouse here. We got the navy."

"We got *Indians!*"

"Nope. I ain't runnin' twice from no Indians. Besides, I got my musket and can shoot as good as any man."

For an answer Mrs. Russell seized his heavy relic of a rifle off the wall and thrust it at him. She all but threw the powder pouch into his lap. "If'n you can load that worthless old thing, Mr. Russell, faster'n I can run 'round this here cabin twice, then I reckon we'll stay! But if'n you can't, then I reckon you can start packing your duds—and no sass!"

Louisa, stirring Mynez's porridge, was drawn by a flash of movement outside her window. *Goodness!* she thought, going over for a closer look. *Has Mrs. Russell taken complete leave of her senses?* She hurried outside and stood in the mist, waiting. Sure enough, Mrs. Russell came huffing around the far corner of Sheriff Tom's house, and kept right on running around again!

"Where's the fire!" called Louisa.

"Ain't no fire! I'm runnin' for my life!" The plump woman disappeared around back, skirts hiked so high her stockings showed.

"Will you watch Mynez?" Louisa tugged off her apron and handed it to Mandy through the door.

"Iron hot? I start hankies first, huh?" asked Mandy.

"No, wait until I get back. I'll be gone only a minute!" She crossed the small yard and was coming up to her neighbor's front door when Mrs. Russell careered around the corner again, skirts bunched, knees pumping. "Come on in," the older woman gasped, charging up the stoop ahead of Louisa. Louisa followed.

"Ah-*ha!* You ain't even got the powder all in!" Mrs. Russell gasped. She stood in the middle of the cabin floor, hands on her hips, struggling for breath.

Mr. Russell, Louisa saw, sat by the table where he was madly trying to ram gunpowder down the muzzle of his musket.

"Now, Mother," he said, "I didn't agree . . ."

"Agreein' ain't got nothin' to do with it! If'n I was an Indian, I'd have killed you ten times!"

Over by the fire Sheriff Tom stroked his beard and winked at Louisa then tipped his head back, peering around his mother at his red-faced dad. "Start packing, Paps! I'll get Terry to help me row you over."

Louisa never did figure out what it was all about, but by noon the whole family was gone. Sheriff Tom, with Charles Terry to help, rowed the whole kit and caboodle fourteen miles across the bay: Mr. and Mrs. Russell, Mary Jane, Emma, Nancy, their husbands, Robert, Alonzo, and the two youngest orphans. Johnny, though, refused. He was too frightened to leave sight of the *Decatur,* and after considerable discussion it was finally agreed that he'd stay with Louisa during the day, but spend his nights aboard ship with the marines.

The *Decatur* gave Kate Blaine sanctuary as well—hoisting her up the davits in her rocking chair, looking a little squeamish, but holding her newborn securely.

"Leschi!"

"What is it?" Startled by the dark look on the face of his runner just in from Seattle, Leschi pulled up from a lounging position in his wickiup near Stuck Creek.

"The fire ship is fixed! She is launched, her big guns back on!"

Leschi grimaced, and motioned his runner to come into the small shelter and sit by Annie's fire. "I was afraid of that. Owhi took too long crossing the mountains. We have to make new plans now. He hasn't got enough men to fight the fire ship. Where is he?" he asked suddenly. "Has he crossed the lake yet?"

"*He* has, but not the whole camp."

"We have to strike the fort first," mumbled Leschi, thinking out loud. "Get the weapons . . . then together attack Seattle. Can you take me to him?"

"Leschi!" protested Annie, a round-faced woman. "Your supper!"

"You eat, skinny woman!"

27

Thursday, January 24

For three nights guard had been maintained, when on the 24th the *Active* reappeared at Seattle, having on board Captain Keyes, Special Agent Simmons, and Governor Stevens...

—Hubert Howe Bancroft, historian
in *History of Washington, Idaho, and Montana*

The swarthy, headstrong little Governor had been inclined to make the most of the Indian War and exaggerate rather than belittle the danger of the settlers. But for reasons that remain obscure, he ridiculed the idea of an attack on Seattle. He went ashore and made a speech to the citizens, ending with the words: "I tell you there are not fifty hostile Indians in the territory, and I believe that the cities of New York and San Francisco will as soon be attacked by Indians as the Town of Seattle."

—Archie Binns, historian
in *Northwest Gateway*

For three nights Captain Ganesvoort held vigilant guard along Seattle's backwoods, waiting for Indians that never came—and for Suwalth and Yoke-Yakeman, whom he'd sent into the forest to learn more. While he waited, rumors sifted, as if on wings. Leschi *wasn't* with Owhi. Leschi *was* with Owhi. There weren't a thousand Indians, only a hundred. No, *hiyu,* many! A thousand? *Hiyu!*

In the middle of all this confusion and anxiety, Thursday afternoon the 24th, Governor Stevens unexpectedly arrived, disembarking from the *Active* with Captain Keyes and Indian Agent Mike Simmons.

Louisa took Johnny and Mynez with her down to the cook-house to hear what the governor had to say, hurrying along, constantly glancing over her shoulder to the trees. Johnny tugged on her hand, apparently as scared as she.

It had gotten so that Louisa marveled almost hourly at their still being alive—but they arrived without mishap. The Do-Nothing men were in attendance, so were men like Mr. Yesler and Uncle Tommy. A few naval officers. She found Ursula and Abbie Jane and some other women sitting in a tense huddle near the back, whispering back and forth, the meeting not yet begun. Suddenly she missed her sister. If only Mary were here, it wouldn't seem so lonely and scary. *But tomorrow David will be home!*

Buoyed by this comforting thought, she smiled and wedged in next to Abbie Jane, Mynez on her shrinking lap, and Johnny squeezing in on the bench the best he could.

"Did your mother," Louisa asked Abbie Jane, "get moved into the Bells' house all right?"

"Yes, and Olivia is doing so much better. You were kind to let my brothers build the room—"

"I'm sure Dobbins—"

"Did you ever hear from him?" Abbie Jane asked, at the same time reaching over the toddler on her lap to tap one of her four boys sitting in front of them. Instantly all four quit misbehaving and looked straight ahead.

"Mrs. Denny, may I go sit with my friend, Sergeant Corbine?" Johnny pointed out one of the naval officers.

"Yes, of course, darling," said Louisa. "And tell him he must come for supper tonight. He likes my clam chowder."

"Yes'm."

"You're keeping busy, Ursula," she said. "What are you making?"

Though she had Eugenia on her lap, Ursula worked around her daughter, knitting furiously. "A toque for Suwalth," she said, fingers flying in a blur of busywork that apparently helped channel her nervous energy. "If he's out scouting, I really dislike the idea of him getting killed by accident. I swear, Lieutenant Phelps is getting positively wolfish these days, you can see it in his eyes. So I figured if Suwalth wore a blue hat there could be no mistakes."

"It's a good idea," said Louisa. "I should make one for Yoke-Yakeman. Do you have any more of that blue yarn?"

"Shh, the governor," whispered Mrs. Horton.

The very sight of him, Louisa realized, turned her stomach; and she wondered if she'd ever felt such loathing for another human being. But for this man they wouldn't be sitting here frightened for their lives. They wouldn't be separated from their husbands and pulled away from their homes. She wouldn't be frantically reciting Bible verses to herself every night. Johnny King's mother would be alive, taking care of her own son. Johnny wouldn't be a haunted child, wouldn't startle at every sound, wouldn't cling to adults and cry so easily. She hoped the governor had something to say to redeem himself.

He did not.

He dismissed their fear as groundless—and so much as called Suwalth and Yoke-Yakeman agitators and the rest of them fools. The mountain passes, he said, were closed by heavy snowfall. Impossible to get through. Besides, he'd just returned from Nez Perce and Coeur d'Alene country, and seen many other tribes, both going and coming. "And I tell you," he announced, "there are not fifty hostile Indians in the whole territory."

"He's crazy," whispered Ursula to Louisa.

227

"If a pip-squeak like him can get through a snowy mountain pass," whispered Abbie Jane on Louisa's other side, "I expect the Indians can!"

The governor suddenly laughed. "I believe the cities of New York and San Francisco will as soon be attacked by Indians as this town of Seattle!"

"He *is* crazy!" declared Ursula, staring at him, open-mouthed.

Captain Ganesvoort, who'd been leaning up against the squared logs beside her, squatted down, level with the women seated on the bench. "He's not crazy, Mrs. Wyckoff. He's alarmed by this latest desertion. People panic, flee the territory, it doesn't reflect well on him. So he's trying to minimize things, keep people from deserting—"

"Then I guess he's preaching to the wrong congregation!" snapped Ursula. "No one here has run off!"

The captain snorted his agreement.

"He started this war and now he's laughing at us because we're scared out of our minds!" she sniffed. "He's a mean man, Captain."

"Captain Ganesvoort?" Louisa leaned around Ursula to speak with him. "He's calling for a whole new army of volunteers. But if there's less than fifty hostiles in the territory, why's he doing that?"

Captain Ganesvoort gave her a helpless shrug.

"*I* believe he's *drunk!*" muttered Mrs. Horton.

"Whatever he is, good luck," said Abbie Jane primly, jiggling the littlest boy on her lap. "Because I'm not letting *my* husband sign up for another round of this when he gets home tomorrow!"

Would David sign up again? The whole notion caught Louisa off guard. Ursula put down her knitting, dug around in her pockets, then handed Louisa a handkerchief. Gratefully Louisa took it and wiped her eyes.

"Hush up, we got no reason to cry just now," hissed Ursula sternly. "Tomorrow maybe, but not yet."

28

Friday, January 25

[The governor] assured the pioneers that there was no danger and expressed the belief that New York and San Francisco were not safer from attack than Seattle was at that very moment.

Fortunately Captain Ganesvoort had been in closer touch and knew local conditions better. A few days previous he had sent an Indian scout over to Lake Washington to find out what was going on. The scout returned on the [morning] of the 25th, shortly after the *Active* with Governor Stevens aboard had sailed away, with the startling news . . .

—Roberta Frye Watt, Katy Denny's daughter
in *Four Wagons West*

*I*n the morning, four days after the Klikitat crossed the snowy winter mountains and now crossing the lake, Suwalth started down the steep lake trail into Seattle. At the bottom of the hill, Lieutenant Phelps glanced at his watch. Seven o'clock. *Where in the world was the order for his ex-*

hausted men to fall back? Suddenly, in the flat light of dawn, he caught sight of movement. Without thinking, he raised his rifle and fired up the trail. Suwalth came howling out of the trees. Phelps popped up his rifle again. A wiser man stayed his hand and Suwalth plunged down the remaining trail madder than a wet hen. Amazingly, he passed the startled lieutenant without a sideways glance and hurried into the cookhouse. He had a report to deliver: Clakum's friendly Duwamish had joined the hostiles and were ferrying them across Lake Washington in canoes—putting them ashore just one and a quarter miles east of Seattle!

Within minutes everyone knew. The Do-Nothings, after months of mocking all danger, panicked. They packed up what they could and fled for other points on the Sound—taking whatever boat was in dock, not caring about the destination. Olympia, Fort Steilacoom, Port Madison, Whidbey Island—anywhere but Seattle.

Captain Ganesvoort ordered Lieutenant Phelps to buy Suwalth a new coat, his shabby flea-bitten jacket having been perforated by Phelps's bullet; then he sent word down to the Wyckoffs' to see if Ursula was finished knitting that hat yet. Finally, he ordered the upper floor of the blockhouse prepared for the women and children. They'd sleep there from now on. The marines trying to catch a nap, he said, would have to do it in the cookhouse.

Uncle Tommy brought his Conestoga out of the livery and hitched up Tib and Charlie. He started at the Plummers' house on the southeast end of the Point and worked his way north, stopping at each house and piling into the back of the wagon whatever the ladies presented him with: feather mattresses, blankets, pillows, clean diapers for the babies, children's toys, dolls, and food.

Louisa, frantic with fear, raced around her own cabin, trying to figure out what she should pack. Her nightgown? No . . . no place to dress! She'd have to sleep fully clothed! But her stomach was getting so big! She hated the constriction!

I'll just have to swallow my pride, she decided, *and take my gown. Maybe the ladies will be kind and turn around.* What about candles? *We need candles! WHERE ARE THE MATCHES?*

"What you doing?"

She'd forgotten all about Mynez! Sitting patiently on her little chamber pot and wiggling her bare toes in the cougarskin rug.

"Are you finished?"

"My done. What you doing?"

"Tonight we're sleeping in the blockhouse. I'm packing our blankets."

"Oh."

"Let's get you dressed and your hair brushed."

"My don't want to sleep in blockhouse, Mama."

"It's better than running there in the middle of the night, isn't it? And sitting on the floor and shivering to death?"

Mynez had to think about that.

When Uncle Tommy pulled up an hour later, his four daughters jumped off the wagon and came running in to say that Madam Damnable had thrown a block of wood at their father!

Uncle Tommy rubbed the back of his head gingerly. "Can you beat that? I simply went up and asked if she needed a hand with her bedding. She came at me like I was some kind of varmint!"

"She called him *terrible* things!" said fifteen-year-old Eliza Ann. "*Shocking* things!"

"Pa says it's not the wood that hurt so much as the words!" giggled thirteen-year-old Susannah.

"She's worse than any sailor I know," grumbled Uncle Tommy, still rubbing his sore head. "I suppose not even the Indians scare her. Is this all you want to go up to the fort, Lousia? Just these blankets and the one pillow?"

"I don't want to send the mattress," she said in dismay. "I sometimes nap during the day. And Mynez has to have her nap."

"You can't sleep on the floor all night. The floor can get pretty hard."

"Well I was going to ask Mandy, or maybe Widow Holgate, to help me lay in some cedar boughs, then cover them with that spare sheet there."

"We can help get the cedar!" volunteered Susannah cheerfully.

"Don't you have your own beds to set up?" Louisa asked, gazing around at the eagerly nodding heads.

"It's not going to take us forever," Eliza Ann said. "Besides, this will be fun!"

Fun?

"Cedar gives me hives," said Mary Jane, the eldest, just turned seventeen the week before. Already she had Mynez in her arms, touching noses and tickling her. "I'll watch Mynez, though."

"Girls, take Mrs. Denny's things out to the wagon," said their father suddenly. "I'll be along in a minute."

"Yes, Pa!"

"Shall I take Mynez?" asked Mary Jane.

"Put her coat on first," he told her.

The minute the girls were gone and the door shut, Louisa turned to Uncle Tommy. "Are they really only a mile and a half away?"

He came over and hugged her. "Nothing's going to happen today. You needn't fret about that," he said compassionately. "It'll take the rest of today and maybe the better part of tomorrow for that many Indians to cross the lake."

"But Suwalth says they've been crossing for two days! What if they're already here?"

"We're in God's hands, Louisa. And remember, today David will be home."

David! "I forgot, I totally forgot," she gulped. "I got so frantic—"

"That can happen when we lose our heads," he said dryly, smiling at her.

"I've packed nothing for him."

"I have a suggestion."

"What?"

"Bake something for the blockhouse. We're going to get hungry there the same as anywhere."

"I didn't think about that."

"I need to go, will you be all right? I can check in later."

For lack of a hanky, she self-consciously seized her apron and blew her nose. "I'm fine now. David's coming home."

29

Friday Evening, January 25

The same afternoon seventy-odd Seattle volunteers landed on the beach from canoes and straggled into the village. They had not come to defend Seattle but to lead a civilian life. Their three months' term of enlistment had expired on that inconvenient day. They had left the Duwamish blockhouse punctually at the hour of expiration, and that evening they were mustered out in front of Yesler's log cookhouse and the company disbanded.

—Archie Binns, historian
in *Northwest Gateway*

The endless wait was over! Louisa couldn't get enough of David, and she sat on their bed wreathed in smiles, watching him thoroughly suds and scrub himself down—his first all over scrub in five weeks! Mynez couldn't get enough of him either, and she kept them laughing, trying to get into the tub with him!

"No, no! Nno-o-o you don't, Missy!" Over and over he had to pry her little hands off the tub rim and unfold her leg, away from the water. "No, no, silly girl!"

"My wants to have a bath, Papa!"

Finally he seized her ankle and pretended to shake her leg off. She squealed with glee. "Now you leave your foot on the rug," he told her, leaning over and planting her foot square on the floor.

"But, Papa, My want a bath wiff you."

"In this dirty water?" He wrinkled up his nose.

She bent down to look. He pointed to pine needles and flotsam. She looked up at him. "You have a suvvy face, Papa," she said solemnly.

David laughed with delight.

"Soft and fuzzy," Louisa explained.

"Where does she keep coming up with these words?" he asked, smiling warmly at Louisa.

"It's a good word."

"It *is* a good word!" he agreed.

"Actually, *I* think you look like a porcupine," she told him. He rubbed his cheeks with both hands.

"What?" She tried not to smile as a marvelously mischievous look stole over his face.

"What if I told you I *like* my beard like this?"

"You don't!" She laughed right back at him.

"I do!"

"You do not! All over the place? Sticking out everywhere?"

"I guess I look like Charles Terry!"

"Not in a million years! He has a pointed nose. And it's bony and sticks up."

"You don't like that?"

"He looks like an elf! Your nose is *soooo* much nicer, softer…" She searched for a word. "More *genteel!* More *manly!*"

He laughed joyfully, exploring the tip of his nose with a thumb and two fingers. "How is Charles anyway?"

"He went over to Port Madison this week with the Russells—"

His eyebrows went up. "They have a sister or something over there, don't they?"

She realized then that he didn't know anything about the Klikitat, or how scared everyone was. "I don't know, Mrs. Russell didn't say, but the whole family went—Did you know Mary Ann was gone? I wrote and told you."

He nodded. "Arthur must be worried about Seattle."

"He was worried about the *Decatur* so long in disrepair. Anyway," she barreled on, "the Russells took the youngest orphans with them, but Johnny refused. He's been staying with me; right now he's helping Uncle Tommy haul hay for the horses. At night he goes to the *Decatur.*"

"You say Charles went over with them?"

"Tom needed his help with the rowing. But he might come back, I don't know. Tom is."

David grinned. "Things must be heating up between Charles and Mary Jane."

"They're very closemouthed about it. Oh! Guess what."

"What?"

"Guess."

"I'm not going to guess, Liza."

"Come on, please. Just try. Oh, but you'll never guess, not in a million years!"

"That's why I'm not going to try."

"One guess! *One!*" she pleaded.

"Liza."

"What?"

He splashed water at her, and she lunged backwards on the bed. "All right, all right, I'll tell you. Edmund Carr and Olivia Holgate are engaged!"

"They are? That's great! When?"

"I don't know. Oh, and David, the saddest thing happened." She told him all about the shooting.

"How's Milton doing?"

"He seems to be the least affected. Olivia's a nervous wreck. Mynez . . . what are you doing?"

"Taking off my clothes."

"Why?"

"So My not get socks and dress dirty in Papa's water."

"You're not getting in Papa's bath. Put your socks back on."

"Here, give me your socks," said David. "No, one at a time. Now, put your foot up here, that's a girl." She sat on the cougarskin and stretched up her leg, resting her ankle on the rim of the tub. David gently tugged her sock back on. "Now, your other foot. All right, Missy, back up. I'm getting out. Louisa, is that someone at the door?"

"Such a wee little knock must mean Johnny," she guessed, getting off the bed. "He knows you're here and is probably shy."

"Better let him in."

"Goodness! You're soaking wet!" she declared, pulling open the door.

"Yes'm," said Johnny. Watch darted in, shaking rainwater everywhere and making Mynez shriek.

"I can see Uncle Tommy must have put you to good use," Louisa told Johnny.

"Yes'm. But we're not done yet, ma'am," he whispered, glancing briefly at David who, after clouting Watch, was busy pulling on a clean pair of long johns.

"No?" asked Louisa, a little puzzled by his behavior. "Did you come home to get a cookie then?"

"No. Uncle Tommy sent me." Again he glanced at David. "To fetch your pa."

"Oh," said Louisa.

David pulled on a clean shirt. "Hello, Johnny. Did Uncle Tommy say why he wants me?"

"Yes, sir. There's new Indians on the Point, sir. Chief Tecumseh. He wants to talk to you."

David glanced up sharply at Louisa. She felt her heart trip.

"I better go see what that's all about, Liza."

237

"Oh, David, I haven't told you yet."

"Told me what?"

"The Klikitat, they've crossed the mountains and joined Leschi. They're—oh, David, we've been so afraid—we're supposed to sleep in the blockhouse—"

He grabbed his jacket.

"David, your shoes and socks!"

"Where are they?"

She pulled a box from under the bed and dug around, found the socks, which he tried to pull on without bothering to sit down, hopping on one foot and taking too long. In exasperation he finally sat down at the table. He had the one sock on, heel up. "How long ago did they come through?" he demanded.

"Yoke-Yakeman brought the report Monday, four days ago. But Suwalth says they've been crossing the lake for two days! Oh, David, I've just been praying and praying, *begging God*, for you to get home before they got here."

"If Tecumseh's come in, it means the hostiles are right on his heels. They're probably out there right now, somewhere in the woods, sizing us up." She must have let out a cry, because he was on his feet, holding her.

"Shh, shhh," he murmured. "It's all right, I *did* come home . . . you're not alone anymore."

"Sir?"

David turned around.

"He said to hurry."

"Yes, of course. Where're my boots?"

Louisa pointed to the hearth.

"Papa, you go away again?" whined Mynez, going over and putting her hand on his knee while he jammed on his boots, first one and then the other.

"I'll be back, darling." He stood up. "Give me half an hour, Liza. Okay?"

"You won't do anything without telling me first, will you?" she begged.

"I won't, I promise. Johnny, you ever ride on your pa's shoulders?"

"Yes, sir. Lots of times, sir."

"I might be a pretty docile mare in comparison, but do you want to give it a try?"

"Yes, sir! I would, sir!"

"Climb into the saddle then." He squatted down, Johnny gave a jump. David eased back to his feet, hitching the boy into place. "Half an hour," he told Louisa, leaning over to give her a kiss. "I'll leave you my rifle."

"You didn't even get a chance to trim your beard!"

"The gun's loaded, all you have to do is pull the trigger."

She bit her lip.

"Half hour, Liza."

30

Friday Night, January 25

On the afternoon of the 25th another chief from the lake district east of Seattle, called Tecumseh, came into town with all his people, claiming protection against the hostile Indians, who, he said, threatened him with destruction should he not join them in the war upon the settlers.

—Hubert Howe Bancroft, historian
in *History of Washington, Idaho, and Montana*

*D*avid was right. The hostiles had driven Tecumseh's band in from the south end of Lake Washington because he had no wish to participate in an attack against Seattle—planned for sometime tonight. Owhi, Leschi, Coquilton, Nelson, Kitsap the Younger, Kanasket—they were all but a mile and a half away, said Tecumseh, preparing for war. In talking with him further, in his own language, David learned even more: that the hostiles had first divided into two columns under Coquilton and Leschi in order to attack Fort

Steilacoom and Seattle simultaneously; that their divided force was so large they expected to capture both places, which were to be sacked and burned and everyone murdered; but that when they learned the *Decatur* had been repaired, they concluded to combine both divisions and concentrate their attack on Seattle in order to secure the gunpowder and the vessel at the same time. The news couldn't have been worse.

Captain Ganesvoort gratefully and immediately granted Tecumseh and his band asylum, assigning them the unoccupied ground on the south end of the Point, between the bluff and Madam Damnable's hotel. He then set about establishing an even tighter line of defense, augmenting his marines with some of the volunteers who'd just mustered out. Agreeing to reassemble if they could serve under a young man called Piexotto (Charles Hewitt was too ill with rheumatism to continue), fifty of seventy men put themselves back into the war. Some of these men Ganesvoort stationed behind the stores on Commercial Street, facing the lagoon. Others he posted outside the blockhouse with Sergeant Corbine or up in the bastion. Those with families he gave the night off; someone had to be with the women and children inside the blockhouse.

Night settled in. Husbands and fathers home, families reunited, the blockhouse was packed. David and Louisa, as uncomfortable on the floor as everyone else (despite the mattress David had insisted on bringing up from the house), curled up in each other's arms, rubbing noses and touching each other in the dark. Their disappointment at not being alone this first night together paled in the dread that it might be their last night at all.

Outside an overcast sky and soft mist nearly hid the moon, certainly the stars: an ominous calm. Along the line of alert marines and volunteers nothing above a whisper could be heard. Officers noiselessly kept ward over every part of their command. Captain Ganesvoort, at times coming out of the cookhouse where headquarters had been set up, paced the line without speaking; though he offered encouragement by way of a soundless clap on the shoulder, a firm handshake, a nod. But for the occasional drunken guffaws of the refractory ex-volunteers drinking to their health down at Mr. Plummer's bar, and an occasional barking of dogs, a near quiet prevailed.

Inside the blockhouse, his voice barely distinguishable amongst the snoring and Sally Bell's laborious breathing, David whispered to Louisa. "Did you know Governor Stevens tried to convince Captain Ganesvoort to abandon Seattle and go with him on the *Active* to Bellingham."

She raised up on her elbow to see if she could see her husband's face in the glow of moonlight coming through a crack in the log. Their eyes met in an intimate exchange.

"Captain Ganesvoort more or less told him he was a fool," David whispered. "He left in pretty high dudgeon."

"Good riddance." Louisa sank back into his arms. "What would we do without Captain Ganesvoort?"

He found her hand and held it over his heart. "I don't know."

"He's an answer to prayer."

"Yes."

"Mary Ann kept saying he's our guardian angel."

"We need one."

Outside, fifty yards away, three Indians came out of Suwalth's shack. Wrapped in blankets, their heads covered, they skirted quietly past the blockhouse and started across the Sawdust to the Spit. Lieutenant Phelps saw them coming. He waited until they were just a few paces away, then stepped into their path, startling them. "What are your names?" he asked in Chinook. "What business do you have at this hour of the night?"

"Lake *tillicum*," they answered. "We've been to visit Suwalth."

242

Careful scrutiny of their faces satisfied Phelps they were indeed strangers, no doubt Tecumseh's lake Indians. He told them to go back to their camp on the Point. "And keep within bounds," he warned, "otherwise you'll be shot."

They gave a satisfactory grunt and hurried on. An hour later an owl hooted. Several more responded, both to the south and north. Lieutenant Phelps glanced both ways. *The Indians moving in?* Suddenly he spotted Suwalth coming out of the woods, muttering to himself, headed towards his encampment and gesticulating wildly. *Where had he been?* Phelps didn't trust Suwalth and watched suspiciously from the shadows. A dozen paces short of the lieutenant, Suwalth suddenly stopped, stamped the ground violently a few times, then turned and headed for the Point. Another owl hooted. Nervously Phelps went up and down his line, cautioning everyone this might be it.

Inside the blockhouse Louisa heard the owls as well, and involuntarily stiffened. *They sounded so close!* David heard too, and jerked up, his hand automatically searching the floor for his loaded rifle. Watch, at their feet, looked up.

"Oh, David, is this it?" whimpered Louisa, glancing at his immobile posture, Watch's ears—and Mynez noisily sucking her thumb under her covers. David didn't answer, but remained rigid a long time, his profile in the dimness as still as a blackened photograph. Finally he relaxed, and lay back down.

"I love you, David," Louisa whispered.

"I love you too."

31

Saturday, January 26

Daybreak saw the village unattacked, with blue uniformed sentries standing guard in the morning mist, and light blue woodsmoke going up sluggishly from the chimneys of cabins and frame houses at the edge of the forest.

On the sloop-of-war in the bay, and on the lumber bark Brontes, lying a cable's length to the south, brown coal smoke went up from the "Charlie Nobles" of the galleys, and there was a smell of coffee and breakfast cooking. The weather was not cold for January, and there was no snow on deck or on the ground ashore; but the morning had its sting of cold and it was a good time to think about breakfast.

—Archie Binns, historian
in *Sea in the Forest*

e're still alive," whispered David, kissing Louisa awake and smiling down into her face. Somehow she'd fallen asleep. Slowly she opened her eyes. "Is it morning?"
"Yes."

"What do you think they're waiting for?" she asked him.

He chuckled softly, happy to be alive. "Since when were you a pessimist?"

Others awoke, and though the blockhouse was still very dark, the scattered yawns and expressions of surprise and delight at having come through the night unscathed soon nudged the sleepyheads out of slumber. "The good Lord's granted us another day," chirped Widow Holgate, getting up and fluffing her pillow.

"Yes, but don't think those Indians went away!" declared Ursula. "They're biding their time."

"Well they're not likely to attack during the day, they never do," said Uncle Tommy, easing to his feet. "Come on, girls," he prodded the four lumps at his feet. "Those cows'll be bawling if we don't shake a leg."

"Tom," said David, "I'll do the milking."

"No, this is your first day back, and you have guard duty in a bit—"

"What time is it?" someone asked.

"*George Junior!*" screeched Ursula all of a sudden. "You leave your sister alone! Stop it, I say! Stop it, stop it! *Right now!*"

No one lingered. All hurried back to their own homes through the pale light of winter's dawn, a few moaning good-naturedly over stiff joints, everyone happy to stretch and get the kinks out of their legs and rush, shivering, to their necessary houses, which was Louisa's priority.

When she got to their cabin David had the candles lit to push back the shadows. A cheerful fire crackled in the fireplace. A fleeting moment of normalcy! Overwhelmed, she threw herself into his arms. "Oh, that every morning was like this!" she declared, kissing him with a loud smack and making him blink in surprise. He laughed and hugged her, and caught her up in his arms.

"What you doing, Papa?"

245

David laughed out loud. "Is that all she says anymore?" he asked, looking into Louisa's merry brown eyes. "'What you doing?'"

"Enjoy it. The next question will be 'why?' Orion's been driving everyone *crazy* with his whys."

Down on the Point, next to Mr. Plummer's henhouse, Captain Ganesvoort watched two blanket-wrapped Indians cross over the sandbar from Tecumseh's camp to the mainland. "What do you suppose they're doing, Morris?" he asked the lieutenant who manned the howitzer.

"There's a good clam bed over there. I suppose they're hunting for breakfast."

"I could use breakfast myself," said Captain Ganesvoort, training his spyglass on the trees directly across the lagoon a hundred or so feet away. Slowly he swept his sight the full length of the forest, south to north. Nothing. "Looks like that's it," he said, "we can fall back," and he collapsed the spyglass and slipped it into his breast pocket.

He ordered his four divisions to fall back one on the other, beginning at the far end of the Point. The men were eager to move. Hungry and exhausted, they knew breakfast and hammocks awaited them aboard ship. Lieutenant Morris's crew dragged their muddy brass howitzer to Mr. Yesler's wharf, and left it under guard. Piexotto came to tell David the marines were being withdrawn from the blockhouse. David kissed Louisa and Mynez good-bye, grabbed his rifle, and hustled up the knoll with Watch.

Mynez went over to the door. Standing on tiptoe, she tried to reach the latch. "Papa not eat his breakfast," she whined.

"We'll have to make him some biscuits," sighed Louisa, fear rushing in now that she was alone. "When they're done, we can take them up to him."

"Where Papa go?"

"Just to the fort." Louisa led her to the window and helped her climb onto a stool. "There, do you see him?"

246

"What he doing?"

"Looking for Indians."

Mynez seemed satisfied with the answer. She waved, but David didn't respond. She tried again. "Mama, Papa not wave to My."

"Perhaps he can't see you, darling."

"But My see him! Mama! Mama!" she shrieked. "My see Johnny!"

Louisa wondered if her little charge would come down to the house, but he seemed satisfied to stay at the fort with David and the other men taking up the post. He'd found Corbine and was shinnying up one of the young sergeant's legs. "Mynez, if I leave you by yourself on the stool, can you be careful of the lamp? It's right behind you on the table here."

"Where you go, Mama?"

"I have to make the biscuits. You'll be careful?"

"My *always* careful."

She was sifting the weevils out of the flour, and wondering in the back of her mind where the Indians might be, when Mynez announced that Mandy was coming.

"Yoke-Yakeman no come home all night!" a very worried Mandy gasped, letting herself in.

"What about Suwalth?" Louisa asked. "Do you know where he is?"

"No," said Mandy, wringing her hands.

"They must be out scouting."

"*Wake,* no," said Mandy, and she started to cry. *"Hy-hu cultus Siwash."* Too many bad Indians. "I not know where look."

"Have you asked down at the Point? Maybe Chief Tecumseh knows where he is."

"Yes," said Mandy, and she darted out the door.

A half hour later, aboard ship, Kate Blaine finished nursing her baby. "Will you get a skiff, dear," she asked her husband, "so I can go ashore today?"

"Absolutely not!" he answered, pulling on the last of his clothes.

"But I am well enough. I'd like the exercise."

"Walk around the deck then," he offered. "I'll go see about breakfast, dear, I hear the men coming back." Hand on the doorknob, he said, "What shall I tell the steward this morning? Tea or coffee?"

"Shh!" She held up a hand. The gruff voice of Henry Yesler could be heard through the thin wall.

"Captain, a *klootchman* just informed me there are a lot of Indians back of Tom Pepper's house."

"A *klootchman?*"

"Yes, Yoke-Yakeman's wife."

"I've been looking for him! She didn't happen to say where he was, did she?"

"He's at Williamson's. Tecumseh had visitors last night— Leschi and Owhi. Yoke-Yakeman couldn't shake them until just a short time ago, and hightailed it over to the store. An imminent attack is planned. Mandy, apparently out looking for Yoke-Yakeman, caught up with him at Williamson's. He sent her straight to me."

"John, bring me my boots!"

"It could be another false alarm, sir. Last night, remember, we thought—"

"I'd rather answer twenty false alarms than be caught napping once!"

"Then never mind, Captain, just send the lieutenant with the howitzer."

"No, sir! Where my men go, I go too! John, my boots!"

The voices died away. "Oh, my dear husband, what is to happen to our friends?" whispered Kate in a tight, hollow voice.

Mr. Blaine rushed over to the bed and sat down. "We must be away from here, dear. It's a most inauspicious land."

"But our mission, Mr. Blaine!"

"I will look upon our retreat as duty; I would be gratified to have you look upon it in the same light." He took her trem-

248

bling hand. "'It is not in man that walketh to direct his steps,'" he quoted. "The Lord will order our ways aright, my dear."

The *Decatur*'s hungry crew, having just sat down to breakfast, moaned when the sound of the long-roll summoned them on deck. Minutes later they found themselves headed ashore, their longboats creaking and jerking forward over the choppy gray sea as well-muscled crewmen belabored the oars in long, hard pulls. Captain Ganesvoort, leaving Officer Middleton in command of the ship's battery, accompanied Mr. Yesler and Lieutenant Phelps's fourteen-man division; and while the skiff leapt forward in jumps and starts, he kept his eyes peeled on the high wooded bluffs behind the village, searching for movement or the glimmer of gunmetal. He saw only the soft blue woodsmoke wafting sluggishly from the chimneys of the little cabins and frame houses along the forest's edge.

"Seems peaceful enough," he told Yesler, and then glanced back over his shoulder to his sloop of war where she stood by, ready to fire her guns. A cable length to the south the lumber bark *Brontes,* awaiting her load from the river, lay idly at anchor. Brown coal smoke spiraled lazily from the "Charlie Nobles" of both galleys, and with a stab of sharp hunger Ganesvoort actually smelled his coffee and uneaten breakfast! Another sniff. Alas, only the salty sea scent!

"For the love of Mike . . ." muttered one of the marines.

Ganesvoort turned back, surprised to see a flurry of friendly Indians hurrying to place their chattels into canoes and pushing out to the bay. When their own boat ground ashore and came to rest, the men leaped out. Suwalth's sister waddled past the captain as fast as she could, obviously crazed with fright.

"What's the matter?" asked Captain Ganesvoort, intercepting her.

"*Hi-hu Klikitat copa Tom Pepper's house!*" Nancy shrieked, pointing back over her shoulder to the woods. "*Hi-hu Kliki-*

tat—!" Before completing the sentence a second time, she plunged headforemost into a waiting canoe.

"Looks like they're here at last," said Lieutenant Phelps darkly. "Though I don't suppose they'll show themselves until nightfall."

"Get your men under cover and to sleep," the captain ordered briskly, "so they can be rested and ready when the Indians do appear. I'll have their meals sent to them onshore. But first—are you coming Yesler? I'm going down to the south end to have Morris lodge a shell at Tom Pepper's house. That'll tell quick enough if anyone's there."

Louisa pulled on her oven mitt and checked the biscuits. Done!

"Sojers, Mama!"

Through the window Louisa could see the marines piling out of their longboats onto the wharf and beach to race across the Sawdust, guns in hand. "How long have they been coming in like that, Mynez?"

"What you say?"

"How long—never mind," mumbled Louisa. *Mynez couldn't understand such a question.* She stood clutching her hot pan, not knowing whether to be frightened or simply curious. The oarsmen, she noticed, spun their emptied boats back around and headed again for the ship. *To bring more men in?* She stepped closer to the window. Why were some of the Indians flipping their dugouts right side up and getting in? *BOOOOOM!*

She must have jumped four inches. The rattling, deep-throated thunder of the howitzer shattered the air, shook the plates on the shelf, and took her breath away. Simultaneously a chorus of bloodcurdling, high-pitched yipping erupted from the forest behind the house and sent a chill straight up her back. A shell screeched over the village rooftops, exploded, and was quickly followed by the crash of musketry! Mynez toppled off her stool. Screaming, she picked herself up and came flying across the room to Louisa, plowing into her knees.

Louisa couldn't move. She stood paralyzed, holding her pan of biscuits, frozen by the thunder of the furious fusillade and terrible, ear-piercing yowl of the Indians. *"Mama!"* screamed Mynez again, frantically clawing Louisa's dress, trying to get up. Mandy burst through the door. Louisa suddenly came to her senses, flipped her biscuits into the deep hem pocket of her apron, dropped the pan, grabbed Mynez's hand, and raced after Mandy. Another shell whistled overhead and they all but stumbled off the stoop. *"Mama! Mama!"* Mynez wailed, Louisa dragging her along, bullets whistling past, biting into the ground all around them and spitting up mud.

Such a running for the fort!

Mr. Butler, his dirty trousers from Fort Duwamish taken by his industrious wife and put to soak in a hot tub of sudsy water, jumped into his wife's red flannel petticoat, and ran.

Ed Hanford, dropping his breakfast fork, seized two of his five boys, one in each arm. Abbie Jane picked up the baby. The eldest grabbed the rifle. Seven-year-old Cornelius was on his own steam and the whole family fairly flew across the Sawdust for the fort, muskets knocking slivers from the fences and stumps around and in front of them. Suddenly Cornelius remembered he'd left the door open. He started back, but saw the heads of four Indians rise up over a fir log beside the house, muskets drawn. Forget the door!

William Bell lumbered up the knoll with Sally. The girls raced ahead, Laura with baby Austin. Virginia reached the fort first, dove past the legs of Piexotto, who was in her path as she entered the blockhouse, knocking him to the ground with a scramble that added to the panic.

Pell-mell from north and south, everyone ran as they'd never run before, converging on the knoll. "We ran so fast our bones bent under us," said Doctor Williamson later. Louisa was hardly conscious of anyone; she knew only her need to get to safety. Suddenly she saw David. He'd spotted her, and was racing toward her. One of the Kirkland girls came running up beside her, brushing Lousia's left shoulder. At the same time the crack of gunfire burst in their ears, and Louisa screamed as she felt heat on her left temple. The Kirkland girl crumpled into the ground.

"David!" yelped Louisa, veering away.

"Run!" he screamed at her, giving her a shove, at the same time squatting down and scooping up the girl. Terror stricken, Louisa stumbled on, dragging Mynez, clutching her apron. *Where was Mandy?* She could hear David coming up hard behind her. *"Go, go, go, go, go—"* he yelled. "Liza, *RUNNNNN!"*

She was through! David hurtled in. *"Make way!"* he bellowed, pushing and shoving past the door, trying to make space for Sarah Kirkland.

Louisa, still holding Mynez's hand and clutching her apron of biscuits, dropped weakly to her knees beside the lifeless fifteen-year-old girl. *This could be her! Lying here dead!* Sarah's five sisters crowded in, wailing and shrieking, reaching down but afraid to touch. David hastily picked up Sarah's hand, turned it over, and felt her wrist for a pulse. "She's alive!" he shouted. "Where is she shot?"

"I don't know!" Louisa panicked, looking all over.

Suddenly the girl blinked.

Everyone gasped.

"Get her out of the way!" bellowed Lieutenant Piexotto. *"More people coming in!"*

David scrambled around, grabbed Sarah under the arms, and started backing through the press of people, dragging her across the dirt floor. Her sisters stumbled along beside her, grabbing her dress, her apron, trying to reassure themselves she was really and truly alive while she looked up at them all with a dazed and bewildered expression. "Look!" said one of the sisters. "A ringlet is missing!"

Louisa felt her own temple. The bullet had come right between them, clipped Sarah's hair, and made her faint. *Oh dear God,* Louisa prayed, squatting awkwardly to gather Mynez into her arms and stifle her terrified crying, *you really, truly, are with us!*

"You are *NOT* going out there!"

Louisa whirled around. Widow Holgate stood in the narrow path of sunlight stealing through the doorway, her face blotched pink with fury and fear. "I said *no!* I mean *no!*"

"I'm not a baby!" Young Milton edged toward the sunlight, rifle in hand.

"Your brothers are out there! I won't have all three of you shot and killed!"

"Ma'am!" shouted Piexotto over the din of cross fire and whistling shells from where he stood guard, hip against the doorjamb, arm stretched across. "We need everyone we got! A thousand Klikitat—"

It was all Milton needed. Ducking under Piexotto's arm, he came up outside. The next thing Louisa knew his body flew straight back, knocking Piexiotto's arm aside. Milton landed with a crash on the floor just inside the door, flat on his back, arms and legs flung straight out.

"Jesus—" Piexotto sprang away from the door and dropped to his knees beside the boy. Milton's eyes stared vacantly up. A bloody hole bore through his head between his sightless eyes. *"Dear Jesus,"* Piexotto prayed, whipping out his hanky. *"Dear Jesus but I'm sorry ..."* Hastily he spread the hanky over the face.

Widow Holgate fainted, folding at her knees like a spent accordion. Children screamed and hid in their mothers' skirts. Everyone else stood benumbed, the same thought racing through their minds. *The bullet hole was in the exact same place as Jack Drew's, the man Milton killed just one week ago.*

32

Saturday Morning, January 26

As the Indians reloaded, young Milton Holgate, carrying the fowling piece with which he had defended his sister, ducked under the arm of Lieutenant Piexotto of the volunteers at the blockhouse doorway. He received an Indian bullet between the eyes and died instantly, the youngest and the first to fall in the Battle of Seattle. David Denny and the lieutenant carried him to a niche under the stairway where the body of Lieutenant Slaughter had lain after they brought him out from his defeat in the White River valley.

—Gordon Newell, historian
in *Westward to Alki*

One young man (a Mr. Holgate I believe) . . . was shot in the face. I was terribly frightened, sick and faint with fear. I begged and pleaded and insisted on being taken to the *Decatur.*

—Dr. John King
in a letter written years later to Ezra Meeker

*D*avid was the first of the stunned crowd to move. Outside, bullets spattered the squared timber walls of the fort, shells of returning fire whistled and shrieked overhead, the noise almost deafening. David inched forward, placing his hand on people's shoulders or arms to let them know he wanted to get by. Numbly they shifted until at last he came to the body.

"Piexotto," he hollered hoarsely, his throat tight, "let's get him under the stairs, out of sight!" Piexotto nodded. "You take his ankles, I'll get him under the arms!" Suddenly in the struggle to lift the body, Milton's head flopped back and the hanky dropped away. Blood pooling in the wound drained onto the floor, splashing David's boots. Mrs. Holgate, who'd just revived, let out a strangled whimper, and Olivia and Abbie Jane, almost as helpless with grief and fear as their mother, shielded her from the gruesome sight. A child started to wail in sheer terror. "It's Johnny King!" Irene Neely shouted at Louisa.

"Come on, Mynez!" By the time Louisa reached the boy he was sick with fear, had vomited all over the floor and soiled his pants, and was repeatedly banging his head against the logs, screaming to be let out. "I want to go to the *Decatur!*" he wept. "Take me to the *Decatur!*"

A pitiful sight. His clothing stained, his brow beginning to bleed from knocking it on the wall.

"Johnny?" Louisa reached out a hand but he was too crazed with fear to recognize her. "Johnny," she tried again. *"Johnny!"* But Johnny was lost in his terror; he couldn't hear. *What was she to do?* Someone pounded down the stairs right behind her, thrust her aside and pushed a rifle into her hands. *Corbine!* she thought gratefully, watching the young sergeant pick up the boy and crush him to his chest.

"Oh, Corbine," Johnny sobbed, throwing his arms around his special friend. "Take me to the ship! Please take me to the ship!" Another shell shrieked overhead. *"Please! Please!"* he screamed, grabbing so tightly that Corbine gagged and choked, and had to tear at the boy to loosen his awful stranglehold.

255

"Corbine! We've got to get him out of here!" David pushed through, shouting over yet another rattling BOOM! of the howitzer. *"If not for his sake, for everyone else's!"*

"Righto! There's some hatchets and saws around here somewhere, Denny! We can cut a door in the back wall, facing the beach! He can semaphore Middleton he wants to go aboard!"

"But will anyone come get him?"

Corbine looked at David in disbelief.

And so while David set to work and mothers counted their children's noses, crying with relief and praying in gratitude to find everyone accounted for, the marines who guarded the fort started urging them all upstairs.

"What all that noise, Mama?" whimpered Mynez, holding her hands to her ears.

"Guns!" Louisa shouted back, at the same time motioning to the marines that she would stay with David.

"What Papa doing?"

"Making a door!"

David leaned into his drill, turning the crank furiously. Sawdust and yellow curls of fir peeled away from the revolving bit and fell to the floor in a sweet-smelling pile. Next the saw . . . now the drill again . . . then the saw again. Finally he pulled back and gave a hard kick. A block of wood fell through. Another kick. Another block of wood.

Johnny needed no instruction. He clambered through the hole in a flash. Corbine handed out the flags. Standing behind the blockhouse Johnny made his signal and Louisa, turning Mynez over to David, peered through the splintery opening.

"They're coming to get him!" she cried in joy. "No, Johnny, *no!*" she yelled, reaching out, grabbing his hand. "Don't go until they get to the beach!" He danced and hopped, hardly able to restrain himself. Finally, the dinghy just ten yards offshore, he took off, sprinting down the embankment, over the logs and sand, bullets twanging over his head, racing past the three-inch howitzer planted on the beach, belching smoke and shot the other way over his head. He kept on running, splashed into the water, and plunged forward—slower, slower—the water rising up around his waist. The dinghy reached him. Strong arms reached out, grabbed him, hauled him aboard dripping wet. Louisa watched him nose-dive as spent bullets dropped in the water all around them. The oarsman jerked his oars, spun the boat about, and the little skiff fairly leaped and skipped over the bay, away from danger.

Louisa drew back. "He's safe," she breathed, and for the first time since the battle began, allowed herself to sit down, dropping into the sawdust and wood chips beside David and leaning almost luxuriously against the solid wall behind her. Suddenly she looked down. She was still clutching her apron. "Oh, David . . ." She started to laugh in giddy, weak hysteria. "Look, David, I brought you your breakfast!"

The thundering noise of war did not go unnoticed elsewhere on the Sound. At Port Madison fourteen miles away seven men loaded into a skiff and rowed hard for Seattle—five millhands plus Seattle's Charles Terry and Sheriff Tom Russell.

On the Port Madison reserve, Chief Seattle paced back and forth on the beach in front of his Ole Man's House. What his thoughts were, no one knew; though his anguish was plainly evident. Frequently he paused to stare miserably across the inlet to the island standing between him and the village named for him on the mainland.

Farther to the north, in Bellingham, the *Active* reversed her engines and headed toward the town where not twenty-four hours before the governor had scoffed at all possibility of attack.

In Seattle the Indians had spread themselves in a ragged, two-mile arc beginning at the Bells' abandoned house a mile north of town and stretching as far south as the Hanfords' abandoned claim below the Point—with the majority congregating along the ridge of trees behind Tom Pepper's house. There, secreted in the woods, but prevented from coming any farther by the *Decatur*'s cannon and the steady volley of the sailors and citizens holding the west side of the lagoon, the battle settled into a long-range duel. Neither party could approach the other across the sandbar without inviting certain death, so they blazed away at each other over the dank marsh separating them.

For two hours the fiery exchange kept up. At one point Lieutenant Dallas, a blanket draped over himself to keep warm, stepped out in front with his spyglass to get a better look. A bullet whistled through his blanket between his arm and side. Another bullet knocked the nipple off the musket of the man next to him. Both men backtracked out of range.

Frustrated by the standoff, some of the Indians circled back through the trees to reinforce their center. In minutes the new concentration charged the Sawdust. Lieutenant Phelps, his fourteen-man unit, and the Seattle citizens under Lieutenant Piexotto saw them coming—tumbling down the hill behind the cookhouse, tearing through the bushes, filling the air with their bloodcurdling, high yips and howls.

"Don't fire until I give the order!" shouted Phelps. David, squatting behind a mossy log, rifle primed and ready, waited, heart in his throat. *If the Indians broke through—*

"FIRE!"

David squeezed his trigger! A deafening roar, billows of blue smoke! The Indians fell back, dragging their dead and taking up shelter behind the trees and logs—but shooting back in dogged determination!

At this point the seven men from Port Madison arrived. Seeing where the fragile link in the line of defense was, they raced across the Sawdust. "Looks like I nearly missed the fun!" puffed Charles, dropping down beside David and propping his rifle on the log. He squinted down the barrel, taking aim.

"Hey there, Charles!" shouted David gratefully.

Sheriff Tom knelt on the other side. "We got a game of pop-and-shoot here? Rather than charge-and-shoot?"

"You missed the charge, Russell! They're taking cover! Their muskets don't shoot any farther than a man can spit!"

"Lucky for us!"

Middleton on the *Decatur* saw the new concentration of gun smoke and repositioned his cannon. In minutes his shells screamed directly over the Sawdust, exploding into the wooded hill. Huge trunks of trees splintered open; the patter of grapeshot peppered against their trunks sounded like hail. Still the Indians held, gunning back from their stumps and logs.

"Holy Moses!" whispered Charles, white-faced behind his unruly black beard. "These are brave buzzards!"

"What was that about fun?" David grunted.

Sensing that stealth might dislodge them, he, Walter Graham, Charles, and Tom decided to work their way up the beach under cover of the bluff to Arthur's house. Furtively they crawled through the underbrush and in through the front door. David crouch-walked across the floor, shinnied up the ladder to the loft, and knocked out a shingle on the east side of the roof, near the peak—everyone hoping to get a clear shot at the enemy. But the minute the board came crashing down a shower of bullets struck the roof. They got out and back to the beach considerably quicker than going in.

Inside the fort the terrified women tried to comfort the children and pray for protection while listening to the roar of the cannon, the explosion of her balls and shells, the sharp report of the howitzer, the incessant rattle of small arms, and the uninterrupted whistling of the bullets—all mingled with the furious yells of the Indians. The blanket-wrapped body of Milton Holgate lying beneath the stairs below added to

259

the untenable anxiety. Occasionally they could hear Indian women screaming encouragement to their warriors; and the cruel, piercing cheers always sent shivers up Louisa's spine.

Hours went by. She wondered about David, where he was, what he was doing, *was he alive?* Just when her fright seemed to overwhelm her, and the uncertainty of what was happening outdoors became intolerable, she'd remember her own narrow escape—*everyone's* narrow escape, for they were all here, weren't they? She'd remember and calm down. Many things she didn't understand. Milton's gruesome, seemingly retributional death, for one. But she knew a kind Providence watched over them. And in this hope she would place David's life.

There was no other hope.

33

Saturday Afternoon, January 26

All the best accounts indicate that Indian "Jim" [Yoke-Yake-man] and the squaw saved the lives of many of the inhabitants; it was their reports that caused the *Decatur* to commence the battle and thus prevent the rush of the hostiles on the cabins of the settlers, thereby giving the latter time to reach the blockhouse, and at the same time enabling the troops to return to their stations on the beach and streets.

All at the reservation [of Port Madison] was quiet until the evening of January 24th, when word came to Chief Seattle from Teatebash that a large band was on the point of attacking the Town of Seattle. . . . On the morning of the 26th the cannonading at Seattle could be plainly heard and all knew that the attack was in progress.

—Clarence Bagley, historian
in *History of Seattle*

About three in the afternoon the firing slowed down and finally petered out. *"Hyas muckamuck! Hyas muckamuck!"* Lots of food! Lots of food! the Indian women called to their men; and as the battle smoke thinned Louisa caught the unmistakable scent of roasting beef.

Good-bye Hay Barn, Hardy Axe Handles, Texas, Loco, Portia, Juliet, and Pied, she thought for it wasn't too hard to guess where the Indians had come by their lunch. But Seattle's women wasted little time in grief over their pet animals, or in tears over the loss of the milk and butter. A boy had died and a soldier had been killed.

To their great joy their own men had come through the long hours of battle unharmed. A few had had their hats shot off. Charles Terry lost a lock of hair. David Denny somehow ripped his trousers. Nothing worse. The *Decatur*'s guns had done their job, and when Captain Ganesvoort stopped by a few minutes later the women were weepy with appreciation.

"This thing's not over," he told them straight, "and I have to withdraw my men—" Instant cries of distress went up. "They've been thirty-six hours without sleep or food," he explained, "and are desperate for both. But first, I want all noncombatants out of the way. We'll be taking you aboard ship. I'll start loading some of you onto the sloop of war, the rest of you we'll put on board the lumber bark."

"Oh, Mama! Do we really get to go on the ship?"

"Is it true, Mama? The soldiers will take us—"

"Ma! Ma! Did you hear?"

"Mrs. Bell, you first," said the captain. "Are you up to it?"

"Yes, I think so."

"I'll take you out myself. The rest of you, Corbine will see to. You'll move in groups, under guard. No dogs, no cats. Move quickly, the lull won't last forever."

Louisa refused to go, and though David argued, it was half-spirited. Neither wanted to be separated from the other. Soon it was only them and the other men settlers in the blockhouse with Sergeant Corbine's marines—left behind to guard them. Shivering in the cold January afternoon, they all agreed they had to somehow obtain some food.

David Graham volunteered to sneak into Louisa's house to bake biscuits for everyone. Four or five others said they'd try for the Borens' a hundred yards away, where the Bells and Holgates lived and where William Bell said he had a well-stocked cupboard of sugar, flour, pork, and potatoes. Walter Graham thought he might be able to get some water from the cookhouse pump. Other men, fearing the Indians might try to sneak in after dark and rob and plunder their homes, dashed out to retrieve what provisions, guns, and other valuables were left behind. The Indians, hearing them, fired shots through the trees, but the *Decatur,* standing by, lobbed another round of shells. The Indians pulled back to finish their lunch.

Across the Sound Chief Seattle turned away from the beach and purposefully strode up to the Ole Man House. His mind was made up. *Leschi should not have enlisted the help of his uncle Owhi.* Everything considered and swept aside, this one thing remained: *Owhi.*

Seattle summoned his runners to assemble the people. When they were gathered, he spoke quickly and determinedly: "When Leschi came to us one moon ago I told everyone here that if ever there was cause to shed blood I would be on the warpath night and day. Today Owhi, my enemy, attacked those with whom I've pledged friendship. This he should not have done."

"You are certain it is Owhi who leads this battle across the Sound?" someone asked.

Seattle nodded to Teatebash, who stood. "It is true," said the runner. "Salmon Bay Curley sent this news to me two nights ago."

A great murmur of discontent ran through the crowd seated in the meeting room of the Ole Man House. Years ago Owhi had come from the east to capture and enslave them. Chief Seattle had saved them.

263

"Who will put their name with mine," asked Seattle, "on a paper our friend Doc Maynard will send to his big chief? Who will pledge to defend the whiteskins from Owhi?"

Hands flew up.

Seattle turned to Econ-O-Lin, One-Eyed Tom, and Stuttering George. "I know your business here. Your fires may burn tonight, but there will be no rush to kill whiteskins here. Tell Leschi my heart is with him, but it is also with the people who protect us from the treacherous Haida and other northern tribes—and tribes led by men like Owhi. Go now," he commanded.

At four o'clock Owhi commenced the battle again by swooping down on what appeared to be an unguarded village. The immediate explosion of shells from the *Decatur* and a stout return from the men at the blockhouse sent him scrambling back into the trees. A desultory exchange on both sides continued off and on until dusk, when Captain Ganesvoort, back on shore, decided to send out Suwalth and Yoke-Yakeman to see what was happening.

The two men returned just after dark, breathless. The enemy, they reported, planned to burn every building as far north as Henry Smith's abandoned farm, clear down to the Duwamish River. The conflagration of flames would light the night sky and signal all the Indians on the beach, across the Sound, and northern tribes to join the attack.

"We can't let that happen!" said Ganesvoort sternly.

"They're piling kindling and brush around and under the houses," warned Suwalth.

Ganesvoort hurried someone out to the *Decatur* with an order for Middleton: "Bombard the shoreline as far as your shells will reach—give it everything you've got!"

Fifteen minutes later the shriek of cannonball and shot, one after the other, came whistling through the night, exploding so quickly and furiously the very earth shook. Louisa, resting in the blockhouse, seized Mynez and hurtled down the blockhouse stairs and flew across the floor to the door in new fear. "David!" she shouted into the darkness and shadows and blinding flashes of streaking color. "David! David! What's happening?"

He appeared out of nowhere, Watch too, coming up on her right, and nearly scaring her to death. "Oh, David, what's happening? Are there more Indians?"

He took Mynez. "No, but they're burning everything!" he shouted above the thudding cacophony. "Henry's house is already in flames!"

"Oh, David, our Swale!" she cried. "All our hard work! Gone!"

"Put your arms around me," he told her. She did, laying her cheek against his cold jacket. "We have each other," he told her.

When the shelling stopped at last, it left their ears ringing, a droning buzz that wouldn't go away. Mynez, crying, hands over her ears, whimpered, "Bad noise over?"

"Soon. But the noise can't hurt you," said David, holding her fiercely. "And Papa has you."

Their ears were still ringing when suddenly from the woods came Chinook words as sharp and deadly as pistol shots.

"If you have ears, listen! I am Coquilton! I speak for Leschi! We will come back with twenty thousand warriors from the north to finish what was begun! We will come to you from the woods! We come to you from the water! This is what we say, listen! We WILL return—BEFORE ONE MOON IS GONE!"

Louisa pressed her face into David's coat.

"Come on," he said, "it's time for bed."

"Denny?"

David twisted around. "Captain?"

"A new crew is coming out to relieve Corbine. We're heading back. I'd like to extend to you and your wife the use of my cabin tonight. I think your wife—"

Louisa started to object.

265

"Please," he told her, his kindly, tired face looking pale in the thin moonlight.

"Well?" David asked her, jostling her a little to encourage her to reconsider.

"It does sound nice," she admitted.

"This way then."

Louisa couldn't remember being so tired. Or so cold. She kissed Watch good-bye at the beach. "The marines will take care of you," she whispered, rubbing his silky ears and then climbing into the waiting longboat, grateful to feel the hard bench beneath her. David sat down beside her, Mynez in his lap. A calm night, clear, the stars so close they seemed to beckon, teased her to reach out and take hold. If she wasn't so weary she might have been tempted to try.

Someone gave the longboat a shove. Soon they were creaking and gliding smoothly across the night water, the men who rowed too tired to do much more than nudge their oars. To the north Louisa could see the fire at Smith Cove, a small flicker of orange flame. She twisted around to look in the direction of her own dear home in the Swale. The Bells' empty house, she saw, was burning high on the bluff. But nothing beyond. "David," she whispered, "maybe they won't burn our house."

He craned his neck a little.

"Do you think?" she asked.

"Don't get your hopes up, Liza," he said tiredly. "It could be burning for all that, and just be hidden by the trees."

"At least we stopped them from burning down the whole town," the captain told Louisa, seeing her discouragement, "and stopped their signal from going out."

"But do you think they may still try?"

He glanced southeast to John Holgate's and Ed Hanford's claims a mile beyond the Point where two fires burned like candles in the night. "They've made good their escape," he said. "By the way, Denny," he said to David, "those friends of yours are good men—Suwalth and his nephew. I'm not sure how the day would have gone if Yoke-Yakeman hadn't managed to warn Williamson what was up."

"I understand it was a close call."

"What's ironic is that I saw Owhi and Leschi leaving this morning about seven, crossing the sandbar. But Morris and I hardly gave it a thought. We thought they were some of Tecumseh's bunch, out scrounging clams for breakfast."

"Seven?" said David, puzzled.

"It was seven all right. Because right after that I had the troops fall back. Why?"

"Why did Yoke-Yakeman wait so long then? Leschi and Owhi gone, why not say something right away? Before you left for the ship?"

"Leschi left Nelson behind."

Ahhh, thought David.

"But don't ask me how Yoke-Yakeman finally eluded Nelson. I don't know. All *I* know is that if Yoke-Yakeman hadn't gotten away, and if Mandy hadn't come by when she did—"

"Don't talk about it anymore," said Louisa.

David took her hand. "It's over. Don't worry anymore."

"It's not over, you heard Coquilton."

David didn't answer; neither did anyone else.

On board the *Decatur* fifteen minutes later the captain ushered them into his cabin. "It can be a wee bit tight for me at times," he apologized, "so it'll be cozy for the three of you. I hope you don't mind. I see a servant brought some hot water. Good. Can I get you anything else before I leave?"

"Uh, no . . ." stammered David, suddenly overwhelmed by the captain's generosity. The warmth and tidiness, the sheer safety he was being offered almost made him dizzy.

"Breakfast at eight bells then," and Captain Ganesvoort shut the door.

"Oh, David, look!" Louisa stumbled straight for the berth. "A real feather mattress!"

"Get your clothes off and climb in," he told her. "I'll take care of Mynez."

She couldn't get undressed fast enough.

By the time David had Mynez asleep on the floor and himself sponged clean, Louisa was asleep. She'd promised to stay awake.

But look at her, he thought with gratitude to God for bringing them through the day. *A war cry won't wake her.*

He blew out the lamp, then slipped into the incredible comfort of the clean flannel sheets and the amazing luxury of the feather mattress. With a weary sigh he pushed Louisa over a little to make room for himself; then drew her hands over his heart and slid his legs alongside hers. It was not a wide berth, cozy was right, which suited him just fine.

34

Sunday, January 27

At noon on the 27th the *Active* with Governor Stevens on board, steamed into the bay.

—Clarence Bagley, historian
in *History of Seattle*

The people of Seattle buried young Holgate and young Wilson beside the White Church and prepared for another attack, which they all expected. The volunteers and marines put up a second blockhouse and began building a stockade around the town.

—Archie Binns, historian
in *Northwest Gateway*

*I*n the morning the pioneers and friendly Indians wandered from one end of town to the other, agog. *Utter devastation.* Behind the buildings whole trees had been uprooted by the shelling, others split open by solid shot, underbrush everywhere flattened by showers of grape and canister. Homes were riddled with bullets, walls gouged through with musket balls, everything inside ransacked and turned upside down by the pilfering Indians. What the men in the blockhouse hadn't been able to save during yesterday's short lull had been spirited away or tossed outdoors as insignificant by the retreating enemy. Children raced to collect and count the bullets littering the floors and the ground outside. Scouts, Indian and white, headed into the forest to determine the fuller extent of damage.

Folk took comfort that only two of their own had been killed in such terrible destruction. *What if Captain Ganesvoort hadn't made his decision to surprise the enemy before the Indians had attacked while everyone in Seattle was sitting down to breakfast? What then? How many more of them would be dead?* Surely a kindly Providence watched over them all!

Being Sunday, and having everything to be grateful for, Reverend Blaine nevertheless did not hold service. He was too busy making arrangements to sell his property to Charles Terry and packing the few things of value that the Indians had left. The next ship in, he said, he and his wife would take. God had called him on, he informed them. To where, he wasn't yet certain. "But God does work in mysterious ways, his wonders to perform."

The first ship in was the Active. Governor Stevens rowed ashore at noon, and to the tight-lipped crowd gathered in the bullet-pocked cookhouse he acknowledged that he'd been wrong and entreated them not to lose heart or to leave. "Do not talk of leaving in this, our hour of adversity," he begged, "but stay 'til the shade of gloom is lifted. Gather heart! Rescue the territory from its present difficulties! To those faithful, the war's end will prove your prosperity!" He went on to say that Seattle could not be given up, else ten thousand men could not subdue the Indians. "You are the key to the Sound! Stay, and I promise vigorous steps shall be taken to save your city!"

Captain Keyes, in company with the governor, motioned it was time to leave. He was worried about the reports of Leschi attacking Fort Steilacoom, and within minutes the *Active* steamed away. This time Governor Stevens did not entreat Captain Ganesvoort to abandon the town. Nor did he take Reverend Blaine with him.

Left behind, Reverend Blaine agreed to conduct the funeral service planned for the young marine and Milton Holgate. At three o'clock everyone packed the little white church beneath the dark forest skirt. A half hour later they huddled in the rain to see their slain laid to rest. Widow Holgate, her head bowed and tears coursing her cheeks, suddenly began, softly, to sing:

> Lord Jesus, think on me,
> And purge away my sin;
> From earthborn passions, set me free,
> And make me pure within.

Few knew the words—but it was the widow's song.

> Lord Jesus, think on me,
> Amid the battle's strife;
> In all my pain and misery,
> Be thou my health and life.

Her voice had grown stronger, and, with her eyes gazing peacefully upon the hastily built coffin of her son, she took hold of her daughters' hands—Abbie Jane's and Olivia's. Abbie Jane reached for her husband's hand. Olivia took Edmund Carr's. They in turn each took the hands of those next to them: Edmund, Louisa; Louisa, David; David, Henry Smith. Henry Smith took little Alice Mercer's hand in his own large one, and Alice slipped her other hand into her father's.

Uncle Tommy took Mr. Bell's hand; Mr. Bell took Mr. Yesler's. All through the crowd they reached out to each other, and Louisa, learning the unfamiliar tune, began to hum along with Widow Holgate as she courageously finished the song.

> Lord Jesus, think on me,
> Nor let me go astray—
> Through darkness and perplexity
> Point Thou the heavenly way.
>
> Lord Jesus, think on me,
> That, when this life is past,
> I may th'eternal brightness see,
> And share Thy joy at last . . .

The last words seemed to linger in the air. The rain fell quietly, pattering against their umbrellas and bonnets, and dripped off the leaves in the mangled underbrush behind the church. Over the bay a seagull wheeled. Reverend Blaine cleared his throat. "Amen. And now, dust to dust, ashes to ashes, we commend your souls, Robert Wilson and Milton Holgate, to the Lord God who made us all."

After the funeral the men partitioned the upper floor of the blockhouse into small rooms for each family staying there; and when night came on, those not on guard rested on beds made on the floor. But only the children seemed to sleep this night, for it was a melancholy little group, two of their number fresh in their graves, the rest worried for their own futures.

"David?" Louisa whispered, seeking his face in the dark with her hand.

He slid his hand over hers. Automatically their fingers entwined. He lifted their hands to his lips and kissed each of her knuckles.

"I talked with Mandy," she whispered, relishing the cool softness of her dear husband's lips against her skin, the brush of his beard on her wrist.

"Is she all right?"

"Yes. She went down to the Point after coming to warn me. But a lot of the friendlies were so scared of the hostiles they went to Alki. She said Suwalth sent Nancy over there."

"He told me. Some went clear over to Port Madison. They weren't so sure we could repulse the hostiles."

"Mandy says the shells saved us."

"The shells, God, luck, friends . . ."

"She said the hostiles understood how the grape and canister could cut down the trees and tear up the earth. But the shells that struck and laid quiet for a time on the ground and then shot off again? They thought the shells had to be bad medicine. They wondered if the evil spirits they'd invoked against us had turned against them."

"Maybe when we wish evil against someone it *does* come back on us."

"David? What's wrong?"

He chewed on her knuckles lightly, then kissed them again. "I've hardly had time to talk with you . . . since coming back from Fort Duwamish. That seems like a long time ago, doesn't it? But it's only been two days."

"Did Yoke-Yakeman say something?"

"He said a lot of things."

"Like what?"

"Well . . . one thing he said . . . when Leschi first planned to attack us? He didn't want to hurt any of the settlers, only the soldiers and marines. I guess he'd figured a way to do it. But then Owhi arrived through the mountains and told him about Chief Peo-Peo-Mox-Mox."

"The Oregon volunteers killed Peo-Peo-Mox-Mox, didn't they?"

"Yes."

"And Leschi didn't know?"

"Oh, I'm sure he knew. He just didn't know *how* he died. *None* of us were told that," he said bitterly.

Beginning to get a sense of how deeply David was troubled, Louisa quietly loosened her fingers from his and began running her hand over his chest, as if to calm a baby with colic. She didn't know what else to do.

He said, "Do you remember how upset I was when I got back from White River? Because the Indians had mutilated the men so terribly, the ones we'd been forced to leave behind the night Slaughter was killed? Corporals Barry and Clarendon? Do you remember how upset I was?"

How could she forget?

"Do you remember?"

"Yes."

"The mutilation I saw," he said in a strained voice, "was nothing compared to what the Oregon boys did to the Walla Walla chief."

"Worse?" she gasped, sitting up in surprise, and to get her breath.

"Shh!" He pulled her back into his arms. "Much worse, Liza. They even dug him back up after he was buried to continue their deprivations—"

"Don't tell me, don't tell me that part!" She made an effort to cover her ears.

"Shhh . . . shh . . . I won't. But Owhi *did* tell Leschi. And I can't help but wonder if this is why he changed his mind about killing the settlers. Because if they'd broken through yesterday, they'd have killed all of us and not thought twice!"

"This is what's bothering you? That Leschi's—"

"From the beginning," David interrupted her, "Leschi's been in the right, you know that. Shoot, we *all* know that. That he's restrained himself as well as he has is astonishing. But when you start adding everything up—Peo-Peo-Mox-Mox, McAllister, Eaton, the governor, the wretched treaty— *what's he supposed to do?* And I have to ask myself why I'm fighting him. Why *am* I, Liza?"

"I didn't think that you *were,* David."

"I was yesterday."

"In self-defense."

He sighed. "It's *always* been self-defense. From the very beginning it's been self-defense. Kill or be killed. And that's the trouble with war, I think. Politicians set up the game and send us off, and we're all so desperate for our miserable little lives that we willingly kill just to keep on breathing. You want to know what's worse? Men actually get so they enjoy the killing. 'Let's go kill Indians,' they say, and they laugh. They *laugh,* Liza! I've heard them! Men I call my friends! And do you think those Oregon boys *wept* while doing what they did to Chief Peo-Peo-Mox-Mox?"

"Shhh," she cautioned. His voice had grown hard and as taut as every muscle in his rigid body.

"I once asked you," he went on, dropping his voice to a low, harsh whisper, "how the Indians could be so barbaric as to mutilate the dead. It fairly tore out my heart to see such debaseness of the human soul. Now I know. Something unspeakable happens in war. Every perversion, everything vile, throws off its shadow and becomes alluringly glorious. Men gloat in the blood they spill, Liza. And if it isn't enough, they desecrate and defile, and to live with themselves afterward they call it good. I dare say bits and pieces of Peo-Peo-Mox-Mox's body will circulate this territory for a long time to come. And the real tragedy? People will actually look up to the evil in the men who did the butchering."

"Surely not!"

"I know they will," he said with conviction. "You know what else?" he whispered hoarsely, pulling her in close. "If it weren't for you and Mynez and the new baby, I'd give it up now. I'd go back to the Swale. And if the Indians in their wrath killed me, so be it. Because I'm sick of being on the wrong side of this war, Liza. I don't *want* to fight Leschi. I never did. And if ever there's anything holy in war maybe I might find it fighting *with* him, not against him. But then I look at you.

And I see all over again the lifeless bodies of those settlers at White River—" Suddenly he started to cry. She could feel the shudders go through his body, the breath in his lungs catch painfully in his throat. "—and I know," he whispered into her ear, his tears wetting her skin, "I would rather die than let this happen to you."

"Maybe we should just go back . . ." she whispered. "Forget all this and take our chances."

"The baby?" he whispered. "Mynez?" he asked. "Can we risk them?"

"That's too easy to answer. We can't."

"You're right, we can't . . . No more than Leschi can let go either, and let his whole tribe die a slow death on that reservation Governor Stevens insists they live and die on."

"Will he come back, do you think?" she suddenly asked.

"He'll at least try. But don't worry," he whispered, kissing her, his composure regained. "There's to be a meeting in the morning to discuss how we can fortify the town."

Louisa thought through everything David had said. And if she tried to make any sense of the hopeless plight, for both whites *and* Indians, she came right to Governor Stevens.

"Hey, I nearly forgot . . ." David whispered.

She tipped back her head to see his comforting face. Such a sensitive, fine man. But oh! how it led him to suffer over right and wrong, and to instill a deep love and appreciation for the Indians!

"I forgot to tell you something else Suwalth told me today, Liza."

"What?" she sniffed, for she'd started to weep quietly, feeling sorry for them all—David, Leschi, for everyone.

"He told me that all of the houses outside Seattle for miles around have been burned to the ground—with the exception of two."

She thought her heart might stop. What was David telling her? She held her breath, hardly daring to hope.

"Uncle Tommy's," he said, "and ours."

276

She threw her arms around him and snuggled in close. "Oh, my darling David, is it really true? But it can't be! It just can't! It's too *good* to be true! *Is it?*"

"Shhh, shh!" He started to laugh a little, and she wiped her eyes at the happy sound and at the wonderful shaking of her husband's body as he stifled his growing laughter. "Would I lie?" he protested.

"No, of course not! But maybe Suwalth—"

"Liza, either the house is standing or it isn't!"

"But why? Why did they leave it—"

"We'll probably never know. But now," and he rolled her over onto her own space of floor, "it's time to go to sleep. Dream about the Swale, Louisa. Dream about going home when this is over."

Home . . . What a wonderful word! She had resigned herself to never seeing her wonderful little house in the Swale. But now, miraculously, it was hers again! In minutes she *was* asleep, the war and all of David's burning questions and terrible torment forgotten. She dreamt of her sweetbriar coming into bloom.

35

January into February, a fortnight

Coquilton, on the 28th, sent word by a Lake Indian, "that within one moon he would return with 20,000 warriors, and, attacking by land and water, destroy the place in spite of all the war-ship could do to prevent."

—Lieutenant T. S. Phelps, *Decatur*
in *Reminiscences of Seattle*

Old General Wool eventually responded to the territory's pleas for help. On January 30 [29], the steamer *Republic* set 200 regular army soldiers ashore at Steilacoom with their new commander, a strapping Colonel named Silas Casey.

—J. A. Eckrom, historian
in *Remembered Drums*

*W*ithin days of the attack against Seattle, Colonel Casey, sent by General Wool, and two companies of the Ninth Infantry arrived at Fort Steilacoom, bringing the total

278

number of regulars on the Sound to nearly a thousand men. Along with Captains Keyes and Maloney—like Governor Stevens in Olympia—Casey took over the command and started putting together a comprehensive, aggressive war policy that would commence, God willing, in a fortnight.

During this same fortnight, Seattle's pioneers furtively barricaded their town against Leschi's promised return.

Thirty hours after the battle, and bearing another warning from the hostiles, Clakum had arrived in a downpour of rain—only to discover the town already spurred by fear, and plans for its fortification drawn. Every able-bodied man was either working on the second blockhouse or standing home guard under "Captain" Judge Lander.

David was summoned from his work on the new blockhouse to translate. The message turned out to be a repeat of the hostile's first warning. *They'd be back within the month.* "Will they?" he asked Clakum.

"Halo." Yes.

Knowing that the Lake Washington subchief had been drawn into the war against his wishes, David told him of the arrangements being made to move Tecumseh and Suwalth's friendlies over to Alki or across the Sound, away from Leschi. Did he want to go with them? *Halo,* yes, Clakum confessed, but his band was being held hostage by Owhi and Leschi. Reluctantly he returned to the forest, and Judge Lander's scouts secretly followed.

In the morning, the drenched scouts (another day of pelting rain) returned to report that Leschi was camped only five miles away on Lake Washington and in no obvious hurry to leave. Yesler hastily donated seventy thousand feet of sawed lumber awaiting shipment so construction could begin immediately on the proposed stockade: two parallel fences, five feet high, a foot and a half apart, the intervening space to be packed solid with sawdust to make it bullet-proof. The enclosure would run from Plummer's house

279

on the Point, north along the shoreline; up behind the cook-house, past the parsonage and White Church; then west over the bluff down to the water's edge. Almost all the village would be included.

Captain Ganesvoort, to give his howitzer greater mobility through the mud, ordered the roads from the wharf to the Point graded. An ambitious project. Stumps had to be uprooted, logs hauled, piled, cradle-hills leveled, an esplanade built across the lagoon to enable the gun to sweep from one end of town to the other. Stumps too big to be extracted with levers had to be burned, their fires kept alive day and night. All in the pouring rain.

Driven by fear and unwilling to stop for the rain, the men adopted a costume that allowed them to remain outdoors for hours: warm underwear; heavy marine trousers tucked into high cowhide boots; five blue flannel shirts; a folded blanket draped around the neck, crossed in front and secured with a cartridge belt or pin; and a slouch hat. When the rain let up they simply tugged off four of their five flannel shirts and hung them to dry near a stump fire. When the rain started in again all they had to do was slip back into their shirts and carry on.

Madam Damnable, however, was not so easily circumvented. Captain Ganesvoort's howitzer road had to pass right by her Felker House. For whatever reason the coarse, harsh Irish hotel manager disliked everyone. At best she was a terrible woman; her tongue, Indian dogs, and apron of stones and wood sticks a terror to all. But the worst of her hatred she reserved for the marines.

When the first division started in with their picks and shovels on Friday, the first of February, they were startled out of their wits by the sudden blast of her approach. Out she came like a red-faced fury with an apron of rocks and three savage dogs. At first the marines stared in stupefied surprise, not sure what she meant. When they knew—they

280

scattered, away from her barrage of stones and biting dogs, their ears ringing with curses not even *they* knew!

After that the four divisions judiciously avoided her section of the road, happy to work elsewhere. When all else was finished, the second division began the Felker House stretch.

After two blows of their picks the cursing banshee with her man-eating dogs and a new apronful of stones came at them like a tornado from hell. The men gave way before the storm, officers too, fleeing as if Satan himself was after them.

The third division's turn! Plucking up what courage they could muster, Lieutenant Phelp's fourteen men assessed their task. For once the house appeared deserted. Not a sound came from its silent walls. Not even a dog was seen tethered out back. Encouraged, they sprang to work with the energy of desperate men. The road rapidly progressed, the house was reached, nearly passed, when suddenly the door banged open and out she flew, a demon in petticoats, a bolt from a catapult! To the men's astonishment, the air seemed instantly filled with sticks, stones, curses, and dogs! They blanched, wavered, *and though they'd withstood the charge of hundreds of hostiles just days before,* they now broke in a panic, scattering in all directions to escape the hellish hatred of Madam Damnable!

Captain Ganesvoort lost his patience. Enough was enough. "I'll just have a wee talk with her," he told his lieutenants. "Surely she knows the road is a military necessity."

"But Captain—"

"Tut, tut, Drake, I'm sure she's a reasonable woman, if reasonably approached." Ganesvoort straightened the lapels of his uniform jacket and strode over to the hotel. He knocked on the door, waited, introduced himself, and started to speak—

Being at close range he got clobbered right between the eyes. He came tearing back at a clip with the harridan and her dogs in hot pursuit, rocks, dogs, and curses flying. He didn't look back. "Do your duty," he barked at the four lieutenants while holding the bridge of his broken nose and hastening on. "This road *will* be finished."

Yes, but how? Lieutenant Hughes suggested they go in at night—*but the nights were quiet, the dogs alert, and Madam Damnable never slept!* Lieutenant Phelps thought they could send in the whole force—*but what was an entire ship's crew against the one woman?* Lieutenant Drake wondered about a diversion, half the crew out front, the other half attacking the road out back—*but two parties could be stoned as easily as one!*

Two more days they tried, each time driven back. Finally, February the 12th and at their wits' end, the fourth division under Lieutenant Dallas started. Boldly they struck their blow, picks into the ground. Like a flash, out darted the she-devil with her usual arsenal in hand. Peremptorily she ordered them off the lot.

Lieutenant Dallas, supported by Sam Silk, a *huge* man, quartermaster, and an old-time salt, ventured to parley. But no more than a dozen words passed his lips than she let fly with a billet aimed straight for his teeth, accompanied by a torrent of abuse and threats. Lieutenant Dallas peremptorily *did* leave the lot—and left Sam Silk to his own devices.

Sam, arms folded over his massive chest, closely, curiously scrutinized the masculine woman. "What do you mean?" he suddenly bellowed even as she reached again into her bumpy apron, "you dreadful old harridan, raising perdition like this? I know you, you old curmudgeon! Many the time I've seen you howling thunder around Fell's Point, Baltimore! You're a cursed pretty one, ain't you?"

So taken aback by reference to her past, Madam Damnable let go of her apron; rocks, stones, and sticks spilling down around her boots. With one glance of concentrated hatred, she bolted. The thunderclap of her front door was the last anyone heard of her! And three days later, February the 15th, the fortifications were in place: stockade, road, esplanade, and blockhouse—just a few days over a fortnight of construction.

For the women and children confined to the fort during these dark, fearful days there was no such comic relief to dispel their fear. Crowded, cold, the hours endless, the tedium untenable—not even a window in the blockhouse to give visual respite—there was only fear.

And increasing hunger. With the friendlies being sent away, there were fewer and fewer Indian men with whom they could trade for fresh game; and their butchered or stolen cattle meant no milk to drink either. The children cried and couldn't be comforted. Susannah Mercer recalled years later how she and her sisters mourned the loss of their new pet cow—Hardy Axe Handles. Oh, how they'd looked forward to the milk and butter!

In the middle of all this sadness and discomfort Sally Bell lay dying in her bed. Her little girls did what they could to make her comfortable where there was no comfort. Each evening she'd whisper, "Your dear little hands have brought me everything I needed today."

To keep off their despair Louisa started sewing an American flag, and invited the ladies to join. They used blue, white, and red flannel, and though the stitches taken in the dim light of the darkened fort were not so fine as they'd like, they agreed no Betsy Ross flag could be more precious! Some of the women, when it was too dark to see or their eyes grew tired, rested by folding a hem and sewing for awhile with their eyes shut.

Oddly, crowded though they were and living on top of each other like bees in a hive, they remained in wonderful harmony. Afraid the Indians might kill them, they wanted to die in peace with each other. Besides, the discomfort they shared was luxury compared to what they'd endured on the Oregon Trail; and when tempers flared, one or the other of them would start a story that soon brought smiles and reminded them all of their relative, current good fortune.

"Remember when we spilled the peach cobbler? How we thought we might just die of disappointment?"

"We was just coming out of Snake River Canyon . . ."

"Holy Moses, but I thought he was a goner!"

"I think a part o' me died when we left my little one in her grave."

And so they comforted each other.

When the fortifications were at last announced done, there was some relief to the conditions. The children could play outdoors now, the women could stretch their legs. Gratefully they took short walks along the beach, and down to the Point—surprised to see a tidy, civilized little town. *Where were all the stumps and underbrush?*

Families whose cabins were inside the stockade felt safe enough to return to their homes during the day and attend household duties, returning at sundown to sleep.

Families who lived at a distance or whose homes had been destroyed, remained; sharing the single stove, taking turns with the cooking, fetching water from Mr. Yesler's cookhouse pump.

At first thrilled to be let out of the fort, Louisa soon discovered that the new stockade was just a bigger pen—holding her a prisoner of war as surely as the blockhouse had done, fear of Leschi's return no less real. When David came home that first afternoon for supper, he found her stirring thin soup at the stove. She was in tears. "I can't seem to help it anymore," she said.

"You have enough to cry about, I should think," he told her, shrugging out of his wet shirts, one by one.

"Is Leschi still camped at the lake?" She dried her eyes on her apron, trying to get hold of herself so they could eat supper without her ruining it.

"So far as Judge Lander can figure. Shall I sit Mynez up to the table?"

"Please. Why does he just sit there, David? I mean, why doesn't he attack us, like he said he would? Why must he sit like a cat, watching us, unnerving us all?"

"I expect he's waiting for reinforcements from Kamiakin or the Haida. Sit down, Liza, you look so tired. I'll pour the soup."

"I don't want to go back to the blockhouse tonight."

"Shall we stay here then?"

"I'm too scared to stay here. What if Leschi comes back tonight?"

"I guess we better go to the blockhouse then."

For Arthur, as Speaker of the House in Olympia, this fortnight following the attack was the longest of his life as the closing business of the legislative session dragged on and on, and on: approving Chief Pat Kanim's offer of fifty-five warriors to bring in Leschi; debating whether or not to accept Chief Seattle's pledge of one hundred fifty warriors; expanding Governor Stevens's original call to arms to include eighteen companies with twenty captains, twenty first lieutenants, eighteen second lieutenants and 1,002 noncommissioned officers and privates for the territorial militia—a total of 1,060 men; projecting war costs: one million dollars—away and above what it would have cost to provide the Indians fair reserves in the first place; drawing up memorials for Acting Governor Charles Mason to take back to Washington City, including a demand for the removal of General Wool; learning from Colonel Casey what the army intended to do to hasten the war's end; and granting the divorce of Diana Collins from Luther Collins

Finally, came adjournment. That same afternoon Arthur shepherded his family aboard a steamer going north. The next evening, putting into Elliott Bay, he was dismayed to see the red glow of fires burning against the darkened skyline. Nauseous fear swept over him and Mary Ann as they gazed in horror at what used to be Seattle. *David . . . Louisa . . . little Mynez! What's happened to them?* he thought with sick dread even as Mary Ann leaned over the rail and threw up.

36

February into March, a month

February, 1856, the several volunteer companies being duly organized and equipped, a start was made for the spring campaign. Governor Stevens determined to establish a line of blockhouses along the old military road, in which to house supplies, open communication across the mountains, and drive back any hostile bands that might have crossed to this side during the winter. It was known by this time that most of the depredations have been the work of the Yakima and Klikitat tribes . . .

—Urban E. Hicks, private
in *A Small World of our Own*

"Mary!"

Excitedly, Arthur pulled Mary Ann back from the rail and spun her around. "I'm all turned around! The fires, they're on the Duwamish River! Not Seattle!"

Mary Ann, rubbing her coat sleeve over her mouth, looked out to where Arthur pointed.

"*That's* east!" Arthur declared, pointing beyond her shoulder.

Oh, the blessed, tranquil, black night sky! Seattle was safe! Leschi hadn't—"Oh, Arthur, you're never wrong, I thought sure . . . Arthur, you're *never* wrong!" she repeated, turning to face him. *"But I'm so glad you were this once!"* and she threw herself weeping into his arms.

"Well, for heaven's sakes," he blustered, patting her clumsily on the back. "I can understand crying beforehand, when we thought the city was all ash, but now, when we know it isn't—"

"Muckle sum!" She buried her cold nose in his scratchy beard.

"Hey, who's telling me to shut up?"

"I am!" and she giggled suddenly.

The fires Arthur and Mary Ann saw were from Leschi's war party, at last dispersing and assuaging their resentment by burning every home, barn, and fence along the Duwamish River as they went. No longer could they wait for Chief Scowell with his northern Haida warriors, or Qualchin, son of Owhi, from Yakima. Food had given out and they needed better shelter from the weather. Also, One-Eyed Tom, Econ-O-Lin, and Stuttering George had come in from Chief Seattle's reserve. That's when Leschi had given the orders to strike camp. *But we'll be back, once we're organized again,* he thought to himself grimly while leading Owhi and the others to his secret camp on Green River near the base of the mountains. As to how things might have gone had Owhi listened to him, and they'd attacked Steilacoom first and gotten better rifles . . . This he didn't want to think about.

Even as Leschi withdrew to Green River Colonel Casey and Governor Stevens made their move, simultaneously deploying all of their forces into the field. By mid-February hundreds of their scouts and soldiers were combing the forests for hostiles, not stopping for snow, rain, or swollen rivers, but keeping up a continuous, dogged pursuit over every known trail—and the many hidden ones too, keen woodsmen-soldiers ferreting out the unmarked forest paths. Scarcely would they return from one foray than they'd be ordered out again while all over the Sound blockhouses and supply depots went up with lightning speed, opening the way for communication and movement of supplies along Military Road between Olympia, Fort Steilacoom, and Connell's Prairie, the last open place before entering the mountains.

Additionally, small bands of Chehalis, Squaxin, and Cowlitz natives—hired by Stevens and led by their Indian agents—came up from the south to help scour the woods and swamps; and from the north came Chief Pat Kanim with fifty-five warriors, his sole purpose being to collect twenty dollars for every hostile Indian head he severed, forty dollars for every chief, and eighty dollars for the coveted head of Leschi—*gruesome payment promised by Little Man In Big Hurry*. And so the net was set and tightened.

Leschi was but two days in his Green River camp when Pat Kanim found him. Had the dogs not barked a warning this might well have ended the war. Shouting over the river that separated them, Pat Kanim announced he wouldn't leave until he had Leschi's head. Leschi, surprised by the betrayal, bellowed back he did not think so. Ten hours later, several men dead, two beheaded, Leschi furtively, quickly, retreated to White River, leaving men like Stahi, Sluggia, his brother Quiemuth—warriors without families, who could move easily and quickly—to strike back with fantastic retaliation. Over the next weeks they zeroed in on isolated farmers and pioneers. Teamster Northcraft, driving oats from the fort out to the Yelm Prairie depot. William White, coming home from church with his family. John Bradley, plowing his fields. Ruthlessly they wielded their advantage, and whatever relief might have been felt around the Sound and in Seattle at Leschi's withdrawal was short-lived. *Leschi was not done!*

The army and government responded to the atrocities from all fronts—Yelm Prairie, Montgomery Prairie, Lemmon's Prairie, Muckleshoot Prairie—but whenever and wherever they flushed out a band of warriors the hostiles always attacked and drubbed them. They knew the country; how to hide, where to flee. So Colonel Casey started watching them, and then began emulating them by sending out his own patrols in short, swift forays designed to surprise, kill, and withdraw before a return fire could be made. He also copied their tactics by setting up small ambushes of three or four men along the trails at night. It was in this way he accidentally captured Kanasket, Leschi's first lieutenant and nemesis, coming down Elhi Hill onto Lemmon's Prairie one clear morning at dawn.

Private Hehl, about to give up his ambush, suddenly caught the glimmer of gunmetal in the morning's early sunlight, and fired. The bullet pierced Kanasket's shoulder, plowed down his backbone, and, as his friends dissolved back into the woods, he fell with a scream of brutal pain to the ground, his legs paralyzed—though he came up at the waist fast enough when Private Hehl and his friends approached. Shrieking his defiance and hatred of white men, Kanasket, despite his agonizing pain, struck out at all who came within reach, stabbing with his spear, wielding his new Kentucky rifle like a club, finally whipping out a butcher knife and shrieking in Chinook, "I am Kanasket! Kill me! I hate you! I would kill you if I could! *Kanasket, tyee, memaloose nika! Nika memaloose Bostons!*"

It took two men to disarm him, and then drag him into camp by his heels, still fighting and twisting from the waist and shouting, "*Now witka, Kanasket, niker!* Kill me!" The soldiers gathered around to watch him die, his wound clearly mortal and horrible. "I have always hated whiteskins! I will always hate you! My voice is for war! The voice of my people is for war!"

Colonel Casey ordered his hanging. The men looked about for rope and tree. When they approached him again he fought back with such savagery that one man later wrote he'd never beheld such hatred in a human face; it was like looking at a demon. *"My heart is wicked toward you! Kill me! My heart will always be wicked toward you!"* he growled, seizing the arms that came at him, and biting through the flesh. He spit skin and blood into the faces of those closest to him. Having enough, Corporal O'Shaughnessy put the muzzle of his gun to the war chief's head and without waiting for an order to the contrary, pulled the trigger.

Standing on the top of Elhi Hill and overlooking Lemmon's Prairie, Leschi listened stoically, unblinking, to Kanasket's men who brought the terrible news. Such a vainglorious, proud man, Kanasket. Arrogant and boastful. So sure of himself, so demeaning of others. *Why then do I feel so sad?* wondered Leschi. *Why am I lost, bereft, why is my heart torn with anguish?* But he knew the answer. Kanasket had known how to fight—the enemy and their own faltering spirits. It was Kanasket's hatred of the whiteskins and his unfaded vision of the past that had kept them united and strong.

But if Leschi's heart was torn with anguish, his mind was tormented with worry as well. For he felt keenly the tightening net to which he and his followers were being subjected. Hunted like cougars, driven place to place, they were now suffering the desperate pinch of want. Children cried with hunger. Women shivered in ragged shawls. Old men with walking sticks tottered about on skinny legs. *The hunter and the hunted,* thought Leschi, staring down at the cluster of white, bell-shaped tents just beginning to show themselves in the winter's thin daylight.

At first he'd faced but the one army, the pioneer volunteers. Then the regulars had come with their blue uniforms, yellow, red, and orange stripes down the legs. Now the worst of all, his own kind. Pat Kanim, he knew, was in Seattle, turning in his severed heads for payment. But he'd be back. As would all the enemy—volunteers, regulars, his own race. Down there on Lemmon's Prairie was but the front line, the hunters narrowing in.

Leschi shook off his depression. He had no time for self-pity. Taking the reins of his now skeletal cayuse, he leapt gently onto her back. His enemies were many and united, yes, but Stahi, Sluggia, and Quiemuth were back; and they'd brought with them all the available fighting men along the Nisqually River from Muck Creek to the Mashel in the hills. Even without Kanasket to stir their hatred, they would manage until Qualchin arrived.

Like everyone else barricaded behind Seattle's stockade, David and Louisa kept track of the war through their newspapers:

MARCH 1: While on his way to reconnoiter with Colonel Casey, Lieutenant Kautz was ambushed at the White River ford at approximately half past nine, Saturday past.

Receiving news of their distress, our able commander, Col. Casey, at once sent Captain Keyes with fifty-four men from Lemmon's Prairie, led by an Indian youth, on a forced march in an attempt to rescue Kautz's company, arriving at the river where it was clearly uncrossable.

Keyes sized up the situation and told the Indian lad that he would shoot him on the spot if he didn't lead them to the real crossing.

"Halo, nike kumtux," the lad responded in Chi-

nook jargon, "Yes, I understand."

He then conducted them through the woods to a spot where the river spread out broad and shallow.

With their cartridge boxes slung around their shoulders, the soldiers crossed over, but it was tough going; the water was icy cold and it came up to the armpits of the shorter men. It was 3:00 by the time Keyes and his soldiers were safely across with their powder dry.

They then moved against the Indians and they retreated.

One man was killed, nine wounded.

"I don't know why I keep reading the paper, David," sighed Louisa late one afternoon in early March. They were seated at the table, sharing the lamp. "Maybe it's because I keep hoping for some *good* news. But it's always the same old fighting. Over and over and over. They just fight in different places, that's all."

"At least it's nowhere near us right now," he mumbled, snapping his section of the paper. "And at least it's soldiers in line of fire. Not us." The door suddenly banged in, startling them. Arthur was on the stoop.

Louisa sighed and gave him a stern scowl, though she knew it would never discourage Arthur's lack of consideration for others' privacy. She might as well count him an Indian in that regard and consider him incorrigible.

"Can you come down to the Sawdust for a minute, Dave, and take a look at what Pat Kanim's brought in? When we gave Stevens the go-ahead in the Legislative Assembly to hire him, we didn't authorize—"

"Arthur?" queried Louisa, narrowing her eyes a little at him. "What's going on?" Something in his voice suggested everything from anger to incredulity to personal distress.

293

David heard it too, and was pulling on his boots. "Wait! I want to go!" she said, her mind made up.

"I don't think you better, Louisa." Arthur banged his boot toe nervously into the floor. "Especially in your condition. It could bring on labor."

"Oh, don't be so melodramatic, Arthur! Come on, Mynez, we're going for a walk," she declared.

"Liza!" he erupted. "You can't take Mynez! He's brought in two severed heads!"

She was so shocked she dropped Mynez's coat. Arthur reached down and snatched it up, handed it back to her. Her mouth, she realized, was still hanging open and she snapped it shut. "He's claiming Stevens agreed to pay him twenty dollars for every head!" said Arthur. "Forty for a chief's—"

"I get the picture, never mind," she said quietly. Then, *"He actually chopped the heads off?"*

"I don't think we need to discuss this in front of Mynez," said David sternly.

"Are you coming with me then, Dave?" Arthur asked.

"If I have to, I will. Louisa?"

"I don't want to go anymore!"

When David came back, his face was ashen and when she set out the pancakes for supper, he couldn't eat.

"Not even a *bite?*" she asked.

"No . . ."

"You didn't go and *look* at them, did you?"

"Kanim was standing there, holding them by the hair, Liza."

She set Mynez up to the table and tied on her bib. "I don't understand why he just didn't take them to Olympia. He knows where Stevens lives."

"Olympia's too far out of the way, and he's anxious to get back to the field."

"But why here?"

"He thought Captain Ganesvoort could take them to Stevens."

294

She picked up the spatula. "Somehow, I can't imagine him wanting anything to do with it."

"What choice does he have? Pat Kanim threatened to leave them at the cookhouse. Yesler had a fit." David flopped into the rocking chair. "You know, this war has gotten so—" He couldn't find the right word.

"Demented?" she tried.

He shut one eye. "Not quite the right word, but it'll do. Things are to the point, Liza, where I don't know who I'm afraid of more—Leschi or Governor Stevens."

She scooped the top pancake off the tier and turned it onto Mynez's little saucer. It took her daughter but a second.

"M!" she shrieked. *"My got a M!"* and she clapped her hands in delight. "Papa, Papa! My got a M!"

David got up and went over, then shook his head wearily and smiled even more wearily at Louisa. "You do think of the craziest things."

"I made you a 'D,'" she said hopefully.

"A 'D' I can eat," he told her.

After supper, just as they were getting ready to go to the blockhouse for the night, someone else came to the door. When Louisa answered the knock, she was surprised to see an Indian. "Clakum?" she asked, suddenly recognizing him in the moonlight. Goodness, what was he doing here? she wondered, stepping aside. *How did he get away from Leschi?*

As soon as he saw David he was talking a blue streak in Duwamish, and Louisa's heart started thumping in alarm so fast it hurt. What had happened? They were being surrounded? Leschi was back? Someone was dead? Suddenly David smiled.

"What, what is it?" She couldn't remember seeing David so happy, not in a long time! "David, what is it? What's he saying?"

"Sit down."

She sat on the stool, her huge stomach cramming against her lungs, making her breathing uncomfortably shallow.

"Clakum says Leschi's band is having a terrible time, Liza. Everyone's starving—"

"That's not why you're smiling."

"No, of course not. It makes me sad to hear things are that grim. A lot of people, Clakum says, are defecting and turning themselves in. Last week thirty people surrendered to Colonel Casey—"

"Is that how Clakum got away? Everyone's breaking up?" Suddenly she sat up straight with new, vibrant energy. *"The war is over?"*

His smile vanished. "No."

"Oh." She slumped back down.

"No, it's not over, not by a long shot. Qualchin got through Naches Pass with a hundred more of Kamiakin's best warriors."

"Then why were you smiling? It is so discouragingly bleak!"

His smile came back. "Because Clakum told me *why* the Swale and Uncle Tommy's house weren't burned!"

She blinked, and looked up at Clakum. "Why?" she whispered, hardly knowing what to think.

"*Leschi* said not to burn our house. And Nelson spared Uncle Tommy's too."

"I don't understand," she gasped, flabbergasted. "Leschi and Nelson, they specifically said not to burn our houses?"

"Remember last fall, just before I went to White River? For the first time? When Ben Wetmore kicked that bucket an Indian was filling at Yesler's pump?"

People, she knew, still talked about that day, and about how David had shamed Ben Wetmore.

"Remember that?" His eyes were all joy and wonder.

"Yes . . . but, David, what, I still don't understand!"

"That Indian was Leschi."

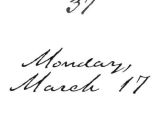

37

Monday, March 17

Madge Decatur was born in Fort Decatur in the year of the Indian War, on March 16th, 1856. "Madge is such a dainty thing!" people said.

—Emily Inez Denny, Madge's big sister
in *Blazing the Way*

The outlying homes that were not burned were those of David and Louisa Denny and Thomas Mercer. These two families had always treated the Indians with particular kindness and, even in the heat of battle, the Indians had returned the kindness.

—Gordon Newell, historian
in *Westward to Alki*

For David and Louisa and Uncle Tommy Mercer the war was over. The fighting might continue for awhile, and Leschi might even return to Seattle, but if in the heat of battle he'd singled them out for protection there was no need anymore for the two families to live in fear.

But if they were surprised by this turn of events, no one else was. Surprised at Leschi, yes, but not that it was the Dennys and Mercers upon whom he'd bestowed the kindness.

And so David and Louisa waited only for the baby to be born—Madge Decatur Denny—before going home. As if anxious to be there herself, Madge Decatur arrived a day early, just missing David's birthday. Louisa, euphoric with her new beautiful daughter, *and oh, she was so so beautiful,* thought it a fine and noble thing for Madge to do! Because now, on her father's birthday, they could all go home. *Home!*

Could it truly be?

The birth had been exceptionally easy, and Louisa, after having had such a hard time with Mynez two years before, decided she was made for having babies. "I'm going to have a dozen more!" she declared when Mary Ann put tiny Madge into her arms for the first time. "What a *wee* thing!" she exclaimed, roving her eyes over the baby's tiny nose and pink cheeks, her mass of curly yellow hair.

"She looks like a buttercup," said Mary Ann.

"Where did she get all this hair? It's like fluffy fine gold!"

"I've never seen a prettier baby, Liza. And she's as sweet as a doll too." Gently Mary ran her fingers through the baby's blond curls, yellower than Rollie's, and looser. Like spun flax, Mary thought.

The birth had been so easy and quick that Henry Smith decided there was no reason in the world for Louisa to stay in town, not if she and David were still disposed to going home. Which they were. And so as soon as Monday morning, the 17th, dawned—a frail, pretty day with a hint of sun in the sky—David and Uncle Tommy scurried about, packing the last-minute things: pots, pans, mattresses, bedding, clothes. For a week they'd been going out to their claims, taking the big items and getting ready for their move back. Now there was little to do but go.

The Mercer girls called good-bye to their friends, Becky Horton, Dorcas Phillips, Katy and Nora Denny, then clambered into their father's Conestoga. David carried Louisa down the blockhouse stairs. She blinked in the sunlight when they came out.

"Do you remember," she whispered when he stepped up with her still in his arms onto a stump behind the wagon, "our last night in Illinois? When you caught me sneaking my father's mirror into Pa's wagon?"

"You were as pretty as a picture that night."

"I remember thinking then that if you would just, *please dear God,* if you would just kiss me, I'd never *ever* be happier."

"I didn't do it, did I?"

"No."

"Shame on me."

"You could now!"

"What?" he teased, "in front of all these people?"

Arms around his neck, she smiled, narrowing her eyes enticingly at him.

The kiss was everything he did best all rolled into one. The crowd cheered and clapped. Louisa blushed.

"Well I didn't mean for you to go overboard!"

"Yes, you did!" he laughed. Carefully he climbed over the backboard, maneuvering her in his arms as easily as he might a child, and lowered her, sitting up, to the mattress Uncle Tommy and the girls had fixed for her. She looked around at the familiar narrow girth of the wagon. Not much room in these.

"David . . . it feels almost as if we're starting over again, headed for the Oregon Trail!"

"We're at the *end* of the trail, Liza."

"Are we *really* going home?"

"Yes." He kissed her tenderly. "Are you comfortable, Mrs. Denny?"

"Oh, David, let's hurry!"

How good God is! she thought in a rush, watching David clear the backboard with a graceful leap and drop to the ground below. Here she was, not only married to David Denny, but she was going home to her wonderful house, built by her beloved husband and spared so unexpectedly by Leschi, and she had two beautiful, sweet little girls! *Oh, Pamelia,* she whispered to the heavens, *you were so right! Spring does come again!*

Mary Ann handed over wee Madge.

"Oh, Mary, I'm so happy!"

"I still can't believe Leschi spared your house! But then I don't know why I'm surprised. We all know how kind David and Uncle Tommy are to the Indians. There now," she fussed, tugging down on Madge's little knit bonnet. "I've just changed her diapers. I think she should sleep all the way home. Mynez, darling," she called, "do you have a kiss for your Auntie Mary?"

Mynez, not understanding what was going on but enjoying all the excitement, crawled over the miscellaneous paraphernalia to give her aunt a slobbery kiss while everyone outside, one by one, came up to say good-bye.

Mrs. Butler cried into her husband's hanky.

Mrs. Yesler passed over a basket of rolls.

"I'll be praying for you," whispered Widow Holgate, "that the Lord will keep you safe out there."

"We have no reason to fear," Louisa assured the widow. "Not anymore."

Uncle Tommy whistled.

Time to go!

"Good-bye! Good-bye!" everyone called.

Louisa felt the wagon drop a little as the men jumped up onto the wagon seat in the front. Watch barked and trotted up alongside the wagon to where David sat.

"Good-bye!" hollered Arthur. He leapt up onto the stump in a single bound, hauling Rollie and Orion up with him.

Louisa waved, and blew kisses. Mynez stood at the backboard and blew kisses too.

The wagon lurched. Louisa, holding fast to Madge, automatically shot out an arm to steady Mynez.

"I'll hold her!" volunteered Mary Jane, taking a firm hold on Mynez and helping her to wave at everyone.

"Good-bye, good-bye!"

The wagon rumbled forward, gaining momentum through the stockade. The gate swung shut behind them. Then they clattered onto the rickety bridge that spanned the deep ravine just north of town. They were rattling off the planks onto the muddy, stumpy trail when Uncle Tommy suddenly whipped off his cap and shrieked, "Whoopeee!"

"Pa!" the girls chorused in frank shock at their father's uncharacteristic burst of enthusiasm.

"Girls!" he shouted back at them, waving his hat in the air. "We're going home!"

When he veered off the road, wagon jouncing, and entered a high grassy, meadow, it fairly took Louisa's breath to see her home. But there it was! The Swale!

What a dear, dear, *pretty house!* she thought, her heart pounding as she craned her neck to look, and she hugged her little baby close. Yes, everything just as she remembered . . . *though the logs aren't as golden,* she thought with a critical eye. A year's weather had dulled the smooth, peeled surface—but it gave the place a rather solid and substantial look that she liked very much.

"Whoa! Whoa there, Tib! Charlie!" Uncle Tommy pulled to a stop twenty feet from the house. The girls hopped out the back of the wagon. Mary Jane reached in for Madge, and Eliza Ann took Mynez. David came around to help Louisa and when she was at last standing on the precious, wonderful land that was theirs, she took her husband's steadying hand and slowly turned.

Her house, her garden, the little necessary house with twin seats. The chicken coop. David's smokehouse. The old stubborn stump that wouldn't come out.

"What you doing?" asked Mynez, gazing up curiously. "You have 'nother cinder in your eye?"

Louisa hardly heard her, she was so captivated at just being here. Two hundred yards behind the house stood the virgin forest, hazy in the spring sunlight, golden rays spilling through the dark green boughs to make a delightful, enchanted wood. Oh, how she had missed this! *Such a beautiful, wonderful, lonely place!*

But there was nothing frightful about the loneliness. The lush meadowlands opened to the south, drawing the eye, and there, in all her majesty, stood Mount Rainier, a dome of brilliant white snow floating in the sky. The majestic mountain had been, and would always be, an eternal landmark that rooted her and David to this place. Here was peace and here peace had been all along.

"Are you up to walking?" David asked. "Or shall I carry you to the door?"

"Let me walk, it's only a few feet," she said, stepping forward through the dewy grass. He matched her step for step, hand under her elbow, Mynez and the others hurrying ahead with armfuls of blankets and pillows. Watch leaped along, then darted off, his nose drawing him thither and yon. At the front porch David helped her up the two steps. At the top she stopped to look down on her sweetbriar, planted along the rail. "David, look, the leaves are beginning to bud!"

"Must be spring." He grinned. "Coming inside?"

"Yes."

Again, everything as she remembered. David's marvelous fireplace, so big that Katy used to be able to stand up in it. The tall bookcases, built on either side of the hearth. Ma and Pa's pictures, she saw, had been brought back and were on the mantel, just as before. The floor was nicely swept, the cougarskin rug put down. Her kitchen, which occupied the

302

opposite side of the room, had been meticulously scrubbed by the Mercer girls. Her big regulation ship's stove fairly gleamed from the polishing.

"You should have seen the cupboards, Mrs. Denny!" Susannah declared, all the girls showing her at once just how clean everything was. "Mice, mice, everywhere!"

"Father thinks you had skunks too," said Eliza Ann.

"Skunks!" Louisa recoiled.

"Oh, we aired everything out!"

Her bedroom, built off the back wall, looked inviting and luxurious! *Such space!* she thought. Especially after being so cramped in the blockhouse! All but sleeping on top of everyone in town! Under her bed were David's lockers, built so they could easily be pulled out, clothes and blankets put in, and then shoved back underneath, out of sight. The window, she realized, had been washed. How hard the girls had worked! There was her oak washstand—with a vase of fresh ferns. "You're too thoughtful," she told Eliza Ann. Next to the stand, a vacant corner, where someday—when she and David were rich—she would have an armoire.

David came in with the mattress and dropped it into place on the bed frame. Straightening up, he stood grinning at her. "I can't believe we're home. Can you?"

"No."

Uncle Tommy poked his nose through the door. "Girls, see if you can rustle up some sheets and get the bed made for Mrs. Denny. I've put her quilt out here on the table. *Clean* sheets," he added. Then suddenly he pointed to the rocking chair. "There's the linens. In fact, one of you clear everything off the chair and bring it out here. Mrs. Denny looks like she could use a sit."

"Yes, I could," she admitted.

"Alice, that's the job for you, I think!" declared Uncle Tommy to his youngest, and he playfully pointed his finger at her like a pistol.

"Yes, Pa!"

Louisa lowered herself into the chair after Alice pushed it across the floor for her, idly watching David as he hung up their hats on the back of the door. Her ratty old sunbonnet. His knit cap. The children's bonnets. Misty-eyed from the overwhelming reality of being home, she felt a big lump grow in her throat. *They were home, they truly were.* For nothing could say it so well as the sight of their hats all hanging in a row along the top of the door.

Uncle Tommy brought in one more load of wood. Louisa could hear the younger girls outside, throwing a bit of feed into the coop for the chickens, brought out the day before. And then Mary Jane was handing her the baby. Time for the Mercers to go; they were anxious to get out to their own homestead and get moved in.

While Louisa unbuttoned her dress to nurse the baby, David and Mynez went outside to say good-bye. "Thanks again, Uncle Tommy!" David hollered from the porch.

"We'll bring breakfast over in the morning! Tell Liza to sleep in, if she can! Giddyup there, girls!"

"Hey, where they go?" asked Mynez, tugging on David's pants, watching the wagon bounce across the meadow and disappear into the trees. "Papa! Where they go?" she repeated sharply.

"They're going home."

She laughed. "But that the wrong way, Papa!"

He laughed, too, and reached down to pat her head. "Nope, Missy Mynez, for once that's the *right* way," and he scooped her up and brought her indoors.

"When *we* go home, Papa?" she asked, slithering out of his arms head first, trusting him not to drop her.

"This *is* home!"

She laughed again, giggling. "This not home, silly! My not live here!"

Louisa felt new things stirring in her when she went to bed that night, the frogs outside singing with spring madness in all the wet places of the Swale. This night was the beginning of life far different than she and David had ever known—and they were here to meet it. They would meet it stronger because they'd known despair and fought it to a standstill. And they'd value their life and everything they possessed far more because it had been taken away from them, *and then so amazingly given back.*

She slid her hand into David's, whispering, "Who would have thought it was Leschi that day, way back last fall."

He threaded his fingers through hers, rubbing the end of his thumb against her palm. "It was a simple thing, Liza. And it makes me sad it should have meant so much to him."

"But not everyone is like you, David. Leschi wanted to thank you."

"Should a man be thanked for normal human courtesy?" He groaned suddenly. "Oh, dear . . ."

"*What?*"

"I forgot all about the chickens. I have to go lock the door so the raccoons can't get in."

"Hurry back."

"I will."

Outside the moon was clear and bright, the stars a million prickles of light. David stepped off the porch conscious of the teeming chorus of frogs swelling loudly from the creek that ran between his place and the Mercers'. They were fairly mad with spring, and hearing them he felt a wave of contentment and purpose. In the morning he would begin spring plowing!

Following the bob of his lamplight, Watch at his side, he headed for the coop, listening to the frogs, feeling the cold blades of grass tickle his bare ankles. And then suddenly he was conscious of Leschi. For a moment he stopped. An amazing man. A man who loved justice. David hurried on. The frogs fell silent. He locked the coop and started back.

"Come on, Watch," he whispered at the door. "Bedtime."

Louisa was half asleep when he slipped in shivering beside her. The quilt was warm and comforting. Beneath the colored squares and patches it was their own little world, where everything belonged just to them and no one else. He was glad to be here. "Liza?"

"Mmm?"

"Why did you marry me?"

She slid into his waiting arms, murmuring the answer she always gave him whenever he asked. "Because there were no other men around . . ."

"No, you married me because you love me, Liza."

"Because I love you . . ." She kissed his chest. "Because I was *born* to love you."

David smiled.

Outside, the frogs started up again.

Inside, jostled when the door swung shut and still aswing, were four hats—two little bonnets, a sunbonnet, and a cap.

Afterword

The result of the war was that the Indians got all that they contended for.

—John Boatman, pioneer
quoted in Ezra Meeker's *Pioneer Reminiscences*

Leschi lost, and won.

He was forced to flee through the snowy mountains to eastern Yakima about the same time David and Louisa returned to the Swale. The war in western Washington bumbled along with sporadic skirmishes, massacres, outbreaks, and other acts of violence until finally Governor Stevens capitulated. In August, after ten months of fighting, a million dollars spent, and untold lives lost, Stevens sat down with the elders of the Nisqually nation and redrew the boundary lines—granting them all of the land Leschi had requested in the first place.

Sadly, two and half years later, after three lengthy, heated trials, Leschi was sentenced to death by hanging. This is his statement to the court:

307

I do not see that there is any use of saying anything. My attorney has said all he could for me. I do not know anything about your laws. I have supposed that the killing of armed men in war time was not murder; if it was, the soldiers who killed Indians were guilty of murder, too . . .

I went to war because I believed that the Indians had been wronged by the white men, and did everything in my power to beat the Boston soldiers, but for lack of numbers, supplies, and ammunition I have failed. . . . As God sees me, this is the truth.

He crossed himself, and said:

Ta-te mono,
Ta-te lem-mas,
Ta-te ha-le-hach,
tu-ul-li-as-sist-ah.

There is the Father,
this is the Son,
this is the Holy Ghost;
these three are all one and the same, Amen.

At his execution six weeks later Leschi reiterated his innocence and stated that he would not be the first to die under false evidence. "But if I can die for my people I am willing. Christ died for others."

His executioner, when the deed was done, said, "I have executed an innocent man."

In Seattle today there are two parks to commemorate the lives of Leschi and David Denny, two men whose natures were so remarkably similar but whose lives, because of their race, drastically differed.

Leschi Park is situated on the same shoreline of Lake Washington where the war party camped after attacking the city on the 26th of January 1856. A monument commemorates his life and death.

Denny Park is but a sliver of its original size, the city having eaten into it over the years, but was donated to the city by David and Louisa as a much larger piece. The fragment that is left sits near the Seattle Center—which was, of course, once upon a time, the old family Swale.

Bibliography

Anderson, Eva Greenslit. *Chief Seattle.* Caldwell, Idaho: The Caxton Printers, 1943.

Bagley, C. B. *History of Seattle: From the Earliest Settlement to the Present Time.* 3 vols. Chicago: S. J. Clarke, 1916.

———. *History of King County, Washington.* Chicago: S. J. Clarke, 1929.

———. *Indian Myths of the Northwest.* Seattle: Lowman & Hanford, 1930.

———. *In the Beginning: Early Days on Puget Sound.* Seattle: The Historical Society of Seattle and King County, 1980.

———. *Pioneer Seattle and Its Pioneers.* Seattle, 1928.

———. *Scrapbook.* Vols. 1, 5, 12, 15. Seattle: University of Washington, Northwest Collections.

Bancroft, Hubert Howe. *History of Washington, Idaho, and Montana,* Vol. 31 of *The Works of Hubert Howe Bancroft.* San Francisco: The History Company, Pub., 1890.

Bass, Sophie Frye. *Pig-Tail Days in Old Seattle.* Florenz Clark, artist. Portland: Binford & Mort, 1937.

———. *When Seattle Was a Village.* Florenz Clark, artist. Seattle: Lowman & Hanford, 1847.

Bennet, Roberta A., ed. *A Small World of Our Own.* Walla Walla, Wash.: Pioneer Press, 1985.

———. *We'll All Go Home in the Spring.* Walla Walla, Wash.: Pioneer Press, 1984.

Binns, Archie. *Northwest Gateway: The Story of the Port of Seattle.* Portland: Binford & Mort, 1941.

———. *Sea in the Forest.* Garden City, N.Y.: Doubleday & Co., Inc., 1953.

Blaine, David and Catherine. Letters 1849–1856.

311

Blankenship, George E. *Lights and Shades of Pioneer Life on Puget Sound.* Olympia, Wash., 1923.

Bonney, W. P. *History of Pierce County, Washington.* Vol. 1. Chicago: Pioneer Historical Publishing Company, 1927.

Boring, Mel. *Sealth—The Story of an American Indian.* Minneapolis: Dillon Press, 1978.

Brewster, David, and David M. Buerge. *Washingtonians: A Biographical Portrait of the State.* Seattle: Sasquatch Books, 1989.

Broderick, Henry. *Picturesque Pioneers.* Seattle: Dogwood Press, 1967.

Buchanan, Laura D. *Souvenir of Chief Seattle and Princess Angeline.* Portland: Binford & Mort, 1909.

Buerge, David M. *The Man We Call Seattle.* n.d.

Carpenter, Cecelia. *Fort Nisqually: A Documented History of Indian and British History.* Tacoma: Tahoma Research Center, 1986.

———. *Leschi: Last Chief of the Nisqually.* Tacoma: Tahoma Research Center, 1986.

———. *Tears of Internment: The Indian History of Fox Island and the Puget Sound Indian War.* Tacoma: Tahoma Research Center, 1996.

———. *They Walked Before: The Indians of Washington State.* Tacoma: Tahoma Research Center, 1977.

Cleveland High School. *The Duwamish Diary.* Seattle: Seattle Public Schools, 1949.

Conover, C. T. *Pioneer Reminiscences.* Seattle: Museum of History and Industry, n.d.

Cook, Jimmie Jean. *"A Particular Friend, PENN'S COVE": A History of the Settlers, Claims, and Buildings of Central Whidbey Island.* Coupeville, Wash.: Island County Historical Society, 1973.

Denny, David. *David's Diaries.* Seattle: Museum of History and Industry, n.d.

Denny, Emily Inez. *Blazing the Way.* Seattle: Rainier Printing Company, 1909.

Dorpat, Paul. *494 More Glimpses of Historic Seattle.* Seattle: Mother Wit Press, 1982.

———. *Seattle Now and Then.* Seattle: Tartu Publications, 1984.

Downie, Ralph Earnest. *A Pictorial History of the State of Washington.* Seattle: Lowman & Hanford, 1937.

Dryden, Decil. *Dryden's History of Washington.* Portland: Binford & Mort, 1968.

Dunbar: *Scrapbook.* Vols. 5 & 6. Seattle: University of Washington, Northwest Collections.

Eckrom, J. A. *Remembered Drums: A History of the Puget Sound Indian War.* Walla Walla, Wash.: Pioneer Press, 1989.

Edson, Lelah Jackson. *The Fourth Corner: Highlights from the Early Northwest.* Bellingham, Wash.: Cox Brothers, 1951.

Eide, Ingvard. *Oregon Trail.* Rand McNally and Co., 1972.

Emmons, Della Gould. *Leschi of the Nisquallies.* Minneapolis: T. S. Denison & Co., 1965.

Evans, Elwood. *History of the Pacific Northwest: Oregon and Washington.* Vol. 1. Portland: North Pacific History Co., 1889.

Evans, Jack R. *Little History of Lenant F. Thompson.* Seattle: SCW Publications, 1992.

———. *Little History of North Bend—Snoqualmie, Washington.* Seattle: SCW Publications, 1990.

Fonda. *Scrapbook.* Vol. 1. Seattle: University of Washington, Northwest Collections.

Franzwa, Gregory. *The Oregon Trail Revisited.* St. Louis: Patrice Press, Inc., 1972.

Frisbie. *Scrapbook.* Vol. 1. Seattle: University of Washington, Special Collections.

Gates, Charles Marvin, ed. *Readings in Pacific Northwest History: Washington 1790–1895.* Seattle: University Bookstore, 1941.

Glassley, Ray H. *Indian Wars of the Pacific Northwest.* Portland: Binford & Mort, 1972.

Grant, James. *History of Seattle, Washington.* New York: American Publishers and English Co. Pub., 1981.

Green, Frank L. *Thomas M. Chambers Collection.* Tacoma: Washington State Historical Society, 1972.

Guie, Dean H. *Bugles in the Valley.* Yakima, Wash.: Republic Press, 1956.

Hanford, Cornelius. *Seattle and Environs.* 3 vols. Seattle: Pioneer Historical Pub., 1924.

Hawley, Robert Emmett. *Skqee Mus: Or Pioneer Days on the Nooksack.* Bellingham, Wash.: Miller & Sutherlen Printing Co., 1945.

Hemphill, Major General John A., and Robert C. Cumbow. *West Pointers and Early Washington.* Seattle: The West Point Society of Puget Sound, Inc., 1992.

Hilbert, Vi. *Huboo.* Seattle: University of Washington Press, 1980.

James, David. *From Grand Mound to Scatter Creek.* Olympia, Wash.: State Capital Historical Association of Washington, 1980.

Johansen, Dorothy O., and Charles M. Gates. *Empire of the Columbia.* New York: Harper and Row, 1967.

Johnson, Jalmar. *Builders of the Northwest.* New York: Dodd, Mead & Co., 1963.

Jones, Nard. *Puget Sound Profiles: Stories about the People, the Places and the Past of Puget Country.* Vol 1. Puget Sound Power & Light Co., n.d.

———. *Seattle.* New York: Doubleday, 1972.

Jordon, Mrs. Harry E. *Incidents in the Life of a Pioneer Woman.* The State Association of the Daughters of the Pioneers of Washington, n.d.

Judson, Katharine Berry. *Early Days in Old Oregon*. Portland: Binford & Mort, 1916.

Judson, Phoebe Goodell. *A Pioneer's Search for an Ideal Home*. Lincoln: University of Nebraska Press, 1984.

Karolevitz, Bob. "Seattle Transit." *Seattle Times*, 24 May 1964.

Kellogg, George Albert. *A History of Whidbey's Island* 1934.

Kelly, Plympton. *We Were Not Summer Soldiers: The Indian War Diary of Plympton J. Kelly, 1855–1856*. Tacoma: Washington State Historical Society, 1976.

Lage, Laura Tice. *Sagebrush Homesteads*. Yakima, Wash.: Franklin Press, Inc., 1967.

Leighton, George R. *America's Growing Pains*. New York: Harper & Brothers, 1939.

LeWarne, Charles P. *Washington State*. Seattle and London: University of Washington Press, 1986.

Litteer, Loren K. *Bleeding Kansas*. Kansas: Champion Publishing, 1987.

McDonald, Lucille. "Seattlites Recall Cable Car Days." *Seattle Times,* 19 September 1955.

———. *Washington's Yesterdays*. Portland: Binford & Mort, 1953.

McDonald, Norbert. *Distant Neighbors: A Comparative History of Seattle and Vancouver*. Lincoln: University of Nebraska Press, 1987.

McDonald, Robert. "Railroading in Seattle." *Seattle Sunday Times*, 31 December 1944.

———. *"Seattle's Mayors."* Bellingham Public Library vertical file: Seattle History.

Meany, Edmond S. *History of the State of Washington*. New York: The Macmillan Co., 1910.

Meeker, Ezra. *Pioneer Reminiscences of Puget Sound*. Seattle: Lowman & Hanford, 1905.

———. *Seventy Years of Progress in Washington*. Tacoma: Allstrum Printing, 1921.

———. *The Tragedy of Leschi*. Seattle: Lowman & Hanford, 1905.

Metcalf, James Vernon. *Chief Seattle*. Seattle: Catholic NW Progress, n.d.

Monaghan, Jay. *Civil War on the Western Border*. Lincoln: University of Nebraska, 1985.

Montgomery, Elizabeth. *Chief Seattle—Great Statesman*. Champaign, Ill.: Garrard Pub. Co., 1966.

Morgan, Murray. *Skid Road: An Informal Portrait of Seattle*. Seattle: University of Washington Press, 1951.

Morgan, Murray, and Rosa Morgan. *South on the Sound: An Illustrated History of Tacoma and Pierce County*. Woodland Hills, Calif.: Windsor Publications, Inc., 1984.

Morgan, Murray, and Rosa Morgan, with Paul Dorpat. *Seattle, a Pictorial History*. Norfolk: The Donning Co. Pub., 1982.

314

Museum of History and Industry, Manuscript Files:
  "Battle of Seattle"
  Denny, A. A. Memorial album.
  Denny, Emily Inez. "By the Blazing Shore."
  ———. Biography of Princess Angeline.
  Denny, John. Biography.
  Denny, Louisa Boren. Manuscript.
  ———. Interviews.
  Denny, Sarah Latimer. *Bass Collection.*
  Graham, Susan Mercer. "Fort at Seattle."
  Kellogg, David. Manuscript.
  Russell, Alonzo. Memoirs.
  Smith, D. H. "Early Seattle."
  Wyckoff, Eugenia McConaha.
  Wyckoff, George McConaha Jr. Letter to mother.
  Yesler, Henry. Letters.
  Yesler, Sarah. Letters.
Neils, Selma. *The Klickitat Indians.* Portland: Binford & Mort, 1985.
Nelson, Gerald B. *Seattle: The Life and Times of an American City.* New York:
  Alfred A. Knopf, 1977.
Newell, Gordon. *Totem Tales of Old Seattle.* Seattle: Superior Pub., 1956.
  ———. *Westward to Alki.* Seattle: Superior Pub. Co., 1977.
Nicandri, David, and Derek Valley. *Olympia Wins: Washington's Capital
  Controversies.* Olympia, Wash.: Washington State Capital Museum,
  1980.
Oates, Stephen B. *To Purge This Land with Blood.* Amherst, Mass: University of Massachusetts Press, 1970.
Pacific Telephone & Telegraph Co. *Growing Together.* Bellingham Public
  Library vertical file: Seattle History, July 1958.
Peltier, Jerome. *Warbonnets and Epaulets.* Compiled by B. C. Payette. Montreal: Payette Radio, n.d.
Phelps, T. S. *Reminiscences of Seattle: Indian War of 1855–1856.* Seattle:
  The Alice Harrison Co., 1880.
Pierce, Frank Richardson. "The Bell Rang Nine Times." *Seattle Times,* 9
  September 1962.
Pioneer & Democrat, 1852–1856. Seattle: University of Washington, Suzalo
  Library.
Post-Intelligencer. Seattle, Washington.
Potts, Ralph Bushnell. *Seattle Heritage.* Seattle: Superior Pub., 1955.
Prater, Yvonne. *Snoqualmie Pass: From Indian Trail to Interstate.* Seattle:
  The Mountaineers, 1981.
Prosch, Thomas. *A Chronological History of Seattle.* Seattle: Museum of
  History and Industry.

———. *David S. Maynard and Catherine T. Maynard.* Seattle: Lowman & Hanford, 1906.

Puget Sound Courier, 1854–1856. Seattle: University of Washington, Suzalo Library.

Raymond, Steve. "Remember When Seattle Had Cable." *Seattle Times,* 8 August 1865.

Records of King County Clerk: Third Territorial District Court 1852–1889. RBD Washington State Archives, Regional Depository at Bellingham.

Redfield, Edith Sanderson. *Seattle Memoirs.* Boston: Lothrop, Lee and Shepard Co., 1930.

Richards, Kent D. *Isaac I. Stevens: Young Man in a Hurry.* Pullman, Wash.: Washington State University Press, 1993.

Rucker, Helen. *Cargo of Brides.* Boston: Little, Brown, 1956.

Sale, Roger. *Seattle: Past to Present.* Seattle: University of Washington Press, 1976.

Sanderson, Edith. *Seattle Memoirs.* Boston: Lothrop, Lee and Shepard Co., 1930.

Seattle, Chief Moses. *"How Can One Sell the Air?"* Summertown, Tenn.: The Book Publishing Company, 1992.

Seattle's First Physician. Clinics of the Virginia Mason Hospital. December 1932, Vol. 12.

Seattle Times. Seattle, Washington.

Smith, Helen Krebs. *With Her Own Wings: Historical Sketches, Reminiscences, and Anecdotes of Pioneer Women.* Portland: Beattie & Company, 1948.

Smith, Herndon, ed. *Centralia: The First Fifty Years.* Centralia, Wash.: The Daily Chronicle & F. H. Cole Printing Company, 1942.

Snowden, Clinton. *History of Washington.* New York: The Century History Co., 1909.

Speidel, William. *Doc Maynard: The Man Who Invented Seattle.* Seattle: Nettle Creek Pub., 1978.

———. *Sons of the Profits.* Seattle: Nettle Creek Pub., 1967.

Stevenon, Shanna. *Olympiana: Historical Vignettes of Olympia's People and Places.* Olympia, Wash.: Washington State Capital Museum, 1982.

Stewart, Edgar I. *Washington: Northwest Frontier,* Vol. 2. New York: Lewis Historical Publishing Company, Inc., n.d.

Tavo, Gus. *The Buffalo Are Coming.* New York: Alfred A. Knopf, 1960.

Thompson, Margaret. *Genealogical Notes—Denny Family.* Seattle Public Library, Main Office.

Trafzer, Clifford, and Richard D. Scheuerman. *Renegade Tribe: The Palouse Indians and the Invasion of the Indian Pacific Northwest.* Pullman, Wash.: Washington State University Press, 1986.

Trotter, F. I., F. H. Loutzenhiser, and J. R. Loutzenhiser, eds. *Told by the Pioneers,* Vols. 1–3. U.S. Works Progress Administration, 1938.

Vaughn, Wade. *Puget Sound Invasion*. Seattle: Leschi Improvement Council, 1975.

Walkinshaw, Robert. *On Puget Sound*. London: J. P. Puttnam's Sons, 1929.

Warren, James. *King County and Its Queen City: Seattle*. Historical Society of Seattle and King County. Woodland Hills, Calif.: Windsor Publications, 1981.

Watt, Roberta Frye. *Four Wagons West*. Portland: Binford & Mort, 1931.

Winthrop, Theodore. *The Canoe and the Saddle*. New York: Dodd, Mead and Co., 1862.

Wright, Robin K. *A Time of Gathering*.

The Sweetbriar Series— the unfolding of history and love

Like the sweetbriar that grows in the great city of Seattle, the memory of two remarkable people will live on forever . . .

Over half a million readers have enjoyed Brenda Wilbee's popular historical series that reveals the courage, strength, and faith of Seattle's first family. You will be inspired by the characters of Louisa Boren Denny and David Denny, two unforgettable people whose love endures the wilderness trail, war, separation, and losses. This well-loved series is a timeless mix of faith, romance, and adventure that offers hope to people of all ages.

Brenda Wilbee is an award-winning author and historian who lives in the Seattle area. Her nine books include the Sweetbriar series, which chronicles Seattle's earliest history.

Louisa Boren Denny's name went down in history. Her story will touch your heart—forever. Relive one of the most thrilling chapters in American history and share in an enduring love.

Newlyweds David and Louisa Denny, founders of Seattle, are finally seeing the firstfruits of their labors. But beneath the heady air of prosperity runs a current of fear. They and their fellow settlers will soon face escalating—and justifiable—Indian unrest.

0-8007-5619-3
Paper (5 1/2 x 8 1/2)
288 pages
FC
$11.99

Indian war has erupted east of the mountains. Will it spread to the West? To Puget Sound? To Seattle? Soon David is called to leave his new family, and Louisa must rely on hope and faith in God that her husband will return safely.

0-8007-5661-4
Paper (5 1/2 x 8 1/2)
272 pages
FC
$11.99